"*Madame Bovary* has a perfection that not only stamps it,
but that makes it stand almost alone."
Henry James

"No writer that we know of devoted himself with such a
fierce and indomitable industry to the art of literature...
He did not think that to live was the object of life; for him the
object of life was to write; no monk in his cell ever more
willingly sacrificed the pleasure of the world to the love of
God than Flaubert sacrificed the fullness and variety of life
to his ambition to create a work of art."
W. Somerset Maugham

"Yes! Flaubert is my master."
Oscar Wilde

"The whole of Flaubert, the whole fight for the novel
as '*histoire morale contemporaine*' was a fight against
maxims, against abstractions, a fight back towards a
human and/or total conception."
Ezra Pound

ALMA CLASSICS

Madame Bovary

Gustave Flaubert

Translated by Christopher Moncrieff

ALMA CLASSICS

ALMA CLASSICS LTD
London House
243-253 Lower Mortlake Road
Richmond
Surrey TW9 2LL
United Kingdom
www.almaclassics.com

Madame Bovary first published in French in 1856
This edition first published by Alma Classics Ltd (previously Oneworld
Classics Limited) in 2010
Reprinted September 2010
This new edition first published by Alma Classics Ltd in 2013
English Translation © Christopher Moncrieff, 2010
Notes and Extra Material © Alma Classics, 2010

Printed in Great Britain by CPI Cox & Wyman

ISBN: 978-1-84749-322-4

Contents

Madame Bovary   1
   Part One   3
   Part Two   59
   Part Three   195
   Note on the Text   298
   Notes   298

Extra Material   307
   Gustave Flaubert's Life   309
   Gustave Flaubert's Works   317
   Adaptations   329
   Select Bibliography   331

Gustave Flaubert (1821–80)

Achille-Cléophas Flaubert,
Flaubert's father

Anne Justine Caroline Flaubert,
Flaubert's mother

Élisa Schlesinger

Louise Colet

Flaubert's birthplace in Rouen

The surviving pavilion from the Flaubert estate in Croisset

A caricature by Lemot of Flaubert
dissecting Emma Bovary

Madame Bovary

Part One

1

W<small>E WERE DOING PREP</small> when the Headmaster came in, followed by a respectably dressed new boy and a porter carrying a large desk. Those who were asleep woke up, and everyone stood up as if caught unawares in the middle of their work.

The Headmaster gestured to us to sit down; then, turning to the head of studies:

"Monsieur Roger," he said quietly, "I'm putting this pupil here in your charge, he will start in the third form. If his work and behaviour merit it he can move up to a higher class, as befits his age."

Standing in the corner behind the door, so we could hardly see him, the new boy was a country lad, about fifteen years old and taller than the rest of us. His hair was cut straight across his forehead like a village choirboy, he looked well behaved and very self-conscious. Although he wasn't broad-shouldered his suit jacket, made of green woollen cloth with black buttons, was tight under the arms, and through the slits in the cuff facings you could see red wrists that weren't used to being covered up. His legs, in long blue socks, appeared from under yellowish trousers that were hiked up by braces. He was wearing stout shoes, unpolished and heavily studded.

We began reciting our lessons. He was all ears, listening closely as if to a sermon, not daring to even cross his legs or lean on his elbow, and when the bell went at two o'clock the head of studies had to tell him to go and sit down with the rest of us.

When we came into the classroom it was our routine to throw our caps onto the floor so as to have our hands free; you had to fling it from the doorway, under the bench, so that it hit the wall and made a lot of dust; it was *the done thing*.

But, either because he hadn't noticed this operation or daren't follow suit, when prayers were over the new boy still had his cap on his knees. It was one of those composite pieces of headgear that was a combination of a fur hat, czapka,* bonnet, otter-skin cap and nightcap, in short one of those sad objects whose mute ugliness has the same depths of expression as the face of an idiot. Egg-shaped and bulging with whalebone, it began at the front with three sausage-like hoops; next, divided by red strips, were diamond patterns, first made of velvet then of rabbit skin; after that came a kind of bag which terminated in a many-sided cardboard shape covered in elaborate braiding from which hung, at the end of a long piece of string, a small cross made of gold thread by way of a tassel. It was new; the peak gleamed.

"Stand up," said the teacher.

He stood up; his cap fell on the floor. The whole class laughed.

He bent down to pick it up. His neighbour nudged him and he dropped it, he picked it up again.

"Set aside your helm," said the master, who was a man of wit.

There was an outburst of schoolboy laughter that flustered the poor lad so much that he didn't know whether he should keep his cap in his hand, leave it on the floor or wear it. He sat down again and laid it in his lap.

"Stand up," repeated the master, "and tell me your name."

In a stammering voice the new boy came out with an unintelligible name.

"Again!"

The same stammered words could just be heard beneath the jeers of the class.

"Louder!" shouted the master. "Louder!"

With utmost resolve the new boy opened his enormous mouth, and at the top of his voice, as if shouting to someone, let out the word: *Charbovari*.

Immediately a great rumpus broke out, rose to a crescendo of high-pitched shouts (we screamed, we yelled, we stamped our feet, we chanted: *Charbovari! Charbovari!*), and then ran on into isolated notes, quietening down with great difficulty and sometimes breaking out again along the benches, where muffled laughter sprung up here and there like a firecracker that hasn't quite gone out.

Meanwhile order was gradually restored under a hail of punishments, and the master, who had managed to catch Charles Bovary's name, having had it dictated, spelt out and read back to him, told the poor devil to go and sit on the slackers' bench in front of the rostrum. He started to make a move but hesitated.

"What are you looking for?" asked the master.

"My ca—" said the new boy timidly, looking round anxiously.

"Five hundred lines for the whole class!" exclaimed by a furious voice put a stop to another outbreak, as if it were the *Quos ego.** "Keep quiet, will you!" added the angry teacher, wiping his brow with a handkerchief that he had taken from under his mortar board. "And as for you, new boy, you will copy out for me twenty times the verb *ridiculus sum.*"*

Then, in a more gentle voice:

"I see you've found your cap then; they haven't stolen it!"

Everything calmed down. Heads bent over satchels, and for two hours the new boy behaved perfectly, despite a few ink pellets that were flicked at him from pen nibs, splattering his face. But he wiped it off with his hand and kept still, eyes lowered.

That evening during prep, he drew a line under his work, cleared away his few belongings, carefully tidied up his paper. We saw him working away conscientiously, looking up every word in the dictionary and taking great pains. Thanks to this willingness he probably wouldn't have to go down a class; for although he knew his rules well enough, his turn of phrase didn't have much style. It was the parish priest who had started him off in Latin, his parents having delayed sending him to school for as long as possible in order to save money.

His father, Monsieur Charles-Denis-Bartholomé Bovary, a former assistant military surgeon compromised by some scandal over conscription around 1812, and forced to leave the service at around that time, had made the most of his personal advantages along the way to get his hands on a dowry of sixty thousand francs that came with the daughter of a hosiery merchant who had fallen for his fine bearing. A handsome fellow, a braggart who made his spurs jingle, grew his sideburns to join up with his moustache, wore rings on his fingers and dressed in garish colours, he had the look of a gallant, the ready gusto of a commercial traveller. Once married he lived off his wife's fortune for two or three years, dining well, getting up late, smoking large porcelain pipes, not coming home at night until after the shows finished and always in cafés. His father-in-law died leaving very little; he was vexed, started up *in manufacturing*, lost money then retired to the country where he was going to *make his name*. But since he knew little more about farming than he did about printed calico, rode his horses instead of putting them to work, drank his cider from bottles instead of selling it in casks, ate the best poultry in his yard and waxed his hunting boots with the fat from his pigs, he soon came to the conclusion that it was best not to get involved in any more ventures.

For two hundred francs' rent a year he found a place in a village on the borders of the Pays de Caux and Picardy, a sort of part farm, part mansion; and, disgruntled, consumed with regrets, blaming the Almighty, envious of everyone, from the age of forty-five he shut himself away, saying he was sick and tired of humanity and had decided to live in peace and quiet.

His wife had been madly in love with him at first; she had adored him in thousands of slavish little ways that pushed him even further away from her. Once cheerful, outgoing and full of affection, as she got older (in the way stale wine turns sour) she became awkward, whining, highly strung. She had suffered a great deal, without complaining at first, when she saw him chasing after all the sluts in the village and coming home at night indifferent and stinking of drink from all those dreadful places! And then her pride rebelled. But she kept quiet, swallowing her anger in a mute stoicism that stayed with her till her death. She was forever doing the shopping, doing business. She went to the lawyers, to the magistrate, remembered when bills of exchange were due, got them deferred; at home she ironed, sewed, did the laundry, kept an eye on the workmen, settled the invoices while Monsieur, who never troubled his head about anything, and in a permanent state of sulky sluggishness from which he only ever roused himself in order to insult her, sat by the fire smoking and spitting in the ashes.

When she had a baby it had to be put with a wet nurse. Then once he came home, the brat was royally spoilt. His mother fed him on jam; his father let him run around barefoot and, playing the philosopher, even said that they might as well let him go naked, like a young animal. Contrary to his wife's maternal leanings he had a particular manly ideal of childhood, and tried to educate his son accordingly, wanting to bring him up the hard way, like a Spartan, to make sure he had a strong constitution. He sent him to bed without any supper, taught him to swig rum and jeer at religious processions. But, being quiet by nature, the boy didn't respond to his efforts. His mother trailed him round with her all the time; she cut out pieces of cardboard for him, told him stories, talked to him in endless monologues full of mournful cheerfulness and chattering little attentions. In her isolation she

8

transferred all her threadbare, shattered vanities onto his young head. She dreamt of high-ranking positions, saw him grown, handsome, witty, well established as a civil engineer or magistrate. She taught him to read, even how to sing one or two short sentimental ballads on an old piano of hers. But to all this, the response of Monsieur Bovary, who cared little for literature or the arts, was that *there was no point!* Would they have enough to support him through the state schools, buy a position for him or set him up in business? Besides, *with a bit of nerve a man always gets on in life.* Madame Bovary bit her lip, and the boy roamed the village.

He went off with the ploughmen, threw clods of earth at crows to drive them away. He ate blackberries along the embankments and minded the turkeys with a long pole, tossed hay at harvest time, ran in the woods, played hopscotch in the church porch when it was raining, and on feast days begged the verger to let him ring the bells, so he could hang on to the great long rope and let it lift him off the ground.

And he grew like an oak. Soon he had strong hands, a ruddy complexion.

When he was twelve, his mother was finally allowed to arrange for him to start his education. They asked the parish priest to take it on. But the lessons were so short and irregular that they were of little use. They were done at odd moments, hurriedly, standing in the sacristy between a baptism and a burial; or else the priest would send for his pupil after the angelus* when he didn't have to go out. They would go up to his room, settle down: midges and moths fluttered round the candle. It was warm, the child fell asleep; and it wasn't long before the old fellow was nodding off as well, hands clasped on his belly and snoring loudly. At other times, when the priest was on his way back from taking the viaticum* to the sick and spotted Charles up to mischief in the fields, he would call him over, lecture him for a quarter of an hour, then make the most of the opportunity to get him to conjugate verbs under a tree. Then the rain would interrupt them, or some acquaintance walking past. Yet he was always pleased with him, even said the young man had a good memory.

But Charles wasn't allowed to stop there. Madame was tireless in her efforts. And, either out of shame or, more likely, weariness, Monsieur gave in without a fight, and so they waited for another year until after the lad's first communion.

Another six months went by; and the following year Charles was sent off to school full-time in Rouen; his father took him at the end of October, during the Saint-Romain fair.

None of us would be able to remember a thing about him now. He was a boy not given to excesses, who played at break time, worked at his studies, listened in class, slept soundly in the dormitory, ate heartily in the refectory. His guardian was an ironmonger in the Rue Ganterie who took him out once a month, on Sundays after his shop was shut, sent him for a walk down to the harbour to look at the boats, and then brought him back to school by seven o'clock in time for supper. Every Thursday evening he wrote a long letter to his mother, in red ink and with three wax seals; then he looked through his history books or read an old copy of Anacharsis* that was lying around in the prep room. On walks he chatted to the servant, who was from the country too.

As a result of applying himself he was always around the middle of the class; once he even got a certificate of merit for natural history. But at the end of his remove year* his parents took him away from school to study medicine, convinced he would be able to pass the *baccalauréat** on his own.

His mother found him a room on the fourth floor in l'Eau-de-Robec, with a dyer and cleaner she knew. She arranged for his board, got some furniture for him, a table and two chairs, sent an old cherrywood bed from home, and bought a small cast-iron stove with a supply of firewood to keep her poor boy warm. Then after a week she left, having exhorted him endlessly about behaving himself now he was on his own.

When he read the lesson timetable on the notice board it made his head spin: anatomy classes, pathology classes, physiology classes, pharmacy classes, chemistry classes, plus botany, clinical studies and therapeutics, not to mention hygiene or medicine itself, all names whose origin he knew nothing about and which were like so many doors to inner temples filled with venerable darkness.

He didn't understand a word; listen though he might, he couldn't grasp it. Nonetheless he worked, took notes in bound notebooks, attended every class, didn't miss a single ward round. He did his minor daily tasks like a horse in a manège, going round and round with blinkers on, unaware of the grinding work it is doing.

To save him money his mother sent a piece of roast veal every week by special delivery, which he had for lunch the next day when he got back from the hospital, stamping his feet to keep warm. Then he had to rush back to class, to the lecture theatre, the poorhouse, and walk home from the other side of town. In the evening, after the scanty dinner his landlord provided, he went up to his room and got on with his work, his wet clothes steaming on him in front of the red-hot stove.

On fine summer evenings when the warm streets are empty, when servant girls play shuttlecock outside their front doors, he would open the window and lean on the sill. The river ran past below, yellow, purple or blue between the bridges and railings, turning this part of Rouen into an unsavoury version of Venice. Crouched on the bank, workmen washed their arms in the water. On poles projecting out of attics, skeins of cotton dried in the breeze. Over the rooftops opposite stretched a great clear sky and a red sunset. How wonderful it must be over there! The coolness of the beech grove! And he would breathe in deeply through his nose to try and smell the good country smells that never reached him here.

He got taller, thinner, his face took on a doleful expression that made it almost interesting.

Of course there came a time when he broke every resolution he had made. One day he missed the ward round, the next day his classes, and gradually, relishing this state of idleness, he stopped going at all.

He began frequenting inns, developed a passion for dominoes. Shutting himself away every night in a filthy barroom to knock on marble-topped tables with small pieces of sheep's bone marked with black dots to him seemed a priceless act of freedom that raised his self-esteem. It was an initiation into life, gave him access to forbidden pleasures; and as he went in he grasped the doorknob with almost sensual delight. Many things that had been held back inside him now opened out; he memorized verses that are sung to welcome people, became keen on Béranger,* learnt to make punch and finally found love.

Thanks to this groundwork he failed the public-health officer's exam. And they were waiting for him at home that evening to celebrate his success!

He set off on foot and stopped on the outskirts of the village, where he asked someone to fetch his mother and told her everything. She made excuses, blamed his failure on the unfairness of the examiners and bolstered him up, taking it on herself to sort things out. Only five years later did Monsieur Bovary actually discover the truth; but it was water under the bridge, so he accepted it, in any case being incapable of imagining that any son of his could be a fool.

So Charles got back to work and prepared every subject for his exam, learnt all the questions off by heart. He passed with reasonable marks. What a great day for his mother! They gave a big dinner.

Where was he to practise his profession? In Tostes. There was only an elderly doctor there. Madame Bovary had been waiting for him to die for years, and the old chap still hadn't shuffled off before Charles was set up opposite him, as his successor.

But it wasn't enough to have raised her son, have him trained in medicine and discovered Tostes to practise it in: now he needed a wife. So she found one for him: the widow of a bailiff from Dieppe, who was forty-five and had a private income of twelve hundred livres* a year.

Despite being ugly, as dried up as an old prune and blowsy as a spring day, Madame Dubuc didn't want for suitors. To achieve her aim old mother Bovary had to oust every one of them, and she was even wily enough to outmanoeuvre a pork butcher who had the clergy's backing.

In getting married Charles had anticipated the advent of a better situation, imagining that he would have more freedom, that he would be able to do as he liked with his time and money. But it was his wife who was the master: in company he had to say this and not that, eat fish on Fridays, dress the way she saw fit, do as she told him and chase up clients who didn't pay. She opened his mail, spied on his comings and goings, and listened through the partition wall of his consulting room whenever he was with a female patient.

She had to have her hot chocolate every morning, her never-ending little attentions. She was forever complaining about her nerves, her chest, her moods. The sound of people walking about made her ill; when they went away she found the loneliness unbearable; when they came back it was undoubtedly to watch her die. When Charles came home in the evening she brought her long thin arms out from under the bedclothes, put them round his neck and, making him sit on the edge of the bed, started telling him her troubles: he was forgetting her, he loved someone else! She'd always been told that she would be unhappy; and she ended up asking him for some syrup mixture for her health, and a little more love.

2

O NE NIGHT AT ABOUT ELEVEN O'CLOCK they were woken by the sound of a horse stopping outside the front door. The maid opened the attic window and altercated for a while with a man in the street below. He had come to fetch the doctor; he had a letter. Shivering, Nastasie went down and opened the locks and bolts one by one. The man left his horse and followed her straight into the house. From under his woollen hat with grey tassels he took a letter wrapped in a piece of old cloth and genteelly presented it to Charles, who sat up in bed to read it. Standing next to him, Nastasie held a lamp; out of modesty, Madame turned to the wall so just her back was visible.

The letter, sealed with a small blue wax seal, begged Monsieur Bovary to come to the farm at Les Bertaux straight away to mend a broken leg. From Tostes to Les Bertaux it was a good six leagues, taking the shortcut through Longueville and Saint-Victor. It was a dark night and young Madame Bovary was afraid her husband might have an accident. So it was decided that the groom would go on ahead. Charles would leave in three hours' time, when there was a moon. They would send a boy to meet him, to show him the way to the farm and open the gates.

At about four in the morning, wrapped in his coat, Charles set off for Les Bertaux. Still drowsy from his warm bed, he let himself be rocked off by the gentle pace of his horse. Whenever it decided to stop at the ditches ringed by thorns that are dug beside ploughed fields, Charles, waking with a start, soon remembered the broken leg, and racked his brains to remember the different fractures he knew. The rain had stopped; it was almost daybreak, and birds sat motionless on the bare branches of the apple trees, ruffling their little feathers in the chill morning wind. The flat countryside stretched away into the distance as far as the eye could see, and clumps of trees round the farms made dark purple patches at odd intervals on the vast grey surface that merged into the dreary colours of the sky on the horizon. Now and then Charles opened his eyes; but soon tiring and giving way to sleep again he fell into a sort of doze in which, recent experiences becoming confused with memories, he saw doubles of himself, student and husband at the same time, lying in bed like a moment ago, walking through an operating theatre as he used to. In his mind the smell of

13

poultices mingled with the fresh smell of dew; he heard the metal rings of bed curtains sliding along their rods, his wife sleeping... As he was going through Vassonville he noticed a young lad sitting in the grass beside an embankment.

"Are you the doctor?" the boy asked.

At Charles's reply he picked up his clogs and set off at a run ahead of him.

As they made their way, the public-health officer took from what his guide was saying that Monsieur Rouault must be a well-to-do farmer. He had broken his leg the night before on his way back from eating *galette des Rois** with a neighbour to celebrate Twelfth Night. His wife had died two years ago. He only had "Mam'selle his daughter" with him now, who helped him keep house.

The ruts got deeper. They were almost at Les Bertaux. The young boy disappeared through a gap in the hedge, and then reappeared at the end of a yard to open the gate. The horse slid on the wet grass; Charles bent down to avoid the branches. Guard dogs barked from outside their kennels and dragged on their chains. As he arrived at Les Bertaux his horse took fright and shied badly.

It was a fine-looking farm. Through the open top half of the doors in the stables, big plough horses could be seen eating peacefully from new hay racks. Alongside the outbuildings was a large pile of steaming manure, and among the turkeys and chickens five or six peacocks were pecking about, a luxury of the Cauchois farmyard. The sheep pen was long, the barn tall, its walls as smooth as the skin on your hand. Under the Dutch barn stood two large carts and four ploughs, with whips, collars and full sets of harness whose blue wool fleeces were finely coated with dust from the haylofts. The courtyard, planted with evenly spaced trees, sloped up to the house, and the cheerful sound of geese rang out from over by the pond.

A young woman in a blue merino wool dress with three flounces came to the door to greet Monsieur Bovary, whom she took to the kitchen where there was a good fire going. Lunch was bubbling away everywhere in different-sized pots. Damp clothes were drying inside the fireplace. The shovel, tongs and the nozzle of the bellows, all enormous, shone like burnished steel, while round the walls were ranged a vast array of kitchen utensils, which sparkled occasionally in the bright light from the kitchen lamps and the early sunshine that came through the windows.

Charles went upstairs to the patient. He found him in bed, sweating under the covers, his nightcap thrown across the room. He was a short fat man, fifty years old, with pale skin, blue eyes, bald at the front and wearing earrings. On a chair beside him was a large carafe of brandy from which he helped himself now and then to cheer himself up; but the moment he saw the doctor he became less agitated, and instead of cursing and swearing as he had been doing for the last twelve hours, he began to groan weakly.

It was a simple fracture, no complications. Charles couldn't have wished for anything easier. So, remembering his former teachers' bedside manner, he soothed the patient with jokes and witticisms, those medical cajoleries that are like the oil used to lubricate the scalpel. Someone went to get a bundle of slats from under the cart to use as splints. Charles chose one, cut it into lengths and smoothed it with a piece of broken glass while the maid tore up sheets to make bandages and Mademoiselle Emma tried to stitch some small pads. Because she took a long time to find her needlework box, her father started to get impatient; she didn't reply, but as she sewed she kept pricking her fingers, and then sucking them.

Charles was surprised at how white her nails were. They were shiny, an almond shape polished cleaner than ivory. Yet her hands weren't so pretty, perhaps not pale enough, and slightly rough around the joints; they were also too long, and their outline and contours lacked softness. Her most beautiful feature was her eyes; although brown, they appeared to be black because of her eyelashes, and she looked straight at you with innocent audacity.

Once the dressing was applied, Monsieur Rouault invited the doctor to *have a bite* before he left.

Charles went down to the dining room. Two places with silver tumblers had been laid on a small table at the foot of a large, canopied four-poster bed whose calico cover was printed with Turkish figures. From a tall armoire facing the window came the smell of irises and damp sheets. Sacks of corn were lined up on the floor in the corners. It was the surplus from the granary next door, up three stone steps. By way of decoration, hanging from a nail in the middle of the wall, whose green paint was flaking off under the saltpetre, there was a pencil sketch of Minerva's head in a gilt frame, under which was written, in Gothic script: "To my dear Papa".

At first they talked about the patient, then the weather, how cold the winter was, the wolves that roamed the fields at night. Mademoiselle Rouault didn't much enjoy the country, especially now she had to look after the farm virtually all by herself. As the room was chilly she shivered as she ate, partly revealing her fleshy lips, which she had a habit of biting when she wasn't talking.

Her neck appeared from a white, turned-down collar. Her hair, whose two black headbands were so smooth that they seemed to be a single piece, had a fine parting down the middle, which deepened according to the contours of her head; almost covering her ears, it was swept back into a heavy chignon, with a waviness round the temples which the country doctor now noticed for the first time. Her cheeks were rosy. She wore a tortoiseshell lorgnette looped through two buttons of her bodice, like men did.

After going up to say goodbye to old man Rouault, when Charles came back to the dining room before leaving, he found her standing with her forehead resting on the window and looking out at the garden, where the beanpoles had been blown down by the wind. She turned round.

"Are you looking for something?" she asked.

"My riding crop, actually," he replied.

And he began rummaging about on the bed, behind the doors, under the chairs; it had fallen on the floor between the grain sacks and the wall. Mademoiselle Emma spotted it; she leant over the sacks of corn. Out of courtesy Charles hurried across, and as he stretched out his arm he felt his chest brush against the young woman's back, which was bent forward in front of him. She stood up, blushing deeply, and as she handed him the leather whip she looked over his shoulder.

Instead of coming back to Les Bertaux three days later as promised, he returned the next day, and then regularly twice a week, not counting the odd unexpected visits that he made as if inadvertently.

What was more, everything went well; the leg healed without complications, and when after six weeks old man Rouault was seen walking unaided in his orchards, people began to regard Monsieur Bovary as a man of considerable ability. Old Rouault said he wouldn't have had better treatment from the best doctors in Yvetot or even Rouen.

As for Charles, he never once asked himself why he enjoyed coming to Les Bertaux. Had he done so he would have probably put his enthusiasm down to the seriousness of the case, or perhaps the money he hoped to make. Yet was that why his visits to the farm made such a delightful break from his dreary routine? On those days he got up early, set off at a gallop, spurred his horse on, then dismounted to wipe his feet on the grass and put on his black gloves before going in. He liked the thought of arriving in the yard, feeling his shoulder against the gate as it opened, the cock crowing on the wall, the boys running to meet him. He liked the barn and the stables; he liked old man Rouault, who clapped his hand in his and called him his saviour; he liked Mademoiselle Emma's little clogs on the scrubbed flagstones in the kitchen; their high heels made her slightly taller, and when she walked in front of him the wooden soles lifted up and made a brisk clacking sound noise against the leather of her boots.

She always saw him off from the top step of the front entrance. If his horse hadn't been brought round, she would wait there. They had said goodbye, they didn't say any more; a breeze would get up round her, blowing the downy hair on the nape of her neck every which way, or tossing the apron strings tied at her waist, which twirled like streamers. Once, during the thaw, the bark of the trees in the courtyard was streaming, snow was melting on the roofs of the farm buildings. She was standing on the doorstep; she fetched her umbrella, opened it. Shining through the dapple-grey silk, the sun cast shifting plays of light across the white skin of her face. In the balmy warmth beneath it, she smiled, and raindrops could be heard falling one by one onto the tightly stretched moiré.

When Charles first started going regularly to Les Bertaux, young Madame Bovary made a point of asking after his patient, and had even selected a nice new page for Monsieur Rouault in the account book that she kept in duplicate. But when she heard that he had a daughter, she made enquiries, and she discovered that Mademoiselle Rouault, brought up in a convent with the Ursulines,* had had, as they say, *a good education*, and therefore knew her geography, as well as how to dance, draw, do tapestry and play the piano. It was the last straw!

"So that's why his face lights up when he's going to see her," she thought, "and why he wears his new waistcoat, even though it might get spoilt in the rain? Oh, that woman! That woman!..."

And instinctively she hated her. At first she made herself feel better by dropping hints. Charles didn't get them; next, by making casual remarks that he chose to ignore for fear of trouble; and finally with point-blank rudeness, to which he didn't have an answer. How come he kept going back to Les Bertaux when Monsieur Rouault had recovered, and they still hadn't paid? Ah, it was because there was someone there, *a person* who knew how to make conversation, an embroiderer, a wit. So that was what he liked: he had need of young ladies from town salons! And she went on:

"Old man Rouault's daughter a town lady! Come off it! Their grandfather was a shepherd, they've got a cousin who was nearly hauled up in front of the bench for giving someone a nasty injury during an argument. There's no point putting on airs, turning up to church on Sunday in a silk dress like some countess. And if it weren't for last year's rape crop the poor old bloke would have had a hard time paying his debts!"

Out of apathy Charles stopped paying calls at Les Bertaux. Héloïse made him swear not to go there again, with his hand on her missal, and after many sobs and kisses in a great outpouring of love. So he obeyed; yet the boldness of his desire protested against his servile behaviour, and out of naive hypocrisy he considered that forbidding him to see her was like giving him the right to love her. Besides, the widow was scrawny; she had long teeth; she wore a little black shawl all year round which came halfway down her back; her hard waist was corseted in dresses like scabbards, which were too short and showed her ankles with the ribbons of her wide shoes criss-crossed over grey stockings.

Charles's mother came to see them occasionally; but after a few days her daughter-in-law's company seemed to sharpen her tongue; and like a pair of knives they were soon whittling away at him with comments and criticisms. He shouldn't eat so much! Why offer a drink to all and sundry who came to the door? And it was sheer pig-headedness to refuse to wear flannel!

And then early in the spring a solicitor from Ingouville, who managed the widow Dubuc's capital, did a moonlight flit, taking all the money from his practice. It was true that as well as her share in a boat which was valued at six thousand francs, Héloïse still had her house in the Rue Saint-François; and yet out of this fortune that so much had been heard about, nothing apart from a few sticks of furniture and one or two bits and pieces had found their way to the marital home. The situation needed clarification. The house in Dieppe turned out to be mortgaged to the hilt; as for what she had entrusted to the lawyer, God only knew, and the share in the boat didn't amount to more than a thousand écus. So the woman had been lying! Smashing a chair on the ground in fury, Monsieur Bovary senior accused his wife of bringing misfortune on their son by hitching him to such a nag, whose harness wasn't worth a tick. They came to Tostes. There were explanations. There were scenes. In tears, Héloïse threw herself into her husband's arms, begging him to stand up for her. Charles tried to take her side against his parents. They got angry and left.

But *the blow had been struck*. A week later as she was hanging out washing in the yard, she started coughing up blood, and the next day while Charles had his back turned closing the curtains, she said: "Oh my God!" gave a sigh and fainted. She was dead! It was quite a surprise!

After the funeral, Charles went home. There was no one downstairs; he went up to the bedroom, saw her dress hanging at the back of the alcove; and then leaning on the writing desk, he stayed there filled with painful musings until evening. After all, she had loved him.

3

ONE MORNING, old man Rouault came to bring Charles the payment for his mended leg; seventy-five francs in forty-sou pieces, and a turkey. He had heard about his loss, and did what he could to comfort him.

"I know all about it!" he said, patting him on the back. "I was in your position once! When I lost my poor dear departed I went out to the fields to be all alone; I threw myself down under a tree, I called on the Lord, said silly things to him; I wanted to be like the moles that were hanging from the branches, with worms crawling about in their bellies, in other words dead. And when I thought that at that very moment other people were with their dear little wives, hugging them tight, I thrashed my stick on the ground; I was as good as mad, I wouldn't eat a thing; the thought of going to the café by myself sickened me, you wouldn't credit it. But very slowly, one day at a time, spring following winter and autumn coming after summer, it slipped by little by little, bit by bit; it went away, left me, what I mean to say is that it got less, because there's always something left deep down inside you, like, how would you say... a weight, just here on your chest! But since fate treats us all the same, we shouldn't let ourselves waste away neither, or want to die just because other folk are dead... You have to make an effort, Monsieur Bovary; it'll pass! Come and see us; my daughter thinks of you now and then, she says you've forgotten her. It's nearly spring, see; we'll have you over to shoot a rabbit in the warren to take your mind off things."

Charles took his advice. He went back to Les Bertaux; to him it was just like the last time, five months before. The pear trees were in flower and old Rouault was on his feet now, coming and going, which made the farm livelier.

Thinking it was his duty to lavish as much courtesy as possible on the doctor because he was still grieving, he urged him not to think of taking his hat off, spoke to him quietly as if he were ill, even pretended to be annoyed that lighter dishes hadn't been prepared for him, such as *pots de crème** or pears baked in the oven. He told stories. Charles found himself laughing; but memories of his wife immediately came back to him and filled him with gloom. But then they brought coffee, and he stopped thinking about her.

He thought about her less the more he got used to living alone. The charms of his new-found independence soon made solitude more bearable. He could eat when he liked, come and go without having to give explanations, stretch out on the bed whenever he felt tired. So he cosseted himself and accepted the consolations that came his way. In any case, his wife's death hadn't done him any harm professionally, because for the last month people had been saying: "That poor young man! What a shame!" His reputation spread, his practice grew; what was more, he could go to Les Bertaux whenever he liked. He hoped for nothing in particular, he was happy for no obvious reason; when he brushed his sideburns in the mirror he thought his face looked nicer than before.

One day he arrived at about three o'clock; everyone was out in the fields; he went into the kitchen but didn't see Emma at first; the shutters were closed. Sunlight came through the wooden slats and reached across the flagstones in long thin stripes that broke up on the edges of the furniture and quivered on the ceiling. Flies climbed up the used glasses on the table, buzzing as they drowned in the cider dregs at the bottom. The daylight that came down the chimney gave a velvety softness to the soot on the back plate, and tinted the cold ash slightly blue. Emma sat sewing between the window and the fireplace; she wasn't wearing a scarf, and he could see droplets of perspiration on her bare shoulders.

As was the country custom she offered him a drink. He said no, she insisted, and finally suggested with a laugh that he have a glass of liqueur with her. She got a bottle of curaçao from the armoire, reached down two small glasses, filled one to the top, put almost nothing in the other and then, having clinked it with his, lifted it to her mouth. Since it was virtually empty she had to tip her head back to drink; and in that position, with her lips extended, neck craning, she laughed because she couldn't taste anything, while between her shapely little teeth the tip of her tongue gently licked the bottom of the glass.

She sat down again and got on with her work, darning a pair of white cotton stockings: she tilted her head forward as she worked; she didn't speak, nor did Charles. A draught came under the door and blew dust across the stone tiles; he watched it drift, all he could hear was a drumming in his head, and the distant clucking of a chicken hatching eggs in the yard. Every now and then Emma cooled her cheeks by putting the palms of her hands on them, which she cooled in turn on the knobs of the large firedogs.

All summer she had been complaining of dizzy spells; she asked if bathing in the sea would be of any use; she began to talk about the convent, Charles about his school, words and phrases came to them. They went up to her room. She showed him her old music exercise books, the little books she had got as prizes, crowns of oak leaves forgotten at the bottom of a wardrobe. She told him more about her mother, the funeral, even showed him the flower bed in the garden where she picked flowers to take to her grave on the first Friday of every month. But their gardener didn't have the first idea; you simply couldn't get good staff! She would have liked to live in town, if just for the winter, although perhaps the long hot summer days made the countryside seem even more boring. And depending on what she was talking about, her voice was clear, high-pitched or suddenly languid, gradually trailing off into what was almost a murmur when she spoke to herself; sometimes cheerful, opening her innocent eyes wide, then with their lids half-closed, her expression shrouded with ennui, mind wandering.

On the way home that night, Charles went back over the words she had said one by one, trying to remember them, to give them more meaning so as to have a picture of the life she had lived before he met her. But in his mind's eye he could never see her any differently from how she was when he saw her the first time, or when he left her a moment ago. And he wondered what would become of her if she were to marry, and to whom? Oh dear! Old man Rouault was wealthy, and she... she was so beautiful! Emma's face kept coming back to him, and something droned in his ears like the humming of a top: "Yet if you get married! If you get married!" That night he couldn't sleep, he had a lump in his throat, he was thirsty; he got up to have a drink from his water jug and opened the window; the sky was full of stars, there was a warm breeze, dogs were barking in the distance. And he turned and faced the direction of Les Bertaux.

Thinking he had nothing to lose in any case, Charles resolved to make his proposal when the opportunity arose; but every time it arose, the fear of not getting the right response made him lose his tongue.

Old man Rouault wouldn't have been upset to get his daughter off his hands, as she was little use to him around the house. Inwardly he forgave her, realizing she was more interested in culture, an ill-starred occupation since you never saw a millionaire among them. Far from having made a fortune, the old man lost money every year; because even if he did well at market, where he enjoyed plying the tricks of the trade, proper agriculture, which involved the domestic running of the farm, didn't suit him at all. He wasn't keen on putting his shoulder to the wheel, and didn't spare any expense when it came to his comforts, expecting to be warm, well fed, and to sleep in a comfortable bed. He liked a good glass of cider, lamb cooked rare, a tot of Calvados to lace his coffee along with well-whipped cream. He had his meals on his own in front of the kitchen fire, at a small table that they brought him with everything laid on it, like at the theatre.

So when he noticed that Charles blushed when he was anywhere near his daughter, which meant that one of these days he was going to be asked for her hand, he mulled it over. He thought he was rather *puny*, which wasn't quite the type he'd have wished for; but people said he conducted himself decently, was careful with money, highly educated, and therefore probably wouldn't quibble too much about the dowry. And since old man Rouault was going to have to sell off twenty-two acres of *his estate*, owed a lot to the builder, a lot to the saddler, and the shaft of the wine press needed repairing, he said to himself:

"If he asks, I'll give her to him."

Around the time of Saint-Michel,* Charles spent three days at Les Bertaux. The third day went by like the previous two, the minutes and hours dragged past. Old man Rouault took him off for a walk; they went along a sunken lane, they were about to go their separate ways; it was the moment. Charles waited till they got to a bend in the hedge, and when they had gone past it he finally mumbled:

"Monsieur Rouault, sir, there's something I really want to ask you."

They stopped. Charles went quiet.

"Tell me what it is then!" said old man Rouault, laughing quietly. "As if I didn't know already!"

"Father Rouault… Father Rouault… " Charles stammered.

"I couldn't ask for better," the farmer went on. "And although the girl is probably of the same mind, we still need to ask her opinion. So you be off then; I'm going to make my way home. If it's yes, you won't need to come back, do you hear, on account of the other people, and besides she'd be too overcome. But so as you won't fret, I'll push the shutter open, right against the wall: you can see it from out back, if you lean over the hedge."

And he walked off.

Charles tied his horse to a tree. He ran along the pathway; he waited. Half an hour went by, then he counted another twenty-nine minutes on his watch. Suddenly there was a noise against the wall; the shutter had been flung open, the catch was still shaking.

The next morning he was at the farm by nine. When he walked in Emma reddened slightly, giving a little laugh to put on a show of composure. Old man Rouault kissed his future son-in-law. They started discussing practical arrangements, although they had plenty of time, because it wouldn't have been proper to hold the wedding before Charles came out of mourning, which would be in spring the following year.

Winter was spent waiting. Mademoiselle Rouault busied herself with her trousseau. Some of it was ordered from Rouen, while she made up shifts and nightcaps based on fashionable styles. During Charles's visits to the farm they chatted about the preparations for the reception, wondered which rooms to use for the dinner, mused over the number of courses that would be needed and what to have as entrées.

Emma had wanted to get married at midnight, by torchlight; but old man Rouault couldn't make head or tail of the idea. So there was a wedding dinner for forty-three people that lasted for sixteen hours, started again the next day and went on for several more days after that.

4

THE GUESTS ARRIVED EARLY IN CARRIAGES, in carrioles, two-wheeled carts, ancient cabriolets without hoods, furniture wagons with leather curtains, the young people from neighbouring villages standing up in rows in carts, holding on to the side so they didn't fall over, going at a trot and being badly jolted about. They came from ten leagues away, from Goderville, Normanville and Cany. Everyone from both families had been invited, broken friendships were patched up, they had written to acquaintances whom they hadn't seen for ages.

Now and then there was the sound of a whip cracking on the other side of the hedge; soon the gate opened: a carriole drove in. Galloping up to the front steps it pulled up sharp, and discharged its passengers from every side, who got out rubbing their knees and stretching their arms. The ladies, in hats, were wearing town dresses, gold watch chains, capes with the ends crossed over under their belts, or little coloured scarves fastened to the back of their dresses with pins, which let the napes of their necks show. The boys, dressed the same as their fathers, looked uncomfortable in their new clothes (many of them were wearing their first pair of boots today), and next to them, not uttering a word and in the white dress she had worn for her first communion and let down for the occasion, was a tall girl of between fourteen and sixteen, probably their cousin or elder sister, red-faced, bewildered, hair plastered with rose pomade and terrified of getting her gloves dirty. As there weren't enough stable boys to unharness the carriages, the gentlemen rolled up their sleeves and set to work themselves. Depending on their social position they wore tailcoats, frock coats, jackets, short morning coats: fine clothes that enjoyed the esteem of an entire family, and which only came out of the wardrobe for grand occasions: frock coats with long skirts fluttering in the breeze, with stand-up collars, pockets as deep as sacks; jackets of heavy material, usually worn with a cap with a brass-edged peak; cut-off morning coats with two buttons side by side at the back like a pair of eyes, and whose skirts seemed to have been sawn off from the same piece by the local carpenter. Others (but of course they would be sitting at the far end of the table) wore their best smocks with the collar turned down over the shoulders, fine pleats at the back and an embroidered belt low on the waist.

Shirt fronts were thrown out like breastplates! Everyone was freshly trimmed, with their ears exposed, they had had a good close shave; some of them, who had got up before dawn when there wasn't enough light to wield the razor by, had slanting gashes under their nose, or chunks as large as three-franc pieces missing from their chins, chafed raw by the journey in the fresh air which had mottled all these big, white, radiant faces with pink blotches.

As the town hall was only a half-league from the farm they walked there, and came back the same way after the church service. The procession, which began as a single colourful streamer that rippled through the countryside, meandering along the narrow footpath between the unripe corn, soon got longer and broke up into separate groups, all dawdling to chat. The fiddler led the way, his violin decked with scalloped ribbons; next came the bride and groom, the parents and relatives, friends in no particular order, with the children at the back, who amused themselves by plucking oat hulls from the stems, or played around while no one was looking. Emma's dress, which was too long, trailed on the ground; she stopped to gather it up now and then, gently brushed off grass and tiny thistle heads with her gloved fingers while Charles waited empty-handed. Old man Rouault, wearing a new silk hat and with the cuffs of his black tailcoat hiding his hands, had Madame Bovary senior on his arm. Monsieur Bovary senior, who in his heart of hearts despised all these people, and so had just come in a military-style redingote with a single row of buttons, was plying pot-house gallantries to a blonde country lass. She just nodded, blushing, not knowing how to reply. The rest of the party were discussing their own affairs, or playing tricks behind each other's backs, carried away by the thought of the coming festivities; and if you listened hard you could hear the scraping and screeching of the fiddler, still playing across the fields. When he noticed that everyone had fallen way behind he stopped to get his breath back, took his time putting more resin on his bow so the strings squeaked better, and then set off again, jiggling the neck of the violin up and down to mark time. The sound of his playing scared off the birds for miles around.

The table was set up under the Dutch barn where the carts were kept. On it were four sirloins, six chicken fricassees, some braised veal, three gigots of lamb, and in the middle a nice roasted suckling pig, flanked by four andouille sausages with sorrel. On each corner stood decanters of eau de vie.* Bottles of sweet cider foamed round the corks, and every glass was filled with wine. Great dishes of golden cream, which shuddered with the slightest jolt of the table, had the newly-weds' initials drawn on their smooth surface in perfect arabesques. They had found a *pâtissier* from Yvetot to make the tarts and the nougat. As he had only recently set up in the area, he had gone to a great deal of trouble; for dessert he personally brought over a special wedding cake that raised gasps. The base was a blue cardboard square made to look like a temple, with porticos, colonnades and stucco statuettes, the recesses dotted with stars of gold foil; on the floor above was a keep in the shape of a *gâteau de Savoie*, with tiny fortifications made of angelica, almonds, raisins and orange quarters; and finally on the very top, which was a grassy meadow with rocks, lakes of jam and boats made of empty hazelnut shells, was a small Cupid sitting on a chocolate swing, whose two posts were topped with fresh rosebuds in place of bosses.

They ate till evening. When people were tired of sitting down they took a stroll in the yard or had a game of *bouchons** in the barn; then they came back to the table. Towards the end, a few nodded off and began snoring. But when coffee was served everything came back to life; and then the songs started, people did feats of strength, they lifted weights, played "under my thumb", tried lifting carts on their shoulders, told risqué jokes, kissed the ladies. Come evening when it was time to leave, the horses would barely fit between the shafts, having gorged themselves to the gunnels with oats; they kicked, reared, broke their harnesses, their masters cursed or laughed, and all night long there were runaway carrioles going flat out along the local roads in the moonlight, leaping ditches, jumping the stony stretches, hugging embankments with women leaning out of the door to grab the reins.

Those who stayed on at Les Bertaux spent all night in the kitchen, drinking. The children were asleep under the benches.

The bride had begged her father to be spared the customary jokes. Nonetheless, one of the cousins who was a fishmonger (and who had given two soles as a wedding present), had just started squirting water out of his mouth through the keyhole when old man Rouault managed to stop him in time, and told him that such unseemly behaviour was out of keeping with his son-in-law's responsible position. The cousin took this explanation with bad grace, however. To his way of thinking, old man Rouault was being stuck-up, so he went off into a corner with four or five others who by chance had all been given cheap cuts of meat more than once, and thought they had been treated inhospitably too, and were whispering in veiled terms about their host and wishing ruin on him.

Madame Bovary senior had been gritting her teeth all day. She hadn't been consulted about the bride's dress, or the organization of the wedding feast; she went to bed early. Instead of joining her, her husband sent out for cigars from Saint-Victor and smoked till daybreak, drinking kirsch toddies, a brew that was unknown to the rest of the gathering, and which in his eyes raised his standing even higher.

Charles wasn't naturally given to pranks, and didn't excel himself at the reception. He gave lacklustre replies to the witticisms, puns, double entendres, compliments and ribald remarks that people regarded as their duty to launch at him from the first course onwards.

The next day, in contrast, he seemed a different man. The day before he was the one who would have been taken for a virgin, while the bride gave nothing away. Even the shrewdest people didn't know what to make of her, and when they walked past them they did their utmost to try and fathom her out. But Charles didn't hide anything. He called her "my wife", spoke to her familiarly as "*tu*", enquired after her to everyone, looked for her everywhere, and took her with him round the yards, or was seen between the trees in this distance with his arm round her waist, leaning over her as they walked and crumpling the bodice of her dress with his head.

Two days after the reception, husband and wife left: Charles wasn't able to be away for longer because of his patients. Old man Rouault had them taken back in his carriole, and went with them as far as Vassonville. There, he kissed his daughter one last time, got out of the carriage and headed back. When he had gone a short way he stopped, and as he watched the carriole disappear, its wheels spinning in the dust, he gave a deep sigh. He remembered his own wedding day, his past life, his wife's first pregnancy; he too had been overjoyed the day he took her from her father's house and back to his own, when he carried her behind him on the pillion, trotting through the snow – because it was around Christmas time and the countryside was completely white; she had held on to him with one arm, her basket hanging over the other; the long lace of her Cauchois coif fluttered in the breeze and occasionally brushed his lips, and when he turned round she was there, close to him, at his shoulder, her rosy little face smiling quietly beneath the gold front-piece of her bonnet. To warm her hands she put them on his chest now and then. But that was years ago! Their son would have been thirty by now! Then he looked back and saw the road was empty. It made him feel as sad as a house without furniture, and, fond memories mingling with dark thoughts in a mind fogged by all the revelry, for a moment he felt a longing to go for a walk over by the church. But he was afraid the sight of it would make him even gloomier, so he went straight home.

Monsieur and Madame Charles arrived in Tostes at about six o'clock. The neighbours came to the windows to see their doctor's new wife.

The old maidservant appeared, greeted her, apologized that dinner wasn't ready, and while they were waiting got Madame to take a look round her house.

5

THE BRICK FAÇADE GAVE DIRECTLY ONTO THE STREET, or more exactly the main road. Inside the front door hung a coat with a short collar, a bridle and a black leather cap, while a pair of leggings covered in dried mud lay on the floor in a corner. To the right was the dining room, the part of the house where one ate and entertained. Canary-yellow wallpaper, broken up by a frieze of pale flower garlands, fluttered on its slack cloth backing; white calico curtains edged with red braid hung at the windows, and glinting on the narrow mantelpiece stood a clock with a head of Hippocrates between two silver-plated candlesticks under oval glass shades. On the other side of the hallway was Charles's surgery, a small room about six paces across, with a table, three chairs and an office armchair. Volumes of the *Dictionnaire des sciences médicales*, their pages uncut, but whose bindings showed signs of having been sold and resold many times, were almost the sole occupants of the pine bookcase. During consultations the smell of baking came through the dividing wall, while in the kitchen they could hear patients coughing in the surgery as they poured out their tales of woe. Next, and opening onto the courtyard and the stables, was a large ramshackle room with an oven, which was used to store wood, wine and goods they had bought, and was full of old bits of metal, empty barrels, broken farm implements and other dusty objects whose purpose it was impossible to guess.

The garden, longer than it was wide, ran between two wattle-and-daub walls covered in apricot trees on espaliers, down to a thorn hedge that divided it from the fields. In the middle stood a sundial made of slate on a stone plinth; four flower beds filled with spindly wild roses were spaced out evenly round a square plot of more useful and important plants. At the far end, beneath some small fir trees, a plasterwork priest was reading his breviary.

Emma went up to the bedrooms. The first wasn't furnished; but the other, the marital bedroom, had a mahogany bed in an alcove with red hangings. On the chest of drawers stood a box covered in seashells, and on the writing desk by the window, in a carafe, was a bunch of orange blossom tied with white satin ribbon. It was a bridal bouquet – the other woman's bouquet! She stared at it. Charles noticed, picked it up and took it to the attic, while, sitting in an armchair (they were bringing in her things and putting them down around her), Emma thought about her own bridal bouquet, which was packed away in a cardboard box, and wondered what would happen to it if she were to die.

She spent the first few days contemplating the changes she would make to her house. She took the glass shades off the candlesticks, had new wallpaper hung, the staircase painted and benches put round the sundial in the garden; she even asked how to go about getting a pond with a fountain and some fish. While her husband, knowing she enjoyed going out for drives, finally found a second-hand *boc*,* or buggy, which with its new lamps and stitched leather mudguards looked almost like a tilbury.

So he was happy, without a care in the world. A quiet dinner together, a walk along the road in the evening, the way she put her hand up to her headbands, the sight of her straw hat hanging from the window catch, and many other things besides that Charles had never imagined being a source of enjoyment, were what now made up his ongoing state of happiness. Side by side in bed in the morning he watched the sunlight touch the down on her fair cheeks, partly covered by the scalloped side flaps of her nightcap. Seen from close up her eyes seemed bigger, especially when her eyelids fluttered as she woke; black in shadow, dark blue in daylight, they appeared to be made of different layers of colour which, heavier in their depths, became lighter nearer the enamel-like surface. His own eyes would sink into them, he would see his head and shoulders reflected in miniature, with the scarf round his head and the top of his nightshirt unbuttoned. He would get up. She would come to the window to see him off, and lean on the sill between two pots of geraniums, draped in her dressing gown. Out in the street Charles fastened on his spurs on the marker stone, and she would keep talking to him from above, while nibbling off tiny pieces of petals or leaves which she blew to him, and which, fluttering, floating, tracing semicircles in the air like a bird, would land on the ungroomed coat of the old grey mare that stood stock still at the door. Once mounted Charles would blow her a kiss; she would wave back, close the window, and then he set off. And on the main road whose long ribbon of dust stretched endlessly away, along sunken lanes where trees bowed down like cradles, on paths where the corn reached up to his knees, with the sun on the back of his neck and morning air in his nostrils, heart filled with the bliss of the night, spirit at peace and flesh content, he would go on his way chewing over his happiness like someone who can still taste the truffles that they have just eaten for dinner.

Up till now, what had been good about his life? Was it when he was at school, shut away behind high walls, all alone among classmates who were richer or better at lessons than him, who laughed at his accent, made fun of his clothes, and whose mothers came to visit with cakes hidden in their muffs? Was it later when he was studying medicine, and was always too broke to go to the dance hall with his mistress, some little factory girl? Then he lived for fourteen months with the widow, whose feet were like blocks of ice in bed. But now, and for the rest of his life, he had a pretty wife whom he worshipped. His whole world was contained in the silky contours of her petticoats; he would reproach himself for not loving her enough, and long to see her, and he would hurry home, go upstairs, heart pounding. In her room Emma would be getting dressed; he would come in without making a sound, kiss her on the back, she would give a little cry.

He couldn't stop himself from constantly touching her comb, her rings, her headscarf; sometimes he kissed her full on the cheeks, or gave her lots of little kisses all the way up her bare arm from the fingertips to the shoulder; and she would push him away, bored and half-smiling, like you do with a child who hangs round your neck.

Before she got married she had believed she was in love. But when the happiness that should have come from this love didn't materialize, she thought she had made a mistake. And so Emma tried to understand exactly what was meant in real life by the words *bliss*, *passion* and *rapture,* which had always sounded so beautiful in books.

6

S HE HAD READ *PAUL ET VIRGINIE** and had dreamt about the little bamboo house, the Negro Domingo, the dog called Fido and especially the sweet friendship of a kind young brother who picks red berries for you from great big trees taller than a church steeple, or runs barefoot over the sand to bring you a bird's nest.

When she was thirteen her father took her into town to put her in a convent. They stayed at an inn in the Saint-Gervais quarter, where they ate supper off plates painted with designs telling the story of Mademoiselle de la Vallière.* The legendary tales, scratched off in places by knife marks, all extolled religion, kind-heartedness and the grandeur of the court.

For the first few days, far from being bored at the convent she enjoyed the company of the nuns, who kept her amused by taking her to the chapel, which was down a long corridor leading off the refectory. She rarely played at break time, knew her catechism, and was always the first to answer the curate's difficult questions. Living constantly in the tepid atmosphere of the classroom, among pale women who carried rosaries with brass crosses, she was lulled by the mystic languor that rose from the incense at the altar, the cool water in the stoup and the glow of candles. Instead of paying attention during Mass she looked at the devout, sky-blue-edged illustrations in her book, where she liked the sick sheep, the Sacred Heart pierced by arrows, and poor Jesus falling over as he carried his cross. To mortify herself she would try and go a whole day without food. She would think up vows to fulfil.

At confession she made up minor sins so she could stay on her knees in the darkness for longer, hands clasped, her face close to the grill, listening to the whispers of the priest. The comparisons between fiancés, spouses, heavenly love and eternal marriage that came up continually in sermons aroused unexpected feelings of sweetness deep down in her soul.

Before evening prayers in the prep room they had a reading from a religious book. On weekdays it was a summary of a Bible story, or from Abbé Frayssinous's *Lectures*, and on Sunday, for relaxation, passages from the *Génie du christianisme*.* The first few times, how closely she listened to the high-sounding lamentations of romantic melancholy repeated in every echo of heaven and earth! If she had grown up above a shop in the working district of a town she might have been open to nature's all-pervading poetry, which we normally only encounter in books. But she knew the countryside too well; she was familiar with bleating flocks, milking and ploughing. Accustomed to tranquil scenery, she looked for dramatic events. She only liked the sea when it was stormy, green fields when they were scattered with ruins. She had to get some kind of personal benefit from things, and she dismissed as useless anything that didn't immediately satisfy her heart's desire – being more of a romantic than an artist, searching for emotions rather than a landscape.

At the convent there was a spinster who came in for a week every month to work in the linen room. Under the wing of the archdiocese, a member of an old gentry family ruined during the Revolution, she ate at the nuns' table in the refectory and always had a chat with them before going back to work. The boarders often slipped out of study periods to go and see her. She knew all the courtly songs from the last century, and sang them quietly as she sewed. She told stories, brought you the news, did shopping for you in town, and secretly lent the older girls novels that she kept in the pockets of her apron, and which the gel in question would devour chapter by chapter in the breaks between lessons. They were about love affairs and lovers, with ill-used ladies fainting in lonely houses, postillions murdered at every staging post, horses killed on every page, dark sombre forests, hearts in torment, vows, sobs, landaus in the moonlight, nightingales in groves, *gentlemen* as brave as lions, as meek as lambs, virtuous like no one on earth, always well-dressed, and who wept buckets. For six months at the age of fifteen, Emma inhaled the dust from these ancient pages. As with Walter Scott later on she became enamoured of things historic, dreamt of oak chests, guardrooms and minstrels. She would have liked to live in an old manor house like the chatelaines in long bodices who spent their days under trefoil arches, leaning on the stonework with their heads in their hands, watching a distant cavalier with a white plume galloping across the countryside towards them on a black horse. She made a religion out of Mary Stuart, was zealous in her veneration of renowned or ill-fated women. For her, Joan of Arc, Héloïse, Agnès Sorel, La Belle Ferronnière and Clémence Isaure stood out like meteors on the dark expanse of history, where, here and there, still prominent but deeper in shadow and quite unrelated, were St Louis and his oak tree, the dying Bayard, some of Louis XI's ferocious deeds, something of St Bartholomew, the Béarnais's plume, as well as the memory of the painted plates that sang the praises of Louis XIV.*

The sentimental ballads she sung in music lessons were always about little angels with golden wings, Madonna-like women, lagoons, gondoliers, tranquil compositions which, behind the silly style and careless playing, gave her glimpses of the alluring dream world of romantic reality. Some of her classmates brought keepsake albums that they had been given as Christmas or New Year presents back to the convent with them. They had to keep them hidden, it was quite a performance; they would read them in the dormitory. Daintily holding the beautiful satin covers, Emma stared with bedazzled eyes at the names of authors unknown to her who, beneath their piece, usually signed themselves *Comte* or *Vicomte*.

As she blew the tissue paper that covered the engravings, making it lift then fall back gently over the page, she would shudder. At the balustrade of a balcony was a young man in a short cloak, clasping in his arms a young woman in a white dress with a purse at her girdle; or anonymous portraits of English ladies with blond curls who looked at you with big bright eyes from beneath round straw hats. You saw them parading in carriages gliding through parkland, with a greyhound racing in front of a team of trotting horses ridden by two young postillions in white knee breeches. Others lay dreaming on sofas with opened letters beside them, and gazed at the moon through half-open windows draped in black curtains. A tear on their cheek, ingénues would feed turtledoves through the bars of a Gothic cage, or, with their heads tilted to one side, smilingly play "he loves me, he loves me not" with a marguerite, their fingertips turned up like long pointed shoes. And then there were sultans with long pipes reclining rapturously under arbours in the arms of bayadères; Giaours,* Turkish scimitars, Greek caps, and especially those pallid fantastical landscapes with palms and pine trees at the same time, tigers on the right, lions on the left, Tartar minarets on the horizon, Roman ruins in the foreground, kneeling camels – the whole thing surrounded by nice clean virgin forest, and with a long vertical beam of sunlight shimmering on the water where, standing out like white scratches on a steel-grey background, swans swim away into the distance.

Above Emma's head, the shade of the oil lamp on the wall lit up all these pictures of the world, which passed before her eyes one by one in the silent dormitory, to the distant sound of a late cab that was still out on the boulevards.

When her mother died, she cried a lot for the first few days. She made a funerary tableau with some of the deceased's hair, and in a letter home to Les Bertaux full of gloomy reflections on life, she asked to be buried in the same tomb. The old man thought she was ill and came to see her. Inwardly Emma was gratified to think she had managed to reach the pale existence's singular ideal at her first attempt, something never achieved by ordinary hearts. And so she let herself drift away into Lamartine-like* meanderings, listened to harps by lakes, songs about dying swans, falling leaves, pure virgins who went to heaven, and the voice of the Everlasting Lord ringing out in the valleys. She soon became bored but refused to admit it, carried on out of habit and then through vanity, and was surprised to feel soothed eventually, and with no more sadness in her heart than wrinkles on her brow.

The Sisters, who had greatly overestimated her calling, were astonished to find Mademoiselle Rouault apparently slipping through their fingers. But they had lavished so many church services on her, so many retreats, novenas and sermons, preached so much about the respect owed to saints and martyrs, given so much good advice

34

about maidenly modesty and the salvation of the soul, that she did what a horse does when you drag it by the mouth: she pulled up sharp, and the bit came out from between her teeth. Her spirit, so clear in its enthusiasms, which had loved the church for its flowers, music for its sentimental songs and literature for its heated excitements, now rebelled against the mysteries of the faith in the same way that it was irked by the discipline that was alien to her nature. When her father took her away from the convent they weren't sorry to see her go. In fact the Mother Superior felt that lately she had become most disrespectful towards the community.

When she first came back to live at home, Emma delighted in ordering the servants about, and then sickened of the country and missed the convent. The first time Charles came to Les Bertaux she saw herself as much disillusioned, having nothing more to learn or feel.

Yet anxiety about her new situation, or perhaps annoyance at the presence of this man, was enough to make her believe that the wonderful passion which up till then had always been like a great bird with pink feathers soaring among the splendour of heavenly poetic skies, finally belonged to her – and yet she wasn't able to picture the peace and quiet in which she was now living as the happiness she had dreamt of.

7

Y ET SOMETIMES she felt this was the best time of her life, the honeymoon as people call it. To savour its sweetness you had to set off for lands with high-sounding names where matrimony can look forward to a time of mellow idleness! In post-chaises, beneath blue silk awnings, you drive gently up steep paths listening to the postillion singing, echoed by goat bells in the mountains and the muffled sound of waterfalls. At sundown you inhale the scent of lemon trees in little bays, and in the evening, alone on the terrace of a villa with your fingers intertwined, you gaze at the stars and make plans for the future. It seemed to her that some places in the world make you happy, like a plant that won't grow in any other soil. How she could have leant on the balcony of a Swiss chalet, or shut away her sadness in a cottage in Scotland with a husband dressed in a black velvet tailcoat with long skirts, and who wore soft boots, a pointed hat and lace cuffs!

She might have wished to confide all this to someone. But how do you describe an intangible malaise which changes appearance like the clouds, swirls like the breeze? She lacked the words, and thus the opportunity, the courage.

And yet if Charles had wanted this, if he had suspected it, if just once his eyes had seen into her thoughts, she believed that a great plenitude would suddenly be released from his heart, like ripe fruit falls from a tree when you shake the espalier. But although their private life became ever more intimate, something inside her detached itself, loosening her ties with him.

Charles's conversation was as flat as a pavement, and other people's ideas and thoughts passed by on it in their everyday clothes without arousing any emotion, laughter or dreams. When he lived in Rouen, he said, he had never once wanted to go to the theatre and see actors from Paris. He couldn't swim, fence or shoot a pistol, and one day he wasn't able to explain an equestrian term that she had come across in a novel.

Yet shouldn't a man know everything, excel at many different pursuits, introduce you to the power of the passions, the niceties of life, to all its mysteries? This man taught her nothing, knew nothing, wished for nothing. He thought she was happy; and she resented him for his steadfast tranquillity, his unruffled sluggishness, even the happiness she gave him.

Sometimes she would draw, and it was a great diversion for Charles to stand and watch her bent over her sketch, screwing up his eyes so he could see her work properly, or rolling pieces of bread into balls with his thumb. When it came to the piano, the faster her fingers flew, the more he marvelled. She struck the keys assuredly, ran them up and down the keyboard without stopping. Shaken about in this way, the old instrument, which was out of tune, could be heard at the other end of the village if the window was open, and the bailiff's clerk, walking along the main road hatless and in slippers, papers in hand, would often stop to listen.

What was more, Emma knew how to run the house. She sent out patients' accounts in well-phrased letters that didn't sound like a demand. When they had neighbours over for lunch on Sunday she always managed to produce an attractive dish, knew how to serve pyramids of greengages on a bed of vine leaves, pots of jam upturned on a plate, and talked of buying bowls for a *rince-bouche** for after dessert.

All this reflected well on Bovary.

Charles began to think more highly of himself for having such a wife. He would proudly show people two small graphite sketches by her in the dining room, which he had had put in heavy frames and hung from long green cords. After Mass he could be seen at his front door in handsome tapestry slippers.

He would come home late, at ten o'clock or sometimes midnight, and ask for something to eat. Since the maid had gone to bed it was Emma who got it for him. He would take off his frock coat to be more comfortable at table. He would tell her the names of everyone he had met one after another, the villages he had been to, the prescriptions he had written and, satisfied with himself, he would finish the rest of the boiled beef with onion sauce, peel some cheese, crunch on an apple, empty his carafe, then take himself off to bed where he fell asleep on his back and snored.

As he was used to wearing a nightcap, his scarf wouldn't stay in place over his ears; so in the morning his hair would be in a mess, in his eyes and white with down from the pillow, whose string fastenings came undone during the night. He wore short stout boots with two thick pleats on the instep, angled outwards towards the ankle, while the uppers went straight down, as tight as if they were on a wooden foot. He said they were "perfectly good enough for the country".

His mother approved of such thriftiness; she came to see him as she always had in the past, whenever she had had a row at home; and yet Madame Bovary senior seemed biased against her daughter-in-law. She thought she was "too grand for people of their means"; firewood, sugar and candles "disappeared as if it were a large household", and the amount of charcoal logs used in the kitchen was enough to cook dozens of meals! She tidied the linen cupboards and taught her to keep an eye on what the butcher delivered. Emma accepted her advice – Madame Bovary was lavish with it – and all day long the words *daughter dear* and *mother dear* went back and forth, accompanied by a slight curl of the lip as they said nice things to each other in voices shaking with rage.

In Madame Dubuc's day, the older woman had felt she was still the favourite; but now Charles's love for Emma seemed like a betrayal of her affection, an invasion of her territory, and she observed her son's happiness in sorrowful silence, like someone who has lost everything looks through the windows of their former home and sees other people sitting down to dinner. To jog his memory she would remind him of the troubles he had had, the sacrifices he had made and, comparing them with Emma's omissions, told him that it wasn't sensible to worship her to the exclusion of all else.

Charles didn't know how to reply; he respected his mother and adored his wife; he regarded the judgement of the first as unerring, while believing the other to be beyond reproach. Once Madame Bovary had left he would venture one or two of his mother's most innocuous comments, couched in the same terms; but Emma would swiftly put him right, and send him back to his patients.

Yet following what she regarded as sound theories, she wanted to demonstrate her love. In the garden in the moonlight she would recite all the passionate verses she knew, sing him sighing, melancholy adagios; but afterwards she felt as calm as before, while Charles, apparently unmoved, showed no sign of being more in love.

When she didn't manage to raise a spark from his heart like this, and unable to understand what it was that she couldn't feel, as if she only believed in things that never expressed themselves in any conventional way, she simply concluded that Charles's passion had given all it had to give. His effusiveness had become predictable; he would kiss her at particular times. It was the same with other couples, like a dessert that you know is coming after a dull dinner.

A gamekeeper whom Monsieur had cured of pneumonia gave Madame a little Italian greyhound bitch; she would take it for walks, since she sometimes went out to be alone for a while, so as not to have to be forever looking at the garden or the dusty road.

She would go all the way to the beech grove at Banneville, near the deserted house that stood on the corner at the edge of the fields. In the ditches there were tall reeds with sharp-edged leaves.

She would look to see if anything had changed since the last time. She found foxgloves and stock in the same places, nettles round large stones, lichen on the three windows whose permanently closed shutters were spotted with mould, their iron bars rusted. Her mind would wander aimlessly at first, like her greyhound, who ran round in circles in the open countryside, yapping at yellow butterflies, chasing shrews or nibbling poppies beside a cornfield. Then gradually her thoughts would settle, and sitting prodding the grass with the tip of her parasol, Emma would say to herself:

"My God, why did I get married?"

And she wondered if there might have been a way, by some other combination of circumstances, of meeting another man; and she tried to picture what these events that had never happened might have been, this different life, this husband she didn't know. Because there was nothing quite like him. He might have been handsome, witty, distinguished, attractive, like the men her old classmates at the convent had no doubt married. What were they doing now? In towns, with the sound and stir of the streets, the buzz of theatres and the bright lights of balls, they lived lives where a heart could unfold, where senses could spread their wings. But for her, life was as cold as an attic with a north-facing window, and that silent spider, ennui, spun its web in all the shadowy corners of her heart. She remembered prize-giving days when she used to go up onto the platform to collect her little wreaths. She had a lovely manner, with her plaited hair, white dress and open sloe-coloured shoes, and when she came back to her seat, gentlemen would lean over to pay her compliments; the courtyard would be full of barouches, people said goodbye to her from carriage windows, the music teacher bowed as he went past with his violin case. How long ago that was! How long ago!

She called Djali, put her between her knees, ran her fingers over her long slender head, and said:

"Come on, give your mistress a kiss, you never have anything to be sad about."

Then, studying the melancholy expression on the svelte animal's face, which gave a big yawn, she would soften and, comparing it to herself, talked to it as if comforting someone who is suffering.

Sometimes a gust of wind, a sudden sea breeze would come bowling across the flatlands of the Pays de Caux, bringing a salty freshness to the fields. The rushes hissed, the beech leaves rustled with a sudden shiver, while the swaying treetops went on with their great murmuring. And she would pull her shawl round her and get up.

On the wide path, green daylight filtering through the leaves would light up the moss that crunched softly beneath her feet. The sun was setting; through the branches the sky was red, and the lines of identical trees seemed like a dusky brown colonnade on a gold backdrop; seized with fright she would call out to Djali, then hurry back along the road to Tostes, where she would collapse into an armchair and not say a word all evening.

But around the end of September, something extraordinary happened; she was invited to La Vaubyessard, the home of the Marquis d'Andervilliers.

A junior minister during the Restoration, the Marquis, who wanted to return to politics, was preparing his official candidacy for the Chamber of Deputies. In the winter he often went out distributing firewood, and at the Departmental Council was always making vigorous demands for new roads in his district. During the summer he had had an abscess in his mouth, which Charles had cured almost miraculously by using a lancet at exactly the right moment. When his estate manager, sent to Tostes to pay the bill for the surgery, got back in the evening, he told him he had seen some splendid cherries in the doctor's little garden. Coincidentally, cherry trees wouldn't grow at La Vaubyessard; the Marquis asked Bovary for some cuttings, made a point of coming to thank him in person, noticed Emma, thought she had a nice figure and didn't speak or behave like a country girl; so up at the chateau they didn't think it would be overstepping the bounds of condescension, or committing a gaffe, to invite the young couple.

One Wednesday at three o'clock, Monsieur and Madame Bovary set off for La Vaubyessard in their *boc*, a large trunk tied on the back and a hatbox in front of the dashboard. Charles had a box between his legs as well.

They arrived at nightfall, just as the lanterns were being lit in the park to show the way for the carriages.

8

THE CHATEAU, a modern building in the Italian style with two projecting wings and three entrances, lay at the far end of a vast lawn where cows grazed among scattered clumps of tall trees, while shrubs, rhododendrons, mock orange and viburnum paraded their varied clusters of lush greenery beside the curving sandy drive. A river flowed under a bridge; through the mist buildings with thatched roofs could be made out, dotted across meadows bordered by two gently sloping wooded hillsides, while at the back, among banks of flowers and bushes, two rows of outbuildings and stables stood side by side, the remains of the old chateau that had been demolished.

Charles's *boc* stopped in front of the central entrance; servants appeared; the Marquis came over and, giving the doctor's wife his arm, showed her into the entrance.

It was tall with a marble floor, the sound of voices and footsteps echoed like in a church. Ahead was a straight staircase, to the left a gallery overlooking the garden and which led to the billiard room, from whose doorway came the clacking of ivory balls. As she walked through it on the way to the salon, Emma saw men with solemn faces standing round the billiard table, chins nestling on tall cravats, all wearing decorations, and who smiled silently as they wielded the cue. On the dark wood panelling were large gilt-framed pictures with names in black letters at the bottom. She read: "Jean-Antoine d'Andervilliers d'Yverbonville, Comte de la Vaubyessard and Baron de la Fresnaye, killed at the Battle of Coutras, 20th October 1587". And on another: "Jean-Antoine-Henry-Guy d'Andervilliers de la Vaubyessard, Admiral of France and Chevalier of the Order of Saint-Michel, wounded in action at Saint-Vaast-la-Hougue,* 29th May 1692, died at La Vaubyessard, 23rd January 1693". The rest could barely be made out, because the light from the lamps, which shone directly onto the green baize of the billiard table, threw shadows across the room. Burnishing the rows of paintings, it broke up against them in delicate fishbone patterns that followed the crackling in the varnish; and among all these great dark squares edged in gold, a lighter section of a painting stood out here and there, a pale forehead, two eyes that stared at you, wigs tumbling onto the powdered shoulders of red tailcoats, or the buckle of a garter strap atop a shapely thigh.

The Marquis opened the door to the salon; one of the ladies (the Marquise herself) got up, came over to greet Emma and asked her to sit next to her on a love seat, where she began to talk to her in a friendly way, as if she had known her for years. She was about forty, with handsome shoulders, a hooked nose, a drawling voice, wearing a simple guipure scarf over her chestnut hair, which fell to a point at the back. A young blonde woman sat nearby in a high-backed chair, and the gentlemen, who all wore a small flower in the buttonhole of their evening coats, were chatting to the ladies by the fireplace.

A seven o'clock, dinner was served. The men, who were in greater numbers, sat at the first table in the entrance hall, and the ladies in the second, in the dining room with the Marquis and Marquise.

As she walked in Emma felt herself being bathed in warm air, a fragrance of flowers mingled with fine linen, the aroma of cooked meats and the smell of truffles. The flames of the candelabra threw long reflections in the lids of the silver dishes; the many-sided crystal glasses, misted over with a dull sheen, gave off pale beams of light; bouquets of flowers lined the table, and on the broad-edged plates the napkins, folded like a bishop's mitre, had an oval bread roll placed between their two pleats. The red claws of lobsters hung over the edges of trays; in deep baskets, large pieces of fruit were laid out in tiers on moss; the quail still had feathers, steam rose; while in silk stockings, knee breeches, white cravat and a lace ruffle, sober as a judge, the butler, passing trays of carved meat between the guests, served the piece you chose with a deft movement of his serving spoon. On top of a large porcelain stove with brass beading, a statue of a woman draped from the neck stood motionless, watching the room full of people.

Madame Bovary noticed that some of the ladies hadn't put their gloves in their glass.

At the head of the table, by himself among the women, crouched over his heaped plate, napkin round his neck like a child, an old man was eating, gravy dribbling from his mouth. His eyes were bleary, he wore his hair in a short tail tied up with black ribbon. It was the Marquis's father-in-law, the old Duc de Laverdière, the former favourite of the Comte d'Artois at the time of the Marquis de Conflan's hunting parties at Vaudreuil, and who was said to have been Queen Marie-Antoinette's lover, between Messieurs de Coigny and de Lauzun. He had led a life of wild debauchery, filled with duels, wagers, abducted women, had consumed his entire fortune and terrified his family. Behind his chair a servant was speaking into his ear, telling him what dishes were as he pointed them out, stammering; Emma couldn't take her eyes off this old man with lolling lips, as if he were something extraordinary and exalted. He had been at Court, shared the Queen's bed!

They served champagne *frappé*. Emma shivered all over as the coldness touched her tongue. She had never seen pomegranates or eaten pineapple. Even the sugar seemed whiter and finer than elsewhere.

Then the ladies went up to their rooms to get ready for the ball.

Emma dressed with the scrupulous eye of an actress before her first appearance. She arranged her hair according to the hairdresser's advice, then got into her light barège* wool dress, which was laid out on the bed. Charles's trousers were too tight round the waist.

"The under-straps are going to make it awkward for dancing," he said.

"Dancing?" Emma replied.

"Yes!"

"Have you lost your mind? People will laugh at you, stay in your seat. Besides, it's more fitting for a doctor," she added.

Charles went quiet. He paced up and down, waiting for Emma to finish dressing.

He could see her in the mirror from behind, between two candlesticks. Her black eyes seemed blacker. Her headbands, shifted down slightly towards her ears, shimmered vivid blue; on her chignon a rose quivered on its stem, with imitation dewdrops on the tips of the leaves. She wore a saffron-yellow dress picked out with three bouquets of button roses mixed with greenery.

Charles came over and kissed her on the shoulder.

"Don't touch me!" she said. "You'll crease my dress."

There was a flourish of violins, the sound of a horn. She went down the staircase, trying not to run.

The quadrilles had started. Quite a crowd was arriving. People jostled. She sat on a banquette by the door.

When the contredanse finished, the dance floor emptied except for groups of men who stood chatting and liveried servants carrying large trays. In the line of seated women, painted fans were fluttering, bouquets half-hid the smiles on the faces, and small flasks with gold stoppers turned round and round in half-open hands whose white gloves showed the outline of the fingernails and were gathered in tightly at the wrist. Lace trimmings trembled on bodices, diamond brooches sparkled on busts, lockets on bangles rustled on bare arms. Hair, fixed over foreheads and tied at the nape of the neck, had wreaths, clusters or sprays of forget-me-nots, jasmine, pomegranate blossoms, ears of corn or cornflowers. Sitting peacefully in their seats, scowling mothers wore red turbans.

Emma's heart beat a little faster when, her partner holding her by the fingertips, she stood in line and waited for the bow stroke to signal the off. But she soon settled down, and swaying in time with the orchestra she glided forward with little movements of her head. She smiled at certain subtleties from the violin, which sometimes played a solo when the other instruments had stopped; the distinct sound of gold louis being tipped onto the cloth of the gaming tables came from nearby; then all at once everything picked up again, the cornet let out a resounding note, feet moved in time, skirts puffed out and skimmed, hands touched then parted; the eyes that had been lowered looked up again and stared into your own.

Some of the men (there were over a dozen), aged between twenty-five and forty, scattered among the dancers or chatting in doorways, stood out from the crowd because of a family likeness, despite differences in age, dress or features.

Their clothes, of better cut, seemed to be of softer material, and their hair, gathered in curls at their temples, had the sheen of finest pomade. Their complexion was that of wealth, the shade of white that enhances the pallor of porcelain, the watered shimmer of satin, the shine of beautiful furniture, maintained in the peak of health by a simple and exquisite diet. Their necks moved effortlessly in low cravats; their long sideburns rested on turned-down collars; they dabbed their lips with handkerchiefs embroidered with large initials, and from which rose sweet smells. The older ones looked youthful, while there was something middle-aged about the young men's faces. In their impassive eyes hovered the serenity of appetites satisfied every day; yet behind their delicate manners lay that brutality which shows itself in easy victories where strength flexes its muscles and vanity finds amusement, the mastery of thoroughbreds and the company of fallen women.

Not far from where Emma was standing, a beau in a blue tailcoat was talking about Italy to a pale young woman wearing a set of pearls. They praised the girth of the pillars of St Peter's, Tivoli, Vesuvius, Castellammare and Cassine, the roses in Genoa, the Coliseum by moonlight. Emma half-listened to this conversation filled with words she didn't understand. People were making a fuss of a young man who the week before had beaten Miss Arabelle and Romulus, and had won two thousand louis for jumping a ditch in England. One was grumbling about his racehorses putting on weight, another about the printer who had misspelt the name of his horse.

The air in the ballroom was heavy; the lamps began to dim. People surged into the billiard room. A servant stood on a chair and broke two windows; at the sound of breaking glass, Madame Bovary turned and saw peasants in the garden, their faces at the window looking in. Memories of Les Bertaux came back to her. She saw the farm, the muddy pond, her father in his smock under the apple trees, she saw herself as she was then, skimming cream off pots of milk in the dairy with her finger. But in the sudden dazzle of the present moment, her former life, up till now so clear, completely disappeared, and she began to doubt whether she had lived it at all. But now she was here; and over everything outside the ball there was only darkness. She ate maraschino ice cream from a vermeil scallop dish in her left hand, eyes half-closed, the spoon between her teeth.

Nearby a lady dropped her fan. A man, one of the dancers, walked past.

"Do be so kind, Monsieur," the lady said, "to please pick up my fan, it's here behind the sofa!"

The gentleman bowed, and as he reached out his arm, Emma saw the young lady throw something white, folded in a triangle, into his hat. Picking up the fan, the gentleman respectfully handed it to her; she thanked him with a little nod and began sniffing her bouquet.

After supper, where there were many different wines from Spain and the Rhine, soups made of lobster and almond milk, Trafalgar sponge and all manner of cold meats in aspic that quivered on the tray, one by one the carriages began to leave. Lifting the corner of the silk net curtains, she saw the light of their lamps gliding into the darkness. The wall seats emptied; there were still a few people at the gaming table; the musicians cooled the tips of their fingers on their tongue; Charles was leaning back against a door, half asleep.

At three in the morning the cotillion began. Emma didn't know how to waltz. Everyone was waltzing, Mademoiselle d'Andervilliers herself and the Marquise; there were only the house guests left, a dozen people or so.

Yet one of the waltzers, known familiarly as *Vicomte*, and whose low-cut waistcoat hugged his body, twice came and asked Madame Bovary to dance, promising to guide her and that she would manage perfectly well.

They began slowly, then went faster. They danced round and round, everything was spinning round them, the lamps, the furniture, the panelling and the dance floor, like a disc on a pivot. As they went past the doors the hem of Emma's dress just brushed his trousers; their legs became tangled; he looked down at her, she looked up at him; suddenly she felt listless, she stopped. They set off again; the Vicomte led her off at a quicker pace to the far end of the gallery where, out of breath, she nearly fell, and rested her head on his chest for a moment. Then, still spinning round and round, but more gently now, he took her back to her seat; she leant back against the wall and put her hand over her eyes.

When she opened them, a lady was sitting on a stool in the middle of the salon with three men kneeling in front of her. She chose the Vicomte, and the violin began to play again.

Everyone watched. They came and went, back and forth, her body never moving, her head slightly lowered, him always in the same posture, shoulders thrown back, elbow lifted, chin forward. She knew how to waltz, this one! They danced for a long time and exhausted all the others.

People talked for a little longer, and then after the goodnights, or rather the good mornings, the guests who were staying went up to bed.

Charles dragged himself up the banisters, his legs were giving way under him. He had spent five solid hours standing at the gaming table, watching people play whist without understanding a thing. Once he had taken his boots off he gave a great sigh of contentment.

Emma put a shawl round her, opened the window and leant on the sill.

The night was dark. There were a few spots of rain. She inhaled the damp breeze that cooled her eyelids. The music of the ball was still buzzing in her ears, and she tried hard to stay awake so as to prolong the illusion of this life of luxury that in a short while she was going to have to give up.

It began to get light. For a long time she looked at the windows of the chateau, trying to guess which were the rooms of the people she had noticed the night before. She would have liked to know about their lives, get inside them, be part of them.

But she was shivering with cold. She undressed and curled up under the sheets against Charles, who was asleep.

There were a lot of people at breakfast. It lasted ten minutes; there was nothing to drink of any kind, which amazed the doctor. Then

Mademoiselle d'Andervilliers gathered up all the pieces of brioche in a little wicker basket to feed the swans on the ornamental lake, and they went for a walk in the hothouse, where strange bristly plants were set out in pyramids in hanging vases, out of which trailed long green intertwined tendrils, as if from vipers' nests that were too full. At the far end, the orangery led under cover as far as the outhouses. To entertain the young woman the Marquis took her to see the stables. Above hay racks shaped like baskets, porcelain plates gave each horse's name in black letters. As they walked past the animals tossed their heads, clicked their tongues. The wooden floor in the tack room gleamed like one in a drawing room. Carriage harness was laid out on two revolving stands in the middle, while bits, whips, stirrups and curb chains hung along the wall.

In the meantime Charles asked one of the servants to harness his *boc*. It was brought round to the entrance and, once all their packages had been loaded on, the Bovarys thanked the Marquis and Marquise and set off back to Tostes.

In silence Emma watched the wheels go round. At the other end of the bench seat Charles drove with his arms apart, and the little horse ambled along between the shafts, which were too wide. The slack reins slapped on its hindquarters, which soaked them in lather, while the box tied to the back kept bumping loudly against the body of the *boc*.

They were on the hill at Thibourville when some young gallants suddenly rode past in front of them, laughing, cigars in mouths. Emma thought she recognized the Vicomte; she turned, but all she could see in the distance were heads rising and falling with the uneven rhythm of a trot or gallop.

A quarter of a league further on they had to stop to repair the breeching with a piece of rope.

As Charles was giving the harness a final check he noticed something on the ground between the horse's legs; he picked up a cigar case edged with green silk which had a coat of arms in the middle, like on a carriage door.

"There are even two cigars in it," he said. "They'll do for this evening after dinner."

"So you smoke, do you?" she asked.

"Sometimes, when the opportunity arises."

He put his find in his pocket and whipped up the nag.

When they got home, dinner wasn't ready. Madame lost her temper. Nastasie answered her back.

"Get out!" said Emma. "What a nerve! You're dismissed."

There was onion soup for dinner, and a piece of veal with sorrel. Sitting opposite Emma, Charles rubbed his hands together happily:

"It's good to be home!"

They could hear Nastasie crying. He quite liked the poor girl. She had often kept him company in the evenings, when he was at a loose end after his first wife died. She was the first person he had met locally, he had known her longer than anyone else here.

"Are you really getting rid of her?" he said eventually.

"Yes. Who's going to stop me?" she answered.

After dinner they warmed themselves in the kitchen while their room was prepared. Charles started smoking. He smoked with rounded lips, spitting every few moments, leaning back with every puff.

"You'll make yourself ill," she said scornfully.

He put down the cigar and hurried off to the pump for a glass of cold water. Snatching up the cigar case, Emma threw it at the back of the armoire.

The next day went by so slowly! She walked in the garden, up and down the same old paths, stopping at the flower beds, the espaliers, the plaster priest, studying all these things from the past that she knew so well with a sense of astonishment. How far away the ball seemed already! What was it that put so much distance between the morning of the day before yesterday and this evening? The visit to La Vaubyessard had created a gap in her life, like the crevasses that storms sometimes make in mountains overnight. Yet she was resigned; reverently she put her beautiful outfit back in the chest of drawers along with her satin slippers, their soles yellow from the slippery wax polish of the dance floor. Her heart was the same: by rubbing against wealth it had picked up something that wouldn't come off.

Thus the memory of the ball became an occupation for Emma. Every Wednesday when she woke up she would say to herself: "Ah! A week ago... Two weeks ago... Three weeks ago, I was there!" But gradually the faces became confused in her memory, she forgot the music of the contredanses, she no longer saw the livery and the rooms so clearly; some of the details disappeared, but the regrets remained.

9

W HEN CHARLES WAS OUT, she would often take the green silk cigar case from among the folded linen in the cupboard where she had put it.

She would look at it, open it, even sniff the scent of its lining, a mixture of vervain and tobacco. Whom did it belong to?... To the Vicomte. Perhaps it was a present from his mistress. It had been worked on some rosewood embroidery frame, a pretty little possession that was kept hidden from prying eyes, and had taken many long hours, with the soft curls of the musing female head bent over it. A breath of love had blown through the fine net of the canvas; every stitch of the needle had woven a hope or memory into it, and the intertwined silk threads were all inseparable from that same silent passion. And then one morning the Vicomte had taken it with him. What did people talk about while it lay on those wide mantelpieces between the vases of flowers and Louis XV clocks? She was in Tostes, but he was in Paris now – far away! What was Paris like? It was such an outlandish name! She said it over and over to herself, quietly, just for the pleasure; it rang in her ears like a great cathedral bell; it blazed before her eyes, even on the labels of her jars of pomade.

At night, when the fish merchants drove past under the window in their carts singing 'La Marjolaine',* she would wake up and, listening to the sound of the steel-rimmed wheels that was soon deadened by the soft ground as they left the village, she would think:

"They'll be there tomorrow!" And she would follow them in her mind, up and down hills, through villages, hurrying along the highway by the light of the stars. Then after an unknown distance she always finished up in some vague place where her dream would end.

She bought a map of Paris, and tracing with her finger took herself for rides round the capital. She went along the boulevards, stopped at every corner, between the lines of the streets, at the white squares that represented houses. Eventually her eyes tired, she would close them, and in the darkness would see the flames of gas lamps twisting in the wind, the running boards of barouches as they drew up with a great brouhaha outside the columned entrances of theatres.

She took out a subscription to *La Corbeille*, a woman's paper, as well as *Le Sylphe des Salons*.* She devoured the reviews of first nights, horse races and soirées, not missing a single one, took an interest in singers' debuts, the opening of new shops. She knew the latest fashions, the addresses of good tailors, the best day to go to the Bois de Boulogne or the Opéra. She studied descriptions of furniture in Eugène Sue;* she read Balzac and George Sand, seeking imaginary satisfaction for her inner yearnings. She would bring a book to the dinner table, turn the pages as Charles talked while he ate. Everything she read brought back memories of the Vicomte. She created connections between him and made-up characters. The circle of which he was the centre gradually widened, the halo round his head spread further and further and lit up new dreams.

Hazier than the Atlantic Ocean, Paris sparkled in Emma's eyes, bathed in rose-coloured light. Yet the many bustling lives that were lived on in this hurly-burly were divided into different parts, classified into separate tableaux. Emma only saw two or three of them, which concealed the rest and represented the whole of humanity all by themselves. The world of ambassadors walked on gleaming parquet floors in drawing rooms lined with mirrors, round oval tables covered in gold-fringed velvet cloths. There were dresses with long trains, great mysteries, anguish concealed behind smiles. Next came the sphere of duchesses; they were pale; they rose at four in the afternoon; the women – poor darlings! – wore English lace on the hem of their petticoats, while the men, unknown quantities beneath a frivolous exterior, and whose idea of fun was to ride their horses to death, spent the summer season in Baden and married an heiress when they were forty. In private rooms in restaurants that served supper after midnight, colourful crowds of authors and actresses laughed in the candlelight. They were as extravagant as kings, full of ideals and fantastical frenzies. Theirs was a life above other people's, between heaven and earth, among the storm clouds, with something sublime about it. As for the rest of the world, it was lost, without any definite place, as if it didn't really exist. And the more things resembled each other, the more her mind turned away from them. Everything around her, the boring countryside, the doltish petits bourgeois, the mediocrity of life, seemed to be the exception, a stroke of misfortune in which she was trapped, while beyond it stretched a land of bliss and passion for as far as the eye could see. In her yearning she confused the sensuality of luxury with the pleasures of the heart, a refined way of life with finer feelings. Like tropical plants, didn't love need the proper soil, the right temperature? Sighs in the moonlight, long embraces, tears streaming down hands that you had to let go of, the frenzied excitements of the flesh and the languor of loving affection were inseparable from the balconies of great chateaux filled with idle amusements, boudoirs with silk blinds and deep carpets, cascading jardinières, beds raised on platforms, from the sparkle of gemstones and the aiguillettes on livery.

The boy from the post who came to groom the mare every morning would walk down the hallway in his clumping clogs; his smock was full of holes, he was barefoot in his shoes. So she had to make do with a lackey in short trousers! Once he had finished work he left for the day; when Charles got home he put his horse in the stable himself, took off the saddle and put on its halter, while the maid brought a bale of hay and threw it in the manger as best she could.

To replace Nastasie (who had left Tostes in floods of tears), Emma took on a girl of fourteen, an orphan with a gentle face. She forbade her to wear a cotton cap, taught her to address people in the third person, bring a glass of water on a plate, knock before entering, and to iron, starch, and how to dress her, wanting to make her her lady's maid. The new servant did what she was told without a murmur, so as not to lose her job; but as Madame usually left the key in the kitchen dresser, every night Félicité helped herself to a small supply of sugar that she ate in bed after saying her prayers.

In the afternoon the girl sometimes went across the road to chat to the postillions. Madame would stay upstairs in her rooms.

She wore an open dressing gown over a pleated chemise with three gilt buttons beneath its wide shawl collar. Her belt was made of cord with large tassels, her little garnet-coloured slippers had a cluster of broad ribbon that fanned out across her instep. She had bought a blotter, a writing case, a pen stand and envelopes, although she had no one to write to; she would dust her shelves, look at herself in the mirror, pick up a book and then, musing over the words, drop it in her lap. She longed to travel or to go back to the convent. She both wanted to die and to live in Paris.

Come hail or shine, Charles was off across the fields on his horse. He would have an omelette in a farm kitchen, put his arms into wet beds, get a spurt of warm blood in the face while bleeding someone, listen to death rattles, examine chamber pots, hitch up plenty of soiled underwear; but every night he would come home to a blazing fire, a meal on the table, a comfortable chair and a beautifully dressed, delightful and sweet-smelling wife, without even knowing where the perfume that filled her shift came from, if not from her skin itself.

She enchanted him with a host of little attentions; sometimes it would be a new way of making paper rings for the candles, a different flounce for her dress, or an unusual name for a simple dish, which the maid couldn't remember but which Charles enjoyed to the last mouthful. In Rouen she saw ladies with charms on their bracelets; she bought charms. She wanted two large, blue-glass vases for the mantelpiece, and then an ivory needlework box with a gilt silver thimble. The less Charles understood about all this finesse, the more he fell under its spell. It added something to his worldly pleasures, the joys of hearth and home. It was as if the narrow pathway of his life had been sprinkled with stardust.

He felt well, he looked well; his reputation was established. The country folk adored him because he wasn't proud. He made a fuss of the children, never went to the inn, and won people's trust with his moral standards. He was particularly good with catarrh and chest complaints. Terrified of killing off his clientele, it was rare for Charles to prescribe anything but painkilling remedies, an emetic from time to time, a footbath or leeches. It wasn't that he was afraid of surgery; he was a great one for bleeding people, like horses, and had *a hellish grip* when it came to pulling teeth.

Eventually, *to keep himself informed*, he took out a subscription to *La Ruche médicale*,* a new journal that had sent him its brochure. He would read it after dinner; but the combination of the warm room and the after-effects of a meal meant that he dropped off within minutes; and there he would stay, chin in his hands, hair spread out like a mane round the base of the lamp. Emma would look at him and shrug. Did she have one of those men of few words for a husband, someone who worked at his books all night, and when they finally got to sixty, the age of rheumatism, wore a row of decorations on their badly made black tailcoat! She would have liked the Bovary name, her name, to be renowned, to see it in bookshops, in the newspapers, to be known all over France. But Charles had no ambition! A doctor from Yvetot whom he had recently been on a house call with had humiliated him, and at the patient's bedside no less, in front of the relatives. That night when Charles told her what had happened, Emma lost her temper about his colleague. Charles was touched. He kissed her forehead, a tear in his eye. Yet she was seething with shame, she felt like hitting him, and went out into the passage, opened the window and took a breath of fresh air to calm herself.

"Pathetic man!" she said under her breath, biting her lip. "Pathetic man!"

Because it was him that she was more annoyed with. As he got older he fell into cloddish ways; during dessert he would cut up the corks from the empty bottles; when he finished eating he would run the tip of his tongue over his teeth; he slurped every mouthful of his soup, and as he put on weight his eyes, which were already small, seemed to be pushed up into his forehead by his bloated cheeks.

Emma would sometimes tuck the red hem of his vest back inside his waistcoat, adjust his cravat or hide the faded gloves that he had a habit of wearing; yet despite what he thought, it wasn't done for him; it was for herself, a boost for her ego, nervous irritation. Occasionally she would talk to him about what she had been reading, a passage from a novel, a new play or a piece of trivia from *high society* that the gossip columns were talking about; because after all, Charles was a good listener, someone who always agreed with you. She confided in her greyhound a lot! She would have told the logs by the fireplace and the pendulum of the clock.

Yet deep down she was waiting for something to happen. Like a sailor in distress, her desperate eyes stared out across the isolation of her life, searching for a white sail in the mist on the distant horizon. She didn't know what this stroke of fate would be, which wind would blow it towards her, what shore it would carry her to, whether it would be a rowing boat or an ocean-going ship, filled with worries or enough bliss to make it sink. But each morning when she woke up she hoped it would be that day, and would listen to every sound, leap out of bed, be amazed that it hadn't come, and then at sunset, unhappier than ever, she would wish it were tomorrow.

Spring came. With the warmer weather, when the pear trees were flowering, she had attacks of breathlessness.

As soon as it was July she counted on her fingers how many weeks were left till October, thinking that the Marquis d'Andervilliers might give another ball at La Vaubyessard. But September came and went with no letters, no visits.

After this depression her heart was left empty once more, and then the sequence of identical days began all over again.

They would follow on in succession, always the same, without number, bringing nothing with them! Other people's lives, as un-remarkable as they may have been, at least had the possibility of an event. An adventure sometimes led to endless episodes, reversals of fortune, a change of scenery. But nothing ever happened to her: it was God's will! Her future was a long dark corridor, and the door at the end was locked.

She gave up music. Why play? Who was going to listen to her? Since she would never feel a murmur of rapture flow round her like a breeze while wearing a velvet dress with short sleeves, sitting at an Érard piano* at a concert, striking the ivory keys with her light fingers, it wasn't worth boring herself learning to play. She left her sketchbooks and tapestry in the cupboard. What was the point? What was the point? Sewing annoyed her.

"I've read everything," she thought.

And there she stayed, letting the fire tongs get red-hot or watching the rain.

How miserable she was on Sundays when the bell rang for vespers! In a waking daze she listened to each distorted chime one by one. A cat strolling along the roof would arch its back in the pale sunlight. The breeze blew trails of dust along the main road. Sometimes a dog barked in the distance, and the bell went on with its steady, monotonous ringing that disappeared into the countryside.

In the meantime people would come out of church. Women in polished clogs, farmers in new smocks, their bareheaded children hopping and skipping away in front of them, all of them were going home. And five or six men, always the same ones, would play *bouchons* outside the door of the inn till nightfall.

It was a cold winter. Every morning the windows were iced over, and the milky-white light that came through them, as if through frosted glass, sometimes stayed the same all day. At four o'clock they had to light the lamps.

When the weather was fine she went into the garden. The dew covered the cabbages with silky silver lace whose long bright strands stretched from one to the other. You couldn't hear any birds singing, everything seemed to be asleep, the espaliers covered in straw, the vine like a great

54

sick snake beneath the coping of the wall, where as you got closer you could see woodlice crawling around on their many legs. Under the fir trees by the hedge, the priest in the three-cornered hat reading his breviary had lost his right foot, and there were white pockmarks on his face where the frost had chipped off the plaster.

She would go back indoors, close the door, rake over the coals and, almost fainting in the heat from the hearth, could feel the tedium descend on her again, even heavier than before. She would have liked to go downstairs and talk to the maid, but propriety held her back.

Every day at the same time the schoolmaster, in his black silk cap, opened the shutters of his house, and the local policeman would walk past wearing his sword over his smock. Morning and night the post horses crossed the road in threes to drink from the pond. Now and again the doorbell of one of the inns would ring, and when it was windy the two small brass cups on the sign outside the wig-maker's shop could be heard creaking on their rods. By way of decoration there was an old-fashioned plate pasted onto one of the window panes and a wax bust of a woman with yellowed hair. The wig-maker, too, bemoaned his discontinued calling, his lost future, and, dreaming of a shop in a big town like Rouen, by the harbour, near the theatre, he spent all day walking up and down from the town hall to the church with a gloomy expression on his face, waiting for customers. Whenever Madame Bovary looked up he was there like a sentry in his worsted jacket, with his embroidered silk cap over one ear.

In the afternoon a man's face would sometimes appear outside the dining-room window, tanned and with black whiskers, and which gave a big slow gentle smile showing white teeth. Soon a waltz would strike up, and in a little drawing room on the barrel organ, Tom Thumb-sized dancers, women in pink turbans, Tyroleans in morning coats, monkeys in black tailcoats, gentlemen in short trousers would dance round and round among the armchairs, the sofas, the console tables, reflected in little bits of mirror strung together at the corners with strips of gold paper. The man would turn the handle, looking from side to side or at the windows. Now and then, spitting a long brown spurt of saliva onto the marker stone, he would lift up his instrument, whose stiff strap made his shoulder ache, with his knee; and, first doleful and drawn-out, then merry and brisk, the music came droning out of the box from behind a pink taffeta curtain beneath an ornate brass grille. They were all tunes that were played elsewhere, in theatres, which people sang in drawing rooms, danced to in the evening in the light from chandeliers, echoes from the world that reached as far as Emma. Whirling figures danced endless sarabands in her head, and like a bayadère on a flower-patterned carpet, her thoughts leapt around with the notes, swayed from dream to dream, from sorrow to sorrow. When people had thrown some money into his cap, the man pulled an old blue woollen blanket over himself, slipped his hurdy-gurdy onto his back and trudged away. Emma watched him go.

But it was at mealtimes particularly that she thought she couldn't bear it any longer, in the little dining room on the ground floor with its smoky stove, squeaky door, walls that streamed with damp, its dank flagstones; all life's bitterness seemed to be heaped on her plate, and, along with the steam from the boiled beef it rose from the depths of her being like so many other insipid odours. Charles took a long time over his food; she would nibble hazelnuts or, leaning on her elbow, amuse herself by drawing lines on the oilcloth with the point of her knife.

She let the housekeeping go completely, and when Madame Bovary senior came to spend part of Lent at Tostes, she was most surprised at the changes. She who had once been so meticulous and refined would now go whole days without getting properly dressed, wore grey cotton stockings, lived by tallow candlelight. She kept saying they had to economize, that they weren't rich, adding that she was quite content, very happy, that she really liked Tostes, and other new notions that left her mother-in-law speechless. Not only that, Emma didn't seem inclined to take her advice any more; on one occasion when Madame Bovary took it into her head to say that masters ought to ensure that their servants practised their religion, she gave her such an angry look, such an icy smile, that the poor woman didn't mention it again.

Emma became difficult, temperamental. She would order dishes for herself then not touch them, one day she would only drink fresh milk, the next, one cup of tea after another. Often she would refuse to go out, and then she would be suffocating, open the windows, put on a light dress. When she had ill-treated the maid she would give her presents, or let her go for a walk to the neighbours, just as she sometimes gave all the spare change in her purse to the poor, although she wasn't particularly tender-hearted or easily moved by the feelings of others, like most people from country families who always carry a trace, however slight, of the rough paternal hand deep down inside them.

Towards the end of February, old man Rouault brought over a magnificent turkey for his son-in-law, in memory of his mended leg, and stayed in Tostes for three days. As Charles was busy with his patients, Emma kept him company. He smoked in his room, spat in the fire, talked about farming, calves, cows, poultry and town-council business; so much so that when he left she shut the door after him with a feeling of relief. Not that she hid her disdain for everything and everyone now in any case; she would sometimes come out with unusual opinions, disagreeing with what other people approved of and approving of things that were depraved or immoral – which raised her husband's eyebrows.

Would this ordeal last for ever? Would she never see the end of it? She was every bit as good as people who led happy lives! At La Vaubyessard she had seen duchesses with less lissom figures and less polished manners, and she cursed God for his injustice; she would rest her head on the wall and weep; she envied others their turbulent lives, the masked balls, the unashamed pleasures and the ecstatic abandon that went with them, which she hadn't experienced but which they must surely have produced.

She grew pale and had palpitations: Charles gave her valerian and camphor baths. But everything they tried seemed to make her worse.

On some days she chattered away feverishly; this overexcitement would suddenly be followed by a state of lethargy during which she didn't move or speak. What brought her round was to sprinkle a bottle of eau de cologne over her arms.

Because she never stopped complaining about Tostes, Charles assumed it was probably something in the local area that was making her ill, and looking no further than this, he seriously considered setting up somewhere else.

From then on she drank vinegar to make herself thinner, contracted a dry little cough and completely lost her appetite.

It pained Charles to leave Tostes after four years, just when he was *starting to make a name for himself*. Still, if needs must! He took her to Rouen to see his former teacher. It was a nervous complaint: she had to have a change of air.

After looking round in various places, Charles heard there was a village-cum-market town in the Neufchâtel area called Yonville-l'Abbaye where the doctor, a Polish refugee, had suddenly upped and left the week before. So he wrote to the local pharmacist to find out the size of the population, how far away the nearest other doctor was, how much his predecessor had earned a year, etc. – and, being satisfied with the answers he received, he made up his mind to move some time in the spring, if Emma's health didn't improve.

One day while she was going through a drawer in anticipation of the move, she pricked her finger on something. It was a piece of wire from her bridal bouquet. The buds of orange blossom were yellowed with dust, and the silver-trimmed satin ribbons were fraying at the edges. She threw it on the fire. It went up quicker than a bale of straw. Soon it was like a glowing red bush on the ashes, being slowly consumed. She watched it burn. The little cardboard berries popped, the alloy wire twisted, the braid melted; and the shrivelled-up paper petals that were fluttering around at the back of the fireplace like black butterflies eventually flew away up the chimney.

When they left Tostes in March, Madame Bovary was expecting a baby.

Part Two

Part Two

1

Yonville-l'Abbaye (named after a former Capuchin abbey of which not even any ruins remain) is a large village eight leagues from Rouen between the Abbeville and Beauvais roads, in a valley watered by the Rieule, a small river that gets the wheels of three mills turning at its mouth before it flows into the Andelle, and in which boys like to fish for trout on Sundays.

Leaving the main road at La Boissière you carry on along the flat until you get to the top of the hill at Les Leux, from where there is a view of the valley. The river that runs through it creates what appear to be two separate areas: on the left bank is pasture, on the right everything is cultivated. The meadow rolls away in a line of low hills until it joins up with the end of the grazing land by the village of Bray, while rising gently to the east the countryside opens out into fields of golden corn for as far as the eye can see. The water that flows beside the grass marks out the colour of the fields from that of the furrows with a white stripe, making the landscape look like an enormous coat whose green velvet collar is edged with silver braid.

When you reach the horizon you meet the oak trees of Argueil forest, and the long steep slopes of Saint-Jean hill, streaked top to bottom with irregular red trails; these are made by the rain, and the thin, brick-coloured trickles that stand out against the grey of the large hillside come from all the iron-bearing springs that flow from it into the surrounding area.

Here you are on the borders of Normandy, Picardy and the Île-de-France, a hybrid region where the local accent is as nondescript as the countryside. This is where they make the worst Neufchâtel cheeses in the area, while growing crops is costly because it takes so much manure to fertilize the crumbly soil, which is sandy and full of stones.

Until 1835 there was no passable road to Yonville, but around that time a *major byway* was built, linking the Abbeville and Amiens roads, and which is sometimes used by wagoners travelling from Rouen to Flanders. Yet despite these *new openings*, Yonville hasn't moved on.

Instead of using better farming methods people cling stubbornly to their pasture, less valuable though it may have become, and moving away from the open countryside the slothful village has expanded naturally towards the river. It can be seen from a distance, lying on the bank like a cowherd taking a nap at the water's edge.

Beginning after the bridge at the foot of the hill, a straight road lined with young aspens leads to the first houses in the village. Surrounded by hedges, they stand in yards full of scattered buildings, wine presses, small carts and distilleries dotted around under bushy trees with ladders, poles and scythes leaning against them. Like fur hats pulled over their eyes, thatched roofs come almost a third of the way down the low windows, whose thick convex panes are whorled like the bottom of beer bottles. The odd spindly pear tree clings to a plaster wall with metal bands running diagonally across it, and the doors have a small swivelling gate to keep out the chicks that peck at brown breadcrumbs soaked in cider on the doorstep. Then the yards get smaller, the houses closer together, the hedges disappear; under a window a bundle of ferns sways on the end of a broomstick; there is a blacksmith, then a cartwright's with two or three new carts outside which jut into the road. Next, behind an open fence comes a large white house beyond a round lawn with a statue of Cupid in the middle, one finger to his lips; two cast-iron vases stand either side of the entrance; brass plaques gleam on the front door; it is the notary's house, the village's finest.

The church is twenty paces further along on the other side of the street, just as you reach the square. The small graveyard that surrounds it, enclosed by a wall at chest height, has so many graves that the old headstones lying on the ground form a solid pavement with regular squares of grass in between. The church was completely rebuilt in the last years of Charles X's reign. Its wooden vaulting is beginning to rot at the top, and there are dark holes here and there in its blue surface. Above the door where the organ would be is a rood loft for the men, whose clogs echo on the spiral staircase.

Daylight comes through the plain stained-glass windows and falls obliquely across the pews, which are sideways on to the wall, where kneelers hang from nails here and there, with, written below them in large letters: "Monsieur So-and-So's pew". Further along, where the nave narrows, the confessional stands directly opposite a statuette of the Virgin, wearing a satin robe and a tulle veil scattered with silver stars, her cheeks as crimson as an idol on the Sandwich Islands; and finally, a copy of the Holy Family, a gift from the Interior Minister, placed in a prominent position on the high altar at the far end between four candlesticks, completes the picture. The choir stalls, made of pine, are left unpainted.

The covered market, a tiled roof supported by about twenty posts, takes up almost half the main square of Yonville. The town hall, *built from designs by a Paris architect*, is a form of Greek temple that stands on the corner next to the pharmacist's house. On the ground floor are three Ionic columns, and on the floor above is an arched balustrade, while on the tympanum at the top a French cockerel rests one foot on the Charter* and holds the scales of justice in the other.

But what most catches the eye, opposite the inn the Lion d'Or, is Monsieur Homais's pharmacy! Particularly in the evening, when the oil lamp is lit and light from the green and red jars that adorn the window display pours across the street, and through them, as if by Bengal lights,* you can make out the shadowy figure of the pharmacist bent over his desk. His shop is full from top to bottom with posters in modern English handwriting, round hand and copperplate: Eau de Vichy, Eau de Seltz, Eau de Barèges, depurative extracts, Raspail medicines, powders from Arabia, Darcet lozenges, Regnault paste,* bandages, baths and rinses, laxative chocolate, etc. The sign, which runs all the way across the shopfront, says in gold letters: "Homais, Pharmacist". At the back of the shop, behind a large set of scales fixed to the counter, the word *laboratory* is written above a glass door, which also has *Homais* in gold letters on a black background halfway down.

After this there is no more to see in Yonville. The street (the only one), which is the length of a rifle shot and lined with a few shops, comes to an abrupt halt at the corner. If you leave it on your right and walk along the foot of Saint-Jean hill, you come to the cemetery.

After the cholera outbreak, a section of wall was knocked down and three adjoining acres of ground were purchased in order to extend it; but the new part is virtually uninhabited, graves still being crammed in near the gate just as they always were. The caretaker, who is also the gravedigger and the verger (thus profiting twice from parish corpses), has taken advantage of the unused space to plant potatoes. Year by year, however, his little plot is shrinking, and come another epidemic he won't know whether to rejoice at all the deaths or curse the new tombs.

"You're living off the dead, Lestiboudois!" the priest said to him one day.

These sombre words gave him food for thought, and for a while he stopped; but he still cultivates his tubers, and goes so far as to say that they grow naturally.

Since the events just described, nothing has changed much in Yonville. The tin tricolour on top of the church tower still spins round; the two calico pennants outside the draper's shop still flutter in the breeze; like bundles of tinder, the pharmacist's foetuses rot away in their cloudy formaldehyde, and above the door of the inn the old golden lion, his colour washed out by the rain, still shows off his poodle curls to passers-by.

On the evening the Bovarys were due to arrive in Yonville, the widow Lefrançois, the landlady of the inn, was so busy that she was sweating buckets over her stove. Tomorrow was market day. Before then joints of meat had to be cut up, chickens gutted, soup and coffee made. Plus she had meals to cook for her residents, the doctor, his wife and their maid; roars of laughter rang out in the billiard room; in the small dining room three millers were calling for brandy; firewood blazed, charcoal crackled, and among haunches of raw mutton on the kitchen table, stacks of plates wobbled where someone was cutting up spinach on the chopping board. In the yard chickens and turkeys could be heard squawking as the serving girl chased them to wring their necks.

A man in green leather slippers, cheeks pitted with smallpox and wearing a velvet cap with a gold tassel, was warming his back in front of the fire. Self-satisfaction was written all over his face; he looked as much at peace with life as the goldfinch that was in a wicker cage hanging above his head: it was the pharmacist.

"Artémise!" shouted the landlady. "Break some kindling, fill the carafes, bring some brandy, get a jildy on! I wouldn't mind knowing what dessert to give all these customers you've got waiting! Lor' lumme! The removal lads are starting their racket in the billiard room again! And their cart's still parked out front! The *Hirondelle* will likely smash into it when it arrives! Give Polyte a shout and get him to shift it!... Just think, Monsieur Homais, they must have had fifteen games since this morning and drunk eight jugs of cider!... But they're going to tear my baize for me," she added, watching them from where she was standing, skimmer in hand.

"It wouldn't be a bad thing," replied Monsieur Homais, "you can buy a new one."

"A new billiard table!" exclaimed the widow.

"That one isn't much good any more, Madame Lefrançois; you're not doing yourself any favours, I tell you! You're not doing yourself any favours at all! The aficionados nowadays want tight pockets and heavy cues. They don't play proper billiards any more, everything's changed! You've got to move with the times. Take Tellier…"

Cut to the quick, the mistress of the house reddened. The pharmacist went on:

"Say what you like, his billiard table is nicer than yours. And to give you an example, they've had the idea of putting on a charity game in aid of Poland, or the flood victims in Lyon…"*

"Crooks like that don't frighten us!" put in the landlady, shrugging her ample shoulders. "Come off it Monsieur Homais, as long as the Lion d'Or is here, people will come! We're made of sterner stuff! One of these mornings you'll see the Café Français shut, not us, with a nice bailiffs' notice on its shutters! Change my billiard table," she went on, talking to herself, "when it's so handy for stacking my laundry on, and when I've had as many as six guests sleep on it during the hunting season!… And that sluggard Hivert still hasn't arrived!"

"Are you waiting for him before you serve your gentlemen their dinner?" the pharmacist asked.

"Wait? And what about Monsieur Binet? Bang on the stroke of six you'll see him walk in, because there's no one like him for punctuality. He has to have his place in the small dining room! He'd sooner die than eat his dinner elsewhere! And so fussy about his food! So difficult over cider! Not like Monsieur Léon; he sometimes comes in at seven o'clock, even half-past; he doesn't even notice what he's eating. What a fine young man. Never a cross word."

"That's the difference between someone with an education and an ex-customs officer turned tax-collector, isn't it."

Six o'clock struck. Binet walked in.

He was dressed in a blue frock coat that hung off his skinny frame, and under the turned-up peak of his leather cap, whose flaps were tied up over the top, you could see he was bald at the front, not helped by always wearing a hat. He wore a black waistcoat, a horsehair collar, grey trousers and, all year round, well-polished boots that bulged on both sides because his toes stuck out. Not a hair was out of place in his blond chinstrap beard which, following the line of his jaw, surrounded his long face, with its small eyes and hooked nose, like the border of a flower bed. Expert at cards, a good hunter and with beautiful handwriting, he had a lathe at home that he used to make napkin rings, and cluttered his house with them with the insecurity of an artist and the self-regard of a bourgeois.

He headed for the small dining room, but first the three millers had to be moved, and while his place was being laid, Binet sat in his chair next to the stove without saying a word; then he closed the door and took off his cap, as was his custom.

"He won't wear out his tongue with polite conversation!" said the pharmacist, when he and the landlady were alone again.

"You never get more than a word out of him," she replied. "Last week there were two fabric salesmen here, a pair of young wags who told so many funny stories that I cried with laughter all evening – and he just sat there like a flatfish, never said a thing."

"Yes," remarked the pharmacist, "no imagination, no witticisms, nothing of what makes a man good company!"

"Still, they say he's well off," the landlady countered.

"Well off?" retorted Homais. "Him, well off! Still, I suppose it's possible in his line of work," he added, calming down.

Then he went on:

"Now, if a merchant with a sizeable client list, or a jurisconsult, a doctor, or a pharmacist were so engrossed in their work that they became cranky, even surly, that I can understand; various idiosyncrasies are mentioned in the history books! But at least it's because they've got something to think about. Take me for example, how many times have I looked for my pen to write a label, only to find it was behind my ear all the time!"

Meanwhile, Madame Lefrançois went to the door to see if the *Hirondelle* had arrived. Then she gave a start. A man in black suddenly came into the kitchen. In the fading twilight you could make out a ruddy face and athletic build.

"What can I do for you, Father?" said the mistress of the house, reaching onto the mantelpiece for one of the brass candlesticks that stood in a row on the mantelpiece; "Would you like a drink? A drop of cassis, a glass of wine?"

Politely the clergyman declined. He was looking for his umbrella, which he had left at the convent in Ernemont the other day, and after asking Madame Lefrançois to send it over to the presbytery later on, he headed over to the church, where they were ringing the angelus.

When the pharmacist heard his footsteps fade across the square, he complained about his lack of manners. To his mind, refusing to have a drink was the most unspeakable hypocrisy; all priests were secret tipplers, always trying to bring back church tithes.

The landlady stood up for her parish priest:

"He could bend four of you over his knee. Last year he helped bring in the harvest; he's so strong he carried six sheaves at once!"

"Bravo!" said the pharmacist. "Send your daughters to confession with strapping fellows like him! If I were the government I'd have priests bled once a month. Yes, Madame Lefrançois, every month, a good phlebotomy in the interests of law and order and morality!"

"Do be quiet, Monsieur Homais! You're ungodly! You've got no religion!"

The pharmacist answered:

"I do have a religion, my own, and I've got more of it than all of them put together, with their childish mumbo-jumbo! Quite the reverse, I worship God! I believe in a Supreme Being,* the Creator, whoever he might be, what's it to me, who put us on the earth to do our duty as citizens and fathers; I've no need to go to church, kiss silver platters, put my hand in my pocket to fatten up a bunch of jokers who are better fed than we are! Because we can glorify him just as well in the woods, the fields or even by gazing at the vault of heaven like the ancients did. My God is the God of Socrates, of Franklin, Voltaire and Béranger! I'm for *La Profession de foi du vicaire savoyard* and the immortal principles of '89!* Nor do I give credence to a man of God who wanders the countryside staff in hand, puts his friends up in whales' bellies, cries out as he dies and rises from the dead three days later; utter nonsense, and, more to the point, in total conflict with the laws of physics – which just goes to show, incidentally, that the clergy have always wallowed in base ignorance and try to drag the rest of the population down with them."

He stopped and looked round, because in his agitation the pharmacist thought for a moment he was in a town council meeting. But the landlady wasn't listening; she heard rumbling in the distance. There was the sound of a coach, the clatter of loose horseshoes drumming on the ground, and then the *Hirondelle* pulled up outside.

It had a yellow body with two large wheels that stood as high as the canvas cover on the top, and which stopped passengers from seeing where they were going and scattered dust all over their shoulders. When the doors were shut the narrow windows shook in their frames, and still had mud splattered over them on top of the ancient coat of dust that even rainstorms could never quite wash off. It was drawn by three horses, the lead one harnessed on its own, and when they lowered the sides the bottom bumped on the ground.

Some Yonville residents appeared in the square; they all talked at once, asked for news, explanations, hampers; Hivert didn't know which of them to answer first. It was him who ran the villagers' errands for them. He went to the shops, brought back rolls of leather for the cobbler, scrap metal for the blacksmith, barrels of herrings for his mistress, bonnets from the milliner, toupees from the hairdresser, and all along the road on his way back he would deliver parcels, throwing them over courtyard walls, standing up on the box and shouting at the top of his voice while the horses drove themselves.

He had been held up by an incident; Madame Bovary's greyhound had escaped across the fields. They had whistled it for a good quarter of an hour. Hivert had even gone back half a league, thinking they would spot it, but he had had to get on. Emma had cried, lost her temper, blamed Charles for the calamity. Monsieur Lheureux, a cloth merchant who was in the coach with her, had tried to comfort her with examples of lost dogs that recognized their owner after many years. He had heard of one, he said, that got back to Paris from Constantinople. Another went fifty leagues in a straight line and swam four rivers, and his own father had had a poodle that, after twelve years' absence, suddenly jumped up at him in the street one evening as he was going into town for dinner.

2

EMMA GOT OUT FIRST, then Félicité, Monsieur Lheureux and a nurse-maid, and they had to wake Charles in his corner, where he had fallen fast asleep the moment it got dark.

Homais introduced himself; he offered his respects to Madame, his compliments to Monsieur, said he was delighted to have been able to be of service, adding affably that he had taken the liberty of inviting himself, since his wife was away.

Once in the kitchen, Madame Bovary went over to the fireplace. With two fingers she gathered up her dress at the knee and, lifting it above her ankles, held out her foot in its short boot towards the flames, where a leg of lamb was turning on a spit. The fire lit her up completely, its garish light shining through the weave of her dress, into the smooth pores of her white skin and even her eyelids, which she screwed up every now and then. She flushed bright red from the breeze that was blowing through the half-open door.

On the other side of the fireplace, a young man with fair hair watched her silently.

As he was very bored in Yonville, where he was clerk to Monsieur Guillaumin, Monsieur Léon Dupuis (it was him, the Lion d'Or's other regular) often delayed his meal in the hope that a traveller would arrive whom he could talk to for the evening. On days when he had finished work, not knowing what else to do, he had no choice but to arrive on time and endure a tête-à-tête with Binet from the soup all the way through to the cheese. So he was delighted when the landlady suggested he have dinner with the new arrivals, and they went into the large dining room where Madame Lefrançois had had four places laid to mark the occasion.

Homais asked if he could keep his embroidered cap on, for fear of catching cold.

Then, turning to his neighbour:

"Madame is no doubt slightly weary? One gets frightfully jolted about in our *Hirondelle!*"

"True," replied Emma, "but I enjoy travelling; I like a change of scene."

"It's wretched to be rooted to the same spot all the time," sighed the clerk.

"Unless you're like me," said Charles, "having to be constantly on a horse—"

"Still," Léon went on, addressing Madame Bovary, "I think there's nothing nicer – when you are able to," he added.

"Mind you," said the apothecary, "practising medicine isn't so very difficult in our part of the world; the state of the roads means you can use a cabriolet, and you're usually quite well paid because the farmers are well off. From a medical point of view, apart from the usual cases of enteritis, bronchitis, bilious attacks, etc., we get a few scattered cases of fever now and then during the harvest, but not much of any seriousness, nothing especially noteworthy, apart from a lot of scrofula, which undoubtedly stems from the deplorable standard of hygiene in our farmers' housing. Oh ho! You'll have plenty of prejudice to contend with, Monsieur Bovary, plenty of pigheaded habits that the endeavours of your science are going to come up against every day; because they still resort to novenas, holy relics, the priest, rather than come to the doctor or the pharmacist. Although to be honest the climate isn't at all bad, and we even have a few ninety-year-olds in the district. In winter the thermometer (I've made observations) goes down to four degrees, while in the hot weather it reaches twenty-five, thirty centigrade at most, which makes twenty-four Réaumur, or put another way fifty-four Fahrenheit* (English measurements), no more! – and it's true that we're sheltered from the north wind by Argueil forest on one side, and from the west wind by Saint-Jean hill on the other; yet this heat, which owing to the water vapour given off by the river and the sizeable amount of livestock in the meadows which, as you know, emit a lot of ammonia, that's to say nitrogen, hydrogen and oxygen (no, only nitrogen and hydrogen), and which, soaking up the humus in the soil, mixing all these different emissions together, collecting them in one body as it were, and combining with the electricity in the atmosphere, when there is some, could in the long term generate unhealthy fumes, like it does in the tropics – this heat, as I say, happens to be tempered by the direction it comes from, or rather would come from, which is to say a southerly direction, on the south-easterly wind, which cooling as it passes over the Seine sometimes reaches us suddenly, like the breeze from Russia!"

"Do you have places to go for a walk nearby?" Madame Bovary went on, talking to the young man.

"Oh, very few," he answered. "There's a place they call the Pasture, on the top of the hill at the edge of the forest. I sometimes go there on Sundays with a book, and stay to watch the sunset."

"I think there's nothing lovelier than a sunset," she went on, "especially by the sea."

"Oh!" said Monsieur Léon. "I love the sea."

"Don't you find," Madame Bovary replied, "that the mind wanders more freely on that boundless expanse, and gazing at it elevates your soul, turns your mind to the infinite, the ideal!"

"It's the same in the mountains," said Léon. "A cousin of mine went to Switzerland last year, and he told me that you can't imagine the poetry of the lakes, the magic of the waterfalls, the impression of vastness that the glaciers produce. You see pine trees that are unbelievably tall, huts perched on precipices on the far side of mountain torrents, while a thousand feet below there are whole valleys beneath the clouds. Sights like that must fire the imagination, fill you with prayer, rapture! So it doesn't surprise me that that well-known musician used to play his piano in front of a dramatic view, to stimulate his creative powers."

"Do you play?" she asked.

"No, but I adore music," he answered.

"Don't listen to him, Madame Bovary!" put in Homais, leaning over his plate. "It's pure modesty. Eh, my dear chap? The other day in your room you were singing 'L'Ange gardien'* wonderfully. I could hear you in my laboratory; it sounded like a real actor's performance."

Léon lodged with the pharmacist, where he had a small room on the second floor overlooking the square. He blushed at this compliment from his landlord, who had now turned to the doctor and was listing the main inhabitants of Yonville for him one by one. He provided both anecdotes and information. No one knew quite how wealthy the notary was, *and then there was the Tuvache house*, which caused no end of bother.

Emma went on:

"What kind of music do you like best?"

"Oh, German, it gets you dreaming!"

"Do you know the Italians?"

"Not yet – but I will next year when I go to Paris to finish my law studies."

"As I just had the pleasure of telling your husband," said the pharmacist, "about poor Janoda who ran off; thanks to his extravagance you are going to find yourselves the delighted owners of one of the most comfortable houses in Yonville. The most convenient feature for a doctor is its door onto the Alley, so you can go in and out without being seen. Not only that, it has everything that makes married life agreeable: a laundry, a kitchen with a pantry, a family room, a fruit store, etc.

He was a lively fellow who didn't worry about the expense! He had an arbour built at the end of the garden, by the river, just for drinking beer in during the summer, and if Madame enjoys gardening she could..."

"My wife isn't much interested in that," said Charles. "Although she's been advised to take physical exercise she prefers to stay in her room, reading."

"Just like me," said Léon. "What better than to sit by the fire with a book of an evening, while the wind howls against the windows and the lamp is burning!..."

"What indeed!" she said, staring at him with her big dark eyes wide open.

"Your head empties of everything else," he went on. "Whole hours go by. Without moving you wander through lands that you imagine you can actually see, and entwined with the story your mind gets involved with the detailed descriptions, or follows the twists and turns of adventures. It mingles with the characters; it seems as if it is your own heart that beats beneath their clothes."

"That's so true! That's so true!" she was saying.

"Has it sometimes happened to you," Léon continued, "that while reading a book you stumble across some hazy idea you've had, some vague image that comes back from far away, as if it were the fullest expression of your most untrammelled feelings?"

"I've experienced that," she replied.

"That's why I like poetry particularly," he said. "I find it more tender-hearted than prose, it makes you cry more easily."

"But eventually it becomes wearying," Emma replied "These days I prefer stories that move at a breathless pace, which frighten you. I can't abide ordinary heroes and restrained emotions, like the ones that exist in everyday life."

"It's true that by not touching the heart," the clerk remarked, "such books stray away from Art's true purpose. Among all life's disillusions it's a pleasure to be able to turn your mind to noble natures, pure-hearted affections, scenes of happiness! For me living here, far from the world, it's my only form of entertainment; Yonville has so few opportunities."

"If Madame would do me the honour of making use of it," said the pharmacist, who had overheard these last remarks, "my library of the best authors is at her disposal: Voltaire, Rousseau, Delille, Walter Scott, the *Écho des feuilletons*, etc., and I get various periodicals too, including the *Fanal de Rouen** every day, which has the advantage of covering the Buchy, Forges, Neufchâtel and Yonville districts and the surrounding area."

Dinner lasted two and a half hours; Artémise, the serving girl, dragging her feet unconcernedly on the tiles in worn-out selvedge slippers, brought plates of food one after another, forgot everything, understood nothing and was always leaving the door to the billiard room half-open, which kept banging against the wall.

As he was talking, Léon inadvertently rested his foot on one of the rungs of Madame Bovary's chair. She was wearing a little blue silk cravat which kept her fluted cambric collar as upright as a strawberry; and depending which way she moved her head, the lower part of her face either disappeared into the material or gently lifted out of it. Which was how, sitting next to each other while Charles and the pharmacist were busy chatting, they got into one of those vague conversations in which the random selection of words always brings you back to a fixed point of mutual affinity. The sights of Paris, titles of novels, new quadrilles, the world he knew nothing about, Tostes where she used to live, Yonville where they were, they discussed everything, talked about everything until dinner was over.

When the coffee had arrived, Félicité went off to get their room ready in the new house, and the dinner guests soon called it a day. Madame Lefrançois was asleep by the dying fire, while the stable lad, lantern in hand, was waiting to show Monsieur and Madame Bovary to their house. There were tangles of straw in his red hair, and he limped with his left leg. Once he had picked up the priest's umbrella they made a move.

The village was asleep. The pillars of the covered market threw long shadows. The world was grey, like on a summer night.

As the doctor's house was only fifty paces from the inn, they were soon wishing each other goodnight, and they all went their separate ways.

The moment she walked into the hall, Emma felt the cold from the plaster descend on her shoulders like a damp cloth. The walls were new, the wooden stairs creaked. In the bedroom on the first floor, a whitish light came through the windows, which had no curtains. The tops of trees were just visible, and, farther away, meadows half-shrouded in mist that rose in the moonlight along the river. Heaped in the middle of the room were drawers, bottles, curtain rods, gilt mouldings and mattresses thrown over chairs, bowls standing on the wooden floor, because the two men who had brought the furniture had left everything where it was.

It was the fourth time she had spent the night in an unfamiliar place. The first was the day she went to the convent. The second was when she arrived in Tostes, the third at La Vaubyessard, the fourth was here; each of them had turned out to be the unveiling of a new phase in her life. She didn't believe things could happen the same way in different places, and since the part she had already lived through had been bad, what remained would surely be better.

3

WHEN SHE WOKE UP the next morning she saw the clerk in the square. She was wearing her dressing gown. He looked up and waved to her. She gave a brief nod and closed the window.

All day Léon waited for six o'clock; but when he walked into the inn the only person there was Monsieur Binet, sitting at table.

Dinner the evening before had been quite an occasion for him; never before had he talked for two whole hours to a *lady*. So how had he managed to expound, and in such language, so many things that he wouldn't have said so well before? As a rule he was shy, and behaved with a reserve that had both something of modesty and dissembling about it. People in Yonville thought he was *well mannered*. He listened to older people's views, and didn't seem to have extreme political opinions, which was remarkable for a young man. And he had talents: he painted in watercolour, could sing a treble part, and liked reading works of literature after dinner when he wasn't playing cards. Monsieur Homais held him in esteem for his education; Madame Homais was fond of him for his obliging attitude, for he often went into the garden with the Homais children, who were grubby brats, badly brought-up and pale and sluggish like their mother. As well as the maid to look after them there was Justin, a trainee pharmacist, a distant cousin of Monsieur Homais's whom they had taken in out of kindness, and who also helped around the house.

The apothecary turned out to be the best of neighbours. He apprised Madame Bovary of the local tradesmen, got his own cider vintner to call especially, tasted it for her and saw to it that the barrel was put in a good place in the cellar; then he explained how to go about getting an inexpensive supply of butter, and came to an agreement with Lestiboudois, the sacristan, who as well as his sacerdotal and funerary duties looked after Yonville's most important gardens on an occasional or regular basis, depending on what people wanted.

All this unctuous goodwill on the pharmacist's part wasn't motivated solely by a desire to be neighbourly. There was a scheme behind it.

He had infringed the Law of the 19th Ventôse, Year XI,* Article I, which forbade any individual not holding qualifications from practising medicine, with the result that, having been denounced by a person or persons unknown, Homais had been summoned to Rouen to the private chambers of His Honour the Public Prosecutor. The Judge received him standing, in robes trimmed with ermine, cap on his head. It was in the morning before the court convened. In the corridor policemen could be heard walking past in heavy boots, and what sounded like keys turning in hefty locks somewhere in the distance. The pharmacist's ears rang so much he thought he was going to have a heart attack; he foresaw dark dungeons, his family in tears, the pharmacy sold, his jars scattered far and wide, and he had to go to a café to have a glass of rum and seltzer to set him back on his feet.

The memory of this reprimand gradually faded, and he carried on giving harmless minor consultations in the back of his shop as he always had. But the mayor had a grudge against him, his colleagues were jealous, he had something to fear from everyone; winning over Monsieur Bovary with favours would earn his gratitude, and stop him from speaking out later if he noticed something. So Homais took him *the newspaper* every morning, and often left his pharmacy for a moment in the afternoon to go and talk to the public-health officer.

Charles was miserable; his practice wasn't attracting any patients. He would sit for hours without saying a word, go for a sleep in his surgery or watch his wife sewing. To amuse himself he did odd jobs around the house, and even tried his hand at painting the attic with some materials the decorators had left. But he had money problems on his mind. He had spent so much on repairs at Tostes, on Madame's clothes and on moving that her whole dowry, more than three thousand écus, had disappeared in two years. Then there were the things that had been lost or damaged in transit from Tostes to Yonville, to say nothing of the plaster priest, which had fallen off the cart after a violent jolt and smashed on the cobbles in Quincampoix.

But he had another concern to distract him, a good one, namely his wife's pregnancy. The closer her time came the more he treasured her. Another bond of flesh and blood was being created, giving him the sense of a more complex married life. When he saw her lumbering gait from some way away, her waist becoming chubby around hips that were no longer in corsets, when they sat facing each other and he could gaze at her at leisure, or she looked tired sitting in her armchair, then his happiness knew no bounds; he would get up, kiss her, stroke her face, call her Little Maman, wanted to dance with her, and, half-laughing half-crying, he would come out with all manner of doting little pleasantries which just came into his head. The thought of fathering a child thrilled him. He lacked nothing now. He had experienced life in all its length and depth, and he leant his elbows on the dinner table with a feeling of serenity.

At first Emma was amazed, then wanted it to be over so she would know what it was to be a mother. But not being able to spend as much as she wanted, to have a *bateau* cradle with pink silk curtains and embroidered bonnets, in a fit of pique she gave up the idea of a trousseau and just ordered everything from a woman in the village, without choosing or discussing anything. So she didn't enjoy the preparations that motherly love has such a taste for, and from the very beginning her feelings of affection were perhaps in some way lessened.

But since Charles talked about the child at every mealtime, she was soon thinking about it constantly as well.

She wanted a son; he would be strong and dark-haired; she would call him Georges; and in her hopes this idea of a male child was revenge for all her past helplessness. A man is free; he can travel the length and breadth of lands and passions, cross obstacles, drink deeply of the most distant delights. But a woman is constantly frustrated. Passive and malleable at once, she has the weakness of her flesh against her as well as her subservience under the law. Like the veil on her hat which is held on by a cord, her will is at the mercy of each and every wind, there is always some desire that beckons, some propriety to hold her back.

She gave birth one Sunday, around six o'clock, at sunrise.

"It's a girl!" said Charles.

She turned away and passed out.

Madame Homais soon came rushing over to kiss her, as did old mother Lefrançois from the Lion d'Or. Discreet man that he was, the pharmacist just said a few preliminary words of congratulation through the half-open door. He asked to see the child and thought it was well formed.

While she was recovering she spent a lot of time trying to decide what to call her daughter. To start with she went through all the names with Italian-sounding endings, such as Clara, Louisa, Amanda, Atala; she quite liked Galsuinde, more so Yseult or Léocadie, although Charles wanted them to name the child after his mother; Emma was against it. They went through the calendar from end to end, they asked other people.

"I was talking to Monsieur Léon the other day," said the pharmacist. "He's surprised you haven't chosen Madeleine, which is extremely fashionable at the moment."

But Madame Bovary senior was indignant at the thought of using this sinner's name. As for Monsieur Homais, he had a preference for those that called to mind a great man, an illustrious event or a high-minded idea, and he had baptized his own children accordingly. Thus Napoléon stood for glory and Franklin for liberty; Irma might have been a nod to Romanticism; but Athalie was a tribute to the most immortal masterpiece of French theatre.* Because his philosophical beliefs didn't prevent him from admiring art, the thinking man in him didn't stifle the sensitive one; he was able to distinguish between things, to find a place for imagination and extremism both. In this play for instance, he rejected its ideas but admired the style; he condemned the concept but approved of the details, became infuriated with the characters while being carried away by what they said. Whenever he read a passage from it he went into raptures; but when it occurred to him that the Bible-bashers would exploit it for their own ends he was distressed, and in this tangle of confused emotions he would have liked to give Racine a prize, as well as debate with him for a quarter of an hour.

Eventually Emma remembered that at the chateau La Vaubyessard she had heard the Marquise call a young woman Berthe; and so that was the name chosen. And as old man Rouault couldn't come, they asked Monsieur Homais to be godfather. All his presents came from his shop: six tins of jujube, a whole jar of racahout powder, three boxes of marshmallow, as well as six sticks of sugar candy that he had found in a cupboard. The evening of the baptism they gave a big dinner; the parish priest came; things got heated. As they were getting on to the liqueurs, Monsieur Homais struck up with Béranger's *Le Dieu des bonnes gens.** Monsieur Léon sung a barcarolle, and Madame Bovary senior, who was godmother, a sentimental ballad from the Empire period, and finally Monsieur Bovary senior insisted the child be brought downstairs, and started baptizing her by pouring a glass of champagne over her head. This ridiculing of the first of the sacraments outraged Father Bournisien; old man Bovary responded with a quote from *La Guerre des dieux,** the priest was going to leave; the ladies begged him to stay; Homais intervened, and the clergyman was persuaded to sit down again, and calmly went on drinking his half-finished cup of coffee from the saucer.

Monsieur Bovary senior stayed on in Yonville for another month, where he dazzled the locals with the magnificent silver-braided forage cap that he carried when he went to smoke his pipe in the square. And, being accustomed to drinking large quantities of brandy, he often sent the maid over to the Lion d'Or to get him a bottle, which was put on his son's account; and to scent his silk scarves he got through his daughter-in-law's entire supply of eau de cologne.

Yet she didn't dislike his company. He had seen the world: he talked about Berlin, Vienna, Strasbourg, his time as an officer, the mistresses he had had, the big luncheons he had given, and besides he was always good natured, and on the stairs or in the garden he sometimes even grabbed her round the waist and cried:

"Watch yourself, Charles!"

Old mother Bovary began to fear for her son's happiness, and, afraid her husband might be a bad influence on the young woman, she soon prevailed on him to leave. Perhaps she had more serious cause for concern. Monsieur Bovary was a man who respected nothing and no one.

One day Emma felt a sudden need to see her little girl, who had been put out to nurse with the carpenter's wife, and without looking at the Church calendar to see if her forty days* were over yet, she made her way to the Rolet house at the far end of the village, at the bottom of the hill between the main road and the meadows.

It was midday; all the houses had their shutters closed, the tops of the gables on the slate roofs, which shone in the glare of the bright blue sky, seemed to sparkle like stars in the sunlight. There was a sultry wind. As she walked Emma felt faint; the stones on the pavement hurt to walk on; she was unsure whether to go home or find somewhere indoors to sit down.

At that moment Monsieur Léon appeared from a doorway, a bundle of papers under his arm. He came over to say hello and stood in the shade outside Lheureux's shop, beneath its grey awning.

Madame Bovary said she was on the way to see her baby, but was feeling tired.

"If..." Léon began, not daring to continue.

"Have you got business to attend to?" she asked.

At the clerk's reply she asked him to come with her. By evening it was known all over Yonville, and Madame Tuvache, the notary's wife, announced in her maid's presence that Madame Bovary was compromising herself.

To get to the wet nurse's house they had to turn left at the end of the street, as if going to the cemetery, and take a little path between some yards and small houses which was lined with privet. It was in flower, as were the veronica, the wild roses, the nettles and the sparse brambles that sprung up through the bushes. Through gaps in the hedge, pigs could be seen on a manure heap in the orchards, or cows grazing, rubbing their horns against tree trunks. They walked slowly, side by side, her leaning on his arm and him taking short steps to match hers; ahead of them flitted a swarm of flies, buzzing in the warm air.

They knew the house from the old walnut tree that shaded it. Low with brown roof tiles, there was a string of onions hanging from the attic window. Bundles of thin sticks stood against a thorn hedge surrounded a plot of lettuces, lavender and a few flowering peas growing up stakes. Muddy water ran across the grass, there were various indeterminate pieces of old clothing everywhere, woollen stockings, a red calico camisole and a heavy cotton sheet spread over the hedge. Hearing the gate the nurse appeared, a suckling child on one arm. With her other hand she dragged a poor, puny-looking brat whose face was covered in scrofula, the son of a hosier from Rouen whose parents were too busy with their shop and had left him in the country.

"Come in," she said. "Your little girl's asleep."

In the bedroom, on the ground floor and the only one in the house, was a large bed without curtains against the far wall, while the kneading trough took up the side with the window, which had one of its panes mended with a blue paper sun. In the corner behind the door, sturdy boots with shiny studs were lined up on the flagstone by the washtub, next to a bottle of oil with a feather sticking out of it; a copy of the *Mathieu Laensberg** lay on the dusty mantelpiece among gunflints, candle stubs and bits of tinder. The final piece of detritus in the room was a picture of a winged figure of Renown blowing her trumpet, probably cut out of a perfumer's catalogue, and which was fixed to the wall with six clog nails.

Emma's child was asleep in a wicker basket on the floor. She picked her up in her blanket and began to sing while walking back and forth.

Léon walked round the room; it seemed odd to see this beautiful woman in her nankeen dress amongst all this poverty. Madame Bovary blushed; he turned away, thinking she had seen impudence in his eyes. Then she put the little girl, who had just been sick over her collar, back in her cradle. The nurse wiped it off, assuring her it wouldn't show.

"She's forever doing that to me too, I do nothing but rinse it out! Maybe you'd be kind enough to tell Camus the grocer to let me have a bit of soap when I needs it? It would be more convenient for you, if that's no trouble."

"That's fine, that's fine!" said Emma. "Good day, Mrs Rolet."

And she walked out, wiping her feet on the doorstep.

The woman went with her to the end of the yard, all the time talking about how difficult it was to get up during the night.

"I'm that worn out sometimes, I fall asleep in the chair; so maybe you'd at least give me a nice pound of ground coffee which will last me a month and I can have it with milk in the mornings."

Having been subjected to all this gratitude, Madame Bovary walked off; but she had only gone a short way down the path when the sound of clogs made her turn her head: it was the wet nurse!

"What is it?"

The woman took her to one side under an elm tree and started telling her about her husband, who what with his job and the six francs a year that the captain...

"Get to the point," said Emma.

"Well!" the nurse went on, sighing between every word. "It's just I'm afraid he'll get himself all upset if he sees me drinking coffee by myself; you know what men are like…"

"Since you've got the audacity," Emma told her, "I'll give you some!… You're getting on my nerves!"

"Dearie me, Madame! It's just that on account of his injuries he gets these dreadful cramps in his chest. He says that even cider makes him come over weak."

"Do hurry up, Mrs Rolet!"

"Well," the woman went on, bowing, "if it wouldn't be too much to ask…" – she bowed a second time – "if you wouldn't mind" – and her eyes were begging – "a little jug of brandy," she said eventually, "and I'll rub some on your little girl's feet – they're as soft as the tongue in her head."

Finally free of the nurse, Emma took Monsieur Léon's arm again. For a while she walked quickly; then she slowed down, and as she looked round her eye was caught by the young man's shoulder, the black velvet collar of his frock coat. His chestnut hair, straight and well-brushed, reached down over it. She noticed his fingernails, which were longer than were usually seen in Yonville. Looking after them was one of the clerk's major occupations; he kept a special pocketknife in his writing case for the purpose.

They went back to Yonville along by the river. In summer the lower water level revealed the very bottom of the garden walls, which had steps leading down to the bank. It flowed quickly and quietly, and looked cold; clumps of tall wispy grass bowed with the current, floated on its clear surface like so much loose green hair. Sometimes an insect landed or walked on tiny feet on the tip of a bulrush or the leaf of a water lily. Sunlight ran over the droplets of bubbling blue water which streamed past, bursting; the grey bark of ancient, lopped willow trees reflected in the surface; beyond, all around them, the meadows seemed empty. On the farms it was lunchtime, and as the young woman and her companion walked, all they could hear was the rhythm of their footsteps on the path, the words they were saying, the rustle of her dress on the ground.

The garden walls, which had fragments of broken bottles set into their curved coping, were as hot as greenhouse windows. Wallflowers grew between the bricks; as she went past Madame Bovary snagged off some of their wilting flowers with the edge of her open umbrella, making a cloud of yellow dust, or a piece of honeysuckle or clematis hanging over the wall trailed across the silk for a second, catching on the fringe.

They talked about a company of Spanish dancers who were coming to the theatre in Rouen shortly.

"Are you going to go?" she asked.

"If I can," he replied.

Didn't they have anything else to say? Yet their eyes had far more serious things to discuss; and while they did their best to find commonplaces, they could feel themselves being overcome by the same languor; it was like a constant murmuring deep down in their souls, drowning out their voices. Amazed at this new mellowness, they didn't dream of describing the sensation or of trying to find out what was causing it. Like a tropical shore, future happiness covers the vast empty space that comes before it with its inborn, natural softness, a scented breeze, and you doze off in this state of elation without worrying about horizons that you have yet to see.

In one place the ground had been trodden down by cattle; they had to walk on large green stones spaced out across the mud. She kept stopping to find somewhere to put her boot, and, tottering on the wobbling stone, elbows sticking out, leaning forward at the waist, eyes hesitating, she laughed from the fear of falling in a puddle.

When they got to her garden gate, Madame Bovary opened it, ran up the front steps and disappeared.

Léon went back to his office. His employer wasn't in; he cast his eye over the files, sharpened a quill, but eventually got his hat and left.

He went up to the Pasture at the top of Argueil hill, where the forest began, and he lay on the ground under the fir trees and looked up at the sky through his fingers.

"I'm so bored!" he thought. "So bored!"

Living in this village he could always find something to complain about, with Homais for a friend and Monsieur Guillaumin for a master. The latter, always taken up with business, wearing glasses with gold side pieces and red whiskers over his white cravat, understood nothing of the subtleties of the mind, despite putting on a stiff English manner which had impressed the clerk at first. As for the pharmacist's wife, she was the best in all Normandy, gentle as a lamb, treasuring her children, her father, her mother, her cousins, bemoaning other people's sorrows, letting the housekeeping go downhill, and hating corsets – yet so slow-moving, so dull to listen to, so common-looking and with so little conversation, that despite the fact that she was thirty, that he was twenty, that they slept in next-door rooms and that he spoke to her every day, he had never dreamt she could be anyone's wife, or that there was more of the female to her than just a dress.

Apart from that, what was there for him? Binet, a few tradesmen, two or three innkeepers, the parish priest, and last but not least Monsieur Tuvache the mayor with his two sons: well-off, surly, dull-witted people, farming their land themselves, always having family feasts and quite the most insufferable company.

But on this banal background of human faces, Emma's stood out all on its own, and yet somehow even more distant; for between himself and her he sensed some ill-defined abyss.

So far he had only been to her house with the pharmacist. Charles seemed little interested in inviting him personally, and between the fear of being indiscreet and the desire for an intimacy that he considered as good as impossible, Léon had no idea how to set about things.

4

A S SOON AS THE COLDER WEATHER SET IN, Emma moved out of her room and into the sitting room, a long low room that had a bushy anemone that spread itself in front of the mirror over the mantelpiece. Sitting in her armchair by the window, she saw the villagers go by.

Twice a day Léon went from his office to the Lion d'Or. Emma would hear him coming from a distance; she would lean forward, listening, and the young man would glide past on the other side of the curtain, always dressed the same and without turning his head. But when at dusk, chin in her left hand, she had given up the tapestry work she had started and dropped it in her lap, she would often shudder at the sudden approach of this gliding shadow. Then she would get up and tell them to lay the table.

During dinner Monsieur Homais would arrive. Embroidered cap in hand, he came in quietly so not to disturb anyone, always saying the same thing: "Evening all!" Once he had sat himself down in his place at the table, between husband and wife, he asked the doctor for news of his patients, who in turn would seek his advice about the likely fees. After that they talked about what was *in the paper*. By this time of day Homais knew the contents almost word for word; and he would give an unabridged report complete with journalistic observations on every tale of personal disaster in France and abroad. But as the subject matter ran dry, it wasn't long before he was commenting on the food. Sometimes, half getting up from his chair, he even pointed out the most tender morsel to Madame or, turning to the maid, advised her on the best way to prepare a ragout and the judicious use of seasoning; he dazzled them with talk of aroma, nitrogenous pungency, juices and gelatine. As he had more recipes in his head than his pharmacy had jars, Homais was expert at making jams, vinegars and sweet liqueurs, and knew all about the latest equipment for cooking economically, as well as the art of preserving cheeses and what to do with wine that was going cloudy.

At eight o'clock Justin came to fetch him to close the pharmacy. Homais would give him a sardonic look, especially if Félicité was there, having noticed his pupil was fond of coming to the doctor's house.

"That lusty lad of mine is getting ideas into his head," he would say. "Devil take it, I think he's in love with your maid!"

Yet his more serious failing, and one which Homais criticized him for, was that of constantly listening in to conversations. On Sundays for instance, you could never get him out of the drawing room once Madame Homais had asked him to come and take the children, who were going to sleep in the armchairs and dragging down the backs of the loose calico covers which were too big.

Very few people came to the pharmacist's evening parties, his malicious gossip and political views having gradually alienated him from a long line of respectable folk. The clerk was sure to be there. The moment he heard the doorbell he hurried to greet Madame Bovary, took her shawl and the thick selvedge slippers she wore over her shoes when it had been snowing, and put them under the desk in the pharmacy.

First they had a few games of *trente-et-un*: after that Monsieur Homais would play *écarté** with Emma; Léon stood behind and advised her. With his hands on the back of her chair, he would look at the comb that held her chignon in place. Every time she put down a card her dress rode up on the right-hand side. Her dark upswept hair tumbled down her back, gradually turning a lighter shade of brown before disappearing into shadow. Her coat hung over the sides of her chair, its pleats puffed out on the floor around her. If Léon felt his foot resting on it, he would move it away as if he had trodden on someone.

When the card games were finished, the apothecary and the doctor played dominoes, and Emma would change seats, lean on the table and flick though a copy of *L'Illustration*.* She always brought her fashion notebook. Léon would sit beside her; they looked at the engravings, waiting for each other to finish before turning the page. Often she would ask him to recite poetry; Léon would draw out the words, letting his voice trail away at any passages about love. But the noise of the dominoes irritated him; Monsieur Homais was very good, he would beat Charles by a full double six. Then, having had three games of a hundred, they stretched out in front of the fire and were soon asleep. The flames died down in the ashes; the teapot was empty; Léon would still be reading. Emma listened to him, absent-mindedly turning the lampshade, which had Pierrots in coaches and dancing puppets painted on it. Léon would stop, gesture round the room at his sleeping audience; then the two of them would talk quietly, and what they said seemed sweeter for only being heard by them.

In this way a form of partnership developed between them, a constant exchange of books and ballads; and not being a jealous man, Monsieur Bovary wasn't surprised.

For his name day he was given a fine phrenological head, painted blue and marked with numbers. It was a thoughtful gesture of the clerk's. He had plenty of others, such as running errands for him in Rouen, and, after a novel started a craze for succulent plants, Léon bought some for Madame and brought them back on his lap in the *Hirondelle*, pricking his fingers on their bristly skin.

She had a shelf-cum-balustrade put up at her window to stand her oriental vases on. The clerk had a window box too, and while they were both nursing their plants they would see each other.

Of all the windows in the village there was one that was occupied even more frequently; on Sundays, from morning till night, and every afternoon on clear days Monsieur Binet's scrawny silhouette could be seen in his attic, bent over his lathe, whose dull hum could be heard as far away as the Lion d'Or.

One evening when he got back to his room, Léon found a wool-and-velvet rug with a pattern of flowers on a pale background; he called Madame Homais, Monsieur Homais, Justin, the children, the cook, he told his employer about it; everyone wanted to see this rug: why was the doctor's wife offering such *kindnesses* to the clerk? It seemed odd, and people were convinced she must be *his lady friend*.

You would have thought it was true, the way he was always telling people about her charms, her fine mind, so much so that in the end Binet said bluntly:

"What's it to me? I'm not one of her set!"

He agonized over how best to *declare himself*, and, wavering between the fear of upsetting her and the disgrace of being faint-hearted, he shed tears of despondency and desire. Then he took drastic decisions, wrote letters that he tore up, put it off to a time that he later postponed. He would set off with the intention of risking everything, but the moment he was face to face with Emma his resolve deserted him, and when Charles appeared and asked him to come with him in his *boc* to see a patient, he would agree immediately, take his leave of Emma and go. For wasn't her husband part of her too?

Emma never stopped to wonder whether she loved him. In her view love always arrived suddenly, accompanied by claps of thunder and bolts of lightning – a storm from heaven that bursts over your life, turns it upside down, scatters your intentions like leaves, sweeps your heart into the abyss. She didn't realize that when the gutters are blocked, the rain makes pools of water on the terrace of a house, so she was living in perfect peace of mind when suddenly she found a crack in the wall.

5

IT WAS A SUNDAY IN FEBRUARY, a snowy afternoon. They – Monsieur and Madame Bovary, Homais and Monsieur Léon – had gone to see a linen mill that was being set up in the valley half a league from Yonville. The apothecary had brought Napoléon and Athalie to give them some exercise, and Justin was with them, umbrellas over his shoulder.

Nothing could have been less interesting than this place of interest. It was a long rectangular building with a lot of small windows standing in the middle of a large empty space, where a few rusty mill wheels lay scattered among heaps of sand and stones. It was still in the process of being built, and the sky was visible through the joists of the roof. Tied to the gable, the red, white and blue ribbons on a bunch of straw and ears of corn fluttered in the breeze.

Homais talked. He explained to *the gathering* the future importance of this establishment, calculated the strength of the floor, the thickness of the walls, and regretted not having a metric rule like Monsieur Binet's.

Emma, who had her arm in his, leant gently on his shoulder and gazed at the distant disc of sun, its blinding pallor blazing through the mist; then she turned away: Charles was there. His cap was pulled down over his eyes and his big fat lips were trembling, giving his face a slightly imbecilic look; even his back, that calm, peaceful back of his was annoying to look at, and in the expanse of frock coat she saw the sum total of his prosaic personality.

While she was studying him, drawing a kind of depraved sensual pleasure from her irritation, Léon walked over. Pale with cold his face seemed even softer, more languid; there was skin showing between his cravat and the collar of his shirt, which was slightly loose; the tip of his ear appeared from beneath a lock of hair, and Emma thought his big blue eyes, which were looking up at the clouds, were clearer and lovelier than the sky reflected in a mountain lake.

"Little devil!" cried the apothecary suddenly.

And he rushed over to his son, who had just jumped in a pile of lime to make his shoes white. Under the hail of rebukes Napoléon started to wail, while Justin wiped his feet with a handful of straw. But he needed a knife; Charles lent him his.

"Ah!" she thought. "He keeps a knife in his pocket, just like a peasant!"

It began to freeze, and they headed back to Yonville.

That evening Madame Bovary didn't go over to their neighbours, and after Charles had left, despite being lonely she experienced that sensation of clarity and near immediacy, yet with the greater perspective that memory gives to things. Watching the fire blazing from her bed, she could still see Léon standing there, bending his switch with one hand and holding Athalie's with the other, while she calmly sucked a piece of ice. She thought he was delightful; she couldn't take her eyes off him; she remembered other poses on other days, things he had said, the sound of his voice, everything about him; and she kept saying, offering her lips as if to be kissed:

"Delightful! So delightful!... Does he love someone?" she wondered. "But who?... Why, it's me!"

All at once the proof was there, her heart leapt. The bright firelight quivered joyfully on the ceiling; she lay back, reached out her arms.

Then came the inevitable lament: "Oh, if only Heaven had willed it! Why is it not to be? Who prevented it?..."

When Charles got back at midnight she seemed to wake up, and because he made a noise as he was getting undressed she complained of a migraine; then she casually asked about his evening.

"Monsieur Léon left early," he said.

She couldn't help smiling, and fell asleep with her heart under a new spell.

The next day as evening was drawing in she had a visit from Lheureux the draper. The shopkeeper was a man of many talents.

A Gascon by birth who had become Norman, his southern volubility was coupled with Cauchois cunning. His fat, flabby, clean-shaven face looked like light-coloured liquorice, and his white hair made the crude glint in his little black eyes even brighter. No one really knew what he had been before: some said a wandering pedlar, others a banker in Routot. What was certain was that he could do complex calculations in his head in a way that even frightened Binet. Polite to the point of unctuousness, he always leant forward slightly, like someone who is bowing or offering you something.

Leaving his hat with its crêpe band by the door, he put a green box on the table and began by complaining to Madame, with profuse politeness, about having so far failed to gain her custom. A poor shop like his wasn't in a position to attract a *lady of fashion*: he emphasized the words. But she had only to place an order and he would undertake to supply whatever she wanted, whether haberdashery, lingerie, hosiery or fabrics, because he went into town four times a month. He did business with all the best shops. You could ask about him at Les Trois Frères, La Barbe d'Or or Le Grand Sauvage, all the gentlemen there knew him like the back of their hand! And since he was passing, he had come to show Madame various items that he happened to have, as a result of a most unique opportunity. And he opened the box and took out half a dozen embroidered collars.

Madame Bovary studied them.

"I don't need anything," she said.

Monsieur Lheureux then daintily produced three Algerian scarves, several packets of English needles, a pair of woven straw slippers and, last but not least, four coconut egg cups carved by convicts. Leaning forward with his hands on the table, neck craned, he watched open-mouthed as Emma's eyes hesitated over his wares. Now and then he flicked the unfolded silk scarves as if brushing off a speck of dust; they rustled slightly as they rippled, and green twilight caught the gold flecks in the material and made them twinkle like stars.

"How much are they?"

"A trifle," he answered, "a mere trifle; but there's no hurry; whenever you like; we're not Jews!"

She thought for a moment, but in the end she just thanked Monsieur Lheureux, who replied equably:

"Never mind! Another time – I always manage to come to an arrangement with the ladies, even if not with my own!"

Emma smiled.

"What I mean is," he added good-naturedly after his little joke, "I'm not worried about the money… If needs be I can let you have some."

She looked surprised.

"Ah!" he said sharply yet quietly. "I wouldn't have to go far to get it for you – you can count on me!"

And he asked after old man Tellier, who ran the Café Français, and whom Charles was treating.

"What's the matter with old man Tellier?… That cough of his is enough to shake the place down. I'm afraid it won't be long before he needs a pine overcoat, not a flannel nightshirt. He was a wild one in his youth! People like that, Madame, they've no idea what's what! He's rotted his guts with brandy! All the same, it's a pity to see someone you know pass away."

As he packed away his box he chatted about the doctor's patients.

"I'm sure it's the weather that's responsible for all this illness!" he said, looking out the window with a sour expression on his face. "I'm feeling a bit off-colour myself, I'll have to come and see Monsieur too one of these days, about this pain in my back. Anyway, good evening to you Madame Bovary – always at your service, your humble servant!"

And he closed the door quietly behind him.

Emma had dinner brought up to her room, on a tray by the fire; she took her time over it; everything seemed fine.

"It was very sensible of me," she thought, remembering the scarves.

She heard footsteps on the stairs; it was Léon.

She got up and took the first from a pile of tea towels that were waiting to be hemmed. When he came in she seemed very busy.

The conversation flagged, Madame Bovary kept breaking off every few minutes, while he seemed rooted in self-consciousness. Sitting on a low chair by the fire he turned an ivory cigarette case round in his fingers; she carried on with her sewing, occasionally gathering up the pleats of the material with her thumb. She didn't speak; nor did he, as enthralled by her silence as he was by her words.

"Poor boy!" she thought.

"What have I done to upset her?" he wondered.

Eventually Léon said that at some point he would have to go to Rouen on business.

"Your music subscription has expired, shall I renew it for you?"

"No," she replied.

"Why not?"

"Because…"

And, pursing her lips, she pulled through a long piece of grey thread.

This needlework of hers got on Léon's nerves. The ends of Emma's fingers seemed rough; he thought of a gallant remark, but daren't risk it.

"So you're giving it up?" he went on.

"What?" she said sharply. "Music? Heavens yes! I've got a house to run, a husband to look after, in fact a thousand things, a great many obligations that come before that!"

She looked at the clock. Charles was late. She pretended to be concerned. Once or twice she even said:

"He's so kind!"

The clerk was fond of Monsieur Bovary, but her show of affection came as an unpleasant surprise. Nonetheless he continued speaking highly of him, in fact about everyone, especially the pharmacist.

"Yes, he's a good man!" Emma went on.

"Indeed," said the clerk.

And he started talking about Madame Homais, whose unkempt appearance usually made them both laugh.

"What does it matter?" Emma cut in. "A mother doesn't worry about what she wears."

And she relapsed into silence.

It was the same over the next few days; her views, her behaviour, everything changed. She took the housekeeping seriously, started going to church regularly again and was stricter with the maid.

She took Berthe away from the wet nurse. Whenever they had guests, Félicité would bring her in and Madame Bovary undressed her to show her off. She confessed to adoring children; they were her consolation, her delight, her mad folly, and this cuddling and caressing was accompanied by operatic outpourings that would have reminded anyone except the people of Yonville of La Sachette in *Notre-Dame de Paris.**

When Charles got home he would find his slippers warming in front of the fire. His waistcoats were lined now, his shirts no longer had buttons missing, and it delighted him to see all the nightcaps neatly stacked in the linen cupboard. She no longer turned her nose up at walking in the garden as she once had; she agreed with whatever he suggested, although she had no clear idea what her motives were for giving in without a murmur – and whenever Léon saw him sitting by the fire after dinner, hands on his stomach, feet on the firedogs, cheeks well-fed and rosy, eyes moist with happiness, with his child crawling around on the rug and this slim woman leaning over the back of his chair to kiss him on the forehead, he would think:

"This is madness! How can I ever get close to her?"

She seemed so virtuous and inaccessible that he gave up even the slightest hope.

Yet by renouncing her he put her in an exceptional position. She radiated physical qualities that were never going to be offered to him, and in his heart she kept rising further and further away like a great peak soaring into the distance. It was a pure emotion, the kind that doesn't prevent a person from getting on with their life, which is cultivated for its rarity, and which is more painful to lose than it is a joy to possess.

Emma got thinner, her cheeks lost their colour, her face fell. With her black headbands, big eyes, straight nose, her birdlike and now silent walk, she seemed to pass through life without touching it, bearing the faint mark of some divine preordination on her brow. She was so sad and so calm, so gentle and reserved, that to be with her was to feel yourself falling under an icy spell, in the way you shiver at the scent of flowers mingling with the chill of marble in a church. Nor were other people spared this enchantment. The pharmacist would say:

"She's a woman of many talents. She wouldn't be out of place in a sub-prefecture."

The ladies of the village admired her thrift, the patients her good manners, the poor her generosity.

Yet she was full of lust, anger, hatred. Her long pleated dress concealed a heart in turmoil, her lips never gave voice to their torment. She was in love with Léon, sought solitude in order to delight in the image she had of him. The very sight of him clouded the sensual pleasure of her contemplation. At the sound of his footsteps Emma's heart beat faster, but when she was face to face with him her excitement died down, and all she was left with was a sense of wonder that eventually turned to sadness.

Léon had no idea that when he left her house in despair she would go to the window and watch him walking down the street. She worried about his motives; she watched his face closely; she invented all manner of excuses to go to see him in his room. To her, the pharmacist's wife was lucky to sleep under the same roof, and her thoughts constantly swooped down on this house like the pigeons at the Lion d'Or who came to dip their pink feet and white wings in the gutters. But the more Emma was aware of this love of hers, the more she suppressed it, so it wouldn't be seen, to weaken it. She would have liked Léon to suspect; she imagined chance events, disasters that might make it happen. What held her back was undoubtedly idleness or fear as much as propriety. She believed she had driven him away, that the moment was past, that all was lost. And then there was pride, the pleasure of telling herself: "I'm virtuous", looking at herself in the mirror while striking a resigned pose, which helped her get over the sacrifice that she thought she was making.

The desires of the flesh, the lust for money and the melancholia of passion all merged in a single agony – but instead of turning her mind away she bound herself to it even more closely, stimulated by pain and looking everywhere for opportunities to indulge herself. She was annoyed if food was badly presented or a door left open, bemoaned the velvet she didn't have, the happiness she lacked, the dreams that were too lofty, a house that was too small.

What infuriated her was that Charles showed no sign of suspecting that she was in torment. His certainty that he was the one who made her happy seemed a preposterous insult, and his sense of security about it, a sign of ingratitude. So for whose benefit was she behaving properly? Wasn't he the barrier to all bliss, the root of every misfortune, the sharp buckle of the belt of complexity that was fastened round her?

So she transferred all the hatred that stemmed from her problems onto him, and any attempt to lessen it only made it grow, because this unnecessary pain was just one more reason to despair, and moved the two of them even further apart. She rebelled against her kindness to herself. The mediocrity of married life drove her to extravagant whims, marital affection to adulterous desires. She would have liked Charles to beat her so it would be easier to justify hating him, taking revenge. Sometimes she was amazed at the appalling schemes that came into her mind, but she had to keep on smiling, listening to herself repeating that she was happy, pretending she was, allowing him to believe it!

Yet there were times when this hypocrisy disgusted her. She would be seized by the temptation to run away with Léon somewhere, a long way away, to discover if fate held something new, but immediately a shapeless black abyss opened up inside her.

"Besides, he doesn't love me any more," she thought. "What's to become of me? What help can I expect, what solace, what respite?"

And there she remained, crushed, breathless, lifeless, sobbing quietly, tears streaming down her face.

"Why not tell Monsieur?" the maid would say whenever she came in during one of her attacks.

"It's just my nerves," Emma would reply. "Don't tell him, you'll upset him."

"Oh, you're exactly like the Guérin girl," Félicité would say, "old man Guérin the fisherman from Le Pollet's daughter, who I got to know in Dieppe before I came here. She was that miserable that when you saw her standing on her doorstep it looked as if there was a winding sheet stretched across the door. What was wrong with her was she had a kind of mist inside her head apparently, and the doctors couldn't do nothing about it, nor the priest neither. When it took her bad she'd go off by herself down to the shore, and when the lieutenant from the customs was doing his rounds he'd often find her lying face down on the shingle, crying. But then after she got married it stopped, or so they say."

"But for me," said Emma, "it started after I got married."

6

ONE EVENING as she was sitting by the open window, she was watching Lestiboudois the verger clipping the box trees when suddenly she heard the angelus.

It was early April, when the primroses flower; a warm breeze wafted over the newly dug flower beds, and like women the gardens seemed to be dressing up for the summer festivals. Beyond, through the trellis of the arbour and all around, she could see the river meandering its way through the meadows. Evening mist drifted among the bare poplar trees, tinting their outline into a soft, violet-coloured blur, paler and more translucent than gossamer caught on the branches. The cattle wandered in the distance, she couldn't hear their hooves or their lowing, while the tolling of the bell filled the air with its tranquil lament.

At the constant chime the young woman's thoughts strayed off into memories of childhood and boarding school. She remembered the tall candlesticks that reached above the vases of flowers on the altar, the tabernacle with its little columns. As she used to then, she would have liked to disappear into the long line of white veils that was interrupted here and there by the stiff black cowls of the nuns, bowed over their prie-dieu; at Mass on Sundays, when she looked up she would see the gentle face of the Virgin among the swirls of drifting blue incense. And she would be filled with emotion; she would feel limp and abandoned, like the downy feathers of a bird circling in a storm; and almost unaware of what she was doing she made her way to the church, prepared for any devotions as long as they absorbed her soul, made life go away.

On the square she bumped into Lestiboudois on his way back, because, so as not to shorten his day, he preferred to break off work then go back to it, and so he sounded the angelus when it suited him. Besides, if it was rung early it let the children know it was time for catechism class.

A few of them were there already, playing marbles on the slabs in the graveyard. Others sat astride the low wall, swinging their legs and cutting down the tall nettles that grew between there and the furthermost graves with their clogs. It was the only place of greenery; everything else was tombstones, always covered in a fine layer of dust despite being brushed with the sacristy broom.

Children were running around in slippers as if they were at home, their shouts could be heard above the drone of the bell. It died away each time the heavy rope trailed on the ground as it dropped back down from the tower. Swallows flew past with little cries, slicing through the air as they hurried back to their yellow nests under the tiled roof of the dripstone. Somewhere inside the church a light was burning, the wick of a glass vigil lamp hanging on its chain. From a distance the flame looked like a pale mark trembling on the surface of the oil. A long beam of sunlight fell across the nave, making the side aisles and corners even darker.

"Where's the Father?" Madame Bovary asked a young boy who was playing with the turnstile, which was coming loose from its mounting.

"He's just coming," he said.

At that moment the presbytery door creaked and Father Bournisien appeared; the children rushed helter-skelter into the church.

"Little devils!" the priest muttered. "They never change!"

And picking up a tattered catechism that he had just caught with his foot:

"No respect for anything!"

Then he noticed Madame Bovary:

"Forgive me," he said, "I didn't see you there."

He stuffed the catechism in his pocket and stopped, still swinging the long key to the sacristy between his fingers.

The setting sun was shining straight in his eyes, and made the worsted cloth of his cassock, which was worn smooth at the elbows and frayed at the bottom, look lighter. Grease and tobacco stains ran down either side of the buttons at the front, and there were more around his bands, on which nestled luxuriant, jowly folds of red skin; it was mottled with yellow blotches almost hidden by the coarse hairs of his greying beard. He had just finished dinner and was breathing heavily.

"How are you keeping?" he added.

"Not well," said Emma. "I'm suffering."

"Me too," replied the cleric, "it's this hot weather, isn't it? Amazing how it makes you feel weak. Still, what can we expect! We were born into suffering, as St Paul says. But what does Monsieur Bovary think about it?"

"Oh, him!" she said with a contemptuous gesture.

"What, he hasn't prescribed something?" the man replied, astonished.

"It's not worldly medicine I need," said Emma.

The priest kept glancing into the church, where the kneeling youngsters jostled each other with their shoulders until they collapsed like a pack of cards.

"I'd like to ask—" she went on.

"Hang on, hang on, Riboudet," the cleric shouted angrily, "I'm going to come in there and clip your ear for you, you little scamp!"

Then, turning back to Emma:

"It's Boudet the carpenter's son; his parents are well off, they let him do whatever he likes. But he's a quick learner if it suits him, because he's very bright. So as a joke I sometimes call him Riboudet (like the hill on the way to Maromme), or even 'mon Riboudet'. Ha ha! Mont-Riboudet! I mentioned it to the Monseigneur the other day, and he laughed… Yes, it even raised a laugh from him. And Monsieur Bovary, how is he?"

She seemed not to have heard. He went on:

"Still very busy I expect? Because we – he and I – are definitely the two people in the parish who've got the most to do. Except he takes care of the body," he added with a clumsy laugh, "while me, I take care of the soul!"

She stared at the priest, eyes imploring.

"Yes…" she said. "You ease every hardship."

"Oh, I don't need reminding, Madame Bovary! Only this morning I had to go over to Bas-Diauville because a cow had dropsy, they thought it was a curse. Every one of their cows, I don't see how… But excuse me! Longuemarre, Boudet! Gorblimey, will you give over!"

And he was in the church in a flash.

The children were crowding round the tall lectern, clambering on the precentor's stool, opening the missal; some of them were sneaking off for a look in the confessional. But the priest quickly dispensed a hail of slaps all round. Grabbing them by their collars he picked them up and dumped them on their knees on the stone floor of the choir as if he wanted to nail them in.

"Now, where were we?" he said when he came back to Emma, taking out a large printed handkerchief and sticking one corner between his teeth. "Yes, the farmers have my sympathy."

"There are others as well," she replied.

"Absolutely! The workers in the towns for one thing."

"It isn't them that—"

"Excuse me, but I've known poor wives and mothers there, virtuous women, I promise you, veritable saints, who didn't have a crust to eat!"

"But those who do," Emma went on (and the corners of her mouth creased as she spoke), "those who do have something to eat, Father, but who don't have—"

"A decent fire in wintertime," said the priest.

"What does that matter?"

"I beg your pardon? What does it matter? I think if you're nice and warm, well fed… after all…"

"Oh my God!" she sighed. "Oh my God!"

"Are you feeling indisposed?" he said, coming over to her with a worried look. "It's probably indigestion. You'd best go home, Madame Bovary – have some tea, it'll help get your strength back, or a glass of cold water with brown sugar in it."

"Why?"

And she looked like someone who had just woken from a dream.

"It's just that you put your hand on your forehead. I thought you were having a dizzy spell."

Then, deciding otherwise:

"So was there something you wanted to ask? What is it? I didn't realize."

Her wandering eyes slowly settled on the old man in his cassock. They looked at each other without speaking.

"Me? Nothing… nothing…" Emma repeated.

"Well then," he said eventually, "you'll have to excuse me, Madame Bovary, duty first, you know; I've got to get these tearaways of mine sorted out. We've the first communions coming up, and I'm afraid there are still a few surprises in store for us. As from Ascension Day I'm keeping them in every Wednesday for an extra hour, *and not a minute less*. Poor children! It's never too early to set them on the way of the Lord, as He Himself commended us to do through the words of His Divine Son… Go well, Madame; give my respects to Monsieur Bovary!"

And he went back into the church, genuflecting as he did so.

Emma watched him disappear between the two rows of pews, walking heavily, head tilted slightly to one side, the palms of his hands turned outwards with the fingers half open.

Then like a statue on a swivel she turned on her heel and set off home. She could still hear the priest's booming voice, the clear, high voices of the children behind her.

"Are you a Christian?"

"Yes, I am a Christian."

"What is a Christian?"

"It's someone who, having been baptized... baptized... baptized..."

She held on to the banisters as she climbed the stairs, and once she got to her room she dropped into an armchair.

The pale light from the window slowly faded in rippling waves. The familiar furniture seemed more motionless, sunk in a sea of shadow. The fire had gone out, the clock ticked, and Emma was somehow surprised at all this tranquillity when she was so distraught. But there, between the window and the work table was little Berthe, tottering about in her knitted bootees and trying to get close to her mother so she could grab hold of her apron strings.

"Leave me alone!" she said, pushing her away with her hand.

The little girl came up to her knees, and leaning on them she looked up at her with her big blue eyes, a trickle of saliva dribbling from her mouth onto the silk apron.

"Leave me alone!" the young woman repeated, getting annoyed.

The expression on her face frightened the child, who started to cry.

"Oh, do leave me alone!" she said, pushing her away with her elbow.

Berthe fell against the brass rosette at the bottom of the chest of drawers; she cut her cheek, it started to bleed. Madame Bovary rushed over and picked her up, broke the bell pull, called the maid as loudly as she could, and was just cursing herself when Charles arrived, in time for dinner.

"Look, dear," Emma told him calmly, "the baby fell and hurt herself while she was playing."

Charles assured her it wasn't serious and went to get a dressing.

Madame Bovary didn't go down to the dining room; she wanted to stay and look after her child. As he watched her sleeping, what remained of her anxiety gradually wore off, and she thought it was very silly and very good of her to have got so flustered about such a little thing. Berthe had stopped crying now. Her cotton blanket rose and fell with her breathing. There were big tears in the corners of her drooping eyelids, and beneath the lashes you could just see two pale, deep-set pupils; the plaster was dragging at the skin of her cheek.

"How odd that the child is so ugly!" thought Emma.

At eleven o'clock, when Charles got back from the pharmacy (where he had been given more dressings after dinner), he found his wife standing beside the cradle.

"It's nothing, I promise you," he said, kissing her forehead. "Don't fret my poor love, you'll make yourself ill!"

He had been at the apothecary's house for some time. Although he hadn't seemed particularly upset, Monsieur Homais had done his best to steady him, *cheer him up*. They had talked about the various dangers to children, the carelessness of servants. Madame Homais had personal experience, because she still had the scars on her chest from where a cook had dropped a tray of hot ash down the front of her smock. So like good parents they took precautions. The knives were never sharp or the floors polished. There were strong metal bars inside and outside the windows. Despite having a measure of independence the Homais children never went anywhere unsupervised; at the slightest sign of a cold their father filled them with cough medicine, and even after their fourth birthday they were mercilessly made to wear padded bands round their heads. In fact this was an obsession of Madame Homais's; privately her husband agonized over it, for fear of the effect such compression might have on their mental faculties, and sometimes he even let slip:

"Do you want to make Caribs or Botocudos* of them?"

Charles had tried to interrupt the conversation several times.

"There's something I need to talk to you about," he whispered into the clerk's ear as he went down the stairs ahead of him.

"Does he suspect?" Léon wondered. His heart started to race and he became lost in imaginings.

Eventually, having closed the door, Charles asked him if he could find out what a good daguerreotype might cost in Rouen; it was a surprise for his wife, an exquisite little romantic kindness, a portrait of himself in a black tailcoat. But first he needed "to know the lie of the land"; making enquiries shouldn't be too much trouble for Monsieur Léon, since he went into town almost every week.

Why was this? Homais suspected some *young man's liaison* was behind it, an affair. But he was wrong; Léon wasn't chasing a passing fancy. He was unhappier than ever, and Madame Lefrançois noticed how much food he left on his plate now. She questioned the tax-collector to find out more details; Binet retorted haughtily that he "wasn't in the employ of the police".

Nonetheless, his friend did strike him as odd; Léon would often lean back in his chair, arms akimbo and complain about life in a vague sort of way.

"It's because you haven't enough to keep you occupied," the tax-collector would say.

"Such as?"

"If I were you I'd get a lathe!"

"But I don't know how to use one," the clerk would reply.

"Ah, of course!" the other would say, stroking his chin with a mixture of scorn and satisfaction.

Léon was weary of loving to no avail; he was beginning to feel the despondency that comes from a life that never varies, that has nothing of interest to guide it or any hope to sustain it. He was so bored with Yonville and Yonville folk that the mere sight of certain people and certain houses annoyed him more than he could bear, and he now found the pharmacist, fine fellow that he was, quite insufferable. Yet the prospect of being somewhere different frightened him as much as it appealed.

His anxiety soon turned to impatience, and in the distance Paris beckoned to him with the clamour of its masked balls, the laughter of its grisettes.* Since he had to go there to finish his law studies, why not leave now? What was stopping him? And inwardly he began making preparations; he organized his future activities. In his mind he furnished an apartment. He would lead an artist's life! He would take guitar lessons! He would have a dressing gown, a Basque beret, blue velvet slippers! He even admired the crossed duelling swords over his new mantelpiece, with a death's head and a guitar above them.

The difficulty lay in getting his mother to agree; yet nothing seemed to make more sense. Even his employer encouraged him to go and see another practice, where he would be able to advance his career. So steering a middle course Léon looked for a position as second clerk in Rouen, couldn't find one, and eventually wrote a long detailed letter to his mother setting out his reasons for going to Paris immediately. She gave her consent.

Yet he was in no hurry. Every day for a month Hivert took chests, suitcases and packages back and forth between Yonville and Rouen for him, and when Léon had restocked his wardrobe, had his three armchairs restuffed, bought a supply of silk scarves, in fact made more preparations than for a trip round the world, he kept putting it off week after week until he got another letter from his mother urging him to leave, if he wanted to pass his exam before the holidays.

When the time came for goodbyes, Madame Homais cried, Justin sobbed. Being a stoic Homais hid his feelings, he even wanted to carry his friend's coat down to the notary's, who was giving Léon a lift to Rouen in his carriage. The clerk barely had time to say goodbye to Madame Bovary.

When he got to the top of her stairs he paused, quite out of breath. As he walked in, Madame Bovary almost leapt up.

"I'm still here!" said Léon.

"So I see!"

She bit her lip, the blood rushed to her face and she blushed bright pink from the roots of her hair down to her ruff. She stood leaning on the panelling.

"Monsieur isn't in?" he went on.

"He's out."

And she said it again:

"He's out."

There was a silence. They looked at each other and, mingling in the same anguish, their thoughts embraced tightly like two heaving breasts.

"I'd like to kiss Berthe," said Léon.

Emma went down some steps and called Félicité.

He glanced round, quickly taking in the walls, the shelves, the mantelpiece as if to get inside them, carry them away with him.

But then she reappeared, and the maid brought Berthe, who was dangling a windmill on the end of a string and looking down at her feet.

Léon kissed her on the neck several times.

"Goodbye, dear child! Farewell, darling girl, farewell!"

And he gave her back to her mother.

"Take her away," she told the maid.

They were left alone.

Madame Bovary rested her face on the window, her back turned; Léon slapped his cap gently against his thigh.

"It looks like rain," said Emma.

"I've got a coat," he answered.

"Ah!"

She turned round, head slightly lowered. Light slid down her forehead as if it were marble, without giving any indication of what she had been staring at on the horizon, or revealing her innermost thoughts.

"Goodbye then!" she sighed.

"Yes, goodbye… I must be going!"

They moved closer to each other; he held out his hand, she hesitated.

"In the English style, then," she said, taking it and trying to laugh.

Léon felt it between his fingers, and his whole being seemed to flow out of him and into her damp palm.

Then he let go; their eyes met once more, and he was gone.

Once he was in the covered market he hid behind a pillar to take a last look at the white house with its four green shutters. He thought he saw a shape at the bedroom window, but the curtain came away from its hook as if someone had undone it, the long diagonal folds moved slightly, and then suddenly it moved across the window and just hung there, as motionless as plaster on a wall. Léon set off at a run.

He saw his employer's cabriolet on the road in the distance, with a man in a rough cloth apron holding the horse. Messrs Homais and Guillaumin were talking while they waited for him.

"Kiss me," said the apothecary, tears in his eyes. "Here's your overcoat, dear friend: wrap up warm! Look after yourself! Go carefully!"

"Come along, in you get, Léon!" said the notary.

Homais leant over the mudguard, and choking back the sobs he managed to say two sad words:

"Bon voyage!"

"Goodnight," replied Monsieur Guillaumin. "Let's go!"

They set off, and Homais went home.

Madame Bovary had opened the window looking onto the garden and was watching the clouds.

They were banking up towards the west where the sun was setting, in the direction of Rouen, travelling quickly in dark spiralling scrolls shot through with streaks of sunlight here and there like the gold arrows of a trophy on the wall, while the rest of the sky was pale as porcelain. Then a gust of wind bent the poplars, and suddenly rain was pattering on the green leaves. And then the sun came out again, hens cackled, sparrows flapped their wings in the dripping bushes, pink acacia flowers floated on puddles in the sand.

"He must be a long way away by now!" she thought.

Homais came over at half-past six as usual, while they were having dinner.

"Well!" he said as he sat down. "We saw that young man of ours off this afternoon then."

"So it seems!" the doctor replied. And turning in his chair, he added: "So what's your news?"

"Not much. Except my wife was somewhat overcome this afternoon. You know women, the slightest thing upsets them! Especially mine! But you'd be wrong to try and change them, because their nervous system is more susceptible than ours."

"Poor Léon!" said Charles. "How is he going to manage in Paris?... Will he ever get used to it?"

Madame Bovary sighed.

"Come off it!" said the pharmacist, clicking his tongue. "Gourmet dinners with his friends! Masked balls! Champagne! He'll get on fine, I promise you."

"I don't think he'll change," Bovary protested.

"Nor do I!" replied Monsieur Homais excitedly. "Although he'll have to go with the crowd unless he wants to be taken for a Jesuit. You don't know the life those characters lead in the Latin Quarter, them and their actresses! Besides, students fit in well in Paris. If they've got charm they'll be received in the best circles, there are even ladies in the Faubourg Saint-Germain who fall in love with them, which gives them the opportunity to make excellent marriages eventually."

"But," said the doctor, "I'm afraid he'll... up there—"

"You're right," the apothecary broke in, "and that's the other side of the coin! You have to hang on to your purse there. You're in a public garden, say; some character appears, well dressed, even wearing a decoration, someone you'd take for a diplomat; he comes over; you get talking; he worms his way into your favours, offers you a pinch of snuff or picks up your hat for you. Then you start to get friendly; he takes you to the café, invites you to his house in the country, gets you tipsy and introduces you to all sorts of acquaintances, and nine times out of ten it's just to con you out of your money or involve you in shady deals."

"True," replied Charles, "but I was thinking more of diseases, typhoid fever for instance, which always affects students from the country."

Emma shuddered.

"It's the change of diet," the pharmacist went on, "and the disruption it causes to your system in general. And then there's the water in Paris of course! The dishes they serve in restaurants, all that spicy food ends up overheating your blood and isn't anywhere near as good as a nice *pot-au-feu*, no matter what people say. For my part I've always preferred good plain cooking – it's healthier! When I was studying pharmacy in Rouen I took my meals in the boarding house; I ate with the lecturers."

He carried on airing his opinions and personal likes and dislikes until Justin came to fetch him to make an eggnog that someone needed.

"Not a moment's peace," he cried. "Nose always to the grindstone! I can't go out for a second! You have to be a carthorse and sweat blood! What servitude!"

Then when he got to the door:

"By the way," he said, "have you heard the news?"

"What's that?"

"It's very likely," Homais went on, raising his eyebrows and putting on his most serious face, "that this year's Agricultural Show for the Lower Seine Region will be held in Yonville-l'Abbaye. At least that's the rumour that's doing the rounds. This morning's paper broached the subject. It'll be of the greatest importance for the district! But we'll talk about it another time. I can see the way, thank you; Justin has the lamp."

7

FOR EMMA the next day was dismal. Everything seemed shrouded in a blackness that floated round things, and the depths of her soul were submerged in softly howling sorrow, like the wind in an empty chateau in winter. It was the dream you dream about what will never return, the listlessness that fills you after every event or deed; the pain you feel when some familiar activity is interrupted, when a constant drumming noise comes to a sudden stop.

In the same way as when she got back from La Vaubyessard, when the quadrilles were still whirling in her head, she was filled with desolate melancholy, numb despair. Léon came back to her, taller, more handsome, more sophisticated, more indistinct; although they were apart he hadn't left her, he was there, his shadow still fell on the walls of her house. She couldn't take her eyes off the carpet where he had walked, the empty chairs where he had sat. The river was still flowing, its shallow ripples glided slowly past the banks. They had gone for walks there so often, to the same murmuring of waves over mossy stones. What fine sunny days they were! What fine afternoons, alone together in the shade at the bottom of the garden! He used to read to her, without a hat, sitting on a cane footstool; the cool breeze made the pages and the nasturtiums in the arbour tremble... Oh, he had gone, the sole pleasure in her life, her one and only hope of bliss! Why hadn't she seized this happiness while it was still there? Why hadn't she held on to him with both hands, on her knees, when he wanted to go? She cursed herself for not having really loved Léon; she thirsted for his lips. She yearned to run after him, to throw herself into his arms, to declare: "It's me, I'm yours!" But she worried about the problems this venture might cause, and regret only made her desires more acute.

From then on Léon's memory became the focal point of her ennui; he glowed brighter than an abandoned campfire in the snow of the Russian steppe. She rushed towards it, huddled round it, gently stirred the dying embers, searched everywhere for anything that would keep it going, and her most distant recollections, like her most immediate circumstances, the things she experienced as well as those she imagined, the carnal desires that evaporated, the plans for happiness that broke off in the wind like dead branches, her barren virtue, her shattered dreams, the marital nest, she gathered it all up, took it and used it to kindle the flame of her unhappiness.

Nonetheless the fire died down, either because her supplies of fuel ran out, or because she had heaped too much on it. Love was gradually snuffed out by absence, regret smothered by routine, and the fiery glow that tinted her pale sky crimson fell into shadow and slowly died away. Within her dulled consciousness she even thought her loathing for her husband was the longing for a lover, the flames of hatred the rekindling of affection; but because the storm was still raging, and her passion had burnt away to ashes, and because no help came and no sun rose, there was black night all around her, and she was left there, lost in the terrible cold that pierced right through her.

And then the bad old days of Tostes began again. Only now she considered herself far more wretched, because with the sorrow she felt came the certainty that it would never end.

A woman who has forced herself to make such great sacrifices can allow herself a few extravagances. She bought a Gothic prie-dieu and spent fourteen francs a month on lemons to clean her nails; she sent to Rouen for a blue cashmere dress; she chose the finest scarf in Lheureux's shop; she knotted it round the waist of her dressing gown; and, shutters closed, book in hand, she would lie on the sofa attired in this garb.

She changed her hairstyle regularly: she wore it *à la chinoise*, in loose ringlets, in plaits or parted on one side and brushed like a man's.

She decided to learn Italian: she bought dictionaries, a grammar book, a supply of plain paper. She attempted some serious reading, history and philosophy. Charles would sometimes wake with a start at night, thinking he was being called out to a patient:

"I'm just coming," he would mumble.

But it was just Emma striking a match to light her lamp. Yet it was the same with books as it was with her tapestry, which no sooner begun were cluttering her cupboard; she picked them up, put them down, moved on to something new.

She would have sudden attacks of eccentric behaviour. One day she told her husband she could drink a whole glass of brandy, and as Charles was foolish enough to dare her, she drained it to the last drop.

Despite her scatterbrained manner (that was the word the good ladies of Yonville used), Emma still didn't seem cheerful, and had that permanent tightening at the corners of the mouth that lines the faces of spinsters and people with thwarted ambitions. She was pale all over, white as a sheet; the skin on her nose dragged slightly round the nostrils, and she would look at you with a faraway expression in her eyes. Having found three grey hairs on her temples, she started talking about getting old.

She frequently had blackouts. One day she even coughed up blood, and as Charles fussed around, clearly anxious, she said:

"Ouf! What does it matter?"

He retreated to his surgery; he sat in his chair under the phrenological head, leant on the table and wept.

Then he wrote to his mother and asked her to come and stay, and they had long discussions about Emma.

What was the answer? What was to be done, seeing as she refused treatment?

"You know what your wife needs?" old mother Bovary told him. "A full-time job, manual work! If she had to earn her living like other people she wouldn't get the vapours. It comes from her filling her head with all those ideas of hers, as well as the fact that she's got nothing to do."

"Still, she does keep herself busy," said Charles.

"Oh? She keeps herself busy, does she? What with? Reading novels, inferior books, writings that are against religion, that poke fun at the clergy using opinions borrowed from Voltaire. But all that has consequences, my poor dear boy, and someone without religion always ends up going to the bad."

So it was decided to stop Emma from reading novels. The woman took it upon herself: the next time she went to Rouen she would go to the book-lender's and personally impress on them that Emma must cancel her subscription. Then wouldn't they be within their rights to tell the police if the bookshop still carried on its poisonous trade?

The farewells between mother-in-law and daughter-in-law were terse. In the three weeks they had spent together they had barely exchanged a word, apart from snippets of news and polite remarks at the dinner table, and before they went to bed.

Madame Bovary senior left on a Wednesday, which was market day in Yonville.

Since early morning the square had been jammed with a line of carts that stretched past the houses all the way from the church right up to the inn, one behind the other with their shafts in the air. On the other side were canvas stalls selling rolls of cotton, blankets and woollen stockings, halters for horses and bundles of blue ribbon that fluttered in the breeze. Heavy ironmongery was laid out on the ground between mountains of eggs, and cheeses in wicker baskets with sticky straw protruding from them; near the threshing machines, chickens poked their heads through the bars of low cages and clucked. The crowd was so dense it was at a virtual standstill, and sometimes almost broke the pharmacy window. The shop was always full on Wednesdays, with people crowding in not so much to buy remedies as to ask medical advice, so esteemed was Homais's reputation in the surrounding villages. His hearty self-assurance mesmerized the country folk. They regarded him as the doctor of doctors.

Emma was leaning on her windowsill (she often did: in the country the window takes the place of the theatre and going for walks), and was enjoying the sight of the thronging peasants when she noticed a gentleman in a green velvet frock coat. Although wearing heavy gaiters he had yellow gloves, and was heading for the doctor's house, followed by a farmer who was looking down at the ground thoughtfully.

"May I speak to the master?" he asked Justin, who was chatting with Félicité on the doorstep.

And, taking him for the servant:

"Tell him Monsieur Rodolphe Boulanger de la Huchette is here."

It wasn't proprietorial vanity that made the newcomer add a title to his name, it was simply a way of introducing himself. La Huchette was an estate not far from Yonville; he had just bought the chateau there, along with two farms that he worked himself, although without being overly energetic about it. He was a bachelor, and was said to have *a private income of at least fifteen thousand livres a year*!

Charles came into the dining room. Monsieur Boulanger introduced his employee, who wanted to be bled because he had pins and needles all over.

"It'll flush me out," he replied to every objection they made.

Bovary sent for bandages and a basin, and asked Justin to hold it. Then turning to the farmhand, who had already gone pale, he said:

"Don't worry, old chap."

"No, no," he answered, "get on with it!"

And with a cocksure expression he held out his arm. As the lancet went in, blood spurted over the mirror.

"Move the bowl closer!" cried Charles.

"*Clock that*!" said the farmer. "It's like a little fountain! My blood's really red, isn't it! Must be a good sign, eh?"

"Sometimes people don't feel anything at first," replied the health officer, "but then they pass out, especially the ones with good healthy constitutions."

At this the peasant dropped the cigarette case he was holding. His shoulders jerked, making the chair creak. His hat fell off.

"I thought so," said Bovary, pressing his finger on the vein.

The basin began to shake in Justin's hands; his knees trembled, he went white.

"Wife!" cried Charles. "Where's my wife!"

She was down the stairs in a trice.

"Get some vinegar!" he shouted. "Oh my God, two at once!"

In his excitement he had difficulty putting the compress on.

"Don't worry," said Monsieur Boulanger calmly, holding Justin up in his arms.

And he sat him on the table with his back to the wall.

Madame Bovary started to untie his cravat. There was a knot in the strings of his shirt; for a moment or two her slim fingers tugged around at the boy's neck; then she put some vinegar on her lawn handkerchief, dabbed his temples and blew gently.

The carter woke up, but Justin was still unconscious, his pupils rolled up in the whites of his eyes like blue flowers floating in milk.

"You'd better not let him see that," said Charles.

Madame Bovary took the basin. As she bent down to put it under the table, her dress (a yellow dress with four flounces, a long waist, a full skirt) spread out round her on the tiles of the dining-room floor – and in leaning forward she teetered slightly as she reached out her arms, and the material of her bodice gave way in places where it stretched. Then she went to get a carafe of water, and was just dissolving some pieces of sugar when the pharmacist arrived. The maid had gone to fetch him during the kerfuffle; seeing his pupil with his eyes open he got his breath back. Then, hovering over him, he looked him up and down.

"Fool!" he said. "Young fool! I mean, really! F-O-O-L spells fool! All this over a simple phlebotomy! And you, a strong lad not afraid of anything! You wouldn't think it to see him now, the human squirrel who climbs trees to shake walnuts from the top branches. Proud of yourself are you, I don't think! It's a fine way to carry on if you want to be a pharmacist; you could find yourself sent for in serious situations, in a courtroom, being asked for expert opinions to help judges make decisions – and you'll need to keep your head, speak sense, behave like a man or be taken for an idiot!"

Justin didn't reply. The apothecary went on:

"Who asked you to come here? You're always pestering Monsieur and Madame! Not only that, I need you on Wednesdays. There are twenty people in the shop. I dropped everything because I was worried about you. Go on, be off with you! Quickly! Wait for me and keep an eye on the jars!"

When Justin had got dressed and left, they talked about fainting fits. Madame Bovary had never had one.

"That's most unusual for a lady!" said Monsieur Boulanger. "Some people are very sensitive. At a duel once I saw one of the seconds pass out, simply from the sound of the pistols being loaded."

"For my part," said the apothecary, "the sight of other people's blood doesn't affect me in the least, but if I dwell on it, the thought of my own is enough to make me black out."

Meanwhile Monsieur Boulanger had sent his servant away, making him promise to stop worrying now his supposed illness was cured.

"But because of it I've had the pleasure of making your acquaintance," he remarked.

And as he spoke he looked at Emma.

Then he put three francs on the corner of the table, gave a casual bow and left.

He was soon on the far side of the river (it was the way he always went to get back to La Huchette); Emma could see him under the poplar trees in the meadow, walking more slowly now and then like someone deep in thought.

"Very sweet!" he was saying to himself. "She's very sweet, that doctor's wife! Lovely teeth, dark eyes, pretty feet, holds herself like a Parisian. Where the devil did she appear from? Where did he find her, that lump of a bloke?"

Rodolphe Boulanger was thirty-four; he had a violent nature and a shrewd mind, had known plenty of women and was well versed in the subject. This one seemed attractive, and he reflected about her and her husband.

"I imagine he's very stupid. She's probably tired of him. He's got dirty fingernails and three days' growth. While he's scurrying about after sick people she's darning his socks. And oh, we're so bored! We'd like to live in town, dance the polka every night! Poor little woman! She yawns after making love, like a carp lying on the kitchen table pining for the river. Three gallant remarks and she'll worship you, there's nothing more certain! She'll be tender, delightful!... Yes, but how do I get rid of her afterwards?"

And, putting the various obstacles to his pleasure into perspective, he started thinking about his mistress. She was an actress in Rouen whom he was keeping, and when he had settled on this image of her, which already sated his memory, he told himself:

"Ah! But Madame Bovary is far more attractive – and fresher too. Virginie is definitely getting too fat. She's so tedious with her little pleasures. And there's that craving of hers for the local prawns!"

The countryside was deserted, all Rodolphe could hear was the grass swishing against his shoes, the distant chirp of crickets hiding somewhere in a field of oats. He could still see Emma in her dining room, dressed as she was a moment ago, and he undressed her.

"Oh, I'm going to have her!" he exclaimed, crushing a clod of earth with his stick.

And immediately he began working on the strategies needed for this venture.

"Where will we meet?" he wondered. "How? She'll always have that brat round her neck, and the maid, the neighbours, the husband, every kind of irritation imaginable. Bah!" he said. "It'll be a waste of time!"

Then he began anew:

"But her eyes bore into your heart like drills. And that pale complexion!... How I adore pale women!"

By the time he got to the top of Argueil hill his mind was made up.

"All I need to do is find opportunities. Well then, I'll drop in from time to time, I'll send them some game, poultry; I'll have myself bled if needs be; we'll become friends, I'll invite them over... By Jove!" he added. "There's the Agricultural Show coming up; she'll be there, I'll see her. We'll make a start, and no holding back – that's always the best way."

8

AND COME IT DID, the much vaunted Agricultural Show! From early in the morning of the grand occasion, all the residents were at their doors, discussing the preparations; the pediment of the town hall had been decorated with garlands of ivy; a marquee had been erected in the meadow for the celebration feast, and in the middle of the square, in front of the church, a form of cannon would announce the arrival of His Honour the Prefect and the names of the farmers who had won prizes. The National Guard from Buchy (there weren't any in Yonville) had come to swell the ranks of the local fire brigade, which was commanded by Binet. He was wearing an even higher collar than usual today and, trussed up in his uniform, his body was so rigid that the only part of him that seemed alive was his legs, which moved like clockwork. As there was a long-standing rivalry between the tax-collector and the colonel, to show off their skills they both got their troops drilling separately. First you saw red epaulettes marching past, and then black breastplates. They just kept going back and forth! Never had there been such pomp! The day before several of the villagers had washed their houses, tricolour flags hung from half-open windows, all the inns were full, and as it was a lovely day the starched caps, gold crosses and colourful scarves seemed brighter than snow, shimmering in the sunlight, their gaily coloured patterns livening up the sober monotone of frock coats and blue smocks. As they got off their horses, local farmers' wives took out the large pins that had been holding their skirts round their waists to stop them getting dirty: their husbands protected their hats by covering them with a handkerchief and holding one corner between their teeth.

The crowds came down the main street from both ends of the village. They poured out of alleyways, side streets, houses, the knockers of front doors were heard rattling now and then as ladies in lisle gloves came out to see the festivities. Particularly admired were two tall yew trees hung with Chinese lanterns either end of a platform where the dignitaries would stand; and against the four pillars of the town hall stood four poles, each bearing a small green banner with gold lettering. On the first one it said: "Commerce"; on the second: "Agriculture"; on the third: "Industry"; and on the last: "The Fine Arts".

But the euphoria that lit up every face seemed to fill the landlady of the inn, Madame Lefrançois, with gloom. Standing on her kitchen doorstep she muttered to herself:

"What nonsense! Look at that canvas shack of theirs, what nonsense! Do they think the Prefect is going to enjoy having lunch in that there tent like some circus performer? And they call this song and dance doing good for the village! It's not worth getting the owner of some greasy spoon over from Neufchâtel for! And who's it in aid of? Cowherds! A bunch of vagrants!...

The apothecary walked past. He was wearing a black tailcoat, nankeen trousers, low beaver-skin shoes and, most unusually, a hat – a low silk hat.

"Salutations!" he said. "Forgive me, but I'm in a hurry."

And as the portly widow asked him where he was going:

"I expect it seems odd, doesn't it? Me, who spends more time cooped up in his laboratory than a rat in a piece of cheese."

"What cheese is that?" said the landlady.

"Oh, never mind!" replied Homais. "I was just trying to describe how I'm usually cloistered away in my house, Madame Lefrançois. Today, however, given the occasion, I must really—"

"Ah! You're going over there then?" she said, with a note of contempt.

"That's where I'm going, yes," retorted the apothecary, surprised. "I'm on the advisory committee, aren't I."

Old mother Lefrançois looked him up and down for a moment, then replied with a smile:

"That's as may be! But what have you got to do with farming? Do you know all about it then?"

"Most certainly I know about it, seeing as I'm a pharmacist – or rather a chemist! And, Madame Lefrançois, the purpose of chemistry being knowledge of the reciprocal and molecular processes in every living body in the natural world, it follows that agriculture comes within its sphere! Because the constituents of fertilizer, the fermentation of fluids, the analysing of gases and the effect of noxious fumes – what's all that if not chemistry pure and simple, I ask you?"

The landlady didn't reply. So Homais went on:

"So to be an agronomist, do you think you have to have ploughed the land or fattened poultry? No, you need to know the composition of the substances in question, geological deposits, atmospheric influences, the quality of the soil, the minerals, the water, the density of various bodies and their capillarity, and goodness knows what else! And you have to have in-depth knowledge of the rudiments of hygiene so you can oversee and evaluate the construction of buildings, the animals' diet, and the servants too! And you also need a thorough knowledge of botany, Madame Lefrançois – so you can identify plants, do you hear? Which are beneficial, which harmful, which are uncultivatable and which nutritious; whether it's better to pull them up in one place and sow them elsewhere, to propagate some and kill off others – in short, you have to keep up to date by reading official pamphlets and documents available to the public, always have your eyes open to pick up new improvements..."

The innkeeper hadn't taken her eyes off the front door of the Café Français. And the pharmacist carried on:

"May God make our farmers chemists, or at least make them pay more attention to the recommendations of science! Take me for example, I recently wrote a fine little work, a dissertation of over seventy-two pages called *Cider, Its Production and Effects; Followed by Some New Observations on the Subject*, which I sent to the Agronomical Society in Rouen, and which earned me the distinction of being elected a member, agriculture branch, pomology section – and if my book had been given some publicity..."

But the apothecary stopped, because Madame Lefrançois's mind seemed to be elsewhere.

"Just look at them!" she said. "It's beyond me! A greasy spoon like that!"

And with a shrug that made her jersey ruck up over her bust, she pointed both hands at her rival establishment, from whose doorway came the sound of singing.

"Still, they haven't got long," she added. "In a week it'll be history."

Homais stood back in amazement. She came down the three steps, and leaning close to his ear she said:

"What? You haven't heard? The bailiffs are due this week. It's going to be sold off because of Lheureux. He's bled him white with interest payments."

"What a calamity!" exclaimed the apothecary, who could always find the right words for every occasion.

The innkeeper started giving him the details, which she had heard from Monsieur Guillaumin's servant, Théodore. Because as much as she loathed Tellier she blamed Lheureux: he was a grovelling swindler.

"Well fancy that!" she said, "and there he is in the covered market; he's greeting Madame Bovary, who's wearing a green hat. And she's on Monsieur Boulanger's arm too."

"Madame Bovary!" said Homais. "I must go and pay my respects. Perhaps she'd like a seat in the enclosure, under the portico."

And ignoring Madame Lefrançois, who was calling him back so she could tell him more details, the pharmacist hurried off smiling, striding out, acknowledging people in all directions and taking up a lot of space with the long skirts of his black tailcoat, which fluttered in the breeze.

Seeing him in the distance, Rodolphe started walking faster, but Madame Bovary was soon out of breath; so he slowed down, and said with a cruel smile:

"It's to avoid that fat fellow: you know, the apothecary."

She nudged him.

"What's that supposed to mean?" he wondered.

And as they walked he studied her out of the corner of his eye.

From the side she looked so composed as to be impenetrable. In the bright sunlight her profile stood out against the oval of her hat, with its pale ribbons that looked like reeds. Her eyes, with long curved lashes, looked straight ahead, and although wide open it was almost as if they were held in check by her cheeks, because of the blood pumping gently beneath her delicate skin. The area between her nostrils was tinged pink. She tilted her head to one side, and between her lips you could see the points of her pearly white teeth.

"Is she making fun of me?" wondered Rodolphe.

Yet Emma's gesture was simply a warning, because Monsieur Lheureux was with them, and making occasional attempts at conversation:

"What a glorious day! Everyone is outdoors! There's an easterly wind."

Madame Bovary spoke to him as rarely as Rodolphe did, yet whenever they made the slightest movement Lheureux came up to her, touched her hat and said: "So do you like it?"

When they reached the blacksmith's house, instead of continuing along the road as far as the gate Rodolphe suddenly turned down a footpath, taking Madame Bovary with him. He called back:

"Good day, Monsieur Lheureux! I'll be seeing you!"

"You certainly sent him packing," she said with a laugh.

"Why let people intrude on your privacy?" he replied. "And as I'm fortunate enough to be with you today..."

She blushed. He didn't finish what he was saying. They talked about the lovely weather, how pleasant it was walking on the grass. A few marguerites were growing there.

"Here are some nice little daisies," he said. "There's enough for all the courting couples in the village to make a wish."

Then he added:

"What would you say if I picked some?"

"Are you courting?" she said, giving a little cough.

"Ah ha!" answered Rodolphe, "who knows?"

The meadow filled with people, mothers jostled them with their big umbrellas, baskets and small children. Sometimes they had to move aside for a long line of country folk, serving girls in blue stockings and flat shoes with silver rings on their fingers, and who smelt of milk. Walking hand in hand, they spilt all the way along the pasture from the aspen trees as far as the banqueting tent. But now it was judging time, and one by one the farmers went into a sort of arena marked out by a rope strung between posts.

This was where the animals were, with their heads facing the cord and their hindquarters, all different heights, in a disorderly line. Sleepy pigs prodded their snouts into the ground; calves lowed; ewes bleated; cows rested their bellies on the ground, one hock folded under them, and, chewing slowly, blinked their heavy eyelids at the midges that buzzed round them. Bare-armed carters tugged at halters to rein in rearing stallions which, nostrils flaring, whinnied at the nearby mares. They just stood there quietly, manes dangling, stretching their necks while their foals sat resting in the shade beside them, occasionally coming up to feed, and along this rippling line of bodies packed in side by side a white mane could be seen tossing in the breeze like a wave, or a pair of sharp horns sticking up, the heads of men running. A hundred yards away, and to one side beyond the enclosure, stood a large bull with a ring in its nose and wearing a muzzle, motionless as a bronze statue. A ragged boy held it by a rope.

Meanwhile some gentlemen were walking ponderously between the two rows, examining each animal in turn and then conferring quietly. One, who seemed more important, took notes in a register as he went along. It was the chairman of the panel of judges, Monsieur Derozerays de la Panville. The moment he caught sight of Rodolphe he hurried over with a friendly smile:

"What's this, Monsieur Boulanger?" he said. "Are you deserting us?"

Rodolphe told him he would be there in a moment. But when the chairman had gone he said:

"Heavens, no, I'm not going anywhere. I prefer your company to his."

And while continuing to look down his nose at agricultural shows, Rodolphe showed his blue entry pass to a policeman so they could walk round more easily, and occasionally even stopped at some fine specimen that didn't exactly enthral Madame Bovary. He noticed, and started to make jokes about the Yonville ladies, their clothes; then apologized for his own casual appearance. It was that indecipherable blend of the ordinary and the exotic, at the sight of which the common herd think they have discovered an eccentric existence, a dissolute love life, the tyranny of art and, of course, a contempt for convention which they either find appealing or infuriating. His cambric shirt with pleated cuffs billowed in the wind above his grey twill waistcoat, and under broad-striped trousers he wore a pair of nankeen boots trimmed with patent leather on the legs and the front of the foot. They were so shiny that the grass reflected in them. He trampled down horse droppings, hand in his jacket pocket, straw hat tilted to one side.

"Still," he added, "when you live in the country..."

"It's a waste of time and effort," said Emma.

"True!" answered Rodolphe. "And just think, not one of these good people is capable of understanding the cut of a tailcoat!"

And they talked about provincial mediocrity, the lives it smothered, the illusions it shattered.

"So," said Rodolphe, "I'm sunk in unhappiness—"

"You?" she said, surprised. "I thought you were happy!"

"On the surface, yes, because when I'm with people I put on a jocular mask, but there are times when I've seen a cemetery in the moonlight and wondered if I wouldn't be better off sleeping with the rest of them..."

"What about your friends? Don't you spare them a thought?"

"Friends? What friends? Have I got any? Who cares about me?"

And as he said it he gave a sort of whistle between his teeth.

But they had to move apart because of a man behind them carrying a huge stack of chairs. He was so weighed down that all that was visible were the toes of his clogs and his elbows protruding. It was Lestiboudois the gravedigger, carting chairs from the church through the midst of the throng. Always resourceful when he stood to gain, he had found a way to turn the agricultural show to his advantage; and his idea was paying off, because he couldn't keep up with demand. Hot, bothered villagers fought over the straw seats that smelt of incense, and settled against the broad backs covered in candle wax with something approaching reverence.

Madame Bovary took Rodolphe's arm again; he went on as if talking to himself.

"Oh yes! So much has passed me by! Always alone! If only I'd had an aim in life, if I'd found affection, met someone... I'd have put my all into it, overcome everything, broken with everything!"

"Nonetheless," said Emma, "it seems to me that you don't have much to complain about."

"You don't think so?" said Rodolphe.

"After all..." she went on, "you're free."

She hesitated.

"Rich."

"Don't make fun of me," he replied.

She was just assuring him that she wasn't making fun when the noise of a cannon rang out; in a great rush people immediately headed towards the village.

It was a false alarm; the Prefect hadn't arrived, and the judges were at a loss to know whether to begin the formalities or wait a little longer.

Finally a large hired landau appeared on the far side of the square, drawn by two scraggy horses that a coachman in a white hat was whipping up with all his might. Binet just had time to shout "Take post!" and the colonel to follow suit. They hurried to the stack of rifles. They rushed. Some forgot to fasten their collars. But the official carriage and pair seemed to anticipate this confusion, and prancing in their chain harness the two beasts between the shafts drew up in front of the columned entrance of the town hall at a gentle trot, just as the National Guard and the firemen fell in, marking time to the beat of the drum.

"Shoulder arms!" shouted Binet.

"Halt!" shouted the colonel. "Left dress!"

And, after shouldering arms with a jingle of metal barrel bands that sounded like a brass cauldron bouncing down the stairs, all the rifles were lowered again.

Out of the coach got a gentleman in a short tailcoat with silver braid, quite bald in front and with a great tuft of hair at the back, with a pale face and a kindly expression. His large, heavy-lidded eyes were half closed in order to get a look at the multitude, while lifting his sharp nose and smiling with his sunken mouth. He identified the mayor by his sash, and explained that His Honour the Prefect had been unable to come. He himself was a Prefectural Councillor; then he added a few apologies. In reply Tuvache presented his compliments, the other confessed to being embarrassed, and there they stood face to face, foreheads almost touching, with the panel of judges, the town council, the worthies, the National Guard and the crowd looking on. The Honourable Councillor, his little black tricorn hat held to his chest, repeated his greetings, while Tuvache, bent like a reed, smiled in return, stuttered, tried to find the right words, declared his devotion to the monarchy and the honour that was being done to Yonville.

Hippolyte, the groom from the inn, took the horses from the coachman, and, limping with his club foot, led them under the porch of the Lion d'Or, where a crowd of farmers had gathered to look at the coach. Drums beat, the cannon roared, and the gentlemen filed onto the platform and sat in the red Utrecht velvet armchairs that had been lent by Madame Tuvache.

They all looked the same. Slightly sunburnt, their flabby blond faces were the colour of sweet cider, their bushy sideburns burst out from large stiff collars held up by white cravats with broad bows. All the waistcoats were velvet with shawl collars; all the watches had an oval fob made of carnelian at the end of a long ribbon; they sat with their hands on their thighs, legs slightly apart, the shabby black material of their trousers as shiny as the leather of their stout boots.

The ladies of the company stood behind, between the pillars of the entrance, while the ordinary mortals were in the crowd opposite, either standing or on seats. Lestiboudois had brought the chairs that he had taken to the meadow, and was now running back and forth to the church to fetch more, blocking the way so much with his little business that people had difficulty getting to the steps onto the platform.

"In my view," said Monsieur Lheureux (speaking to the pharmacist, who was walking past on his way to his seat), "they should have put up a pair of Venetian flagpoles there: with something rather stern and sumptuous as novelties, it would have looked really nice."

"Absolutely," replied Homais. "Still, what do you expect? The mayor took everything on himself. Poor old Tuvache hasn't got much taste, he's totally devoid of what's known as artistic sensibility."

Meanwhile Rodolphe had gone up to the first floor of the town hall with Madame Bovary, into the debating chamber, and since it was empty he decided it would be a good place in which to view the proceedings in comfort. He fetched three stools from round the oval table beneath the bust of the monarch, and putting them by the window they sat down.

There was fidgeting on the platform, much whispering and conferring. Finally the Honourable Councillor stood up. It was now known that he was called Lieuvain, and his name was soon passed round the crowd. Once he had gathered up some sheets of paper and studied them, he began:

"Gentlemen, permit me first of all (before speaking to you on the subject of today's gathering, and this sentiment, I am sure, will be shared by all of you), permit me, as I say, to offer due recognition to the higher authorities, to the government, to the monarch, gentlemen, to our sovereign, the beloved King for whom no part of public or private prosperity is a matter of indifference, and who steers the ship of state through the ceaseless perils of a stormy sea with a hand both steady and wise, knowing, moreover, how to respect peace as much as war, industry, commerce, agriculture and the fine arts."

"I think I should move back slightly," said Rodolphe.

"Why?" said Emma.

But at that point the Councillor's voice became extraordinarily loud:

"The time is past, gentlemen," he proclaimed, "when civil dissent brought bloodshed to our public squares, when the property owner, the merchant, even the working man trembled when he went to sleep at night for fear of being woken by the sound of the fire alarm, when the most subversive maxims had the temerity to undermine the foundations..."

"I might be seen from down there," Rodolphe replied, "and then I'd spend two weeks apologizing, and what with my bad reputation..."

"You're maligning yourself, surely," said Emma.

"No no, it's appalling, I assure you."

"However, gentlemen," the Councillor went on, "if, dismissing these baleful scenes from my mind, I shift my gaze to the situation in our beautiful homeland today, what do I see? Everywhere commerce and the arts are flourishing; everywhere new communication routes, like so many new arteries in the body of the State, are creating new connections; our manufacturing centres are busy once more; religion, now strengthened, welcomes every heart; our ports are full, confidence has revived, and at last France can breathe..."

"Besides," Rodolphe added, "perhaps people are right!"

"What do you mean?" she said.

"What!" he said. "You didn't know there are souls in constant torment? One minute they have to have dreams, the next action, the purest passions then the wildest pleasures, they throw themselves into every kind of mad excess."

She stared at him as you would at a traveller just returned from fantastic lands, then replied:

"We poor women don't even have that for amusement!"

"Some amusement: it doesn't bring happiness."

"Does anything?" she asked.

"Yes," he replied, "you stumble across it sooner or later."

"And you have realized this," the Councillor was saying. "You farmers and working men of the countryside! You peace-loving pioneers of a great work of civilization! You men of progress and moral standards! You realize, I say, that political storms are more fearsome than any atmospheric disturbance…"

"You stumble across it sooner or later," repeated Rodolphe, "quite suddenly and when you had given up hope of finding it. And then the clouds on the horizon open and it's as if a voice is crying: 'This is it!' You feel the need to trust this person with your life, to give them everything, give up everything for them! You don't need to explain things to each other, you just know. You've seen each other in dreams." (And he looked at her.) "It's there in front of you at last, the treasure you've searched for for so long; it shines, it sparkles. And yet still you doubt it, you daren't believe it; you stand there dazzled, as if you've walked out of darkness into the light."

As he finished, Rodolphe added a touch of melodrama to what he had just said. He put his hand over his face like someone who suddenly feels faint, then let it fall onto Emma's. She moved hers away. And the Councillor was still reading:

"And who would be surprised at this, gentlemen! Only one who is so blind, so submerged (I'm not afraid to say it), so submerged in the prejudices of another age that he misjudges the spirit of the farming community. Where, indeed, do you see more patriotism than in the countryside, more dedication to the public interest, in a word more intelligence? I don't mean that shallow intelligence, gentlemen, that empty adornment for idle minds, but the profound and reasonable intelligence which concentrates its efforts on striving for useful aims above all else, thus contributing to the common good, to the betterment of all, to supporting the State, which is the fruit born of respect for the law and doing one's duty…"

"Ah, there it is again!" said Rodolphe. "Always duty! I'm bored to death with that word. It's for old duffers in flannel vests, religious maniacs with foot-warmers and rosaries, forever crowing in our ears: 'Duty! Duty!' Duty is having a sense of what is great, by Jove, treasuring what is beautiful, not just accepting social conventions and the disgrace they impose on us!"

"Yet… yet…" protested Madame Bovary.

"No! Why inveigh against the passions? Aren't they the only beautiful thing on earth, the fount of all heroism, ardour, poetry, music, the arts, in fact of everything!"

"But you should take notice of some of society's opinions, comply with its moral code."

"Ah," he replied, "but there are two codes. The little one, the accepted one, the one for men, the one that is forever changing, that yells at the top of its voice and wriggles around on its belly on the ground like that collection of idiots you see out there. But the other one, the eternal one, is all around and above, like the landscape that surrounds us and the blue sky that gives us light."

Monsieur Lieuvain wiped his mouth with his handkerchief. Then he continued:

"But what point is there, gentlemen, in my demonstrating the usefulness of agriculture to you here today? For who is it that provides for our needs? Who supplies us with food? Isn't it the farmer? The farmer, gentlemen, who, industriously sowing seed in the fertile furrows of the countryside, causes the wheat to grow, which, ground into powder by ingenious machines, comes out as what we call flour, and from there, transported to towns and cities, is then given to the baker who uses it to produce food for rich and poor alike. And isn't it the farmer who fattens his numerous herds and flocks in the pasture? For how would we clothe ourselves, how would we feed ourselves without agriculture? Is there any need, gentlemen, to go far to find examples? Which of us hasn't pondered the importance of what we get from that humble creature that adorns our farmyards, which provides soft pillows for our beds, delicious meat for our table and eggs? But I would never finish if I had to list the various things that well-cultivated land produces, like a doting mother is generous to her children. Here it's the vineyard; elsewhere it's cider-apple trees; there, rape; somewhere else, cheeses; and flax, gentlemen – don't forget flax, which over the last few years has seen a sizeable increase and to which I particularly call your attention!"

There was no need for him to call: because every mouth in the crowd was open as if swallowing his words. Beside him Tuvache listened wide-eyed; now and then Monsieur Derozerays's eyelids drooped slightly; while farther along the pharmacist, with his son Napoléon between his legs, cupped his hand to his ear so as not to miss a word. The chins of the other judges were nodding on their waistcoats in approval. Around the foot of the platform the firemen were resting on their rifles; while Binet, motionless, elbow held to his side, kept the point of his sword bolt upright. He might have been able to hear, but he couldn't have seen anything because the peak of his helmet came down over his eyes. The one worn by his second in command, Tuvache's younger son, was even worse; it was enormous and wobbled about on his head, revealing the end of his printed scarf. Beneath it he was smiling with childlike sweetness, and his pale little face, dripping with sweat, had an expression of delight, exhaustion and drowsiness.

The square was packed right the way to the fronts of the houses. People were leaning at the windows, standing in every doorway, while outside the pharmacy Justin seemed lost in wonder at what was before his eyes. Yet despite the silence, Monsieur Lieuvain's voice was borne away on the breeze. It reached you in snippets, broken up here and there by the noise of chairs in the crowd; the long bellow of an ox would suddenly come from behind you, or the baaing of lambs calling each other on street corners. For that was how far the cowherds and shepherds had driven their animals, and they lowed or bleated every now and then as they nibbled at some piece of greenery hanging over their nose.

Rodolphe moved closer to Emma, and said quickly and quietly:

"Doesn't this coven appal you? Is there a single human emotion that it doesn't condemn? The noblest instincts, the purest friendships are persecuted, vilified, and if two poor souls do meet, everything is arranged so they can't be together. Yet try they will, they'll flap their wings, call out. What does it matter? Sooner or later, in six months', ten years' time they'll meet again, they'll love one another, because that's what destiny demands, because they were made for each other."

He sat with his arms crossed, and turning to Emma he looked at her hard, closely. She could make out tiny gold flecks in his eyes, fanning out round his black pupils, and could even smell the pomade that made his hair shine. Then suddenly she felt weak, she remembered the Vicomte who had waltzed with her at La Vaubyessard, and whose beard gave off the same scents of vanilla and lemon, and instinctively she half-closed her eyes in order to breathe it in. But as she did so she sat up in her chair, and saw the old stagecoach *Hirondelle* on the horizon, coming slowly down Les Leux hill trailing a long plume of dust. It was in that same yellow carriage that Léon had so often returned to her; and it was on that same road that he had left for ever! She thought she saw him at his window opposite; then everything became confused, the clouds passed; it was as if she were still waltzing in the Vicomte's arms in the light of the chandeliers, and Léon wasn't far away, he was coming... and yet she could still sense Rodolphe's head beside her. The sweetness of the sensation found its way into her old desires, and like grains of sand in the wind they whirled round in the delicate waft of perfume that was spreading through her soul. She breathed in deeply through her nose several times, to inhale the fresh smell of the ivy at the top of the pillars. She took off her gloves, wiped her hands; then she fanned her face with her handkerchief, while beneath the drumming in her temples she heard the murmur of the crowd, the drone of the Councillor's voice.

He was saying:

"Carry on! Persevere! Don't listen to what habit advises, or to the precipitous suggestions of reckless empiricism! Put your efforts into improving the soil, good manure, the breeding of the equine, bovine, ovine and porcine races! May this show be a peaceable arena for you where the victor holds out the hand of friendship to the vanquished in the hope of greater success! And you, respected and humble servants, whose exhausting toil has never been recognized by any government until now, come and receive the reward for your quiet virtues, rest assured that from now on the State has turned its gaze to you, that it supports you, protects you, that it will accede to all your lawful grievances, and as much as it is able will lighten the load of your painful sacrifices."

Monsieur Lieuvain sat down; then Monsieur Derozerays stood up and began the next speech. His was perhaps not as florid as the Councillor's, but notable for its more pragmatic style, as well as its more specialist knowledge and more sophisticated observations. Praise for the government played a smaller part; religion and agriculture a larger one. The connection between the two could be seen, as well as how they had both contributed to civilization. Rodolphe and Madame Bovary talked about dreams, premonitions, magnetism. Going back to the cradle of humanity, the speaker described the savage times when men lived on nuts and berries in the woods. But then they cast off animal skins and put on clothes of wool, dug furrows, planted vines. Was this a good thing, or were there more drawbacks to this discovery than advantages? This was Monsieur Derozerays's question. From magnetism Rodolphe gradually moved on to affinities, and while the Honourable Chairman quoted Cincinnatus and his plough, Diocletian planting cabbages* and the emperors of China declaring the new year open by sowing seed, the young man was explaining to the young woman that irresistible attractions had their roots in a previous life.

"Take us," he said. "Why did we meet? What whim of fate was responsible? It's probably that from a great distance, like two rivers flowing into each other, our individual trajectories have pushed us together."

And he took her hand; she didn't move it away.

"Overall best arable land!..." called out the chairman.

"Just now, for instance, when I came to your house..."

"...Goes to Monsieur Bizet from Quincampoix."

"Did I realize that I would come with you?"

"Seventy francs!"

"I wanted to leave a hundred times, yet I followed you, I stayed."

"Manure."

"In the same way as I'd stay tonight, tomorrow, other days, all my life!"

"To Monsieur Caron from Argueil, a gold medal!"

"Because never have I found someone's company so utterly captivating."

"To Monsieur Bain of Givry-Saint-Martin!"

"So I'll carry your memory with me."

"For a merino ram..."

"But you'll forget me, I'll just be a fleeting shadow."

"To Monsieur Belot of Notre-Dame…"

"No, I'll still have a place in your thoughts, in your life, won't I?"

"Swine breeding: joint first prize goes to Messieurs Lehérissé and Cullembourg – sixty francs!"

Rodolphe squeezed her hand, it was warm, he felt it tremble like a caged dove that wants to fly away; but whether she was simply trying to free it or responding to this pressure, she moved her fingers.

"Oh, thank you!" he cried. "You aren't rejecting me! You're so kind! You've realized that I'm yours! Let me see you, gaze at you!"

A sudden breeze from the window rucked up the tablecloth, and in the square the farmers' wives' large bonnets lifted up like so many white butterflies fluttering their wings.

"Utilization of oilseed cattle cake," the chairman went on.

He was in a hurry now:

"Flemish fertilizer* – cultivation of flax – drainage – long-term leasing – domestic service."

Rodolphe said no more. They looked at each other. Their dry lips trembled with utter desire, and gently, effortlessly, their fingers intertwined.

"Catherine-Nicaise-Elisabeth Leroux, of Sassetot-la-Guerrière, for fifty-four years of service on the same farm, a silver medal – and a prize of twenty-five francs!"

"Catherine Leroux? Where is she?" said the Councillor.

She didn't appear, and voices could be heard whispering:

"Go on!"

"No."

"Over to the left!"

"Don't be afraid!"

"Oh, she's so stupid!"

"So is she here?" Tuvache exclaimed.

"Yes!… She's here!"

"Let her come up then!"

A small, timid-looking old woman who seemed wizened in her shabby clothes approached the platform. She was wearing heavy wooden clogs and a long blue apron. Her thin face, framed by an untrimmed bonnet, had more wrinkles than a withered Cox's apple, and the sleeves of her red smock hung down over her long gnarled hands. They were so engrained, chapped and hard with dust from the barns, with caustic soda and suint from the wool, that they looked dirty although they had been washed in clean water; as a result of all her years of service they were permanently half open, as if humbly bearing witness to the many hardships she had suffered. There was a monastic rigour about her expression. Nothing sad or sentimental softened this pale gaze. The company of animals had lent her their mute tranquillity. It was the first time she had been in such a crowd of people; and inwardly alarmed by all the flags, the drums, the gentlemen in black tailcoats and the Councillor's gold Croix d'Honneur* she just stood there, unsure whether to walk forward or run away, or why the crowd were pushing her and the judges were smiling at her. So there she stood in front of the beaming burghers, a half-century of servitude.

"Come forward, worthy Catherine-Nicaise-Elisabeth Leroux!" said the Honorable Councillor, who had taken the list of prizewinners from the chairman.

And, looking first at the sheet of paper then at the old woman, he repeated in a fatherly voice:

"Come forward, come forward!"

"Are you deaf?" said Tuvache, leaping out of his chair.

And he shouted in her ear:

"Fifty-four years of service! A silver medal! Twenty-five francs! It's for you."

When she had her medal, she studied it. A beatific smile spread over her face, and as she walked away she could be heard muttering:

"I'll give it to the Father so he can say Mass for me."

"What a zealot!" cried the pharmacist, leaning over to the notary.

The prize-giving was over, the crowd broke up, and now that the speeches were finished everyone went back to his proper place and everything returned to normal; the masters beat the servants and the servants hit the animals, indifferent victors who went home to the cowshed with a crown of laurels on their horns.

Meanwhile the National Guard moved up to the first floor of the town hall, with brioches skewered on their bayonets, the battalion drummer boy carrying a basketful of bottles. Madame Bovary took Rodolphe's arm and he walked her back to her house; they said goodbye at the door, then he went for a stroll in the meadow on his own while he waited for the banquet to start.

The feast was long, noisy and disorganized; people were so packed together there was barely room to move their elbows; the narrow planks that were used as benches almost gave way under the weight of the guests. Food was plentiful. Everyone helped himself to a large portion. Sweat ran down every forehead, and a whitish haze hovered above the table between the hanging oil lamps like mist over the river on an autumn morning. Leaning back against the canvas wall of the marquee, Rodolphe's thoughts were so fixed on Emma that he didn't hear a thing. On the grass behind him servants were stacking dirty dishes; the people either side were talking, he didn't join in; they filled his glass, yet despite the noise that grew louder and louder, in his mind all was silence. He dreamt about what she had said, the shape of her lips; her face shone out of the badges of the shakos as if from a magic mirror; the pleats of her dress hung down the sides of the tent, long days of love unfolded endlessly into the future.

He saw her again at the fireworks display that night; but she was with her husband, Madame Homais and the pharmacist, who was fretting about the risk of stray rockets; he kept on leaving them in order to go and give Binet advice.

Due to excessive precautions the pyrotechnics that were delivered to Mr Tuvache's house had been locked away in the cellar, and so now the damp powder wouldn't light properly and the main set piece, which would have shown a dragon biting its tail, completely flopped. Here and there a poor little Roman candle went off; the gaping crowd began to protest, their yells mingling with the shrieks of women having their backsides felt in the darkness. Emma nestled quietly against Charles's shoulder, and then looking up she watched the brilliant trails of rockets in the night sky. Rodolphe gazed at her in the glow of the Chinese lanterns.

Gradually they all went out. Stars appeared. There were a few spots of rain. She tied her scarf round her head.

Just then the Councillor's carriage drove off from the inn. The coachman, who was drunk, quickly dozed off, and his massive shape could be seen in the distance over the top of the hood between the two lamps, swaying from side to side with the pitching of the coach.

"Frankly," said the apothecary, "they should deal severely with drunkenness! I wish they would write the names of all those who've poisoned themselves with alcohol during the last seven days, on a board on the door of the town hall every week, ad hoc. So when it came to statistics there'd be a form of official record that could be consulted if needs be... But do excuse me."

And he hurried back to the fire-brigade commander.

Binet was on his way home. He was going back to his lathe.

"It might not be a bad thing to send one of your men," said Homais, "or even to go yourself..."

"Do leave me in peace," replied the tax-collector, "there's nothing wrong!"

"Don't worry," said the apothecary when he got back to his friends. "Monsieur Binet guaranteed to me that the proper measures have been taken. No sparks fell anywhere. The pumps are full. Let's go to bed."

"Heavens above, I need it," said Madame Homais, who kept yawning. "Still, we had a really beautiful day for the fair."

Quietly, and with a fond look in his eyes, Rodolphe repeated:

"Yes, really beautiful!"

Two days later a long article on the Agricultural Show appeared in the *Fanal de Rouen*. Homais had put pen to paper the very next morning, with some eloquence:

"Why all the festoons, the flowers, the garlands? Where rushes this crowd of people like a raging tide at sea, beneath the deluge of tropical sun that poured forth its heat on our tillage?"

Going on from this he talked about the farmers' lot. The government was undoubtedly doing a great deal, but not enough! "Take heart!" he cried. "There are thousands of essential reforms, let us implement them!" Then, picking up on what the Councillor had said, he didn't neglect "the military bearing of our militia", or "our most vivacious village ladies", or "the balding old men, patriarchs, some of whom, relics of our immortal phalanxes, still feel their hearts beat faster at the manly sound of the drum". He named himself among the first of the panel of judges, mentioning in an aside that Monsieur Homais, pharmacist, had sent a dissertation on cider to the Agricultural Society. When he came to the prize-giving he described the delight of the winners in eulogistic terms. "The father embraces his son, the brother his brother, the husband his wife. More than one showed off his humble medal with pride, and when he got home to his lady wife, he no doubt wept as he hung it on the wall of his simple cottage."

"At six o'clock a banquet was held in a marquee in Monsieur Liégeard's pasture for all the main participants of the festival. There was an atmosphere of utmost cordiality throughout. Various toasts were proposed: Monsieur Lieuvain, to the Monarch! Monsieur Tuvache, to the Prefect! Monsieur Derozerays, to agriculture! Monsieur Homais, to those two sisters, industry and the fine arts! Monsieur Leplichey, to improvements! That night a dazzling fireworks display lit up the sky. It was a true kaleidosope, one would have thought it was a scene from the opera, and for a moment our little locale was whisked away into a dream from *A Thousand and One Nights*.

"It is worth mentioning that not a single untoward incident disrupted this family gathering."

And he added: "The only ones notable by their absence were the clergy. No doubt the sacristy views progress in a different way. That is your choice, gentlemen of Loyola!"

9

SIX WEEKS WENT BY. Rodolphe didn't come back. Then one evening he finally made an appearance.

The day after the Agricultural Show he had said to himself:

"Don't go back too soon. It would be a mistake."

So at the end of that week he had taken himself off on a hunting trip. When he got back he wondered if it was too late, but then he had told himself:

"If she loved me from the first, then out of impatience to see me again she'll love me even more now. So, on we go!"

He knew his assessment was correct when he walked into the dining room and saw Emma turn pale.

She was alone. It was just getting dark. The little muslin curtains at the window muted the twilight, and sunlight reflected on the gilding of the barometer scattered fiery splinters among the jagged outlines of the anemone over the mirror.

Rodolphe stayed standing; to his polite greetings Emma made little reply.

"I've had business to attend to," he said. "I was ill."

"Was it serious?" she cried.

"Well," said Rodolphe, sitting on a stool beside her, "no, actually!...
It was just that I didn't want to come back."

"Why?"

"Can't you guess?"

And he looked at her again, so intensely this time that she blushed
and looked down. He went on:

"Emma..."

"Monsieur!" she said, moving away.

"Ah!" he replied sadly. "I see I was right not to want to come back;
because that name, the name that fills my heart, which has eluded
me, you forbid me to say it! Madame Bovary!... Oh!... That's what
everyone calls you!... But it isn't your name; it belongs to someone
else!"

And again he said:

"Someone else!"

And he buried his face in his hands.

"Oh yes, I think of you constantly!... The memory of you drives me
to despair! Ah, forgive me!... I must leave... Farewell!... I shall go far
away... so far that you'll never hear of me again!... Yet... today... I
don't know what drove me to you! Because you can't battle with the
heavens, you can't resist when the angels smile on you! You let yourself
be swept away by what is beautiful, lovely, adorable!"

It was the first time Emma had heard such things, and like someone
lying back in a steam bath, her pride gave itself up gently and completely
to the warmth of the words.

"But if I haven't come," he went on, "if I haven't been able to see
you, at least I've gazed at where you live. At night, every night, I get up,
I come here, I look at your house, the roof glinting in the moonlight,
the trees in the garden swaying by your window, and your lamp, a little
glow behind the panes in the darkness. Oh, you didn't realize there was
a poor wretch out there, so near and yet so far!..."

She turned to him, her voice choked with emotion:

"Oh, you are so good!" she said.

"No, I love you, that's all! You mustn't doubt it! Say it to me: a word!
Just one word!"

And Rodolphe slid off the stool onto the floor, oblivious; but there
was the sound of clogs in the kitchen, and he noticed that the dining-
room door was partly open.

"It would be so kind," he continued, getting up, "if you were to indulge a whim!"

It was to look round her house; he wanted to get to know it; and as Madame Bovary saw nothing untoward in this, they were both getting up when Charles came in.

"Hello, Doctor," said Rodolphe.

Flattered at being addressed in this way, Bovary produced a stream of unctuous remarks, and the other man took advantage of this to gather his thoughts.

"Madame was just telling me," he said, "about the state of her health—"

Charles interrupted him – because in fact he was most concerned; his wife had started having feelings of suffocation again. So Rodolphe asked if going out on a horse wouldn't be a bad idea.

"Now there's a thought!... Most certainly! Excellent, ideal! You ought to follow up on it, Emma."

And when she protested that she hadn't got a horse, Monsieur Rodolphe offered her one; she refused; he didn't press the point; then, to justify his visit he explained that his carter, the man who had been bled, was still having blackouts.

"I'll drop by," said Bovary.

"No no, I'll send him; we'll come over, it would be easier for you."

"Oh, jolly good! Thank you very much."

As soon as they were alone he said to her:

"Why didn't you accept Monsieur Boulanger's offer? It was very kind."

She gave a sulky look, made a host of excuses, and finished by saying *that it might look odd*.

"I don't give a fig!" said Charles, spinning round. "You're wrong! Health comes before everything!"

"And how do you expect me to ride when I don't have a habit?"

"Then we'll have to get one for you!" he answered.

The riding habit persuaded her.

When the clothes were ready, Charles wrote to Monsieur Boulanger to tell him that his wife was at his disposal, and that they were counting on his indulgence.

At twelve o'clock the next day, Rodolphe arrived at Charles's door with two fine horses. One had pink pompoms on its ears and a lady's doeskin saddle.

He was wearing tall soft boots, having thought she probably wouldn't have seen anything like them before, and it was true that when he walked up to the door in his long velvet tailcoat and white woollen breeches, Emma was delighted with his appearance. She was ready and waiting for him.

Justin slipped out of the pharmacy to see her, the apothecary stopped what he was doing. He made suggestions to Monsieur Boulanger.

"Accidents happen so easily! Do take care! What if those horses are spirited?"

She heard a noise above her; it was Félicité, tapping her fingers on the window to amuse little Berthe. The child blew a kiss to her mother; she waved back with the handle of her whip.

"Have a good ride!" shouted Monsieur Homais. "And above all be careful! Be careful!"

And he waved his newspaper as he watched them ride away.

As soon as it felt soft ground, Emma's horse broke into a gallop. Rodolphe galloped beside her. Now and then they exchanged the odd word. Head lowered, hand raised and right arm at full stretch, she gave herself up to the gentle lulling rhythm of the saddle.

At the foot of the slope, Rodolphe dropped the reins; they both set off flat out; then at the top of the hill the horses suddenly pulled up, and her long blue veil dropped back down.

It was early October. The landscape was covered in mist. A few trails stretched to the horizon among the outlines of the hills; others drifted apart, rose, disappeared. Through a gap in the folds they sometimes saw a shaft of sunlight on the distant rooftops of Yonville, its gardens by the river, its yards, its walls, the tower of the church. Emma half-closed her eyes so she could pick out her house; never had it seemed so small, this poor village where she lived. From the high ground the valley looked like a vast white lake vanishing into thin air. Clumps of trees stood out here and there like black rocks, and, rising up out of the mist, rows of tall poplars drew shorelines that swayed in the breeze.

On the grass among the nearby fir trees, dusky-brown light swirled round in the warm air. The ground, which was the russet colour of tobacco, muffled the sound of the hooves, and as they walked the horses kicked fallen pine cones ahead of them.

Rodolphe and Emma followed the edge of the wood. She turned her head away occasionally to avoid his eyes, and saw only fir trunks whose unbroken ranks made her feel giddy. The horses snorted. The leather saddles creaked.

As they rode into the forest the sun came out.

"God is watching over us!" said Rodolphe.

"Do you think so?" she said.

"On on!" he replied. He clicked his tongue. The two animals set off.

Some tall ferns beside the track caught in Emma's stirrup. Rodolphe leant over to pull them out as they went along; or he rode close to her to avoid low branches, and Emma felt his knee brush her leg. The sky was blue now. The leaves didn't stir. There were long stretches of flowering heather; clusters of violets were dotted about among ragged clumps of trees whose leaves were grey, tawny or gold. Often they heard a faint flapping of wings skate away beneath the bushes, or the soft, hoarse cry of crows as they flew off into the oak trees.

They dismounted. Rodolphe tied up the horses. She went on ahead, over the moss between the ruts.

Although she picked it up at the back her long dress hampered her, and from behind Rodolphe gazed at her fine white stockings between the heavy black cloth and her black ankle boots, which to him seemed part of her nakedness.

She stopped.

"I'm tired," she said.

"Come on, keep going!" he said. "Take heart!"

After another hundred yards she stopped again and, through her veil, which hung obliquely across her hips from her hat, her face could be seen in a bluish translucent haze, as if she were swimming though azure tides.

"Where are we going?"

He didn't reply. Her breathing was becoming erratic. Rodolphe glanced round, chewed his moustache.

They came to an open spot where some saplings had been felled. They sat on a fallen trunk, and Rodolphe started talking about his love for her.

He didn't frighten her with compliments to begin with. He was calm, sad.

As Emma listened, head lowered, she raked over some wood shavings on the ground with her whip.

But when he said:

"So don't we share a common destiny now?"

She replied: "No! It's impossible. You know that very well."

She got up to leave. He grabbed her wrist. She stopped. Then, after staring at him for a moment with tender, tear-filled eyes, she snapped:

"Let's not talk about it... Where are the horses? Let's go back."

He made an angry, weary gesture. So she repeated:

"Where are the horses? Where are the horses?"

Then with a strange smile, a vacant look in his eyes, teeth clenched, he walked towards her with arms outstretched. She backed away, trembling, stammering:

"You're scaring me! You're making me afraid! Let's go."

"If we must," he replied, his expression altering.

And immediately he was considerate again, affectionate, shy. She gave him her arm. They set off back.

"So what's wrong?" he said. "Why? I don't understand. You probably misunderstood me. In my heart you're a madonna on a pedestal, unshakeable and unsullied. But I need you in order to live! I need your eyes, your voice, your mind. Be my friend, my sister, my angel!"

And he put his arm round her waist. Feebly she tried to free herself. But as they walked he still held on to her.

They could hear the horses nibbling at the leaves.

"No, not yet!" said Rodolphe. "Let's not go! Stay!"

He took her along to a small pond where duckweed covered the surface with green. Wilting water lilies floated motionless between the reeds. At the sound of their footsteps in the grass, frogs jumped out and hid.

"I'm to blame," she said. "I'm to blame. I'm out of my mind from listening to you."

"But why?... Emma! Emma!"

"Oh, Rodolphe!" said the young woman slowly, leaning on his shoulder.

Her dress caught against the velvet of his tailcoat. She tilted her head back, her white throat filled with sighs, and, faltering, in tears, hiding her face, with a great shudder she gave herself.

Evening shadows were falling; through the branches the low sun dazzled her. Vivid patches of light flickered here and there around her, among the leaves or on the ground, as if hummingbirds had scattered feathers as they flew away. Everywhere there was silence; a sweetness seemed to come from the trees; she could feel her heart beat faster again, blood coursing through her veins like a milky stream. Then in the distance, beyond the woods, on one of the other hills she heard a long faint cry, a trailing voice, and she listened to it silently as it mingled like music with the final tremors of her inflamed nerves. Cigar between his teeth, Rodolphe was mending one of the bridles with his knife.

They rode back to Yonville the same way they had come. They saw the old tracks of their horses side by side in the mud, the same bushes, the same stones in the grass. Nothing around them had changed; yet for her something unexpected had happened, something more significant than a mountain moving. Occasionally Rodolphe leant across, took her hand and kissed it.

She looked enchanting on a horse. Upright, slender-waisted, with her knee folded in on her horse's mane, face slightly flushed from the fresh air in the reddish tint of evening.

As they rode into Yonville her horse pranced on the cobbles. People watched from their windows.

At dinner her husband thought she looked well; yet she didn't seem to hear when he asked about the ride; she sat with her elbow on the table, between the two glowing candles.

"Emma!" he said.

"What?"

"I dropped in on Monsieur Alexandre this afternoon; he's got an old filly that still looks very nice, just some grazes on its knees, I'm sure we can have it for about a hundred écus..."

Then he added:

"I thought it would be nice for you, so I asked him to keep it... Actually I bought it... Is that all right? Say something."

She gave a nod of approval; then a short while later she asked:

"Are you going out this evening?"

"Yes. Why?"

"Oh, nothing my dear, nothing."

Once she had got rid of Charles she went up and shut herself in her room.

At first it was like a fit of giddiness; she saw the trees, the tracks, the embankments, Rodolphe, she could feel his arms around her, and all the time the leaves trembled, the rushes hissed.

When she saw herself in the mirror she was surprised at her face. Never had her eyes been so big, so black, so deep. Something delicate was spreading through her whole body, transforming it.

She kept saying to herself: "I have a lover! A lover!" revelling in the thought as if she were going through a second puberty. So at last the joys of love would be hers, that feverish happiness which she had despaired of ever finding. And she entered into something like a state of wonder where everything was passion, rapture, elation; she was surrounded by an infinity of blue, the mountain tops of emotion sparkled in her mind, and everyday existence receded into the distance, far far below in the deep shadows between the high ground.

Then she remembered the heroines in the books she had read, and in their sisterly voices this poetic legion of adulterous women sang songs of enchantment in her mind. She became part of these imaginings, fulfilled the long-held dreams of her youth, seeing herself as the type of lover she had so envied. Not only that, Emma felt the satisfaction of taking revenge. Hadn't she suffered enough! But now she had prevailed, and love, so long suppressed, gushed forth in a great effervescence of joy. She savoured it without remorse, without anxiety or distress.

The whole of the next day went by in new feelings of sweetness. They made vows to each other. She told him her sorrows. Rodolphe interrupted her with kisses and, gazing at him with half-closed eyes she asked him to call her by her name, to tell her again that he loved her. They were in the forest like the day before, in a clog-makers' hut. The walls were straw, the roof was so low that they had to crouch down all the time. They sat leaning against each other on a bed of dry leaves.

From then on they wrote to each other every night. Emma took her letter to the bottom of the garden, near the river, and put it in a crack in the terrace. Rodolphe would come and take it, leaving one of his own, which she always chided him for for being too short.

One morning when Charles had left before dawn, she was seized with a sudden desire to see Rodolphe that very second. It was possible to get to La Huchette quite quickly, spend an hour there and be back in Yonville while everyone was still asleep. The thought made her breast heave with lust, and she was soon halfway across the meadow, walking fast and not looking back.

It was almost daybreak. Emma identified her lover's house from a distance, its two dovetail weather vanes standing out black against the pale light of dawn.

Beyond the farm courtyard was a main building, which had to be the chateau. She walked in as if the walls had parted at her approach. A large straight staircase led up to a corridor. Emma turned a door handle, and suddenly saw a man asleep at the far end of the room. It was Rodolphe. She let out a cry.

"You're here!" he kept saying. "You're here! How were you able to come?… Oh! Your dress is wet!"

"I love you!" she replied, putting her arms round his neck.

Since this first act of daring paid off, every time Charles went out early Emma dressed quickly and crept down the lawn to the riverbank.

When the plank used by the cows had been taken up, she had to go along by the walls beside the river; the bank was slippery; she held on to clumps of wilting stocks so as not to fall over. Then she headed across the ploughed fields where she sank in, stumbled, tripped in her thin boots. In the pasture her headscarf blew in the wind; she was frightened of cows, she ran; she would arrive out of breath, cheeks rosy, her whole presence exuding the clean cool smell of sap, green grass and fresh air. At that time of day Rodolphe would still be asleep. She was like a spring morning coming into his bedroom.

A dull flaxen light filtered in gently through the yellow curtains. Emma felt her way along, the dewdrops that balanced on her headbands creating a topaz halo round her face. Rodolphe took her to him with a laugh, held her in his arms.

Afterwards she would inspect his room, open drawers, comb her hair with his comb, look at herself in his shaving mirror. She often took his big pipe from among the lemons and cubes of sugar by the jug of water on the bedside table, and would put it between her teeth.

Saying goodbye took more than a quarter of an hour. And then Emma cried; she would have liked never to leave Rodolphe. She was driven towards him by something stronger than her, and then one day when she arrived unexpectedly he frowned, as if he were annoyed.

"What's the matter?" she said. "Are you ill? Tell me!"

Eventually, looking serious, he told her that these visits were becoming foolhardy and that she was compromising herself.

10

T HESE FEARS OF RODOLPHE'S gradually took hold of her. At first she had been intoxicated by love, and hadn't thought beyond that. But now it had become essential to her life she was afraid of losing something, and even that this wouldn't bother him. On the way back from his house she would glance round uneasily, studying every shape on the horizon, every attic window in the village from where she might be spotted. She would listen to footsteps, cries, the sound of the ploughs, and she would stop, more pale and trembling than the leaves of the poplars that swayed above her.

One morning when she was coming back she suddenly thought she saw the long shape of a rifle pointing at her. It was protruding at an angle from one end of a small barrel half buried in the grass on the edge of an embankment. Although faint with terror, Emma went on, and then a man appeared from the barrel like a jack-in-the-box. He was wearing gaiters up to his knees, a cap pulled down over his eyes, his lips trembled with cold and his nose was red. It was Chief Fire Officer Binet, on the hunt for wild ducks.

"You ought to have said something!" he cried. "If you see a rifle you should always warn people."

The tax-collector was trying to hide his own fear. A prefectoral order had banned all duck-shooting except in boats, and so however much he respected the law, Monsieur Binet was breaking it. He expected to hear the local policeman coming at any minute. But anxiety only made his enjoyment all the keener, and alone in his barrel he congratulated himself on his good fortune and cunning.

At the sight of Emma he seemed relieved, and immediately struck up a conversation:

"It's none too warm – *it's quite nippy!*"

Emma didn't answer. He went on:

"You're out bright and early."

"Yes," she gabbled. "I've been to the wet nurse who's looking after my child."

"Ah, excellent, excellent! I've been here since the crack of dawn, but it's so foggy that unless you see feathers at the end of your—"

"Good day to you, Monsieur Binet," she said, turning on her heel and walking away.

"And to you too, Madame," he replied curtly.

And he climbed back into his barrel.

Emma regretted taking leave of the tax-collector so abruptly. There was no doubt that he would make awkward assumptions. The story about the wet nurse was the worst excuse to use, because everyone in Yonville knew that the young Bovary girl had been back home for a year. And in any case no one lived out this way; the path only led to La Huchette; so Binet would work out where she was coming from, and wouldn't keep it to himself – he would give the game away, there was no question about it! She spent the whole day agonizing over every possible lie she might have to tell, with the image of the duck-eating idiot constantly before her eyes.

After dinner, noticing she was worried about something, to take her mind off it Charles asked her to come to the pharmacist's house – and the first person she saw in the pharmacy was him: the tax-collector! He was standing at the counter in the light from the red jar, and saying:

"Give me half an ounce of vitriol please."

"Justin," called the apothecary, "bring the sulphuric acid."

Then he turned to Emma, who was about to go upstairs to Madame Homais's room:

"Don't worry, stay here, she'll come down. Warm yourself by the stove while you're waiting... Excuse me... Hello, Doctor..." (because the pharmacist much enjoyed using the word *doctor*, as if by addressing someone else with it some of its glory would be reflected on him) "Be careful you don't knock the mortars over! Get the chairs from the little room; you know we don't take the armchairs out of the drawing room."

Homais was just hurrying out from behind the counter to put his armchair back when Binet asked him for half an ounce of sugar acid.

"Sugar acid?" said the pharmacist contemptuously. "I've never heard of it! Perhaps it's oxalic acid you're wanting? Oxalic, that's it, isn't it?"

Binet explained that he needed a corrosive agent so he could mix up a brass cleaner to get the rust off his hunting equipment. Emma shuddered.

The pharmacist began:

"I must say the weather's not ideal, it's this damp..."

The taxman put in, with a wily expression, "Mind you, it suits some people."

Emma nearly choked.

"Give me some more…"

"He's never going to go!" she thought.

"Half an ounce of rosin and turpentine, four ounces of yellow wax and three half-ounces of bone residue please, to clean the patent leather on my equipment."

The apothecary was just cutting off a piece of wax when Madame Homais appeared carrying Irma, with Napoléon beside her and Athalie behind. She sat on the velvet seat under the window, and the boy squatted on a stool while his older sister hovered round the tin of jujube next to her darling Papa. He was filling funnels, stoppering little bottles, sticking on labels, making up packages. Everyone kept quiet; all that could be heard was the occasional clink of the weights on the scales, a few quiet words as he gave his pupil advice.

"How's your young thing?" Madame Homais suddenly asked.

"Quiet!" cried her husband, who was writing figures in his notebook.

"Why didn't you bring her?" she went on, lowering her voice.

"Ssh!" said Emma, pointing to the apothecary.

But Binet was too absorbed with checking his bill, and probably hadn't heard. At long last he left. Emma heaved a sigh of relief.

"You sound out of breath!" said Madame Homais.

"Oh, it's just that it's rather warm," she replied.

The next day she and Rodolphe gave some thought as to how best to arrange their meetings; she wanted to bribe her maid with a present, but it would be better to find an unobtrusive house in Yonville. He promised to look for one.

All winter, three or four times a week, he came to her garden when it was completely dark. Emma had taken the key out of the gate, and Charles thought it had been lost.

To let her know he was there, Rodolphe always threw a handful of sand at the shutters. She would jump up; but sometimes she had to wait, because Charles had a habit of chatting by the fire and would go on ad infinitum. She would be consumed with impatience; if they could have done, her eyes would have leapt out the window. Eventually she would start to get ready for bed; then she would pick up a book and read quietly as if she were enjoying it. But Charles, who was in bed already, would call down to her.

"Hurry up, Emma," he would shout, "it's getting late."

"Just coming!" she would answer.

Meanwhile, because the candlelight was in his eyes, he would turn and face the wall and go to sleep. And she would slip out, holding her breath, smiling, quivering with excitement, half-dressed.

Rodolphe had a long coat; he would wrap her in it, and putting his arm round her waist, without saying a word he would take her to the bottom of the garden.

They would sit in the arbour, on the same disintegrating cane seat where Léon used to gaze at her so lovingly on summer evenings. She rarely thought of him now! Stars shone through the bare branches of the jasmine. Behind them they could hear the river, occasionally the rustle of dry reeds. Great banks of shadow surged out of the darkness, rising up and then toppling forward with a shudder, like vast black waves come to cover them. The cold night air made them embrace more tightly, the sighs from their lips seemed deeper; their eyes, barely visible, seemed bigger, and in the silence soft words were spoken that tumbled into their souls with a clear crystalline sound which echoed, reverberated, time and time again.

If it was raining they took refuge in the surgery, between the shed and the stable. She would light a candlestick that she had taken from the kitchen and hidden behind the books. Rodolphe made himself at home. The sight of the little library, the desk, in fact the whole room improved his already cheerful mood, and he couldn't help but mock Charles in all sorts of ways, which embarrassed her. She would have preferred him to be serious, even tragic occasionally, like the time she thought she heard footsteps on the path.

"Someone's coming!" she said.

He blew out the light.

"Have you got your pistols?"

"Whatever for?"

"Why… to defend yourself!" replied Emma.

"What, is it your husband? Poor fellow!"

And Rodolphe made a gesture that meant: "I'll crush him with my little finger."

She was awed by his gallantry, despite the feeling of naive and unseemly coarseness that she was experiencing, which shocked her deeply.

Rodolphe thought long and hard about the affair with the pistols. If she had meant it seriously then it was utterly absurd, even offensive, because he had no reason to hate the good Charles, not being exactly eaten up with jealousy – and Emma had also made a solemn vow to him about it, which he thought was in equally poor taste.

What was more, she was becoming overly romantic. They had had to give each other miniatures, cut off locks of each other's hair, and now she wanted a ring, a proper wedding band as a token of their everlasting union. She often spoke to him about evening bells or the *voices of nature*; or she talked about his mother and her own. Rodolphe had lost his mother twenty years before. Yet Emma comforted him with mawkish remarks as if to an abandoned child, and sometimes even said, while gazing at the moon:

"I'm sure they're up there together, and approve of our love."

But she was so lovely! Of all those he had known, few could rival her for innocence! Love without licentiousness was new to him, and by getting him out of his superficial habits it flattered his pride and sensuality both. In his heart of hearts, Emma's elation, which his bourgeois common sense despised, struck him as delightful, because it was intended for him alone. And so, certain of being loved, he didn't let it bother him, and imperceptibly changed his ways.

He no longer used the gentle words that had once made her cry, nor the violent caresses that drove her wild, and so this grand love of theirs, in which she and her life were now submerged, seemed to drain away beneath her like a river into its bed, and she was confronted with the sludge at the bottom. But she didn't want to believe it; she became doubly loving; while Rodolphe concealed his indifference less and less.

She didn't know whether she regretted giving in to him or, on the contrary, whether she adored him even more. The humiliation of feeling weak turned into bitter resentment that only sensual pleasure could mollify. It wasn't affection: it was permanent seduction. He held her in thrall. She was almost afraid of him.

Yet on the surface it was more peaceful than ever, because Rodolphe managed to continue with this act of adultery by simply giving in to her whims, and after six months, when spring came, they found that when they were together they were like husband and wife, quietly keeping the fire going in the marital hearth.

It was the time of year when old man Rouault sent a turkey in memory of his mended leg. A letter always came with the gift. Cutting the string that held it to the basket, Emma read:

My dear children,

I hope this present finds you in good health and that it'll be every bit as good as the others; because if I may say so it seems a bit soft to me, and sturdier. But by way of a change next time I'll send a cock bird, unless you prefer picots;* *and let me have the hamper back please, along with the other two. I've had a mishap with my cart, the roof blew off into the trees one night in a strong wind. And the harvest wasn't none too dandy neither. Anyway, I don't know when I'm going to see you. It's difficult for me to leave the house now I'm on my own, my poor dear Emma!*

There was a break between the lines here, as if the man had put down his pen to reflect for a moment.

As for me I'm fine, except for catching cold at the fair in Yvetot the other day, where I went to hire a shepherd, since I threw mine out on account of him having too much lip. You've always got something to grouse about with those blighters. Besides which he was dishonest.

I heard from a pedlar who was down your way during the winter, and had a tooth pulled, that Bovary is still hard at it. Which doesn't surprise me, and he showed me the tooth; we had a cup of coffee together. I asked him if he'd seen you but he said no, although he saw two horses in the stable, from which I gather business is going well. So much the better, my dearest children, and may the good Lord send you every possible happiness!

It grieves me that I still haven't seen my beloved granddaughter Berthe Bovary. I've planted a fine plum tree for her in the garden, under your window, and I won't let anyone touch it except to make compote for her later on, which I'll keep in the cupboard for when she comes.

Goodbye my dear children. With my love to you, dearest daughter; and to you too, son-in-law, and a kiss on both cheeks for the little one.

> *With all best wishes,*
> *Your loving father,*
> *Théodore Rouault*

For a while she stood there with the rough piece of paper in her hand. It was full of spelling mistakes, and she followed the gentle thoughts that clucked through it like a hen under a thorn hedge. The ink had been dried with ash from the kitchen fireplace, because grey dust fell off onto her dress, and she could almost see her father bending over the hearth to get the tongs. It was such a long time since she had sat next to him on the wooden stool in front of the fire and burnt marsh daisies on the end of a stick, how they crackled in the great tall flames!... She remembered the sunny summer evenings. The foals whinnied as you walked by, and galloped, galloped away... There was a beehive under her window, and when they whirled round in the sunlight the bees would bump against the glass like bouncing golden balls. How happy those times had been! How free! How full of hope! How full of illusions! And now there were none left! She had used them all up on her heart's many adventures, on a long series of different states, first virginity, then marriage, then love – losing them one by one over the course of her life, like a traveller leaves part of his wealth in every inn along the road.

So what was it that made her so unhappy? What was the disaster that had thrown her into disarray? And she looked round, as if it were there that she might find the cause of her suffering.

April sunshine sparkled on the china on the shelves; the fire was blazing; she felt the soft carpet beneath her slippered feet; the light was pale, the air warm, she could hear her child screaming with laughter.

The little girl was rolling around on the lawn, near where they were turning the mown grass. She was lying face down on one of the stacks. Her nursemaid was holding her by the skirt. Lestiboudois was raking nearby, and every time he got closer she leant over and waved her arms in the air.

"Bring her here!" said her mother, hurrying over to kiss her. "I do so love you, my darling girl! I do so love you!"

Seeing dirt in her ears, she quickly rang for warm water and cleaned her up, changed her, put on new shoes and socks, asked a thousand and one questions about her health as if she had just come back from a journey, and then kissing her again with tears in her eyes, she finally gave her back to the maid, who was astonished at such a display of affection.

That night Rodolphe found her more serious than usual.

"She'll get over it," he thought to himself. "It's only a fad."

And the next three times they were due to meet he didn't appear. When he did she behaved coldly, even dismissively.

"You're wasting your time, my sweet…"

He pretended not to notice her mournful sighs or the handkerchief in her hand.

So Emma was repenting!

She even asked herself why she loathed Charles, and whether it might not be better to love him. But her renewed affections had little effect on him, and so she was left in a predicament, feeling a vague impulse to make sacrifices, when the apothecary provided her with a well-timed opportunity.

11

H E HAD RECENTLY READ AN ARTICLE praising a new method of treating club feet, and since he was an advocate of progress he had the patriotic idea that *to put itself on the map*, Yonville ought to carry out tenotomy* operations.

"What's the risk?" he said to Emma. "Let's consider it" (and he numbered off the advantages on his fingers). "Virtually guaranteed success, relief and a better life for the sufferer, overnight fame for the man who performs the operation. Why shouldn't your husband bring comfort to poor old Hippolyte from the Lion d'Or, for instance? Because don't forget, he'll tell everyone who comes in how he was cured, and besides…" (Homais lowered his voice and looked round) "what's to stop me sending a short piece to the newspaper about it? My goodness! An article appears… it gets talked about… and eventually it snowballs! So who knows, who knows!"

It was true that Bovary might make a success of it; there was nothing to make Emma think he didn't know what he was doing. And how gratifying for her to have encouraged him to try something that would set him on the path to fame and fortune? The soundest thing she could rely on was love.

Approached by her as well as by the apothecary, Charles allowed himself to be persuaded. He sent to Rouen for Doctor Duval's great tome,* and every night, head in his hands, he buried himself in it.

While he was busy studying equine feet, varus feet and valgus feet, or rather strephocatopody, strephendopody and strephexopody (or, to put it a better way, the various deformities of the foot, either turned downwards, inwards or outwards), along with strephypopody and strephanopody (in other words, twisting underneath and straightening on the top), Homais was using every possible argument to convince the groom that he ought to have the operation.

"You'll hardly feel a thing, a slight pain maybe; it's just a simple pinprick, like being bled, not even as bad as having a corn removed."

As he thought it over, Hippolyte rolled his bemused eyes.

"Still," the pharmacist added, "it's nothing to do with me! It's for you, an act of pure human kindness! I'd like to see you rid of that ghastly limp, my dear fellow, that swaying in the lumbar region that must hinder you considerably in your work, however much you say otherwise."

So then Homais described how much more energetic and quick on his feet he would feel afterwards, and even led him to believe that it would make him more attractive to the ladies, and the groom gave a gauche smile. Then he struck a blow at his pride:

"Good grief, you're a man, aren't you! What if you'd had to join up, go and fight for king and country?... Oh, Hippolyte!"

And Homais went off, saying that such stubbornness, this blind refusal to take advantage of the benefits of science was quite beyond him.

The poor devil gave in: it was a conspiracy. Binet, who never got involved with other people's business, Madame Lefrançois, Artémise, the neighbours and even Monsieur Tuvache the mayor all advised him, lectured him, made him feel ashamed, but what finally decided him was that *it wouldn't cost him anything*. Bovary even took it on himself to provide the equipment for the operation. This generosity was Emma's idea, and Charles agreed, thinking in his heart of hearts that his wife was an angel.

So with suggestions from the pharmacist he got the carpenter, assisted by the locksmith, to make a form of box construction weighing about eight pounds and using copious quantities of iron, wood, sheet metal, leather, nuts and bolts.

Meanwhile, so as to know which of Hippolyte's tendons to cut, he first had to find out what kind of club foot he had.

His foot formed almost a straight line with his leg, which didn't prevent it from turning inwards, so it was an equine type crossed with a touch of varus or inward-turning type, or even a mild varus type with a pronounced equine tendency. Yet even with this equine foot, which was the size of a horse's hoof, with coarse skin, hard, tight tendons, large toes whose black toenails looked like the nails in a horseshoe, this strephopod charged around like a stag from morning till night. He was always in the square, hopping and skipping round the carts, thrusting his lopsided leg out in front of him. It was almost as if it were stronger than the other one. Because of all the use it got it seemed to have acquired patience and vitality, and before he did any heavy work he liked to make sure that he was standing in a steady position.

Since it was an equine or downward-turning type, it was the Achilles tendon that needed to be cut, even if it meant dealing with the anterior tibial muscle later on, to rid him of the inward-turning condition, because the doctor daren't risk two operations at once, and was already living in fear of damaging a vital part of the anatomy that he wasn't familiar with.

Neither Ambroise Paré, applying a ligature directly to an artery for the first time since Celsus fifteen hundred years earlier; nor Dupuytren when he was about to cut into an abscess through a thick layer of brain tissue; nor Gensoul* when he performed the first-ever removal of an upper jawbone, felt his heart race so fast, his hand shake so much or his mind so on edge as Monsieur Bovary as he came over to Hippolyte with his tenotomic scalpel in his hand. On the table beside him, just like in a hospital, were piles of linen dressings, waxed thread, plenty of bandages, a mountain of bandages, the pharmacy's entire stock of bandages. Homais had spent all morning preparing everything, as much to impress the crowd as to delude himself. Charles pierced the skin; there was a sharp snap. The tendon was cut, the operation was over. Hippolyte couldn't believe it; he took Bovary's hands and kissed them again and again.

"Come along now, calm yourself," said the apothecary, "there'll be plenty of time to show your gratitude to your benefactor later!"

And he went outside and described the operation to five or six onlookers standing around in the courtyard, who imagined that Hippolyte was going to come out walking normally. Once he had fastened the special apparatus onto the patient, Charles went home, where Emma was waiting anxiously for him on the doorstep. She threw her arms round him, they sat down to dinner; he ate heartily, even asked for a cup of coffee with dessert, an extravagance he only normally allowed himself on Sundays when they had guests.

It was a delightful evening, spent talking and sharing dreams. They discussed their future fortunes, improvements they would make to the house; he saw his esteem spreading, his well-being increasing, his wife loving him for ever; and she realized that she felt happy and renewed in these new, healthier and better emotions, and finally had some affection for this poor fellow who so treasured her. Rodolphe was forgotten for the moment; her attention shifted to Charles, and she was surprised to notice that his teeth weren't unattractive.

They were in bed when, despite the cook's protests, Monsieur Homais suddenly came into the room holding a sheet of paper covered in writing. It was the piece he was going to send to the *Fanal de Rouen*. He had brought it for them to read.

"You read it," said Bovary.

So he did:

"'Despite the prejudice that is still so widespread throughout Europe, the light has nonetheless begun to dawn on our countryside. So it was on Tuesday that our little town of Yonville was the scene of a surgical experiment that was at the same time an act of the highest philanthropy. Monsieur Bovary, one of our most distinguished practitioners—'"

"Oh no, you're exaggerating, you're exaggerating," said Charles, choked with emotion.

"No, not at all! You're most welcome!... 'operated on the club foot...' I haven't used the scientific term, because in a newspaper you know... not everyone would understand; the masses need to—"

"Quite," said Bovary. "Go on."

"I'll continue," said the pharmacist. "'Monsieur Bovary, one of our most distinguished practitioners, operated on the club foot of one Hippolyte Tautain, groom for the last twenty-five years at the hotel the Lion d'Or on the Place d'Armes, kept by the widow Lefrançois. The novel aspects of this experiment, as well as the importance accorded to the subject, attracted such a throng of local inhabitants that the entrance to the establishment became quite congested. What was more, the operation went ahead as if by magic, and there were no more than a few drops of blood, as if to prove that the rebellious tendon had finally yielded to the art of medicine. Strangely enough the patient (we witnessed it with our own eyes) didn't show any sign of feeling pain. His condition so far is all one could wish for. Everything points to a quick recovery; and who knows, at the next village fete we might even see our gallant Hippolyte taking part in bacchanalian dances surrounded by a chorus of merrymakers, thereby proving to everyone, with his spirited leaps and bounds, that he is completely cured? So all hail to the noble scientists! All hail to those untiring spirits who devote their waking lives to improving and alleviating the lot of their fellow man! Hail! Thrice hail! Is it not the moment to shout out that the blind will see and the lame will walk! What fanaticism once promised to its elect, science now performs for Everyman! We will keep readers informed about the stages in this remarkable cure as they occur.'"

None of which made any difference five days later, when an aghast Mother Lefrançois came running in, crying:

"Help! He's dying!... I'm going out of my mind!"

Charles rushed over to the Lion d'Or, and seeing him hurrying across the square without a hat, the pharmacist left his shop. He arrived red-faced, out of breath, apprehensive, and asked anyone who was going upstairs:

"What's the matter with our interesting strephopod?"

The strephopod was writhing around in appalling convulsions, making the contraption that encased his leg thrash against the wall and knock holes in it.

Taking great care not to disturb the position of the limb, they took off the box, and were met with a dreadful sight. The foot was so deformed by so much swelling that it looked as if the skin was about to burst, and it was covered in bruises caused by the infamous apparatus. Hippolyte had been complaining about the pain, but no one had taken any notice; so now they had to admit there was truth in what he said, and left it off for a few hours. But no sooner had the oedema gone down than the two scientists saw fit to put the limb back in the appliance, and then tighten it to speed things up. Three days later, since Hippolyte couldn't stand it any longer, they removed the contraption again, and were astonished at what they found. Angry bluish swellings had spread up the leg, as well as blisters out of which seeped a black fluid. Things were getting serious. Hippolyte was becoming restless, and Mother Lefrançois put him in the small dining room next to the kitchen so he would at least have something to take his mind off it.

But the tax-collector, who had dinner in there every day, complained bitterly about his presence. So they moved Hippolyte to the billiard room.

And there he lay under the rough blankets, moaning, pale-faced, in need of a shave, eyes sunken, tossing his head with its sweaty face on the filthy pillow where flies kept settling. Madame Bovary came to see him. She brought fresh dressings and tried to comfort him, cheer him up. Not that he was short of company, particularly on market day when farmers threw billiard balls, fought duels with the cues, drank, smoked, sang and yelled all round him.

"How's it going then? they said, clapping him on the shoulder. "You ain't too full of yourself now, eh! Still, it's your own fault." And he ought to do this, ought to do that.

They told him about people who had been cured by treatments different from his; then by way of consolation they would add:

"You mollycoddle yourself! Get up, why don't you! Who do you think you are, the king? No, don't bother, you old skiver! You don't smell none too sweet!"

Because the gangrene was spreading fast, it was even making Bovary ill. He came every hour, every minute. Hippolyte stared at him with terror-filled eyes and babbled, sobbing:

"When am I going to get better?... Oh, save me!... I'm so miserable! I'm so miserable!"

And the doctor would leave, advising him not to eat anything.

"Don't you listen to him, my lad," Mother Lefrançois would tell him. "They've made you suffer enough already! You'll just get weaker. Here, eat this!"

And she would offer him some nice broth, a slice of roast lamb, a piece of bacon, and sometimes a small glass of eau de vie that he didn't feel up to touching.

Hearing his condition was worsening, Father Bournisien asked to see him. He began by sympathizing, while telling him to rejoice because it was the Lord's will, and to be quick to take the opportunity to make his peace with the kingdom of heaven.

"...Because you've been rather neglecting your duties," said the priest in a fatherly way. "We don't often see you at the divine office. How many years is it since you took communion? I realize your work, the hurly-burly of the world might have taken your mind off your salvation. But now is the time to think about it. Still, don't give up hope, I've known great sinners who just before they stood before the Lord (and I'm sure you're not at that point), begged him for forgiveness, and definitely died a better death as a result. Let's hope you'll set as good an example. And just to be on the safe side, why not say a Hail Mary and an Our Father morning and night? Yes, do it! Do it for me, as a kindness. What will it cost?... Do you promise?"

The poor soul promised. The priest came back regularly over the next few days. He chatted to the landlady, told little stories full of jokes and puns that Hippolyte didn't understand. Then as soon as he had a chance he got back to matters of religion, always putting on the appropriate expression.

His zeal appeared to have the desired effect: the strephopod was soon expressing a wish to make a pilgrimage to Bon-Secours if he was cured, to which Father Bournisien replied that he saw no objection; two precautions were better than one. *There was nothing to lose.*

The apothecary was furious about what he called *priestcraft*; he claimed it was jeopardizing Hippolyte's chances of recovery, and kept telling Madame Lefrançois:

"Leave him alone! Leave him alone! You're upsetting him with this mysticism of yours!"

But the woman would have none of it. He was the one who was *the cause of everything*. And just to be contrary she hung a vessel of holy water at the patient's bedside with a sprig of boxwood.

Yet religion didn't seem any more help to him than surgery, and the unstoppable infection went on rotting its way towards his stomach. However many times they changed the medication or dressings his muscles got weaker every day, and when Mother Lefrançois finally asked if, as a last resort, she could send for the celebrated Monsieur Canivet from Neufchâtel, Charles gave a little nod.

A doctor of medicine, fifty years old, with a good position and a self-assured manner, his colleague laughed disparagingly when he uncovered the leg, which was gangrenous up to the knee. Then, announcing bluntly that it would have to be amputated, he went over to the pharmacy and ranted on about the jackasses who had reduced a hapless individual to such a state. Shaking Monsieur Homais by the lapels of his frock coat, he bellowed across the pharmacist's shop.

"This is a Parisian idea! A typical invention by the gentlemen from the capital! It's like strabismus, chloroform and lithotripsy,* a lot of iniquities that the government ought to ban! But they want to look clever, so they stuff you full of potions without a thought for the consequences. The rest of us aren't as good as they are; we're not learned men, dandies, ladykillers; we're practitioners, healers, we wouldn't dream of operating on someone who's in the best of health! Straighten a club foot! Can a club foot be straightened? It's like trying to get a hunchback to stand upright!"

It pained Homais to hear this, but he concealed his discomfort with a sycophantic smile. He had to tread carefully with Monsieur Canivet, whose prescriptions sometimes got as far as Yonville; so he didn't stand up for Bovary, he didn't make a single comment, and abandoning his principles he sacrificed dignity to the more serious interests of his trade.

The amputation of a leg by Doctor Canivet was a major event for the village! All the residents got up early, and yet despite the crowds the main street had something funereal about it, as if there were going to be an execution. In the grocer's they were debating what the matter was with Hippolyte; the shops weren't doing any trade, and Madame Tuvache, the mayor's wife, didn't budge from her window, so keen was she to see the great surgeon arrive.

He arrived in his cabriolet, driving himself. Since the springs on the right hand side had given way under his considerable weight, the carriage tilted to one side, and on the seat beside him they saw an enormous red leather box whose three brass clasps gleamed authoritatively.

Once he had swept through the front door of the Lion d'Or like a whirlwind, the doctor bellowed to them to unhitch his horse, then went to the stable to see if it had enough oats; for whenever he arrived at a patient's house he saw to his mare and his cabriolet first. People even used to say: "That Monsieur Canivet, he's a quite a character!" And they thought more of him for his unshakeable sangfroid. The world could have come crashing down, it wouldn't have made him change the least of his habits.

Homais appeared:

"I'm relying on you," said the doctor. "Are we ready? Let's make a start!"

Turning red, the apothecary confessed that he was of too nervous a disposition to be present at an operation of this kind.

"When you are a mere onlooker," he said, "the imagination works overtime, you see! Besides, my nervous system is so—"

"Phooey!" said Canivet, interrupting. "You seem more of an apoplectic to me. Not that that surprises me; you pharmacist fellows are always so busy poking around in your kitchens it must affect your health. Take me on the other hand: I get up at four every morning, I shave in cold water (I don't feel the cold), I never wear flannel underwear, I never catch cold, my chest is fine! I live first this way then the next, philosophically, taking life as it comes. Which is why I'm not as squeamish as you, and it's all the same to me whether I cut up a Christian or a turkey. Apart from that it's routine, as they say!... Just routine!"

Then, without sparing a thought for Hippolyte, who was sweating with fear between his sheets, the two gentlemen got into conversation. The apothecary likened the cool-headedness of a surgeon to that of a general; the comparison pleased Canivet, who waxed lyrical about the demands of his profession. He regarded it as a calling, despite it being discredited by public-health officers. Finally getting back to the patient, he examined the bandages that Homais had supplied, the same ones as for the operation on the club foot, then asked for someone to hold the leg. They sent for Lestiboudois, and rolling up his sleeves Monsieur Canivet went through into the billiard room, while the apothecary stayed with Artémise and the landlady, both with their ears pressed to the door and faces as white as their aprons.

Meanwhile Bovary didn't dare leave the house. He just sat by the unlit fire in the dining room, chin on his chest, hands clasped, eyes vacant. "What a mishap!" he thought. "What a disappointment!" Yet he had taken every conceivable precaution. Fate had had a hand in it somewhere. Still, what difference did that make? If Hippolyte died then it would be him who had murdered him. And how was he going to explain to people if they asked about it when he was on house calls? Perhaps he had made a mistake somewhere? He racked his brains but couldn't come up with anything. But even the most well-known surgeons made mistakes. Not that anyone would believe him! Quite the reverse, they would laugh and gossip! Word would spread as far as Forges! All the way to Neufchâtel! To Rouen! Everywhere! His colleagues might write articles against him! There would be a controversy, he would have to issue a reply in the newspapers. Hippolyte might even take him to court. He saw himself disgraced, ruined, lost! And, assailed by a host of conjectures, his imagination bobbed about like an empty barrel out at sea.

Sitting opposite, Emma looked at him; she didn't share his humiliation, she was experiencing another one; that of having believed that

a man like this could amount to something, as if she hadn't seen what a mediocrity he was dozens of times already.

Charles paced up and down the room. His boots creaked on the wooden floor.

"Sit down," she said, "you're getting on my nerves!"

He sat down.

So what had she done (she who was so intelligent!) to misjudge things yet again? More to the point, what appalling compulsion was it that drove her to ruin her life with these unending sacrifices? She reflected on her inclinations for luxury, the hardships her soul endured, the meanness of marriage, family, dreams that fell in the mud like injured swallows, everything she had wanted, everything she had denied herself, everything she could have had! And for what? For what?

An appalling scream rent the silence of the village. Bovary turned deathly pale. She frowned nervously then went back to her thoughts. It was for him, this individual, this man who understood nothing, felt nothing! And there he sat quite calmly, oblivious to the fact that from now on the ridicule attached to his name would sully her as well. She had done her best to love him, she had repented in tears for giving in to the advances of another man.

"Maybe it was a valgus?" said Bovary suddenly, lost in thought.

At the unexpected jolt of these words, which dropped into her thoughts like a piece of lead shot onto a silver plate, Emma shuddered. She looked up to see what he meant; they stared at one another without speaking, as if astonished to see each other, so unaware were they of the other's presence. Charles gazed at her with the blurred eyes of a drunk, while he listened, motionless, to the last screams of the patient, their long-drawn-out sound interrupted by fitful shrieks like the distant howl of an animal having its throat cut. Emma bit her bloodless lips, and, her fingers twisting a wisp of anemone which she had broken off, she fixed her fiery eyes on Charles like a pair of blazing arrows about to be loosed. Everything about him made her angry, his face, his clothes, what he didn't say, his whole personality, in fact his very existence. She regretted her past virtue as if it were a crime, and what remained of it caved in beneath the violent blows of her pride. She revelled in the bitter irony of all-conquering adultery. The thought of her lover came back to her, his allure now breathtaking; she flung herself at it body and soul, swept towards his image by a wave of newfound ardour, and

Charles seemed as remote from her life, as permanently absent, as inconceivable and non-existent as if he had just died, drawn his last breath before her very eyes.

There was the sound of footsteps on the pavement. Charles looked up; through the lowered blinds he saw Doctor Canivet outside the covered market, in the sunlight, wiping his forehead with his silk scarf. Behind him Homais was carrying a large red box, and they both headed towards the pharmacist's shop.

Then with sudden despondent affection, Charles turned to his wife: "Give me a kiss, my dear!"

"Leave me alone!" she said, scarlet with rage.

"What's wrong, what's wrong?" he kept saying, astounded. "Pull yourself together, calm down!... You know I love you!... Come here!"

"That's enough!" she cried in a terrible voice.

And she rushed out of the room, slamming the door so hard that the barometer fell off the wall and smashed.

Charles sank into the armchair in tears, distraught, trying to understand what was wrong with her, imagining it was some nervous complaint, and with the obscure feeling that something malign and incomprehensible was wheeling round about him.

When Rodolphe came to the garden that night he found his mistress waiting for him on the bottom step at the end of the lawn. They held each other tight, and all the bitterness between them melted away like snow with the warmth of their first kiss.

12

THEY BEGAN TO LOVE EACH OTHER AGAIN. Emma often wrote to him in the middle of the day, quite suddenly; then she would gesture to Justin from the window, and he quickly untied his apron and took off for La Huchette. Rodolphe would come; it was a way of telling him that her husband was unspeakable, her existence unbearable.

"Is there anything I can do?" he exclaimed one day, losing patience.

"Oh, if only you would!..."

She was sitting on the floor between his legs, hairbands undone, staring into space.

"What?" asked Rodolphe.

She sighed.

"We could go and live somewhere else... somewhere..."

"You're mad!" he laughed. "It's impossible!"

She kept coming back to it; he pretended not to understand and changed the subject.

What baffled him was all this fuss over something as simple as love. She must have other motives, an objective, something over and above her attachment to him.

For her affection was growing stronger every day, fuelled by her loathing for her husband. The more she gave herself to one, the more she detested the other; never had Charles seemed so unpleasant, to have such squat fingers, to be so dull-witted, to have such coarse manners than when they were together after she had been with Rodolphe. While playing the wife, the woman of virtue, she was inflamed with lust for this face with dark curls over its tanned forehead, for the waist that was strong and yet so elegant, for a man who was so reasoned in his judgements and so passionate in his desires! It was for him she trimmed her nails with the care of a master carver, him for whom there could never be enough *cold cream** on her skin or patchouli on her handkerchiefs. She weighed herself down with rings, bracelets, necklaces. When he was coming she filled her two large blue-glass vases with roses, and arranged herself and her room as if she were a courtesan awaiting a prince. The maid did nothing but launder her clothes; Félicité spent all day in the kitchen, where young Justin, who often kept her company, would watch her at work.

With his elbow resting on the long board on which she was ironing, he eagerly studied all the women's things laid out around him: damask underskirts, headscarves, ruff collars, drawstring knickers that were wide at the hips and narrow at the bottom.

"What's this?" the boy would ask, running his hand over a crinoline petticoat or some hook-and-eye fasteners.

"Don't you know anything?" Félicité would reply with a laugh. "As if your boss, Madame Homais, doesn't wear the same sort of thing."

"Oh yes, well! Madame Homais!"

Then he added, thoughtfully:

"Is she a lady like Madame?"

Félicité was tired of him hovering round her. She was six years older than him, and Monsieur Guillaumin's servant, Théodore, was starting to court her.

"Do leave me in peace!" she said, moving her jar of starch. "Why don't you go crush some almonds; you're always poking your nose into women's business; you'll have to wait till you've started shaving before you meddle with all that, you horrid boy."

"Don't get cross, I'll do her boots for you."

And he reached up onto the mantelpiece and got Emma's shoes, which were thick with mud – mud from meeting Rodolphe – that crumbled in his fingers, and watched as dust drifted slowly in the sunlight.

"Don't worry about spoiling them!" said the cook, who didn't make a fuss when she cleaned them herself, because as soon as they were slightly worn Madame gave them to her.

Emma had a great many in her wardrobe, and got through one pair after another without Charles daring to say a word.

In the same way he had paid out three hundred francs for a wooden leg that she felt was a fitting gift for Hippolyte. The leg itself was covered in cork, it had spring-loaded joints and a complex mechanism, all inside black trousers with a shiny boot on the end. But not daring to use such a fine leg every day, Hippolyte had pleaded with Madame Bovary to get him one that was more practical. And naturally the doctor paid the bill for that as well.

So the groom gradually went back to his old job. He could be seen hurrying round the village like before, and whenever Charles heard the sharp tap of his walking stick on the cobbles he quickly went in another direction.

Monsieur Lheureux the draper had dealt with the order; it gave him an opportunity to come and see Emma. He would talk to her about the latest deliveries from Paris, a thousand and one feminine novelties, proved himself most obliging and never asked for money. Emma succumbed to this easy means of indulging her whims. There was a handsome riding crop in an umbrella shop in Rouen that she wanted to give to Rodolphe. The following week, Monsieur Lheureux put it on the table in front of her.

The next day he came to the house with a bill for 270 francs, not including centimes. Emma was most embarrassed; the drawers of the writing desk were empty; they owed more than two weeks' pay to Lestiboudois, six months' to the maid and many other things besides, while Bovary was still waiting for something from Monsieur Derozerays, who usually settled up with him once a year, around Peter and Paul.*

She managed to stall Lheureux at first, but eventually he lost patience: people were hounding him, he was short of capital, and if some of his bills weren't paid he would have to take back the goods that she had had.

"Fine!" said Emma. "Take them then!"

"I was only joking!" he protested. "It's just the riding crop I'm sorry about. Still! I'll ask Monsieur to give it back."

"No no!" she said.

"Ah ha, I've got you!" thought Lheureux.

And, convinced that he had discovered something, he went off whistling his little whistle and saying to himself:

"So be it! We'll see, we'll see!"

Emma was wondering how to get herself out of her predicament when the cook came in and put a roll of blue paper *from Monsieur Derozerays* on the mantelpiece. Emma pounced on it. There were fifteen napoleons" inside. It was the amount she owed. She heard Charles coming up the stairs; she threw the gold coins into her drawer and took the key.

Lheureux came back three days later.

"I've got a proposition for you," he said. "Instead of the said amount, if you'd like to take out—"

"Here," she said, handing him fourteen napoleons.

The shopkeeper was dumbfounded. To hide his disappointment he offered his profuse apologies, a host of services, all of which Emma turned down; then she stood for a moment with her hand in her apron pocket, feeling the two ten-sou pieces he had given her in change. She resolved to put something aside for later, so she could pay back...

"Ouf!" she thought to herself. "He'll soon forget all about it."

As well as the whip with a silver gilt handle, Rodolphe had been given a seal with the motto: *Amor nel cor*,* plus a muffler and a cigar case exactly like the Vicomte's that Charles had picked up on the road years ago, and which Emma had kept. Yet these gifts humiliated him. Several he wouldn't accept; she insisted, and in the end Rodolphe did as he was told, finding her tyrannical and intrusive.

And then there were her odd notions:

"When midnight strikes," she would say, "you are to think of me!"

If he confessed to not having remembered, then came the rebukes that always led to the inevitable question:

"Do you love me?"

"Certainly I love you!" he would answer.

"A lot?"

"Of course."

"You've never loved anyone else, have you?"

"You didn't think you were my first, did you?" he would laugh.

Emma would cry, and he would do his best to comfort her, larding his objections with witty remarks.

"It's just that I love you!" she would go on. "I love you so much I can't manage without you, do you realize that? Sometimes I yearn to see you, and I'm torn apart by love's anger. I wonder: 'Where is he? Perhaps he's talking to other women? They're smiling at him, he comes closer…' But you don't like any of them, do you? Some of them are more beautiful, but it's me who knows how to love! I'm your servant, your concubine! You're my king, my idol! You're good! You're handsome! You're intelligent! You're strong!"

He had heard this so many times before that it was nothing new to him. Emma was the same as his other mistresses, and gradually the novelty wore off, laying bare the inevitable monotony of passion, which always looks and sounds the same. For all his experience the man couldn't tell the difference between the various and distinct emotions that were concealed beneath these identical phrases. Because licentious or grasping lips had whispered similar words to him before, the trust he had in their spontaneity was minimal. "We need fewer of these overblown speeches," he thought. "They just conceal commonplace affections" – as if the abundance of the soul doesn't sometimes overflow in hollow metaphors, because no one can ever adequately describe what or how much they need, the ideas in their head or the pain they are feeling; human speech is like a cracked pot in which we cook up tunes for bears to dance to, or when we want to call down the moon.

But with the greater analytical sense of someone who holds himself back in any undertaking, Rodolphe saw there were other delights to be had from this love. He regarded a sense of decency as an inconvenience. He treated the matter straightforwardly. He turned love into something malleable and corrupt. It was just a foolish attachment that consisted of admiration for him, sensual pleasure for her, a sensation of bliss that left her drowsy, and her soul sunk into this drunken exhilaration and drowned, shrivelled up like the Duke of Clarence in his vat of malmsey.*

The mere routine of being in love caused Madame Bovary to change her ways. She looked at people more boldly, spoke more openly; she was improper enough to go for walks with Monsieur Rodolphe with a cigarette between her lips, so as *to cock a snook at the world*; and when she was seen getting out of the *Hirondelle* wearing a close-fitting man's waistcoat, those who had doubted finally doubted no longer, and Madame Bovary senior, who had taken refuge at her son's house after an appalling row with her husband, wasn't the least shocked among all the respectable ladies. And there were plenty of other things to displease her: Charles hadn't taken her advice about forbidding novels, for one thing, and she didn't like *the look of the house*; she saw fit to make comments, and on one particular occasion there was a contretemps over Félicité.

The previous evening, as Madame Bovary senior was walking down the corridor she had caught her with a man, who was about forty with a brown chinstrap beard, and who hearing her coming quickly slipped out of the kitchen. Emma laughed; the older woman lost her temper, and said that if you weren't worried about your own morals you could at least keep an eye on those of the servants.

"Which world do you live in?" said the daughter-in-law, with such an impudent look that Madame Bovary senior asked if it was perhaps her own behaviour she was defending.

"Get out!" said the young woman, leaping up out of her chair.

"Emma!... Mother!..." cried Charles, in an effort to patch things up.

But they were both too far gone in their wrath. Emma stamped her foot and kept saying:

"What manners! What a peasant!"

He rushed after his mother; she was beside herself, and spluttered:

"The impertinence! She's a scatterbrain! Or perhaps worse!"

She was going to leave that instant if the other didn't apologize. So Charles went back to his wife and pleaded with her to give way; he got down on his knees; and in the end she said:

"Very well! I will."

And with the dignity of a marquise she held out her hand to her mother-in-law:

"Please forgive me, Madame."

Then going back up to her room, Emma threw herself face down on the bed and cried like a child, her head buried in the pillow.

She and Rodolphe had made an agreement that if something out of the ordinary happened she would fix a scrap of white paper to the blind, and if he happened to be in Yonville he would hurry round to the alley at the back of the house. Emma gave the signal; she had been waiting for three quarters of an hour when she suddenly spotted Rodolphe outside the covered market. She was tempted to open the window, to call out; but he had already disappeared. And she sank back down in despair.

Yet soon she thought she heard someone coming along the pavement. There was no doubt, it was him; she went downstairs, across the courtyard. He was there, outside. She threw herself into his arms.

"Do be careful," he said.

"Oh, if only you knew!" she answered.

And she started telling him everything in a great rush, in no particular order, exaggerating, making up quite a lot, getting so far off the point that he didn't understand a word.

"There there, my darling angel, be brave, you'll get over it, have patience!"

"But I've been patient for four whole years, and suffered!... A love like ours should declare itself before the world! They torment me. I can't stand it any longer! Save me!"

She held him tight. Her tear-filled eyes glinted like fire beneath the surface of the water, her chest heaved frantically; never had he loved her so much; so much that it went to his head and he asked:

"What shall we do? What do you want?"

"Take me away!" she cried. "Oh, get me away from here, I beg of you!"

And she pressed her mouth to his, as if to kiss his consent out of him.

"But..." he answered.

"What?"

"What about your daughter?"

She thought for a moment, then said:

"Never mind, we'll take her with us!"

"What a woman!" he thought as he watched her walk away – because she had just slipped out into the garden, and they were calling her.

Over the next few days, old mother Bovary was amazed at the transformation in her daughter-in-law. For Emma proved to be more amenable, and even took deference so far as to ask her for a recipe for pickling gherkins.

Was it just another game of mutual deception? Or did she, out of a form of sensual stoicism, wish to fully experience the bitterness of what she was about to give up? Yet she paid little heed to it – quite the reverse; she went on with life as if she could taste her future happiness already. It was an endless topic of conversation with Rodolphe. She would lean on his shoulder and whisper:

"Ah, when we're in the post coach!... Can you imagine it? Is it possible? I can almost feel the coach setting off, it'll be like going up in a balloon, as if we're heading for the clouds. You do realize I'm counting the days, don't you?... And you?"

Never had Madame Bovary been so beautiful as she was at this time; it was that indefinable beauty that comes from joy, exuberance, success, when someone's nature is in harmony with their situation. Her lustful desires, her sorrows, the way she experienced pleasure and her still-youthful illusions had burgeoned by degrees, in the way flowers do with feeding, sun, rain and wind. Her eyelids seemed created for the long tender gazes when her eyes would drift away, while her heavy breathing made her nostrils flare, lifted the corners of her fleshy lips that were shaded by dark downy hair. You could have been forgiven for thinking that the coils of hair on the nape of her neck had been arranged by an artist versed in debauchery; they curled down carelessly in heavy folds, waiting for the chance hand of adultery that untied them every day. Her voice took on subtler nuances, as did her figure; there was something indefinable in the fall of her dress and the arch of her foot that had an effect on you. Like when they were first married, Charles thought she was delectable, irresistible.

When he came home in the middle of the night he didn't dare wake her. The porcelain night lamp threw a circle of flickering light on the ceiling, and the closed curtains of the little cot looked like a white cabin rising from the shadows beside the bed. Charles would watch them. He would think he could hear his child's shallow breathing. She was growing, and fast; every few months brought more changes. Already he saw her coming home from school as it was getting dark, laughing and smiling with ink stains on her little blouse, her bag over her arm; then she would have to go away to boarding school, it would cost a great deal; how would they manage? And he would think it over. He had in mind to rent a small farm somewhere nearby, which he could take care of himself every morning before he went off to see his patients. He would keep back some of the income from it, put it in a savings bank; then he would buy stocks and shares from somewhere, anywhere; and in the meantime his practice would grow. He was counting on it, because he wanted Berthe to be well brought up, to have talents, play the piano. Oh, she would be so pretty later on, when she was fifteen, she would wear a big straw hat in summer like her mother! From a distance people would think they were sisters. He imagined her working beside them in the evening in the lamplight; she would embroider slippers for him; she would take care of the housekeeping; she would fill the whole place with kindness and gaiety. And then he thought about getting her settled: they would find her a decent young man with a steady job; he would make her happy; it would last all their lives.

Emma wasn't asleep, she was just pretending to be, and as he dozed off beside her, she kept herself awake with dreams of her own.

Carried off by four galloping horses, she was already a week's journey away, in a new land from which they would never return. On they went, on and on, arms entwined, not speaking. Often, from the top of a mountain they suddenly saw a magnificent city with domes, bridges, ships, whole forests of lemon trees and cathedrals of white marble with storks nesting in their pointed steeples. They drove at walking pace because of the large paving stones, and there were bunches of flowers on the ground everywhere, which women dressed in red bodices offered to them. They heard bells ring, mules bray, the strumming of guitars and the murmur of fountains whose cooling misty spray settled on mountains of fruit piled at the foot of white statues that smiled through the plashing water. And then one evening they came to a fishing village where brown nets were drying in the breeze beside the cliffs and the huts. This was where they would settle. They would live in a low house with a flat roof in the shade of a palm tree, beside the sea at the end of a bay. They would sail in a gondola, swing in hammocks, their daily life would be as easy and comfortable as their silk clothes, as warm and starry as the gentle night sky that they gazed up at. And yet from the vast infinity of this future life which she summoned out of nowhere, nothing special appeared; the days, all glorious, all similar, were like so many waves in the sea; the same ones that washed back and forth all the way to the horizon, boundless, blue, bathed in sun. But then her child would start coughing in her cot, or Bovary would snore louder, and Emma wouldn't get to sleep till morning, when dawn whitened the window panes and young Justin was already out in the square, opening the awnings of the pharmacist's shop.

She sent for Monsieur Lheureux:

"I'll be needing a coat," she told him. "A long coat with a deep collar, lined."

"You're going travelling?" he asked.

"No! But… never mind. I can count on you, can't I? I certainly hope so!"

He gave a little bow.

"And I'll need a trunk," she added, "not too heavy… something convenient."

"Yes yes, I understand, about ninety-two centimetres by fifty, that's the size they come in nowadays."

"And an overnight bag."

"I can see there are going to be ructions," Lheureux was thinking to himself.

"Here," said Madame Bovary, taking the watch from her belt, "have this; you can get money for it."

The shopkeeper objected, said she was misjudging him; they knew each other well; would he doubt her? How silly! Nonetheless she insisted he at least take the chain, and Lheureux had pocketed it and was on his way when she called him back.

"You're to keep everything at your shop. And the coat" – she seemed to think for a moment – "no, don't bring that either; just give me the address of the person who's making it and tell them to have it ready for me."

It was the following month that they were going to run off. She would leave from Yonville as if she were going shopping in Rouen. Rodolphe would have reserved the seats, got the passports, even written ahead to

Paris so they could take the post coach all the way to Marseille, where they would buy a barouche, and from there go on to Genoa without stopping. She would have her luggage sent to Lheureux's shop, and it would be taken straight from there to the *Hirondelle* so no one would suspect anything; but among all this there was never any mention of her child. Rodolphe avoided the subject; perhaps she had forgotten about her.

He needed two clear weeks to finish making various arrangements; then after a week he asked for another two, then said he wasn't well; after which he went off on a trip, the whole of August passed, and then after all the delays they settled on a definite date, the 4th of September, a Monday.

At last it came, the Saturday before.

Rodolphe arrived earlier than usual that evening.

"Is everything ready?" she asked.

"Yes."

They walked round the flower beds then sat on the edge of the wall by the terrace.

"You're unhappy," said Emma.

"No, why?"

Yet he was looking at her oddly, affectionately.

"Is it because of going away?" she asked. "Leaving things you're attached to, your life here? Oh, I understand... But me, I've got nothing! You're everything to me, so I'll be everything to you. I'll be your family, your country; I'll look after you, I'll love you."

"You're enchanting!" he said, taking her in his arms.

"Really?" she said, with a lascivious laugh. "Do you love me? So swear it!"

"Love you? Love you? My darling, I worship you!"

At the end of the meadow a crimson full moon lifted above the horizon. It rose quickly behind the branches of the poplar trees that concealed it here and there, like a black curtain full of holes. First it reappeared, brilliant white, and lit up the empty sky; and then, moving more slowly, it cast a great, endless trail of stars across the surface of the river; the silver glow seemed to spiral down all the way to the bottom, like a headless serpent covered in brightly shining scales, or a gigantic candelabra that streamed molten diamonds. The gentle night spread out around them; the leaves were sheeted with darkness. Eyes half closed, Emma took deep breaths of the cool breeze. They didn't speak, so submerged were they in their all-consuming reverie. The tender feelings of the early days came back and filled their hearts, as lush and silent as the river running by, as soft and gentle as the scent from the mock-orange trees, throwing shadows into their memories more vast and melancholy than those of the motionless willows that stretched across the grass. Nocturnal creatures, hedgehogs or weasels, rustled among the leaves, and now and then they heard a ripe peach fall from the espalier.

"What a beautiful night!" said Rodolphe.

"We'll have plenty more!" replied Emma.

And, as if talking to herself:

"Yes, it's good to travel... But why is my heart so sad? Is it fear of the unknown... the thought of leaving what's familiar... or is it just?... No, it's the effect of too much happiness! I'm so feeble. Forgive me!"

"There's still time!" he exclaimed. "Think it over, perhaps you'll regret it later on."

"Never!" she declared, impulsively.

And, moving closer to him:

"What could go wrong? I'm not going to cross the desert, a chasm or an ocean with you. As long as we're together we'll be closer, more fulfilled as a couple every day! There won't be anything to disturb us, no troubles, nothing to get in our way. We'll be alone, all by ourselves, for ever... say something, answer me."

He kept repeating: "Yes... yes." She ran her fingers through his hair, saying over and over in a childlike voice through her tears:

"Rodolphe! Rodolphe!... Oh, Rodolphe, my darling little Rodolphe!"

Midnight chimed.

"Midnight!" she said. "It's tomorrow already! Just one more day!"

He got up to leave, and as if this were the signal for their escape, Emma suddenly brightened:

"Have you got the passports?"

"Yes."

"You haven't forgotten anything?"

"No."

"You're sure?"

"Absolutely."

"It's the Hôtel de Provence where you'll be waiting for me, isn't it? At midday?"

He nodded.

"Till tomorrow, then!" said Emma, caressing him one last time.

And she watched him walk away.

He didn't look back. She ran after him, and, leaning out over the river between the bushes, she called:

"Till tomorrow!"

But Rodolphe was already on the other side, walking quickly across the meadow.

After a while he stopped, and when he saw her in her white dress, disappearing into the darkness like a ghost, his heart began to pound so wildly that he had to lean against a tree to stop himself from falling.

"I'm a fool!" he said, with a terrible curse. "But what does it matter, she was a good mistress!"

And immediately Emma's loveliness, the delights of their affair came back to him. At first he softened, but then felt repelled by her.

"After all," he exclaimed, "I can't live abroad, be responsible for a child!"

This was what he told himself to justify his decision.

"And besides, the difficulties, the expense... Oh no, no, a thousand times no! It would have been so foolish!"

13

NO SOONER HAD HE GOT HOME than Rodolphe flung himself down at his desk beneath the stag's head trophy on the wall. But once he had picked up the pen he didn't know what to write, and so, leaning on his elbows, he sat thinking. Emma seemed to recede into the past, as if the resolution he had just made had put a vast distance between them.

To recapture something of her he fetched an old Reims biscuit tin from the armoire beside his bed, where he kept the letters that women had written to him; as he opened it it gave off a smell of damp, dust, dry rose petals. The first thing he saw was a handkerchief spotted with faded little marks. It was hers, she had had a nosebleed while they were out walking once; he had totally forgotten. With it was the miniature of herself that Emma had given him, its corners dented; he found her clothes and hair pretentious, her sideways glance a pitiable effect; and then, as a result of studying the picture, conjuring up a mental image of the model, Emma's features gradually became confused in his mind, as if the real and the painted faces had rubbed together and obliterated each other. Finally he read some of her letters; they were full of instructions about the journey, short, detailed and importunate, like business correspondence. He wanted to reread the longer ones, the ones from much earlier; to find them at the bottom Rodolphe disturbed all the others, and without thinking he began rummaging through the heap of paper and objects, coming across a jumble of posies, a garter strap, a black mask, pins and locks of hair – hair! Brown, blond, some of it caught on the metal of the tin and came apart in his fingers.

Strolling down memory lane in this way, he studied the handwriting and the style of the letters, which were as varied as the spelling. They were affectionate or jolly, mischievous or melancholy; there were those that wanted love, those that wanted money. From a single word he could remember a face, the odd gesture, the sound of a voice; although sometimes he couldn't remember anything at all.

For as all these women went rushing through his mind they got in each other's way and lost their individual importance, as if all their loves were identical, worth the same. Picking up a handful of letters at random, for a moment he let them tumble from his right hand into the left, smiling. And then, bored and drowsy, he put them back in the armoire and said to himself:

"What a lot of nonsense!..."

It summed up his opinion, because like schoolboys in the playground, pleasure had so trampled down the soil of his heart that nothing green would grow there now, and what did pass through, being more wanton than any child, never thought to carve its name on the wall as they did.

"Come on," he told himself, "let's make a start!"

And he wrote:

Be brave, Emma! Be brave! I don't want to bring unhappiness to your life...

"After all it's true," thought Rodolphe. "I'm acting in her interests; I'm being honest."

Have you weighed your decision? Are you aware of the abyss I was dragging you into, my poor darling? You haven't, have you? You were setting off madly, full of trust, believing in happiness, the future... Oh, what wretches we are! Insane!

He paused, to think of a good excuse.

"If I told her that I've lost everything?... No, and anyway, it wouldn't make any difference. It would all start up again later on. You can't make women like that see sense!"

Rodolphe thought for a moment, and then added:

I'll never forget you, you must believe that, I'll always be deeply devoted to you; but sooner or later (and this is the lot of all mankind) this passion of ours would have undoubtedly cooled! And then we would have wearied of each other, and who knows, I might have had to suffer the agony of witnessing your remorse, even of sharing in it, because I would have been responsible! The thought of you suffering torments me. Oh, forget me, Emma! Why did I have to meet you? Why were you so beautiful? Was it my fault? O my God! But no, no, just blame fate!

"That word always has the desired effect," he thought.

If you were just one of those trivial women that one meets, then out of selfishness I could have probably ventured something without any risk to you. But that exquisite state of elation, which is both your charm and your agony, blinded you, adorable woman that you are, to the falseness of the situation which we would have found ourselves in. I didn't give it enough thought at first either. I just lay back in the shade of perfect happiness like lying under a manchineel tree, without thinking of the consequences.

"Perhaps she'll think I'm abandoning it all out of meanness... Oh, what does it matter! It's just too bad, we have to put an end to this!"

It's a cruel world, Emma. And wherever we might have gone it would have come chasing after us. You would have been subjected to indiscreet questions, slander, contempt, perhaps even insults. Insults

for you! Oh!... And me, who would like to see you on a throne!
Me, who carries your memory with him like a lucky charm! Because
for all the harm I've done you, I'm punishing myself with exile. I'm
going away. Where? I've no idea, I'm mad! Farewell! Always be good!
Preserve the memory of the poor creature who has lost you. Teach
your child my name so she can remember me in her prayers.

The two candle flames flickered. Rodolphe went and closed the window, then once he had sat down again:

"I think that's all. Oh no, just one more thing, in case she decides to *come chasing after me*."

By the time you read these unhappy lines I shall be far away; I wanted
to leave as soon as possible to avoid the temptation of seeing you
again. I must be strong! I will come back, and perhaps eventually
we'll be able to talk about our past love in the cold light of day.
Farewell!

And he put one last *farewell*, written in two words: *Fare well!* and felt it was in perfect taste.

"How shall I sign it?" he wondered. 'Your most devoted'?... No. 'Your friend'?... Yes, that's it."

Your friend

He read the letter through. It seemed very good.

"Poor woman!" he thought, softening. "She'll think I have a heart of stone. It needs a few tears on it, but I'm not capable of crying; it's not my fault." And pouring a glass of water, he dipped his finger in it and let a big drop fall onto the paper, making a pale blotch on the ink. Then looking for a seal he found the one with the words *Amor nel cor*.

"It doesn't quite suit the circumstances... Pah, so what!"

Then he smoked three pipes and went to bed.

When he got up the next day (around two o'clock, having slept late), Rodolphe went and picked a basket of apricots. He put the letter at the bottom, under the leaves, and instructed Girard his ploughman to take it carefully to Madame Bovary's house. It was his way of communicating with her, sending her fruit or game depending on the time of year.

"If she asks after me," he said, "you're to tell her I'm away travelling. You must give the basket to her, to her personally… Off you go, and be careful!"

Girard put on his best smock, tied his handkerchief round the apricots and, lumbering along in his studded clogs, he made his way unhurriedly to Yonville.

When he arrived Madame Bovary was sorting laundry on the kitchen table with Félicité.

"I've brought something for you from the master," said the man.

She was suddenly filled with apprehension, and as she went through her pockets for some change she stared at the farmhand with frantic eyes, while he looked back in amazement, failing to see why a gift like this should have such an effect on someone. Eventually he left. But Félicité was still there. Unable to bear it any longer she hurried into the dining room as if to take the apricots, where she turned the basket over, tore out the leaves, found the letter, opened it and, as if a terrible fire were raging at her heels, fled horror-struck to her room.

But she saw that Charles was in there; he spoke to her, she heard nothing, and rushed on up the stairs, breathless, befuddled, beside herself, with the terrible piece of paper flapping and snapping in her fingers like a sheet of metal. On the top floor she stopped outside the attic door, which was shut.

She tried to calm herself; she thought about the letter; she had to finish it but didn't dare. But where? How? Someone would see her.

"Here," she thought. "I'll be safe in here."

And she went in.

The heat from the tiles on the roof above was constant, heavy, leaden, it closed round her temples like a vice, suffocating her; she managed to get to the shuttered window, opened the catch, and dazzling sunlight flooded in.

Beyond the rooftops opposite, the countryside stretched away into the distance. Below her the village square was empty; the cobbles on the pavement glistened, the weathervanes on the houses stood motionless; from a lower floor on the corner of the street came a high-pitched droning noise. It was Binet at his lathe.

Filled with nervous rage she leant on the window sill and reread the letter. The more she stared at it, the more befuddled she became. She saw him, heard his voice, threw her arms round him, and the beating of her heart, pounding against her breast like a battering ram, gradually got faster and faster, coming in fits and starts. She looked round, longed for the ground to open up beneath her. Why not have done with it all? What was to stop her? She was free. And she took a step forward, stared at the cobblestones and said to herself:

"Go on! Go on!"

A bright shaft of sunlight shone straight up from below, pulling her bodily towards the abyss. It was as if the square was rising up towards her, the floor swayed like a ship pitching and tossing. She leant all the way out and almost hung there, surrounded by the vast empty space. Blue sky swept through her, air rushed round and round in the void inside her head, all she had to do was give up, let go, and the humming of the lathe went on without stopping, like an angry voice calling to her.

"Wife!" shouted Charles. "Where's my wife!"

She stopped herself.

The thought that she had just escaped death made her almost pass out with terror; she closed her eyes; then she gave a start, feeling a hand on her sleeve: it was Félicité:

"Monsieur is waiting, Madame – supper's ready."

So she had to go downstairs! She had to sit at the dinner table!

She tried to eat. Every morsel almost choked her. She unfolded her napkin as if to examine the mends, devoted herself seriously to this occupation, even counting the threads in the material. Then suddenly she remembered the letter. Had she lost it? Where had she put it? But she was so filled with apathy that she was unable to think of an excuse to leave the table. Her courage deserted her; she was scared of Charles; he knew everything, she was sure of it! And then oddly enough he said:

"It seems we won't be seeing Monsieur Rodolphe for a while."

"Who told you that?" she said, giving a start.

"Who told me?" he answered, slightly surprised at her abruptness. "Girard, I bumped into him outside the Café Français just now. He's gone off travelling, or he's just about to."

She gave a sob.

"Why the surprise? He goes away every now and then to keep himself amused, and why not? There's nothing wrong with that, when you're rich and a bachelor to boot!... He enjoys a good laugh apparently, that friend of ours! Quite the practical joker. Monsieur Langlois was telling me…"

But then the maid came in, so he broke off.

The girl took the apricots from the sideboard and put them back in the basket. Not noticing the blush on his wife's face, Charles asked her to bring them over, took one and bit into it.

"Ah, excellent!" he said. "Here, try one."

And he held out the basket to Emma. But she gently pushed it away.

"Do at least have a smell. Mmm!" he said, wafting the basket under her nose.

"I'm going to choke!" she cried, leaping up.

But she controlled herself and the attack passed; then she said:

"It's nothing, nothing! Just nerves! Sit down, get on with your food!"

She dreaded being pestered, questioned, fussed over and never left in peace.

Charles did as he was told and sat down, spat apricot stones into his palm and put them on his plate.

Suddenly a blue tilbury drove across the square at a fast trot. Emma gave a cry and fell back onto the floor.

After a great deal of thought Rodolphe had decided to go to Rouen after all. And as there was no other way to get from La Huchette to Buchy except via Yonville, he had to drive through the village, and Emma had caught sight of him in the lamplight, which cut through the twilight like a flash of lightning.

Hearing the commotion next door, the pharmacist came running. The table had been overturned, plates and everything; gravy, meat, knives and forks, the salt cellar and oil and vinegar bottles were scattered round the room; Charles was calling for help; Berthe was crying with fright; while Félicité, her hands trembling, was trying to unlace Madame who was having convulsions.

"I'll get some smelling salts from my laboratory," said the apothecary.

And when she opened her eyes as she smelt the little bottle, he said:

"There, I knew it; it's enough to bring anyone back from the dead."

"Say something!" Charles was repeating. "Say something! Come on! It's me, your loving Charles! Don't you know me? Here's your little girl: give her a kiss!"

The child held out her arms to put them round her mother's neck. But, turning away, Emma said in a faltering voice:

"No... no... no one!"

Then she passed out again. They carried her up to bed.

She lay with her mouth open, eyes closed, hands flat on the covers, motionless and white as a sheet. Tears streamed from her eyes and trickled onto the pillow.

Charles stood at the end of the alcove with the pharmacist, who maintained the thoughtful silence that befits life's grave occasions.

"Don't worry," he said, touching his arm, "I think the crisis has passed."

"Yes," said Charles, who was watching her sleep. "She's more settled. Poor woman!... Poor woman!... Another relapse!"

Homais asked what had happened. Charles said that it had come on suddenly while she was eating an apricot.

"Extraordinary!" answered the pharmacist. "Perhaps apricots can bring on a fainting fit! Some people are extremely sensitive to certain smells! It could be a subject worth studying, as much from the pathological angle as the physiological. The priesthood knows its significance, that's why they use incense. It's to dull your perception, bring on a state of rapture, which is easy to achieve with members of the opposite sex in any case, since they're more susceptible than the rest of us. You hear of people passing out at the smell of burning horn or freshly baked bread..."

"Be careful not to wake her!" said Charles quietly.

"And it's not just human beings who are prone to these abnormalities," the apothecary went on, "but animals too. You're obviously not unaware of the peculiarly aphrodisiac effect which *Nepeta cataria*, commonly known as catmint, has on the feline race. To give an example which I guarantee is genuine, Bridoux (one of my old classmates who's now got a pharmacy in the Rue Malpalu in Rouen) has a dog that goes into convulsions at the sight of a snuffbox. He often does it by way of an experiment to show his friends at his house over by Guillaume woods. Would you believe that a simple sternutator* could have such a devastating effect on the bodily functions of a quadruped? It's curious, don't you think?"

"Yes," said Charles, who wasn't listening.

"Which goes to show," the other went on, with a benign, self-satisfied smile, "that there are countless irregularities in the nervous system.

Where Madame is concerned, I have to admit she's always seemed oversensitive to me. So, my dear chap, I wouldn't recommend any of those so-called remedies that claim to attack the symptoms but which really attack the health. No, none of those pointless medications! A proper diet, that's the answer! Sedatives, emollients, calmatives. And don't you think we should perhaps do something about her imagination?"

"What do you mean? How?" said Bovary.

"Ah, that's the question! That is indeed the question: *That is the question*,* as I read in the paper recently!"

But suddenly waking up, Emma cried out:

"The letter? What about the letter?"

They thought she was delirious – and she was: at midnight, brain fever set in.

For six weeks Charles never left her side. He abandoned his patients; he didn't go to bed, he was forever taking her pulse, applying mustard poultices and cold compresses. He sent Justin all the way to Neufchâtel to get ice; it melted on the return journey; he sent him back again. He called in Monsieur Canivet to get his opinion; he sent for his old tutor from Rouen, Doctor Larivière; he despaired. What frightened him most of all was Emma's state of depression; she didn't speak, hear anything, didn't even appear to be in pain – as if body and soul alike had set aside their turmoil.

By the middle of October she was able to sit up in bed, propped on pillows. When he watched her eat her first slice of bread and jam, Charles wept. She regained some strength; she got up for a few hours in the afternoon, and one day when she was feeling better he took her for a walk in the garden holding on to his arm. The sand on the paths was covered in dead leaves; she took one step at a time, dragging her slippered feet, leaning on Charles's shoulder and smiling.

They went right to the end, onto the terrace. She slowly straightened up and shaded her eyes; she looked way, way into the distance; but there was nothing but great bonfires smoking on the hillsides where they were burning the grass.

"You'll tire yourself, my darling," said Bovary.

And steering her gently under the arbour he added:

"Sit here on the bench: you'll be fine."

"No!" she said, her voice trembling. "Not there! Not there!"

She fainted, and that night her illness set in again, only now it took on a more unpredictable character, with more complex aspects. Sometimes she had a pain in her heart, then her chest, her head, her limbs; she had sudden bouts of vomiting which Charles thought might be early symptoms of cancer.

In addition to which the poor fellow had money problems!

14

FOR ONE THING he didn't know how he was going to pay back Monsieur Homais for all the drugs he had had from him; for although as a doctor he wasn't obliged to, it rather embarrassed him. And now the cook was in charge the household expenses were becoming alarming; bills poured in; the tradesmen were muttering; Monsieur Lheureux in particular was harassing him. When Emma's illness was at its height, the man took advantage of the situation to inflate his bill and immediately brought her coat, overnight bag and two trunks instead of one, and a lot else besides. However many times Charles told him he didn't need them, the shopkeeper arrogantly replied that the items had been ordered from him and he wouldn't take them back; besides, it would upset Madame's recovery, so Monsieur would think it over – in other words he would take him to court rather than give up what was due to him and take back his goods. After he had gone Charles told Félicité they were to be sent back to the shop, but it slipped her mind; there were other things to worry about; they forgot all about it. Lheureux redoubled his efforts and, first threatening then whining, he so contrived things that Charles ended up by signing a promissory note that fell due in six months. But no sooner had he signed the agreement than he had a bold idea: to borrow a thousand francs from Monsieur Lheureux. So, looking slightly embarrassed, he asked if there was a chance of getting it, adding that it would be for a year and at whatever rate of interest he liked. Lheureux rushed back to his shop, fetched the écus and made out another promissory note, by which Bovary agreed to pay on demand, the 1st September coming, the sum of 1,070 francs – which with the 180 already specified came to exactly 1,250. At six per cent, plus a quarter per cent commission, and with the administrative charges bringing in at least a third, in twelve months it would make him a 130 francs profit – and he was hoping it wouldn't end there, that they wouldn't be able to honour the agreements, that they would take out new ones, and that eventually, having been nurtured by the doctor as if in a nursing home, his dear little sum would come back to him significantly plumper, fat enough to split the money bags.

In fact everything was going well for him at the moment. He had won the bid to supply cider to the hospital at Neufchâtel; Monsieur Guillaumin had promised him shares in the peat bogs at Grumesnil, and he had an idea for setting up a new stagecoach service between Argueil and Rouen, which would soon put paid to the Lion d'Or's old jalopy, and, being faster, cheaper and carrying more baggage, would put all the business in Yonville his way.

More than once Charles wondered how he was going to pay back so much by next year; he tried to find it, dreamt up various means such as going to his father or selling something. But it would fall on deaf ears with his father, and he had nothing to sell. He found it all so difficult that he put the whole unpleasant business out of his mind. He reproached himself for ignoring Emma as a result of it; as if, because his every thought should be for his wife, he were concealing something from her by not thinking of her all the time.

It was a hard winter. Madame took a long time to recover. When the weather was fine they pushed her armchair over to the window, the one that looked over the square; because she had an aversion to the garden now, and the shutters on that side were permanently closed. She wanted her horse to be sold; what she had once loved she now disliked. Her every thought seemed concentrated on taking care of herself. She stayed in bed and ate light meals, rang for the maid to check about her tisanes or to chat with her. Meanwhile the snow on the roof of the covered market cast its pale still light into the room, and after that came the rain. Day in day out, with a form of anxiety, Emma waited for the unfailing round of minor events which were of little importance to her. The most significant was the arrival of the *Hirondelle* in the evening. The landlady would shout, other voices replied, while Hippolyte looked for trunks on the roof of the coach, his lantern like a star in the darkness. At midday Charles would come home; then he went out again; then she would have some bouillon, and at five o'clock as it was just getting dark, the children coming home from school would drag their clogged feet on the pavement and clatter their rulers on the catches of the shutters one after another.

It was the time when Father Bournisien came to see her. He would ask after her health, tell her the news, and encourage her in her faith with a cosy little chat that had its own particular charms. The mere sight of his cassock made her feel better.

One day when her illness was at its height she thought she was dying, and had asked to take communion. While the room was being got ready for her to receive the sacrament, the chest of drawers cluttered with medicine bottles laid out as an altar, and Félicité scattered dahlia petals on the floor, Emma felt something very powerful moving over her which took away her pain, her every feeling and emotion. Her unburdened flesh no longer weighed on her, a new life was beginning; and as her whole being rose towards God it seemed as if it would be absorbed into this love, like grains of incense turn to smoke and vanish as they burn. They sprinkled holy water on her sheets; the priest took the white host from the ciborium; and faint with heavenly joy she opened her lips to receive the body of the Saviour. The curtains of the alcove billowed gently round her like thick clouds, the glow of the two candles on the chest of drawers seemed like dazzling haloes of glory. Then she let her head drop back down, believing she heard the song of seraphic harps on the air, and in a bright azure sky, sitting on a golden throne surrounded by saints holding green palm branches, she saw God the Father in all his radiant majesty, and who with a sign dispatched angels with wings of fire earthwards to bear her up in their arms.

She kept this glorious vision in her mind as the most beautiful dream it was possible to have, and she tried to recapture the feeling in a less unique way, yet with the same profound sense of sweetness. Stiff with pride, her soul finally found peace in Christian humility, and savouring the pleasure of being weak, Emma looked on as her will was destroyed, opening the way for grace to pour in. In place of worldly happiness there was now a greater bliss, one love above all others, unbroken and unceasing, and which grew eternally! Among her hope-filled illusions she glimpsed a state of purity that hovered above the earth, intermingling with the sky, and which was where she longed to be. She wanted to be a saint. She bought rosaries, wore amulets; she wanted a reliquary set with emeralds to keep beside her bed so she could kiss it every night.

The parish priest marvelled at these tendencies, although he felt that the fervour of Emma's religion made it border on heresy, even excess.

But not being versed in such matters, beyond a certain level he wrote to Monsieur Boulard, the Bishop's bookseller, and asked him to send "something suitable for a member of the opposite sex with a quick mind". Paying as much heed as if he were sending ironmongery to Negroes, the bookseller packed up a random selection of everything the trade currently had by way of pious reading matter. There were handbooks with questions and answers, tracts written in a haughty tone in the style of Monsieur de Maistre, and what claimed to be novels in pink bindings and sickly style produced by seminarists with poetic pretentions or repentant bluestockings. There was: *Give It Some Thought*; *The Man of the World at Mary's Feet*, by Monsieur de ***, recipient of several decorations; *Voltaire's Errors, for the Use of the Young*,* etc.

But Madame Bovary's mind still wasn't clear enough to concentrate on just anything; what was more, she embarked on her reading too hastily. She was angered by the Church edicts; she disliked the arrogance of the polemical works with their relentless pursuit of people she hadn't heard of; and the secular stories drawn from religion seemed to have been written with so little knowledge of the world that, imperceptibly, they pushed her away from the truths she was expecting to have confirmed. She persevered nonetheless, and when the tome fell from her hand she imagined she had been seized with the most exquisite Catholic melancholy that an unworldly soul is able to envisage.

As for memories of Rodolphe, she stored them away in the depths of her heart, and there they stayed, more stately, more motionless than a mummy in its crypt. From this great embalmed love came a fragrance that, touching everything, scented the world of purity where she wanted to live with tenderness. When she knelt at her Gothic priedieu she spoke the same honeyed words to the Lord that she had once whispered in her lover's ear during their adulterous outpourings. She did it to instil faith, but no delight descended on her from heaven, and she would get up aching, with the obscure feeling that she was the victim of an enormous hoax. Yet this quest, so she believed, was just one more good deed, and in her proud devotions Emma likened herself to the great ladies of the past, whose glory had once inspired her in a painting of la Vallière,* and who, trailing the richly bedecked trains of their long dresses with such splendour, withdrew into seclusion to wash Christ's feet with the tears of a heart wounded by life.

She devoted herself to extravagant acts of charity. She made clothes for the poor; she sent firewood to expectant mothers; one day her husband came home to find three vagrants drinking soup at the kitchen table. She brought her daughter back, whom Charles had sent to the wet nurse while her mother was ill. She started to teach her to read, and however much Berthe cried she never got annoyed. Hers was a forbearing world view, an all-embracing compassion. Whatever she talked about her language always expressed ideals. She would say to her little girl:

"So has your tummy ache gone now, my darling?"

Madame Bovary senior could find nothing to reproach her for, except perhaps her obsession with knitting nightshirts for orphans instead of mending tea towels. But worn out by her own domestic squabbles, the woman enjoyed it in this peaceful house, and even stayed on until after Easter to avoid the sarcastic comments from old man Bovary, who made a point of always asking for chitterlings on Holy Friday.

Besides her mother-in-law, whose presence strengthened her with its upright opinions and serious manner, Emma had other company almost every day. There was Madame Langlois, Madame Caron, Madame Dubreuil, Madame Tuvache and, regularly between two and five o'clock, the excellent Madame Homais, who had never really believed any of the tittle-tattle that went round about her neighbour. The Homais children came to see her too; Justin would bring them. He came up to her room with them and stood by the door, not moving or speaking. Without realizing, Madame Bovary would sometimes even start getting dressed. First she would take out her comb, briskly shake her head; the first time the poor boy saw all this hair rolling in dark ringlets down the back of her legs it was like gaining entrance to something new and extraordinary whose magnificence he found alarming.

Emma probably didn't notice his over-attentive silence or his shyness. Now love had disappeared from her life she never suspected it was just a few feet away, beating beneath the rough cotton shirt in an adolescent heart that was receptive to the effusions of her beauty. Besides, everything about her was now cloaked in such detachment, she spoke so affectionately and with a gaze that was so lofty, her behaviour was so changeable, that it was no longer possible to see the self-interest behind her charity or the depravity beneath her virtue. One evening she lost her temper with the maid, who had asked if she could go out and was stammering away in an attempt to find an excuse, when Emma suddenly said:

"So do you love him?"

And, without waiting for a reply from Félicité, who was blushing, she added sadly:

"Off you go then! Enjoy yourself!"

When spring came she made drastic changes to the garden, despite Charles's comments; but he was glad to see her showing an interest in something at last. The more her health improved, the more of it she displayed. First she found a way of getting rid of old mother Roulet the wet nurse, who while she was convalescing had been spending too much time in the kitchen with her two nurslings, as well as her lodger who ate like a horse. Next she unburdened herself of the Homais family, dismissed her other visitors one by one and even stopped going to church regularly, to the great approval of the apothecary, who said to her good-humouredly one day:

"I see you're cutting the cloth!"

Father Bournisien still came every day, after catechism class. He preferred to sit outside in the fresh air, in the bocage, as he called the arbour. It was the time when Charles came home. They were hot; so they would call for sweet cider and drink to Madame's recovery.

Binet would be there, or rather further along, against the wall of the terrace fishing for crayfish. Bovary would invite him for a drink; he proved to be expert at uncorking pitchers.

"You must hold the bottle steady on the table like this," he would say, looking round at the landscape with a satisfied expression. "Then once you've cut the strings, you ease the cork out bit by bit, gently gently, just like they do with bottles of seltzer in restaurants."

But during the demonstration, cider would often spurt in their faces, and each time the clergyman would give an enigmatic laugh and make the same joke:

"It's clear that his joy is overflowing!"

He was a decent man at heart, and wasn't the least shocked when the pharmacist suggested to Charles that to amuse Madame he should take her to the theatre in Rouen to see Lagardy, the distinguished tenor. Surprised at his lack of comment, Homais asked his opinion; the priest admitted that he considered music less harmful for people's morals than literature.

The pharmacist sprang to the defence of letters. The theatre, he argued, helped satirize prejudice, taught virtue in the guise of pleasure.

"*Castigat ridendo mores*,* Monsieur Bournisien! Take Voltaire's tragedies: most of them are skilfully interspersed with philosophical observations that provide the public with lessons in morality, how to be diplomatic."

"I once saw a play called *Le Gamin de Paris*,"* said Binet, "there was this General character who was completely barmy! He sends a son of the family packing for seducing a working-class girl, and who in the end—"

"Undoubtedly!" Homais went on. "There's bad literature the same way as there's bad pharmacy; but condemning the most important of the arts out of hand seems a blunder to me, a medieval notion worthy of the abysmal days when they locked Galileo up in prison."

"I'm well aware there are good books and good authors," the priest protested. "Nevertheless, with people of both sexes gathered together in a delightful room, decorated with worldly finery, as well as those heathen costumes, make-up, torchlight, effeminate voices, it must end up by fostering a certain licentiousness of mind, and give you impure thoughts, unseemly temptations. At least, that's the opinion of the Fathers. After all," he added, taking on a mystical tone as he rolled snuff between his thumb and forefinger, "if the Church forbade theatrical performances it's because it had good reason to; we should bow to its edicts."

"But why excommunicate actors?" asked the apothecary. "They used to take part openly in church services. Yes, they performed in the chancel, a sort of farce called a mystery play during which the laws of decency were often affronted."

The cleric just groaned. The pharmacist continued:

"Like in the Bible: there's more than one... you know... spicy... little detail... things that are quite... bawdy!"

To Father Bournisien's gesture of annoyance he replied:

"Oh, so you'll admit it's not the sort of book to give young people! I'd be annoyed if Athalie—"

"It's the Protestants who advise reading the Bible, not us!" exclaimed the other man, losing patience.

"What does that matter!" said Homais. "I'm surprised in this day and age, the age of enlightenment, that people still insist on banning a form of mental relaxation which is harmless, moral and sometimes even good for the health. Isn't that so, doctor?"

"Undoubtedly," replied the medic noncommittally, either because he thought the same and didn't wish to upset anyone, or because he didn't have any thoughts.

The conversation appeared to be over when the pharmacist decided to make one last sally.

"I've known priests who dressed up in ordinary clothes so they could go and watch dancing girls cavorting."

"That'll be the day!" said the priest.

"Oh yes, I've known them!"

And, enunciating each syllable, Homais repeated:

"I-have-known-them."

"Well, they were wrong," said Bournisien, resigned to hearing anything and everything.

"And there are plenty more where they came from, by Jove!" exclaimed the apothecary.

"Monsieur!..." retorted the cleric, with such a savage look that the pharmacist was quite unnerved.

"What I mean to say," he replied in a less combative tone, "is that tolerance is the surest way to draw people over to religion."

"Very true!" said the other, sitting down again.

But he only stayed a little longer. As soon as he had gone, Homais said to the doctor:

"That was a fine old set-to! Did you see how I got him going!... For goodness' sake take Madame to the theatre, if only to goad the God-botherers for once! If I can get someone to stand in for me I'll come too. But you'll have to be quick! Lagardy will only give a single performance; he's got lucrative engagements in England. He's a bit of a lad, so they say! Rolling in it! He takes his cook and three mistresses with him! All those great entertainers burn the candle at both ends; loose living helps fire their imagination. But they die in the poorhouse because they never think to put anything aside while they're young. Anyway, goodnight, bon appétit – see you tomorrow!"

The thought of the theatre soon took root in Bovary's mind, because he immediately mentioned it to his wife, who said no at first, pleading tiredness, the inconvenience, the expense; but for once

Charles didn't give in, so convinced was he that some relaxation would be good for her. He didn't see any difficulties; his mother had sent three hundred francs which they hadn't been expecting, their debts weren't too huge at the moment, and the promissory notes with Lheureux weren't due for such a long time that there was no need to worry yet. Besides, thinking she was just being tactful, Charles persisted; so much that she finally made up her mind. And the next day at eight o'clock they bundled themselves into the *Hirondelle*.

The apothecary, who had nothing to keep him in Yonville but felt obliged not to leave, heaved a sigh as he watched them set off.

"Bye then, bon voyage!" he said. "Lucky folk that you are!"

And turning to Emma, who was wearing a blue silk dress with four flounces he added:

"You look as pretty as the goddess of love! You'll be *a great success* in Rouen."

The stagecoach took them to the Hôtel Croix Rouge on the Place Beauvoisine. It was one of those inns that can be found in the suburbs of all provincial towns, with large stables and small rooms, chickens pecking at corn under commercial travellers' muddy cabriolets in the yard – decent old lodgings with worm-eaten wooden balconies that creak in the wind on winter nights, permanently full of people, noise and unappetizing food, black tabletops sticky from cups of laced coffee, the thick glass of the windows yellowed by flies, damp napkins spotted with cheap wine stains; and which, forever smelling of the country like a farmhand in his Sunday best, have a café on the street side and a vegetable garden at the back. Charles hurried off straight away to buy tickets. He confused front of house with the circle, the *stalls* with the boxes, asked questions, didn't understand the answers, was referred to the house manager, went back to the hotel, then to the front desk again, in the process doing several tours of the town between the theatre and the main boulevard.

Madame bought herself a hat, gloves and a bouquet. Monsieur was terrified that they would miss the start, and so, without having had time for a bite to eat, they stationed themselves outside the main door of the theatre, which was still closed.

15

T HE CROWD QUEUED UP along by the wall, penned in neatly between the railings. On the corners of nearby streets enormous posters announced in flamboyant letters: "*Lucia di Lammermoor**... Lagardy... Opera..." etc. The sun was shining; people were hot; sweat trickled from curled hair, every handkerchief was mopping a red face; sometimes a warm breeze blew from the river and made the heavy cotton awnings over the doors of the taverns flutter. Yet farther along people were cooled by a draught that smelt of tallow, leather and oil. It was the fumes from the Rue des Charrettes, full of big dark shops where barrels were rolling.

For fear of looking foolish, Emma asked to go for a walk by the harbour before they went in, and Bovary held on tightly to the tickets in his trouser pocket.

The moment they walked into the lobby her heart began to race. Inadvertently she gave a conceited smile as the crowd rushed along the right-hand corridor while she went upstairs to the dress circle. She felt childish pleasure as she pushed the large carpeted doors with her finger; she took a deep breath of the dusty corridors, and once she was sitting in the box she threw back her shoulders with all the nonchalance of a duchess.

The auditorium began to fill, opera glasses came out of cases, and spotting each other from a distance, habitués exchanged greetings. They came here to forget the cares of commerce in an evening of art; although never quite losing sight of *business* they still talked cotton, connoisseur brandy or indigo. There were old faces, expressionless and calm, skin as white as their hair, and which looked like silver medals misted with leaden-grey breath. Young bucks strutted in the stalls, flaunting pink or apple green cravats above their waistcoats; Madame Bovary admired them from above, as they rested the outstretched palms of yellow gloves on the golden heads of their canes.

Meanwhile the candles in the orchestra pit were lighting; a chandelier was lowered from the ceiling, the brilliance of its many glittering surfaces scattering gaiety round the auditorium; then the musicians walked in one after another, and there rose a hubbub of droning double basses, squeaking violins, trumpeting cornets, cheeping flutes and flageolets. Then the three knocks came from the stage; there was a drum roll, the brass section struck up and the curtain rose to reveal a landscape.

It was a clearing in a wood, with a spring on the left beneath an oak tree. Plaids over their shoulders, peasants and masters were singing a hunting song; then an officer appeared, and raising his arms to heaven he called on the dark angel; another man came on; then they left the stage and the hunters began to sing again.

It took her back to the books she had read when she was young; she found herself in a Walter Scott novel. She thought she heard bagpipes echoing though the mist over the heather. Meanwhile, what she remembered of the book made it easier to understand the libretto, and she followed the plot line by line while the elusive memories that came back to her scattered beneath the hail of music. She let herself be lulled by the singing, quivered as if the bows of the violins were playing her nerves like strings. She couldn't take in all the costumes, scenery, characters, the painted trees that shook as people walked past, or the velvet caps, cloaks, swords, all these products of the imagination that moved among the chords as if breathing the air of another world. Then a young woman came on stage, throwing a purse to a sprightly squire. She stood there alone, then a flute was heard, like a babbling brook or the chirping of a bird. Lucia launched bravely into her cavatina in G-major; she was unhappy in love, she wished she had wings. Emma, too, would have liked to escape her life, fly away into an embrace. Then suddenly Edgardo-Lagardy appeared.

He had the magnificent pale complexion that brings the grandeur of marble to the hot-blooded people of the Midi. His strong waist was shown off by a brown doublet; a small chased dagger swung at his left thigh, he rolled his eyes languorously while showing white teeth. People said that a Polish princess, who had heard him singing one night on the beach in Biarritz, where he had gone to unwind, had fallen in love with him. She had ruined herself over him. He dropped her for other women, but these romantic entanglements only enhanced his reputation as a performer. The wily thespian made a point of including a comment about his personal magnetism and sensitive soul on publicity posters. A fine voice, unshakeable self-confidence, more personality than intelligence and more presence than musical ability was what had made the name of this lovable rogue, in whom there was something of the hairdresser and the matador.

From the moment he came on he enthused the audience. He clasped Lucia to him, left her, returned, seemed in despair: he flew into fits of rage then gave poignant moans filled with the greatest tenderness, while notes rose from his uncovered throat along with sobs and kisses. Emma leant forward to see him, sinking her nails into the velvet balustrade of the box. Her heart filled with dulcet laments that lingered to the sound of double basses like the cries of shipwrecked sailors in a storm at sea. In them she recognized the rapture and fear that had nearly killed her. The soprano's voice was nothing more than the echo of her own consciousness, these imaginings that were enchanting her, a fragment of her life. But no worldly person had loved her like this. On that last night in the moonlight when they had said: "Till tomorrow, till tomorrow!" to each other, he hadn't wept like Edgardo did... The auditorium exploded into bravos! They sang the finale of the duet for a second time; the two lovers spoke of flowers on their tomb, of vows, exile, destiny, hope, and when they uttered their last farewell, Emma gave a sharp cry that was lost among the final chords.

"Why is this lord ill-treating her?" asked Bovary.

"He isn't," she replied. "He's her lover."

"But he swears to take revenge on her family, while the other man, the one who came on just now, said: 'I love Lucia and I believe she loves me.' And anyway, he went off arm in arm with her father. Because that's her father, isn't it, the ugly little one with the cock's feather in his hat?"

Despite Emma's explanations, as soon as they got to the *recitativo* in which Gilbert explains his monstrous intrigues to his master Ashton, when Charles saw the mock engagement ring that would deceive Lucia he thought it was a keepsake that Edgardo had sent. Not only that, he admitted he couldn't work out the story – because of the music, which stopped him from hearing what they were saying.

"What does it matter?" said Emma. "Be quiet!"

"You know I just like to understand what's happening," he went on, leaning against her shoulder.

"Shut up! Shut up!" she said, becoming irritated.

Lucia came on supported by her female attendants, a wreath of orange blossom in her hair, paler than her white satin dress. Emma thought of her own wedding day; she saw herself walking to church along the path through the cornfields. Why hadn't she stood her ground, implored like this woman was doing? Instead she had been full of joy, not realizing she was hurling herself into an abyss... Oh, if only she could have put her life into the hands of some strong heart while her beauty was still young, before it was sullied by marriage and disillusioned by adultery, then virtue, affection, sensual pleasure and duty would have become one, and she would never have fallen from the heights of such bliss! But happiness of that kind was a lie, designed to reduce desire to a state of despair. She was acquainted by now with the mediocrity of the passions that art overstated. So, doing her best to turn her thoughts away from it, in this reproduction of her own distress Emma saw just a stage-set fantasia that was only suitable for light entertainment, and when a man in a long black cloak appeared at the back between the velvet door curtains, she smiled in pity and contempt.

He swept off his wide-brimmed Spanish hat; immediately the orchestra and singers launched into a sextet. Flashing with rage, Edgardo's voice dominated all the others. In a bass tone, Ashton hurled murderous insults at him, Lucia gave a high-pitched wail, to one side Arturo's voice hovered in mid-range, the minister's bass baritone droned like an organ, while the women took up their words in a delightful chorus. They stood in a line, gesturing: anger, vengeance, envy, dread, forgiveness and astonishment issued from every mouth at once. The offended lover brandished his sword; his heavy lace collar rose and fell on his heaving breast, he strode back and forth across the boards, gilt silver spurs jingling at the slack ankles of his soft boots. His love must be inexhaustible, she thought, if he can pour it out in such great waves over the crowd. Her disparaging impulses evaporated in the face of this poetic character who overcame her, and drawn to the man by the fantasies inspired by the role that he was playing, she tried to picture his life – the epic, exceptional, magnificent life that she could have led had destiny willed it. They would have met, they would have loved each other! She would have travelled with him through every realm in Europe, one capital after another, sharing his exhaustion and his pride, gathering up the flowers that people threw at him, embroidering his costumes; and then every night, wide-eyed behind the gilt lattice of a grille at the back of a private box, she would have received the outpourings of a soul who sang for her alone; he would have looked at her from the stage as he sang. Then she was seized by a wild thought:

he was looking at her, she was sure of it! She longed to rush into his arms, seek sanctuary in his strength as if it were love personified, to say to him, to cry: "Take me away, carry me off, let's go! I'm yours! I'm yours for ever! My every desire, my every dream!"

The curtain fell.

The smell of the gas lamps mingled with people's breath; the draught from fans only made the air more stifling. Emma wanted to leave, but the crowd was blocking the corridors and she dropped back into her seat, unable to breathe. Afraid she was going to faint, Charles hurried off to the refreshment room to get her a glass of lemon barley water.

He had difficulty getting back to his seat; people jostled him all the way because of the glass he was carrying, and he spilt most of it down the back of a Rouen lady wearing a short-sleeved dress who, feeling the cold liquid running down her spine, shrieked like a peacock as if she were being murdered. Her husband, a mill owner, lost his temper with the clumsy stranger, and while she mopped the stains off her beautiful cerise taffeta dress he muttered in a surly voice about compensation, costs, reimbursement. Charles finally got back to his wife, and still out of breath he told her:

"Crikey, I never thought I'd make it! There are so many people... so many people!"

Then he added:

"You'll never guess who I bumped into? Monsieur Léon!"

"Léon?"

"The very same! He's coming to offer his respects to you."

As he was speaking the former clerk from Yonville came into the box.

He held out his hand with gentlemanly nonchalance: without thinking she offered hers, almost certainly following the dictates of a will stronger than her own. She hadn't felt it since that spring evening when rain was falling on the fresh green leaves, and they had stood by the window and said goodbye. But quickly remembering what decorum required, she shook off the lethargy of her memories and started to babble one word after another.

"Oh, hello!... Goodness! You're here?"

"Quiet!" shouted a voice from the stalls, because the third act was just starting.

"You're in Rouen then?"

"Yes."

"How long have you been here?"

"Get out! Get out!"

People turned round and stared; they stopped talking.

But from now on she wasn't listening; for her the choir of wedding guests, the scene with Ashton and his manservant, the great D-major duet, faded into the distance as if the instruments were playing with mutes and the cast had moved farther away; she remembered the card games at the pharmacist's house, the walk to the wet nurse's, reading under the arbour, the chats by the fire together, everything about that poor, peaceful love of long ago, so discreet, so affectionate, yet which she had quite forgotten. So why had he come back? What trick of fate had brought him back into her life? He stood behind her, shoulder against the partition wall, and now and then she felt herself shudder as the warm breath from his nostrils touched her hair.

"Are you enjoying it?" he said, leaning so close that the tip of his moustache brushed her cheek.

"Heavens no! Not really."

He suggested they go out to have an ice cream somewhere.

"Oh, not yet!" said Bovary. "Let's stay. She's let her hair down; it looks like there's going to be something dramatic."

But Emma wasn't interested in the scene with the madness, and she found the soprano's performance overplayed.

"She's shouting," she said, turning to Charles, who was listening.

"Perhaps... yes... slightly," he answered, wavering between his own simple enjoyment and his respect for his wife's opinions.

Then Léon sighed and said:

"This heat is so..."

"Unbearable! You're right."

"Are you feeling uncomfortable?" asked Bovary.

"Yes, I'm suffocating – let's go."

Monsieur Léon put her long lace shawl gently round her shoulders, and the three of them went to the harbour and sat outside a café.

They began by talking about her illness, although Emma stopped Charles occasionally because she said she was afraid of boring Monsieur Léon; then he told them he was spending two years in a large practice in Rouen to gain experience in business, which was handled differently in Normandy to the way it was in Paris. Then he asked after Berthe, the Homais family, old mother Lefrançois; and since there wasn't much more they could say to each other in her husband's presence, the conversation soon tailed off.

People coming out of the theatre walked past, humming "O my angel, my beautiful Lucia!" or yelling it out at the top of their voices. And then to show he was a man of the world, Léon started to discuss music. He had seen Tamburini, Rubini, Persiani, Grisi – compared with them Lagardy was nothing, despite all his glamour.

"Mind you," put in Charles, who was nibbling a rum sorbet, "they say he's quite superb in the third act; I'm sorry we left before the end, I was just beginning to enjoy it."

"Never mind," replied the clerk, "he'll be giving another performance soon."

Charles said they were leaving the next day.

"Unless, that is," he added, turning to his wife, "you'd like to stay on by yourself, my little puss cat?"

Changing tactics at this unhoped-for opportunity, the young man began praising Lagardy's performance in the final piece. It was magnificent, sublime! So Charles persisted:

"You could travel back on Sunday. Come on, make your mind up! Because if you think for a moment that it won't do you some good, you're mistaken."

Meanwhile the tables around them were emptying; a waiter hovered discreetly. Taking the hint, Charles opened his wallet, but putting his hand on his arm the clerk stopped him, and even remembered to leave some silver as a tip, which he tossed onto the marble with a clink.

"Really," muttered Bovary, "I'm not happy, there was no need for you to…"

The other just shrugged it off with a friendly wave of the hand, and picking up his hat he said:

"So it's agreed then, tomorrow evening at six o'clock?"

Again Charles protested that he couldn't stay away any longer, but there was nothing to stop Emma…

"It's just that…" she said hesitantly, with an odd smile. "I'm not sure if…"

"Well, we'll see, you think it over! Sleep on it…"

And then he said to Léon, who was walking with them:

"Seeing as you're back in our part of the world, I hope you'll come and take dinner off us now and then?"

The clerk said that he would be sure to, because he had to come to Yonville on business in any case. And they went their separate ways at the Passage Saint-Herbland, just as the cathedral clock was striking eleven thirty.

Part Three

Part Three

1

W HILE FINISHING HIS LAW STUDIES, Monsieur Léon had spent a fair
amount of his time at Paris dance halls where he made not
a few conquests among the grisettes, who thought he *looked distinguished*. He was the most respectable of students; his hair was neither
too long nor too short, he didn't spend his whole allowance on the
first day of term, and stayed on good terms with his tutors. As for wild
behaviour, he avoided it as much from timidity as from finer feelings.

When he was reading in his room or under the lime trees in the
Luxembourg, he would often drop his copy of the Code Civil,*
and thoughts of Emma would come back to him. Yet these feelings
gradually faded, to be supplanted by other desires, although they
didn't disappear completely; because Léon had not given up all hope
– there was a vague, uncertain promise that dangled in front of him
like a golden apple on some fantastical tree.

Then, when he saw her again after three years, his passion was
rekindled. He was finally going to have to find a way of making
her his, he thought. His shyness had worn off by now as a result of
keeping loose company, and he returned to provincial life despising
anyone who didn't walk the boulevards in shiny shoes. Meeting a lacy
Parisian lady in the drawing room of an eminent doctor, an important
man with decorations and a carriage of his own, the poor clerk would
almost certainly have trembled like a child, but by the harbour in
Rouen with the wife of this little doctor, he felt secure, already certain
of impressing her. Self-assurance depends on its environment: people
speak differently downstairs to the way they do upstairs, and a rich
woman seems to wear a bodice lined with banknotes, like a breastplate
to defend her virtue.

After he had left Monsieur and Madame Bovary the night before,
Léon followed them at a distance, and seeing them go into the Croix
Rouge he went home and spent all night devising a plan.

The next day at five o'clock he walked into the hotel kitchens, white-
faced, a lump in his throat, with the determination of a coward who
intends to stop at nothing.

"Monsieur's not here," replied one of the servants.

It seemed to bode well. So he went upstairs.

She wasn't flustered when he appeared; in fact she apologized for forgetting to tell him where they were staying.

"Oh, I guessed!" Léon answered.

"How?"

He said he had been guided to her by chance, an instinct. She smiled, and to make up for his silliness Léon explained that he had spent all morning looking for her in every hotel in town.

"So you decided to stay?" he added.

"Yes," she said, "but I was wrong. One shouldn't make a habit of unrealistic pleasures when one is surrounded by a host of things that need doing…"

"I can imagine—"

"No you can't! You're not a woman."

But men have their own afflictions, and the conversation took a philosophical turn. Emma waxed lyrical about the woes of worldly attachments, the perpetual isolation in which the heart lies buried.

To assert himself, or perhaps in artless imitation of her melancholy, the young man told her that he had been phenomenally bored all the time he was studying. Procedure irritated him, he was drawn to other careers, his mother was constantly harassing him with her letters. The more they talked, the more detail they went into about the cause of their woes, glorying in each new revelation. Yet they stopped short of laying bare their every thought, although still trying to find words to express them. She never told him about her passion for another man; he didn't admit to having forgotten her.

Perhaps he didn't remember the suppers he had had with broad-shouldered, broad-minded girls after balls; and she seemed to have forgotten the times when she had run through morning grass to her lover's chateau. The sounds of the town barely reached them; the room seemed tiny, as if purposely designed to draw them closer in their loneliness. Wearing a damask dressing gown, Emma rested her chignon on the back of the old armchair; the yellow wallpaper was like a golden backdrop; her head, her hair with its centre parting, was reflected in the mirror, and the tips of her ears showed beneath her headbands.

"I'm sorry," she said, "it's wrong of me! I'm boring you with my endless complaints!"

"No no, not at all!"

"If only you knew all the dreams I've had!" she went on, looking up at the ceiling with tears trickling from her beautiful eyes.

"Oh, me too! How I've suffered! I used to go out and roam the embankments, submerge myself in the noise of the crowd, unable to drive away the obsessions that hounded me. There was a shop on the boulevard that sold prints, it had an Italian engraving of one of the Muses. She was wearing a loose tunic and looking up at the moon, with forget-me-nots in her long, untied hair. Something made me go back time and time again; I used to stand there for hours."

Then in a trembling voice he said:

"She looked rather like you."

Madame Bovary turned away so he wouldn't see the irrepressible smile that she could feel forming on her lips.

"I often wrote you letters," he said, "then tore them up."

She didn't reply. He went on:

"Sometimes I would dream that fate would lead you to me. I used to think I had seen you in the street; I would run after every cab that had a shawl or a veil like yours fluttering from the window…"

She seemed to have decided just to let him talk. Arms crossed, head lowered, she stared at the bows on her slippers, occasionally wriggling her toes inside the satin.

Yet she sighed:

"What could be more pitiful than shuffling through a pointless existence like mine? If only our sorrows could be of use to someone, we could take comfort from the thought that the sacrifice was worth it."

So then he praised virtue, duty, silent acts of selflessness, saying that he also felt a powerful need to dedicate himself to something, which he wasn't able to satisfy.

"I'd like to be a nun in a hospital," she said.

"Sadly men don't have such sacred vocations," he replied, "and I don't see any profession… apart from medicine perhaps—"

With a slight shrug Emma interrupted him, and then started lamenting the illness that had nearly claimed her life; it was a pity she wasn't in pain now! Immediately Léon was yearning for *the quiet of the grave*, had even written his will one night, asking to be buried in the beautiful velvet-striped quilt that had been a present from her; for that was what they should both have tried to do, become an ideal by which they could now be reconciled with their past. Because words are like a rolling mill, they smooth out our feelings and make them last longer.

Hearing his idea for the quilt, she asked:

"Why was that?"

"Why?"

He hesitated.

"Because I loved you!"

And congratulating himself for clearing this obstacle, Léon studied her from the corner of his eye.

She was like the sky when a sudden gust of wind blows the clouds away. All the unhappy thoughts that had darkened her blue eyes seemed to withdraw; her whole face glowed.

He waited. Eventually she replied:

"It had occurred to me…"

And they talked about the little incidents of that far-off life whose delights and miseries they had just enclosed within a single word. He remembered the clematis in the arbour, the dresses she wore, the furniture in her room, her whole house.

"And our dear little cactuses, how are they?"

"The frost got them in the winter."

"I used to think about them, you know? I often saw them as they were then, with the sun on the shutters on summer mornings… when I saw your bare arms appear from among the flowers."

"Poor, dear friend!" she said, holding out her hand.

Léon immediately pressed it to his lips. Then after taking a deep breath he said:

"You were a sort of mysterious force for me back then, it enthralled my whole existence. I once came to your house, for instance; but you probably don't remember?"

"Yes I do," she said. "Go on."

"You were downstairs in the anteroom, on the top step, about to go out – wearing a hat with little blue flowers, and despite myself, without being asked, I went with you. Yet with each passing moment I became more and more aware of my foolishness, yet I went on walking near you, never quite daring to follow you but not wanting to leave you. When you went into a shop I stayed outside, I watched you through the window, pulling off your gloves and counting out change on the counter. Then you called on Madame Tuvache, they invited you in, and I stood there like an idiot outside the great heavy door that had just closed behind you."

As she listened, Madame Bovary was surprised to realize that she was that old; all these things coming back to her seemed to lengthen her lifespan, as if they were romantic milestones that she was looking back on; now and then, with her eyes half closed, she said quietly:

"Yes that's right!... That's right!... That's right..."

They heard eight o'clock strike on the various clocks in Beauvoisine, a district full of boarding schools, churches and large, deserted hotels. They had stopped talking; yet as they looked at each other they were conscious of a humming noise in their heads, as if an echo had rung out simultaneously from their staring eyes. Their hands were clasped, and the past, the future, memories and dreams all mingled in this sweet rapture. Night's shadows deepened on the walls, where in the half-light the brash colours of four prints showing scenes from *La Tour de Nesle** with captions in Spanish and French stood out brightly. Through the sash window a triangle of black sky could be seen between the pointed rooftops.

She got up and lit two candles on the chest of drawers, then sat down again.

"Well..." said Léon.

"Well?..." she replied.

He was trying to think of a way to resume their conversation when she said:

"How is it that no one has expressed such feelings to me before?"

Ideal natures were difficult to fathom, the clerk exclaimed. He had loved her the moment he saw her, and he despaired to think of the happiness they could have had if by some good fortune they had met earlier, formed an indissoluble bond.

"I've wondered about that," she answered.

"What a dream!" Léon mumbled.

And, gently feeling the blue edging of her long white belt, he added:

"What's to prevent us from starting again?..."

"No, my dear," she said. "I'm too old... you're too young... forget me! There will be others... they'll love you... and you'll love them."

"Not like you!" he cried.

"You're such a child! Please, let's be sensible! It's what I want!"

She pointed out how impossible their love was, that they should keep it as a friendship between brother and sister, like it was before.

Did she really mean it? Emma probably couldn't be sure herself, so preoccupied was she with the delights of seduction, the need to protect herself from it, and, eyes melting as she gazed at the young man, she gently pushed away his trembling hands, their shy caresses.

"Forgive me," he said, moving back.

Faced with such shyness, which was more of a risk to her than Rodolphe advancing with arms brazenly outstretched, she was seized with something approaching dread. Never had a man seemed so handsome. His whole manner exuded innocence. He lowered his long, delicately curved lashes. His velvety cheeks reddened with lust – so she believed – to possess her, and she felt an irresistible urge to put her lips to them. Then, leaning towards the clock to see the time, she said:

"Heavens, it's late! We've been chatting for ages!"

He took the hint and picked up his hat.

"And I've missed the performance! Poor old Bovary, he left me here especially! Monsieur Lormeaux and his wife from the Rue Grand-Pont were supposed to be taking me."

She wouldn't get another chance, as she was leaving the next day.

"Really?" said Léon.

"Yes."

"But I have to see you again," he went on. "There's something I've got to tell you."

"What?"

"Something... serious... important. Anyway... No, look, you can't go, it's not possible! If only you knew... listen... So didn't you understand? You haven't guessed?..."

"Your words were perfectly clear," said Emma.

"No jokes! That's enough! For pity's sake, let me see you again... once... just once."

"Well!..."

She broke off; then, as if changing her mind:

"But not here!"

"Wherever you like."

"Do you want to..."

She seemed to think for a moment, then just said:

"Tomorrow at eleven, in the cathedral."

"I'll be there!" he cried, taking hold of her hands, but she withdrew them.

They were standing now, him behind her and her looking down, and he leant forward and kissed the nape of her neck again and again.

"You're mad! Quite mad!" she said, with a musical little laugh, while the kisses came one after another.

Leaning over her shoulder, he seemed to seek a look of acquiescence. Her eyes, full of icy dignity, met his. He stepped back, ready to leave. Standing in the doorway, he whispered in a shaking voice:

"Until tomorrow."

She just nodded, then disappeared into the next room like a bird.

That night Emma wrote the clerk an extremely long letter, cancelling their meeting: everything was over, and for the sake of their happiness they should never see each other again. But once she had sealed it she was at a loss, because she didn't have Léon's address.

"I'll give it to him personally," she thought. "He'll be there."

The next morning, windows open and singing to himself on his balcony, Léon polished his court shoes several times. He put on white trousers, fine socks, a green tailcoat, sprinkled every last drop of his cologne over his handkerchief and then, having had his hair curled, he mussed it up to make it more natural.

"It's still far too early!" he thought, looking at the cuckoo clock in the wig-maker's, which said nine o'clock.

He read an old fashion magazine, went out, smoked a cigar, walked up and down several streets, then decided it was time and slowly made his way to the square in front of Notre-Dame.

It was a beautiful summer morning. Silver gleamed in silversmiths' windows, slanting sunlight made the cracks in the grey stone of the cathedral sparkle; in the blue sky a flock of birds whirled round the clover-leaf pinnacles; echoing with voices, the square was scented by the flowers that ran round the edge of the cobbles, roses, jasmine, carnations, narcissi and tuberoses interspersed with moist greenery, catmint and pimpernel for the birds; the fountain babbled away in the centre, and among mountains of cantaloupe melons under large umbrellas, bare-headed stallholders were wrapping bunches of violets in tissue paper.

The young man bought some. It was the first time he had bought flowers for a lady, and as he sniffed them his chest swelled with pride, as if this token of esteem for another was reflected back on him.

But he was afraid of being seen, so he strode into the church.

A Swiss Guard* was standing in the entrance, in the left-hand doorway beneath the statue of the Dancing Marianne,* plume in his hat, rapier at his side, staff in hand, more stately than a cardinal and shining like a sacred vessel.

He came over to Léon with the benign and ingratiating smile used by clergy when addressing children, and said:

"Monsieur is visiting, no doubt? Would Monsieur care to see the unusual features of the church?"

"No," said Léon.

And he walked round the side aisles. Then he went out and looked round the square. Emma wasn't in sight. He went back in and along to the choir.

The nave was mirrored in the water of the stoups, as was the foot of the rib vaults and a few panels of stained glass. But the reflection of the paintings, which broke up on the marble edge, stretched over the flagstones like a carpet of many colours. Brilliant sunlight poured through the three open doors, falling through the church in three vast beams. At the far end a sacristan walked in front of the altar now and then, with the sideways genuflection of a pious man in a hurry. Crystal chandeliers hung motionless. A silver lamp burned in the choir, and from the side chapels, the darkened parts of the church, came what sounded like the occasional sigh, followed by the noise of a grille closing which echoed away into the vaults.

Léon walked along by the wall, his tread deliberate. Never had life seemed so good. She would arrive any moment, delightful, restive, glancing behind to see if anyone had seen her, with her flounced dress, gold lorgnette, thin boots, abounding in all manner of finery, things of which he had never known the like, and with the unutterable allure of virtue on the point of yielding. The church was laid out for her like a gigantic boudoir; the vaults bowed down to hear her confession of love in the shadows; the stained glass blazed its colours abroad to light her face, and the censers would fill the air with perfume to announce the coming of an angel.

Yet she didn't come. He sat on a chair, then noticed a blue window where boatmen were carrying baskets. He studied it for a long time, counted the scales on the fish, the buttonholes on their doublets, while his mind wandered in search of Emma.

To one side the Swiss Guard was privately fuming at this character who was taking the liberty of admiring the cathedral all by himself. He thought it was abominable behaviour, stealing as it were, almost sacrilege.

A swish of silk on flagstones, the brim of a hat, a black cope... It was her! Léon hurried over to meet her.

Emma was pale. She walked quickly.

"Read it!" she said, handing him a piece of paper... "Oh, no!"

And she promptly withdrew her hand and went into a chapel dedicated to the Virgin where, kneeling against a chair, she began to pray.

This sanctimonious caprice annoyed the young man; yet there was something attractive about seeing her plunged in her devotions in the middle of their meeting, like an Andalusian marquise; but as she showed no sign of finishing he was soon bored.

Emma was praying, or endeavouring to pray, in the hope that a sudden solution might descend on her from heaven; to draw down divine intervention she feasted her eyes on the splendour of the tabernacle, inhaled the scent from the great vases of blossoming white gillyflowers, listened hard to the silence, which only made the turmoil in her heart become louder.

She got up, and they were about to leave when the Swiss Guard hurried across:

"Madame is visiting, no doubt?"

"Oh no!" exclaimed the clerk.

"Why not?" she replied.

Because her precarious virtue clung to the Virgin, to sculptures and tombs at every opportunity.

So as to do things *in the right order*, the Swiss Guard took them back to the entrance on the square where, with a gesture of his cane, he pointed out a large circle of black cobblestones that had no inscription or engraving of any kind.

"Here," he said grandly, "you see the circumference of the great bell of Amboise. It weighed forty thousand pounds. There wasn't another like it in the whole of Europe. The craftsman who cast it died of joy—"

"Let's move on," said Léon.

The fellow set off again; returning to the chapel dedicated to the Virgin, he opened his arms in an all-embracing gesture and, prouder than a fruit-grower showing off his orchards, he said:

"Beneath this simple slab lies Pierre de Brézé, Lord de la Varenne and de Brissac, Grand Marshal of Poitou and Governor of Normandy, who died at the battle of Montlhéry on the 16th of July, 1465."

Biting his lip, Léon tapped his foot.

"And to your right, the armour-clad gentleman on the rearing horse is his grandson, Louis de Brézé, Lord de Breval and de Montchauvet, Comte de Maulevrier, Baron de Mauny, Chamberlain to the King, Chevalier of the Order and likewise Governor of Normandy, who died on the 23rd of July 1531, a Sunday, as it says on the inscription; and below, the figure about to descend into the tomb represents this same man. You couldn't ask for a more perfect way to portray eternal darkness, could you?"

Madame Bovary took out her lorgnette. Léon watched her, not moving, not attempting to say a word or make a single gesture, so disheartened was he at this choice between prattle and indifference.

The eternal guide went on:

"Next to him the kneeling woman in tears is his wife, Diane de Poitiers, Comtesse de Brézé, Duchesse de Valentinois, born in 1499, died in 1566; and to your left the one holding the child is the Holy Virgin. Now look this way: these are the Amboise tombs. They were both Cardinal Archbishops of Rouen. This one was a minister under King Louis XII. He did a great deal for the cathedral. He left thirty thousand golden crowns in his will for the poor."

Then, still talking, he urged them into a chapel cluttered with handrails, moved a few and revealed a sort of lump that had the look of a clumsily carved statue.

"Once," he said, with a deep sigh, "this used to grace the tomb of Richard Cœur de Lion, King of England and Duke of Normandy. It was the Calvinists who reduced it to this state, Monsieur. Out of spite they buried it beneath the Archbishop's official seat. See, there's the door that leads to the Monseigneur's residence. Let's move on to the Gargoyle windows."

But Léon hurriedly got a silver coin from his pocket and took Emma by the arm. The Swiss Guard stood aghast, baffled by such misplaced largesse when there was still so much for the visitor to see. To remind him he said:

"But the spire, Monsieur! The spire!"

"No, thank you," said Léon.

"Monsieur is making a mistake! It's 440 feet tall, only nine less than the great pyramid of Egypt. It's cast entirely from iron, it—"

Léon fled; it seemed as if his love, which for almost two hours had been petrified inside the church like a piece of its stone, was about to disappear in a puff of smoke up this cut-off length of pipe, this oblong hutch, this renowned chimney that had landed so ludicrously on the cathedral like some outlandish experiment by an eccentric boilermaker.

"Where are we going to go?" she asked.

But he hurried on without answering. Madame Bovary was just dipping her fingers in holy water when they heard heavy breathing behind them, punctuated by the rhythmic tap of a cane. Léon turned.

"Monsieur!"

"What?"

It was the Swiss Guard, carrying about twenty paper-bound tomes balanced against his stomach. They were books "about the cathedral".

"Idiot!" muttered Léon, dashing out of the church.

A young boy was larking about in the square outside.

"Go and find me a cab!"

The lad shot off like a bullet down the Rue des Quatre-Vents, and for a moment they were alone, looking at each other self-consciously.

"Oh Léon!…" she simpered. "Actually… I don't know… whether I ought to!…" Then she added, with a serious expression:

"It would be most improper."

"How so?" protested the clerk. "People do it in Paris!"

And like an incontrovertible argument that one word decided her.

Yet the cab didn't arrive. Léon was afraid she might go back into the church. Then finally it appeared.

"At least go out by the north door!" cried the Swiss Guard, who was still in the entrance. "You can see the *Resurrection*, the *Last Judgement*, *Paradise*, *King David* and the *Damned* in the fires of hell."

"Where is Monsieur going?" asked the cab driver.

"Wherever you like!" said Léon, pushing Emma into the coach.

And the ponderous vehicle set off.

It drove down the Rue Grand-Pont, across the Place des Arts, the Quai Napoléon, the Pont Neuf, and pulled up sharply at the statue of Pierre Corneille.

"Drive on!" said a voice from inside.

The carriage set off again and, letting itself run away on the downward slope after the Carrefour La Fayette, it drove into the railway station at a gallop.

"No, straight on!" shouted the same voice.

The cab headed out through the railings and, soon coming to the Mall, trotted gently under the elm trees. The cabbie wiped his brow, put his leather hat between his legs and drove at speed past the side streets, out to the lawns beside the river.

It went along the pebbled towpath by the river, and for quite a while in the direction of Oyssel, beyond the islands.

But then suddenly it sped off through Quatre-Mares, Sotteville, the Grande-Chaussée, the Rue d'Elbeuf, and made its third stop outside the Jardin des Plantes.

"Keep going!" cried the voice, even angrier now.

And setting off once again it drove through Saint-Sever, along the Quai des Curandiers, the Quai aux Meules, back over the bridge, across the Place du Champs-de-Mars and past the garden of the hospital, where old men in black coats were walking in the sunshine along an ivy-clad terrace. It went back up the Boulevard Bouvreuil, all the way along the Boulevard Cauchoise, then up Mont-Riboudet as far as Deville hill.

Then it came back, and impartially, without instructions, it roamed at will. It was seen in Saint-Pol, Lescure, Mont Gargan, the Rouge-Mare and on the Place du Gaillardbois; on the Rue Maladrerie, the Rue Dinanderie, outside Saint-Romain, Saint-Vivien, Saint-Maclou, Saint-Niçaise – outside the Customs House – at the lower Old Tower, the Trois-Pipes and the Monumental Cemetery. From his seat the driver looked in desperation at taverns. He couldn't understand what sort of motion madness was driving these two people to not want to stop. Occasionally he tried to, only to hear shouts of rage from behind. So he whipped up his two sweating nags even harder, not watching out for bumps, heedlessly running into things, dejected and almost weeping with thirst, exhaustion and misery.

Among wagons and barrels at the harbour, in the streets and at marker stones, local people stared in amazement at this unheard-of thing for a provincial town, a carriage with its blinds pulled down, and which kept reappearing, more tightly sealed than a tomb, pitching and tossing like a ship at sea.

Once, in the middle of the day in open countryside, as the sun was beating down at its fiercest on the old silver lamps, an ungloved hand appeared from behind the yellow canvas curtains and threw away some torn-up scraps of paper, which scattered on the wind and landed like white butterflies in a field of flowering red clover.

Then at about six o'clock the carriage stopped in a lane in Beauvoisine, and a woman got out and walked away with her veil lowered, not looking back.

2

WHEN SHE GOT TO THE HOTEL, Madame Bovary was surprised not to see the stagecoach. But Hivert, who had waited for her for almost an hour, had eventually gone.

Yet there was nothing forcing her to leave, although she had promised to be home that night. Charles was expecting her, and already she felt that craven submissiveness which for many women is both the punishment for and the price of adultery.

She packed hurriedly, paid the bill, hired a cabriolet in the yard and, harassing the groom, urging him on, continually asking what time it was and how far they had come, she managed to catch up with the *Hirondelle* just as it reached the outskirts of Quincampoix.

No sooner had she installed herself in a corner than her eyes closed, and only opened again at the bottom of the hill where she saw Félicité standing outside the blacksmith's house, looking out for her. Hivert reined in the horses, and standing on tiptoe to reach the window of the coach, the cook said cryptically:

"You've to go to Monsieur Homais's right away, Madame. It's urgent."

The village was completely quiet as always. There were small pink heaps steaming on street corners, because it was jam-making time, and everyone in Yonville did it on the same day. But outside the pharmacist's shop a much larger heap was attracting admiration, superior to all the rest in the way a professional kitchen is to a family oven, or a public requirement to mere personal whim.

She went in. The large armchair had been turned upside down, pages from the *Fanal de Rouen* were spread out on the floor between the two pestles. She opened the door from the passage, and there in the kitchen, among brown earthenware jars full of redcurrants, caster sugar, cube sugar, scales on the table, preserving pans on the stove, she saw the entire Homais family, young and old, aprons round their necks and forks in hands. Justin was standing with his head hanging as the pharmacist shouted:

"Who told you to get it from the inner sanctum?"

"What is it? What's the matter?"

"The matter?" replied the apothecary. "We're making jam. It's cooking, but it's boiling over because there's too much, so I ask for another pan. And so out of indolence, out of bone idleness, he goes to my laboratory and takes the key for the inner sanctum from its hook!"

This was the apothecary's name for the closet in the attic that was full of the utensils and materials of his profession. He often spent whole hours in there by himself, labelling, decanting and repackaging; he regarded it as not just a simple shop but a veritable sanctuary, from where all manner of pills, boluses, tisanes, lotions and potions created by his own fair hands would duly issue, and which would spread his fame round the locality. Not another soul set foot in there; he revered it so much that he swept it himself. Because if the pharmacist's shop, open to all and sundry, was his showplace, his pride and joy, the inner sanctum was the refuge where, alone with his ego, Homais could delight in the pursuit of his private interests, and so Justin's blunder seemed to him an act of unspeakable sacrilege; and, redder than the currants, he repeated:

"Yes, the inner sanctum! With the key that's used to lock up the acids and caustic alkalis! To get a spare pan! A pan with a lid, that I might never use! Of vital importance in the delicate processes of our profession! Dash it all! We have to differentiate, not use something that's designed for pharmaceutical work for domestic purposes! It's like carving chicken with a scalpel, or as if a judge—"

"Do calm down!" said Madame Homais.

Tugging at his frock coat, Athalie said:

"Papa, Papa!"

"Leave me alone," the apothecary went on, "leave me alone, dammit! I might as well open a grocer's shop for Heaven's sake! Go on then! Don't show respect for anything! Break it! Smash it! Let the leeches go! Burn the marshmallow! Use the jars for pickled gherkins! Tear up the bandages!"

"But you've—" said Emma.

"Just a second! Have you any idea of the risks you were taking?… Didn't you see anything in the corner on the left, on the third shelf? Speak to me, answer me, say something!"

"I… don't know," stammered the boy.

"Oh, you don't know! Well I do! You saw a bottle made of blue glass, sealed with yellow wax, which contains a white powder, and on which I myself wrote: 'Danger!' And do you know what's in it? Arsenic! And you were going to touch it! Or pick up a pan next to it!"

"Next to it!" cried Madame Homais, clasping her hands. "Arsenic! You could have poisoned us!"

And the children started screaming, as if their insides were already contorting in agony.

"Or poison a patient!" the apothecary went on. "Do you want me to end up in the dock? See me dragged off to the scaffold? Don't you realize how much care I take handling things, despite all the years of experience I've got? I often frighten myself just thinking of my responsibilities! The government tyrannizes us, the ludicrous regulations we're governed by are a sword of Damocles over our head!"

By now Emma had lost any thought of asking why they had wanted her to come, while the pharmacist carried on breathlessly:

"So this is how you thank me for my kindness! This is how you pay me back for the fatherly care and attention I've lavished on you! Where would you be without me? What would you be doing? Who feeds you, educates you, clothes you, provides you with the means of taking up a worthy place in society one day? But you have to put your back into it, get your hands dirty as they say. *Fabricando fit faber, age quod agis.*"*

So incensed was he that he quoted Latin. He would have quoted Chinese or Greenlandic had he known how, because he was in one of those fits of rage when the soul gives us a glimpse of what it contains, like a storm at sea when the surface of the water opens up from the seaweed on the shore to the sand of the ocean bed.

Then he continued:

"I'm beginning to regret taking you on! I'd have done better to leave you to rot in the misery and filth you were born in! All you'll ever be fit for is minding the cows! You've got no aptitude for science! You can barely stick a label on. And you live in my house like a lord, a pig in clover, feeding off the fat of the land."

Emma turned to Madame Homais:

"I was told to come—"

"Oh my Heavens!" the woman broke in, sounding sad. "However am I going to tell you?... It's a calamity!"

But she didn't finish. The apothecary roared:

"Empty it! Scrub it! Put it back! And hurry up!"

And as he shook him by the collar of his smock, a book fell out of Justin's pocket.

The boy bent down to get it. But Homais was quicker, and picking it up he stared at it, mouth and eyes wide open.

"*Conjugal... Love!*" he read, pausing between the words. "Very nice! Very nice! Delightful! And with engravings too!... Oh, this is too much!"

Madame Homais came over.

"No, don't look!"

The children wanted to see the pictures.

"Out!" he ordered.

They went out.

First he strode up and down with the book still open in his hand, eyes rolling, spluttering, puffing, incandescent. Then he came and stood in front of his pupil with his arms folded:

"You've got all the vices then, wretch that you are!... Be careful, you're on a slippery slope!... I don't suppose you stopped to think that this vile book might find its way into the hands of my children, light the touch paper inside their heads, tarnish Athalie's innocence, corrupt Napoléon! He's already developing into a man. In fact are you sure he hasn't read it? Can you assure me—"

"For goodness' sake, Monsieur," said Emma, "haven't you got something to tell me?..."

"That's right, Madame... Your father-in-law is dead!"

Monsieur Bovary senior had died suddenly from a stroke two days before, after getting up from the dinner table, and out of exaggerated concern for Emma's feelings, Charles had asked Homais to break the news gently to her.

He had contemplated what he was going to say, polished it, rounded it out, given it cadence; it was a masterpiece of tact and transition, finely turned, full of subtlety; but his anger swept all rhetoric aside.

Not wanting to hear details, Emma left, because Monsieur Homais had gone back to ranting and raving. Yet he did finally calm down, and started muttering in a fatherly voice while fanning himself with his embroidered silk cap.

"Not that I wholly disapprove of the book! The author was a medical man. It has scientific angles to it that it's not a bad thing for a man to know, which I'd go so far to say that a man ought to know. But later! Later! At least wait till you're a man, when your character is more established."

Hearing Emma knock, Charles, who was waiting for her, came over with his arms outstretched, saying tearfully:

"Oh, my dear love…"

And he leant forward gently to kiss her. But at the touch of his lips she remembered those of the other man, and put her hand to her face with a shudder.

Yet she still said:

"Yes I know… I know…"

He showed her the letter from his mother, in which she described what had happened without cant or sentiment. The only thing she regretted was that her husband hadn't received the last rites, having died in the street, outside a café in Doudeville where he had been at a reunion dinner with some old comrades.

Emma gave him back the letter and, out of decorum, at supper she pretended not to have any appetite. But since he insisted she set to with a will, while Charles sat opposite, utterly devastated.

Occasionally he looked up and stared at her with anguished eyes. At one point he sighed:

"I'd have liked to see him again!"

She didn't say anything. But eventually realizing that she should, she asked:

"How old was he, your father?"

"Fifty-eight!"

"Ah!"

And that was all.

A quarter of an hour later he added:

"My poor mother!… What'll become of her?"

She just shrugged.

Seeing her so withdrawn, Charles took it to be grief, and forced himself not to talk about it, so as not to make the pain any worse for her. Yet stirring up his own he asked:

"Did you enjoy yourself yesterday?"

"Yes."

When the table had been cleared, neither Bovary nor Emma got up, and gradually, the more she reflected, the more the prosaicness of the scene drove any compassion from her heart. He seemed puny, feeble, worthless, a pathetic man in every way. How could she rid herself of him? Would the evening never end? It was as if something was numbing her, like a cloud of opium.

They heard the sharp sound of a walking stick on the wooden floor in the hall. It was Hippolyte, with Madame's luggage. As he put it down he swung his wooden leg round painfully in a quarter circle.

"He doesn't even notice it now!" she said to herself as she watched the poor devil, his mop of red hair dripping with sweat.

Bovary got some coppers from his purse and, seemingly oblivious to how humiliating the mere presence of this man was, standing there like a living rebuke for his inveterate incompetence, seeing Léon's violets on the mantelpiece he said:

"Oh my, what a pretty bouquet!"

"Yes," she said matter-of-factly. "I bought them this afternoon from... a beggar woman."

Charles picked up the violets and, his tear-reddened eyes brightening, he sniffed them gently. She quickly took them and put them in a glass of water.

The next day Madame Bovary senior arrived. She and her son shed many tears together. On the pretext of having things to organize, Emma kept her distance.

The day after that, the three of them had to discuss the funeral arrangements. They took their workboxes and sat under the arbour by the river.

Charles thought about his father, surprised to find he felt so attached to a man who up till now he had believed he hardly loved. Madame Bovary senior thought about her husband. The bad times seemed to have been worthwhile now. Everything faded in the face of those spontaneous regrets born of long years of routine, and as she sewed, every now and then a big tear trickled down her nose and hung there. Emma was thinking that less than forty-eight hours ago they were together, far away from everything and everyone, exhilarated and unable to stop feasting their eyes on each other. She tried to recapture every detail of that one lost day. But the presence of a mother-in-law and husband hampered her. She would have liked not to be able to hear, not to see, so as not to interfere with the contemplation of her love which, however hard she tried, gradually disappeared beneath worldly sensations.

She was unpicking the lining of a dress, the remnants scattered round her; old mother Bovary was squeaking away with the scissors, not looking up from her work, and Charles, in selvedge slippers and the old brown frock coat which he used as a dressing gown, sat with his hands in his pockets without saying a word either; nearby, dressed in a little white pinafore, Berthe was raking the sand on the paths with her spade.

Suddenly they saw Monsieur Lheureux the draper come through the gate.

He had come to offer his services *in view of the sad occasion.* Emma replied that she could manage. But the shopkeeper didn't give up easily.

"Do please forgive me," he said, "but I'd like a private word."

Then lowering his voice he added:

"It's regarding the little matter... you remember?"

Charles blushed scarlet.

"Oh yes!... Of course."

And in his discomfiture he turned to his wife:

"My darling... do you think you could?..."

She seemed to understand because she got up, and Charles turned to his mother:

"It's nothing! Some trifling housekeeping matter I expect."

He had no wish for her to find about the promissory note, fearing what she would say.

Once they were alone, in fairly unambiguous terms Monsieur Lheureux congratulated Emma on her inheritance, and then chatted about nothing in particular, the espaliers, the harvest, his health, which was always *so-so, neither one thing nor t'other.* Because he worked hellishly hard just to make ends meet, despite what people said.

Emma let him talk. These last two days she had been unbelievably bored!

"I see you're completely recovered!" he went on. "Heavens, your poor husband was in a fine old state! He's a good man, although we've had our problems, him and me."

She asked him what he meant. Charles had deliberately not told her about the dispute over the merchandise.

"You know perfectly well!" said Lheureux. "It was over those little luxuries of yours, the travelling cases."

He had lowered the brim of his hat over his eyes and, hands behind his back, whistling and smiling, he looked her straight in the face in the most insufferable fashion. Did he have his suspicions? She stood there, sunk in trepidation. Eventually he went on:

"But we've resolved our differences, and I've come to offer him a new arrangement."

It was to renew the promissory note that Bovary had signed. But of course Monsieur would do as he saw fit; he mustn't fret himself, especially not at the moment when he was going to be snowed under with other worries.

"It might be better for him to get someone else to take it on, yourself for example; with power of attorney it would be simple and convenient, and then we could do some business, you and I…"

She didn't understand. He dropped the subject. And then getting down to business, Lheureux said Madame could do worse than to order something from him. He would send her twelve metres of barège, enough to make a dress.

"The material you have already is good enough for wearing about the house. But you need something for paying calls in. I noticed the moment I came in. I've got a quick eye, me."

He didn't send the cloth, he delivered it in person. Then he came back to take measurements; he found reasons to make other calls, always doing his best to be pleasant, obliging, ingratiating – pledging his allegiance as Homais would have said – never failing to drop helpful hints to Emma about a power of attorney. He didn't mention the promissory note. She didn't give it a thought; when she was just starting to recover from her illness Charles had said something to her about it, but her mind had been in such a whirl since then that she didn't remember. Besides, she was careful not to raise the subject of money; old mother Bovary was surprised, but put her change of heart down to the religious feelings she had developed while she was ill.

But as soon as she had left, Emma had Charles marvelling at how practically minded she was. He ought to make enquiries, check on the mortgages, find out if it was worth putting things up for auction or liquidating assets. She used technical expressions quite arbitrarily, as well as big words such as "bill of exchange", "writ of summons", "contingency fund", and never stopped exaggerating the problems with the estate; and then one day she showed him an example of a standard authority to "manage and administer his affairs, arrange all borrowings, sign and endorse all bills of exchange, pay all sums due, etc." She had benefited from Lheureux's lessons.

Innocently, Charles asked her where the document had come from.

"Monsieur Guillaumin."

And then with all the equanimity in the world she added:

"I wouldn't trust it too much. Lawyers have such a bad name! Perhaps we should get some advice... from... but we only know... Ah, no one!"

"Apart from Léon..." said Charles, who was busy thinking.

Of course, it was difficult to come to an agreement by letter. So she volunteered to go herself. He said it was too much trouble. She insisted. He bombarded her with excessive concerns. In the end, in mock revolt, she cried:

"For Heaven's sake, I'm going."

"You're so kind!" he said, kissing her on the forehead.

The next morning she boarded the *Hirondelle* to Rouen to go and ask Monsieur Léon's advice; she stayed for three days.

3

T HEY WERE THREE FULL DAYS, sublime, glorious days, a honeymoon. They stayed at the Hôtel de Boulogne by the harbour. And there they remained, doors and shutters closed, with the iced cordials that they had sent up every morning and flowers scattered over the floor.

In the evening they took a covered boat and went for dinner on one of the islands.

It was the time of day when caulkers' mallets could be heard echoing against the hulls of ships in the nearby shipyards. Smoke from burning tar drifted through the trees, and large oily patches floated on the surface of the river like sheets of Florentine bronze, rippling erratically in the purple sunlight.

They put in to shore among moored boats whose long cables rubbed the top of their own.

Imperceptibly the sounds of the town grew fainter, the rattle of carts, the clamour of voices, the yapping of dogs on the decks of ships. She untied her hat and they landed on their island.

They sat in the downstairs room of an inn with black net hanging over the doorway. They ate fried whitebait, cherries and cream. They lay on the grass; they kissed under the poplar trees; and like two Robinson Crusoes they would have liked to spend the rest of their days in this little spot, which in their beatific state they thought the most wonderful in the whole world. It wasn't the first time they had seen trees, blue sky, lawns, heard water trickle or the wind rustling in the leaves, but they had probably never admired these things before, as if nature didn't exist then, or only began to be beautiful once their desires were satisfied.

Then, late at night, they came back. The boat followed along the banks of the islands. They sat in the stern, hidden in shadow, not speaking. The square oars rang out in the iron rowlocks; it was like the ticking of a metronome in the silence, while behind them the painter kept up its gentle lapping in the water.

Once, the moon came out, and finding the evening star melancholy, poetic, they couldn't help but hymn the night; she even sang:

> One night we were sailing, do you recall?* etc.

Her soft, melodious voice disappeared across the waves; the breeze bore off the trilling birdsong that Léon heard passing, like wings beating around him.

She sat opposite, leaning against the bulkhead where moonlight came through one of the open shutters of the portholes. Her black dress, its folds fanned out around her, made her look thinner, taller. She held her head up, hands clasped, and looked at the sky. Sometimes the shadow of the willows would plunge her into darkness, only to reappear suddenly like a vision in the moonlight.

Sitting on the deck beside her, Léon found a dark-red silk ribbon.

The boatman studied it:

"Maybe it's from that party I took out the other day," he said. "A right lot of jokers they were, ladies and gentlemen with cakes, champagne, cornets, the whole kit and caboodle! There was one especially, a tall good-looking fellow with a little moustache, he was really funny! And they kept saying something like: 'Come on, tell us a story, Adolphe... Dodolphe...' I think it was."

She shuddered.

"Are you all right?" said Léon, coming closer.

"It's nothing. Probably just the cold night air."

"...And he certainly wasn't short of women neither," added the old sailor quietly, thinking to make conversation with the strangers.

And then spitting into his palms he took up the oars again.

But they had to part. The goodbyes were sad. He would have to send his letters via old mother Rolet, and she gave him such detailed instructions about how to use two envelopes that he was filled with admiration for her guile in the ways of love.

"So you promise everything will be all right?" she asked as they kissed for the last time.

"Yes, of course!"

But afterwards, as he walked back through the streets on his own, he wondered: "So why is she so anxious about this power of attorney?"

4

LÉON WAS SOON ASSUMING AN AIR OF SUPERIORITY among his colleagues, avoiding their company and paying no attention to his work. He just waited for her letters; he read them over and over. He wrote to her. He conjured up her memory with every fibre of his desire. Instead of fading in her absence, his longing to see her again grew so strong that one Saturday morning he got up and left the office.

When from the top of the hill he saw the church tower in the valley, its tin flag turning in the wind, he experienced that sensation of delight mingled with jubilant vanity and self-centred pity that a millionaire must feel when he goes back to the village where he was born.

He loitered round her house. There was a light on in the kitchen. He waited to see her shadow on the blinds. But nothing appeared.

When old mother Lefrançois saw him she let out a cry of surprise, and said he had got "taller and thinner", while Artémise thought he was "browner and more broad-shouldered".

He had dinner in the little dining room like he used to, but alone, without the tax-collector for company, because Binet, *tired* of having to wait for the *Hirondelle*, had brought his mealtime forward by an hour, and now dined at five o'clock sharp, while still maintaining that *the old jalopy made him late.*

Meanwhile Léon made a decision: he would go and call on the doctor. Madame was up in her room and only came down a quarter of an hour later. Monsieur seemed delighted to see him, but didn't leave the house all evening, or the next day.

He saw her on her own late that night, in the alley behind the garden – in the alley, like with the other one! There was a thunderstorm, and they talked under an umbrella in the pale glow of the lightning.

Parting was unbearable.

"I'd sooner die!" said Emma.

She clung to his arm, doubled up with tears.

"Goodbye!... Farewell!... When will I see you again?"

They turned back and embraced again, and she promised she would find a way, any way, and soon, to come and see him at least once a week. Emma was in no doubt. In fact she was full of confidence. She was about to come into some money.

So she bought a pair of yellow curtains with broad stripes for her room, which Monsieur Lheureux peddled to her as being a good price; she had her heart set on a carpet, and Lheureux, saying that it was "as easy as falling off a log", kindly promised to supply one. She couldn't manage without his services now. She would send for him a dozen times a day, and he was there immediately without a murmur, laying out his wares. Still less did people understand why old mother Rolet came for lunch every day, and even paid her special visits.

It was around this time, the beginning of winter, that she suddenly became enthused with music.

As Charles was listening to her one evening, she kept playing the same piece over and over, constantly getting angry with herself, although he couldn't tell the difference.

"Bravo!" he exclaimed. "Very good!... No, you're wrong! Don't be silly!"

"No no, it's atrocious! I'm so rusty."

The next evening he asked her to play him something else.

"If you insist, just to please you."

And Charles was forced to admit that she had lost her touch somewhat. She missed notes, became confused, then stopped abruptly:

"That's enough!" she said. "I ought to have lessons, but…"

And biting her lip she added:

"Twenty francs a time is too much!"

"Yes, rather… it is a bit," said Charles with an inane giggle. "Still, I think we could get them for less; there are unknown musicians who are often better than the famous ones."

"Find one for me," Emma replied.

When he got home the next day, he kept giving her an artful look. Eventually he couldn't contain himself:

"You can be so stubborn!" he said. "I was over at Barfeuchères today. And well! Madame Liégeard told me that her three daughters, who are all at the Convent of La Miséricode, have piano lessons for fifty sous a time, and from a first-class teacher too!"

She just shrugged, and didn't open the lid of the piano again.

But when she walked past it (and if Bovary was there), she would sigh:

"Oh, my poor little piano!"

When she had visitors she would be sure to let you know that she had given up music, and wasn't able to take it up again for serious reasons. Then they felt sorry for her. What a pity! She was so talented! They mentioned it to Bovary. They made him feel ashamed, most of all the pharmacist:

"You're making a mistake!" he said. "We should never let natural abilities go to waste. And just think, my dear fellow, by encouraging Madame to play you'll be saving money on your daughter's musical education later on! For my part, I think mothers should educate their children themselves. It's an idea of Rousseau's, still slightly novel perhaps, but it'll catch on in the end, like breastfeeding and vaccinations."

So Charles brought up the subject of the piano again. Emma replied scathingly that it would be better to sell it. Because in some vague way, to see it go, the poor piano that had given her so much self-satisfaction, was for Madame Bovary like killing part of herself.

"If you want the occasional lesson…" he said, "it wouldn't exactly break the bank."

"But lessons are only any good if you keep them up," she protested.

Which is how she got her husband to agree to her going into town once a week to see her lover. After a month, people were saying that she had made considerable progress.

5

I T WAS THURSDAY. She got up and dressed quietly so not to wake Charles, who would have wanted to know why she was getting ready so early. Then she paced up and down; she went to the window, looked out at the square. Daybreak was making its way between the pillars of the covered market, and on the pharmacist's house, whose shutters were closed, you could see the large letters of his sign in the pale tints of dawn.

When the clock said quarter-past seven she went over to the Lion d'Or, where a yawning Artémise opened the door for her. She raked up some hot coals for Madame from under the ashes. Emma stayed in the kitchen by herself. Now and then she went out into the yard. In no great hurry Hivert was harnessing the horses, while listening to Madame Lefrançois, who, with her nightcap-clad head sticking out of the window, was burdening him with errands and instructions that would have baffled any other man. Emma stamped her booted feet on the cobblestones.

Finally, once he had had something to eat, put on his cape, lit his pipe and picked up his whip, he settled himself calmly onto the box.

The *Hirondelle* set off at a gentle trot, stopping occasionally during the first three quarters of a league to pick up passengers, who stood on the side of the road outside their gates, looking out for him. The ones who had let him know the day before, he waited for; some were still in bed; Hivert called out, yelled, cursed, then climbed off the box and went and hammered on the door. The wind blew through the cracked windows of the coach.

Meanwhile the four bench seats filled up, the coach drove on, apple trees filed past one after another, and between two long ditches of brackish yellow water the road tapered away towards the horizon. Emma was familiar with every inch of the route; she knew that after a certain pasture there was a marker post, then an elm tree, a barn or a roadman's hut; sometimes she closed her eyes to surprise herself. Yet she never lost the distinct sensation of having a long way to go.

Eventually brick-built houses appeared, the roadway reverberated beneath the wheels, and the *Hirondelle* was gliding past gardens where, seen through an open fence, there were statues, ornamental hillocks planted with vines, yew trees trimmed into shapes and a swing. Then in the blink of an eye the town was there.

Like an amphitheatre in the mist, it spread hazily beyond its bridges. Then the open countryside began again, rising without varying all the way to where the pale sky met the blur of the horizon. Seen from above, the landscape was as motionless as a painting; ships at anchor were wedged together in one corner; the river traced a wide curve at the foot of green hills, and the long narrow islands resembled big black fish floating on the water. Great plumes of brown smoke puffed from factory chimneys. The drone of foundries and the clarion chime of churches rose out of the fog. Along the boulevards, leafless trees created a purple undergrowth among the houses, and glistening with rain the rooftops shimmered from many different heights and angles. Sometimes a gust of wind swept the clouds towards St Catherine's hill, sylphlike waves breaking silently against a cliff.

There was something about the lives that gathered here which took her breath away; her heart overflowed, as if the hundred thousand others that were beating in the town had suddenly filled it with the heady fumes of passions that she imagined they felt. At the sight of the place her love began to grow, filling with the rising ferment of faint humming sounds. She poured it out again onto the squares, the esplanades and streets, and the ancient Norman town lay before her like a mighty capital, as if she were driving into Babylon. She hung her hands out of the window, swallowed great breaths of the breeze; the three horses galloped, stones crunched in the mud, the coach swayed, Hivert called out to carts farther along, while townspeople who had spent the night in Guillaume woods made their way gently down the hill in a small family carriage.

They stopped at the toll gate; Emma took off her clogs, changed her gloves, straightened her shawl, and a short way farther on she got out of the *Hirondelle*.

The town was just waking. Shop assistants in silk caps were scrubbing the shopfronts, and on the street corners women with baskets under their arms gave songlike cries. She walked along close to the wall, looking down and smiling beneath her black veil.

For fear of being seen she didn't usually take the shortest route. She plunged into dark sombre alleyways and came out at the end of the Rue Nationale near the fountain, covered in sweat. It was the theatre district, full of taverns and whores. Carts carrying pieces of shaking scenery often drove past close by her. Waiters in aprons poured sand on the paving stones between small green shrubs. There was a smell of absinthe, cigars and oysters.

She turned down a street, and recognized him from the long curly hair beneath his hat.

Léon carried on walking. She followed him to the hotel; he went upstairs, opened the door, walked in... How tightly they embraced!

After the kisses came the words. They told each other about their week, its sorrows, its forebodings, the anxiety over letters; but that was all forgotten now, and they looked into each other's eyes, laughed with sensual delight, called each other by pet names.

The big mahogany bed was in the *bateau* style. The bottoms of its red full-length Levantine silk curtains were gathered in tightly, then flared out at the head of the bed – and nothing was as beautiful as his dark hair and pale skin against their crimson colour when she modestly hid her face behind bare arms.

With its subdued carpet, whimsical decoration and quiet light, the warm room seemed designed for passionate intimacy. When sunlight shone in, the spirelike bedposts, brass curtain hooks and heavy firedogs would suddenly gleam. Between the candelabra on the mantelpiece were two large pink seashells, the sort you can hear the sea in if you hold them to your ear.

How they loved this room of happiness, despite its faded grandeur! The furniture was always in the right place, and they sometimes found hairpins that she had left behind under the base of the clock the Thursday before. They had lunch by the fire on a little pedestal table inlaid with rosewood. Emma cut the meat into pieces and put it on his plate for him, along with all manner of other playful attentions; when champagne bubbles overflowed from the delicate glass onto her rings, she gave a high, licentious laugh. They were so submerged in each other that they imagined this was home, that they would live out their days here like the eternal young couple. They spoke of "our room", "our carpet", "our chairs", she even referred to a gift from Léon as "my slippers", one of her passing fancies. They were of pink satin bordered with swansdown. When she sat on his lap, her leg, too short, dangled in mid-air, with the dainty, backless little shoes just kept on by her bare toes.

For the first time he enjoyed the indescribable subtlety of feminine graces to the full. Never had he known such elegance of speech, such discreet simplicity of dress, this look of a sleeping dove. He marvelled at the transports of her soul and the lace of her skirts. For wasn't she *a woman of the world*, a married woman – in fact a true mistress!

With the variety of her moods, by turn mystical then merry, talkative, secretive, tempestuous, blasé, she evoked a thousand and one desires in him, conjured up instincts or memories. She was the lover from every novel, the heroine from every play, the mysterious *she* from every book of verse. On her shoulders he saw the amber light of *L'Odalisque au bain*; hers was the long bodice of a feudal chatelaine; she looked like *La femme pâle de Barcelone*,* but above all she was an Angel!

As he looked at her he would feel as if his soul had fled his body and flown to her, pouring over her head like a wave, trickling down onto the whiteness of her breast.

He would get down in front of her and, his elbows resting on her knees, he would gaze at her, smiling, and offer her his brow.

She would lean towards him and whisper, as if choked with elation: "Don't move! Don't speak! Look at me! There's something in your eyes which is so good for me!"

She called him "child":

"Do you love me, child?"

But she would barely wait for a reply, so swiftly did her lips fly to his.

On the clock there was a small bronze figure of Cupid that held out its arms with a simpering expression beneath a garland of gilt flowers. They often laughed at it, but when the time came for them to part, everything would seem serious.

Standing face to face they would keep saying to each other:

"Till Thursday!... Till Thursday!"

Then suddenly, taking his head in her hands, she would kiss him on the forehead, cry "Goodbye!" and rush down the stairs.

She would go to a hairdresser's in the Rue de la Comédie to have her hair rearranged in its headbands. It would just be getting dark; they would be lighting the gas lamps in the shop.

She would hear the little bell on the theatre, summoning thespians for the performance, and across the street she would see white-faced men and faded women going in the stage door.

It was warm in the small, low room, where the stove thrummed among all the wigs and pomades. The smell of curling tongs and the greasy hands that wielded them made her feel faint, and she gradually dozed off in her gown. While he was doing her hair, the assistant would often offer her tickets for a masked ball.

But then she had to leave! She walked back through the streets; she came to the Hôtel Croix Rouge; she retrieved her clogs from under the seat where she had left them that morning and squeezed herself into her seat among the impatient passengers. A few got out at the bottom of the hill, and she was left on her own in the coach.

At every bend in the road, more of the lights of the town could be seen, creating a scintillating haze over the mass of houses. Emma knelt on the cushions and lost herself in the dazzling sight. She sobbed, called Léon's name, said tender things, blew kisses that were lost on the breeze.

Walking among the stagecoaches on the hill was a poor wretch who wandered along, stick in hand. His rags hung off him, his face was hidden beneath a battered old beaver hat shaped like a pudding basin; but when he took it off, in place of eyelids were two gaping, bloody sockets. The skin was red and flayed, fluid trickled out of them and congealed into green scabs round his nose, whose blackened nostrils snorted in uncontrollable spasms. When he spoke he tipped his head back and gave a stupid laugh; and his eyes rolled up till their bluish pupils met the edge of his raw, open cuts.

As he walked along behind the carriages he sang a little song:

On hot days when it's nice and sunny
The young girls start to feel lovey-dovey.

The rest was about birds, sunshine, leaves on the trees.

Sometimes he suddenly appeared behind Emma, with his hat off. She moved away with a scream. Hivert came over and made fun of him. He told him he ought to have a stall at the Saint-Romain fair, or jokingly asked after his sweetheart.

While the coach was moving his hat would often suddenly come through the window as he clung to the running board with the other arm and got spattered with mud from the wheels. Weak and whining at first, his voice rose to a shriek. It trailed off into the night like a lament, the expression of some unnamed anguish; and among the jingling of the harness bells, the whisper of the trees and the hollow rumbling of the coach, there was something desolate about it that left Emma distraught. Like a whirlwind in an abyss it went to the very depths of her soul, swept her away to a place of empty, untold despair. But noticing that the coach was tilting, Hivert lashed out at the blind man with his whip. It bit into his sores and he fell into the mud with a howl.

Eventually the *Hirondelle*'s passengers fell asleep, some with their mouths open, others with their chins on their chests, leaning against the person next to them, or with their arm through the strap, rocking with the motion of the carriage. Shining in through the chocolate-coloured calico curtains, the faint light of the lamp swaying above the horses' hindquarters threw blood-red shadows over the motionless people. Drunk with misery, Emma shivered in her clothes, her feet got colder and colder, and she felt death in her heart.

At home Charles would be waiting for her; the *Hirondelle* was always late on Thursdays. Then at last Madame arrived! She gave her daughter the briefest of kisses. Dinner wasn't ready, but what matter! She forgave the cook; the girl seemed to get away with everything nowadays.

Seeing how pale she was, her husband often asked if she was unwell.

"No," Emma would say.

"You're in a funny mood," he would protest.

"Oh, it's nothing, nothing!"

There were days when she would go up to her room the moment she got back, and Justin would be there, walking around quietly, more attentive than the most expert chambermaid. He would lay out matches, the candlestick, a book, a nightdress, turn back the sheets.

"All right," she would say, "that's fine, off you go."

He would be standing there wide-eyed, arms hanging by his side, as if caught up in the threads of a dream.

The whole of the next day would be awful, and those that followed made worse by Emma's impatience to retrieve her happiness – a bitter, grasping lustfulness ablaze with familiar images which burst out in Léon's arms on the seventh day. His passions were concealed by his effusive wonder and gratitude. Emma savoured his love quietly, submerged herself in it, kept it alive with every ploy her affection possessed for fear of losing it.

She often said to him, a note of sadness in her voice:

"You'll leave me, oh yes you will!... You'll get married!... You're no different from all the others."

And he asked:

"What others?"

"Men in general," she answered.

And then, pushing him away listlessly she would add:

"You're unspeakable, all of you!"

One day when they were talking in a philosophical way about worldly disenchantments, she let it be known (either to test his jealousy or perhaps succumbing to a need to express her feelings) that she had loved someone else before him – "But not like you!" she hastened to add, swearing on her daughter's life "that nothing had happened".

The young man believed her, but persisted in asking what *he* did.

"He was a ship's captain, my dear."

Was this a way of preventing him from making more enquiries, while putting herself on a pedestal by claiming to have captured the heart of a man who was clearly warlike, accustomed to flattery?

So the clerk became conscious of his inferior position; he yearned for epaulettes, medals, a title. She must like that sort of thing – and he began to have suspicions about her spendthrift habits.

Yet Emma kept quiet about many of her wilder excesses, such as the longing to own a blue tilbury pulled by an English horse and driven by a footman in top boots to bring her to Rouen. It was Justin who had prompted this fad by imploring her to take him on as her valet, and even if the lack of such a coach did nothing to lessen the pleasure of her arrival, it undoubtedly increased the bitterness of the return journey.

When they talked about Paris, she would often sigh:

"Wouldn't it be wonderful if we lived there!"

"Aren't we happy here?" the young man would answer, stroking her headbands.

"You're right," she would say, "I'm mad; kiss me!"

She was more delightful than ever to her husband, made pistachio caramels for him, played waltzes after dinner. He thought he was the luckiest man alive, and Emma carried on without a care, until one evening when he suddenly asked:

"It is Mademoiselle Lempereur who gives you lessons, isn't it?"

"Yes."

"Hm," Charles went on. "I saw her at Madame Liégeard's this afternoon. I mentioned you, but she doesn't know you."

It was like being struck by lightning. Yet she just replied, unruffled:

"Oh well, she's probably forgotten my name!"

"Perhaps there's more than one Mademoiselle Lempereur in Rouen who teaches the piano?"

"Possibly!"

Then she quickly added:

"I've got the receipts, look!"

And she went to the writing desk, rummaged through the drawers, got all the papers mixed up and became so flustered that Charles made her promise not to worry about a few wretched bills.

"No, I'm going to find them," she said.

And so it was that that Friday, as he was putting his boots on in the dark closet where all his clothes were crammed, Charles felt a piece of paper between the leather and his sock. He pulled it out and read:

Received for three months' lessons and sundry supplies, the sum of sixty-five francs.
FÉLICIE LEMPEREUR
Music Mistress

"How on earth did this get in my boot?"

"It probably fell out of that old box of invoices on the edge of the shelf," she told him.

And from that moment on her life was nothing more than a tissue of lies in which she wrapped her love as if in a veil, to keep it hidden.

It was a necessity for her, an obsession, a pleasure, so much so that if she said that the day before she had walked down the right-hand side of the street, then it must have been the left.

One morning when she had just set off, wearing light clothes as usual, it suddenly began to snow. Charles, who was at the window watching it fall, spotted Father Bournisien in Mr Tuvache's *boc*, which was taking him to Rouen. He went out and gave the priest a thick shawl to give to Madame when he got to the Croix Rouge. As soon as he arrived he asked the innkeeper if the doctor's wife from Yonville was there. The woman told him that she rarely came to her establishment. That evening, finding Madame Bovary in the *Hirondelle* with him, the cleric told her about the confusion, although apparently setting little store by it, because he started singing the praises of a preacher whom the whole cathedral was marvelling at, and to whom all the ladies rushed to listen to.

But even if he didn't ask questions, others might not be so discreet. So she decided it was best to go to the Croix Rouge every time, so people from the village saw her there they wouldn't be suspicious.

One day, however, she bumped into Monsieur Lheureux as she was coming out of the Hôtel de Boulogne with Léon. She was afraid that he might gossip – but he was no fool.

Three days later he came to her room, closed the door and said:

"I need some money."

She told him that she didn't have any to give him. Lheureux began whining, reminding her how obliging he had been.

Of the two bills of exchange that Charles had taken out, so far Emma had only paid one. As for the second, at her request the shopkeeper had agreed to renew it with two others that were not due for quite some time. Then he took out a list of goods on account that still hadn't been paid for: the curtains, the carpet, material for the armchairs, several dresses and various toiletries, which all together came to around two thousand francs.

She hung her head; he continued:

"Even if you don't have cash, you do have *property*."

And he mentioned a miserable little smallholding at Barneville, near Aumale, which didn't bring in very much. It had used to be part of a small farm that Monsieur Bovary senior had sold, because Lheureux knew everything, including how many hectares it was and the names of the people on the neighbouring properties.

"If I were you I'd get rid of it," he said, "and still have money to play with."

She protested that it would be difficult to sell; he was confident he could find a buyer; so then she asked how to go about the sale.

"Don't you have power of attorney?" he asked.

The words were like a breath of fresh air.

"Leave the bill with me," said Emma.

"Oh, there's no need!" Lheureux replied.

He came back the next week, and proudly announced that after many efforts he had managed to find a man called Langlois who had had his eye on the property for quite some time, although he hadn't named his price.

"The price isn't important!" she exclaimed.

Nonetheless they would have to take their time sounding out this character. It was worth making a trip, and since she was unable to, he offered to visit the property and meet Langlois. When he got back he told her that the buyer was prepared to pay four thousand francs.

Emma's face lit up.

"It's a good price, frankly," he added.

She was paid half the amount straight away, but when she went to settle her account the draper said:

"Mercy, it upsets me to see you part with a *considerable* sum like that all at once."

She looked at the banknotes, and then, thinking of all the assignations that these two thousand francs represented, she stammered:

"What? What do you mean?"

"Oh!" he went on, laughing good-naturedly. "You can keep on paying bills for ever. I know what running a house is like!"

And he looked her in the eye, while stroking the backs of his fingers up and down two large sheets of paper that he was holding. Then opening his pocket book he laid four promissory notes on the table, each for a thousand francs.

"Sign these for me," he said, "and you can keep all of it."

She gave a cry of indignation.

"But if I give you the balance," replied Lheureux insolently, "aren't I being of service to you?"

And picking up a pen he wrote at the bottom of the account: "Received from Madame Bovary, four thousand francs."

"What is there for you to worry about, since in six months' time you'll receive the outstanding amount on that place of yours, and I'll set the due date for the last bill of exchange for after it's been paid to you?"

Emma was slightly confused by his machinations; she had a ringing noise in her ears, as if a sack of gold had been emptied on the floor at her feet. Then Lheureux explained that a friend of his called Vinçart, a banker in Rouen, would discount the four bills of exchange, after which he would personally remit to Madame what remained from the actual debt.

But instead of two thousand francs he only brought eighteen hundred, because his friend Vinçart (as was *his due*) had deducted two hundred to cover his commission and the discounting fee.

And then casually he asked for a receipt.

"You understand... sometimes... in business... and with the payment date, if you wouldn't mind."

The prospect of attainable extravagances suddenly opened up in front of Emma. She was wise enough to put a thousand écus aside, which paid the first three promissory notes when they fell due, but by chance the fourth one arrived on a Thursday, and when his wife got back, Charles, distraught, was waiting patiently for an explanation.

If she had failed to tell him about this bill of exchange it was to spare him domestic worries; she sat on his lap, petted him, cooed over him, went through the long list of essential items that had been bought on credit.

"After all, considering how much there is, you have to agree it's not too expensive."

Running out of ideas, it wasn't long before Charles also had to turn to the inevitable Lheureux, who promised to hold off if Monsieur signed two more promissory notes, including one for seven hundred francs payable in three months' time. To make sure that he would be able to honour it, he wrote his mother a plaintive letter. By way of reply she came in person, and when Emma asked him if he had managed to get anything out of her he replied:

"Yes. But she wants to see the bill."

So just as it was getting light the next morning, Emma hurried to Lheureux's shop to persuade him to write out a new invoice, one which wasn't for more than a thousand francs; because to produce the one for four thousand meant she would have had to explain that she had already paid two thirds of it, and thus admit to selling the property, a transaction which the shopkeeper had handled very adroitly, and which no one found out about until much later.

Despite the fact that the individual items were all cheap, Madame Bovary senior wasn't slow to point out that the expenditure was excessive.

"Couldn't you manage without the carpet? Why have the armchairs re-covered? In my day there was only one armchair in a house, for elderly people – at least that's how it was in my mother's house, and I can assure you she was a respectable woman. Not everyone can be rich! Wastage eats up even the biggest fortune! I'd be ashamed if I pampered myself like you do! And I'm old, I need care and attention... What a state to be in! What a state! It's all window dressing, ostentation! Why use silk for linings at two francs a time when you can get ticking for ten sous, even eight, and which is quite good enough!"

Lying back on the love seat, Emma protested as calmly as she could manage:

"Oh, enough Madame, please, that's enough!"

But the other woman continued with her lecture, predicting they would end up in the poorhouse. Still, it was all Bovary's fault. It was just as well that he had promised to cancel the power of attorney...

"What?"

"Oh yes, he assured me," the mother-in-law replied.

Emma opened the window and called Charles, and the poor fellow had no choice but to admit that what his mother had inadvertently told her was true.

Emma slipped away, but soon came back and presented her with a large sheet of paper.

"You're too kind," said the old woman.

And she threw the power of attorney on the fire.

Emma began to laugh, a shrill, piercing laugh that went on and on without stopping: it was an attack of nerves.

"Oh my God!" cried Charles. "See! You're just as much to blame! You come here and cause a scene!..."

With a shrug his mother said that "it was all just put on".

But rebelling for the first time in his life, Charles stood up for his wife; so Madame Bovary senior announced that she was going home. She left the next day, and as he stood on the doorstep trying to dissuade her, she retorted:

"No no! You love her more than you do me, and you're right, it's in the nature of things. As for everything else, you'll see!... Take care of yourself... because as you say, I won't be coming back to cause another scene in a hurry."

Charles wasn't any less contrite towards Emma, who didn't hide the resentment she felt for his not trusting her; it took much pleading on his part before she agreed to take on her power of attorney again. He even went with her to Monsieur Guillaumin's office to set up another one.

"I quite understand," said the notary. "A man of science can't burden himself with everyday matters."

Charles was flattered by the ingratiating remark. Rather than weak, it made him look like a man with more important things on his mind.

How her cup overflowed the following Thursday in the room at the hotel with Léon! She laughed, cried, sang, danced, sent for sorbets, wanted cigarettes, and to him she seemed madly eccentric yet adorable, magnificent.

He didn't realize what she was reacting against to allow herself to be thrust body and soul into life's pleasures. She became fractious, gluttonous, voluptuous; she walked down the street with him with her head held high, without fear of compromising herself, so she said. Yet sometimes she would shudder at the thought of unexpectedly meeting Rodolphe; for although they had parted, she didn't feel totally free from her addiction to him.

One evening she didn't come back to Yonville. Charles was beside himself, and little Berthe, who wouldn't go to sleep without her mother there, cried her eyes out. Justin wandered off along the main road. Monsieur Homais even left his shop.

At eleven o'clock, unable to bear it any longer, Charles harnessed the *boc*, jumped in, whipped up his horse and arrived at the Croix Rouge at two in the morning. No one there. He wondered if the clerk might have seen her; but where did he live? Luckily Charles remembered his employer's address. He set off at a run.

Day was just breaking. He could make out a brass nameplate above the door; he knocked. Without coming to open it someone shouted out and asked what he wanted, roundly cursing people who woke you up in the middle of the night.

The house where the clerk lived didn't have a bell, a knocker or a concierge. Charles hammered on the shutters. A policeman walked by, which scared him, and so he went away.

"I'm going mad," he thought. "She probably went for dinner at the Lormeaux'."

But the Lormeaux family didn't live in Rouen any more.

"She will have stayed on to look after Madame Dubreuil. What? Madame Dubreuil died ten months ago!... So where is she?"

Then he had an idea. He went into a café, asked for the directory and quickly looked up Mademoiselle Lempereur, who lived at number 74, Rue de la Renelle-des-Maroquiniers.

Just as he turned into the street, Emma appeared at the other end; he threw himself into her arms without even kissing her, crying:

"Where were you?"

"I wasn't well."

"What was it?... How?... Where?..."

Putting her hand to her forehead she said:

"At Mademoiselle Lempereur's."

"I thought so! I was on my way there."

"There's no point," Emma told him. "She's just this minute gone out; but don't get so agitated in future. How can I relax if I know that the slightest delay will get you in a state like this?"

This was her way of allowing herself not to feel awkward about her little trips. And she made the most of it in every way, without once troubling her conscience. Whenever she felt a sudden craving to see Léon, she went on the slightest pretext, and as he wouldn't be expecting her she would go to his office to find him.

The first few times it was a joy; but it wasn't long before he had to be honest with her: his employer was complaining about all the distractions.

"Bah!" she said. "Let's go!"

And so he slipped out.

She wanted him to dress in black and grow a pointed little beard so as to look like the portraits of Louis XIII. She asked to see where he lived, thought it was drab; he blushed, she didn't take any notice, and told him he ought to buy curtains like hers; and when he said that it would cost too much:

"Ah ha!" she said, laughing. "You're counting the pennies!"

Every time they met, Léon had to tell her about everything he had done since the last time. She asked him for poetry, verses about her, *a love poem* dedicated to her; but he could never manage to make the second line rhyme, and so eventually he copied a sonnet from a keepsake album.

It was not so much vanity as a desire to please her. He never challenged her ideas; he agreed with all her likes and dislikes; he was her mistress, rather than her being his. Her words of love, her kisses swept him away. Where had she acquired this depravity, concealed so deep down inside her as to be almost unworldly?

6

W HEN HE CAME TO SEE HER, Léon often had dinner with the pharmacist, and out of politeness he felt obliged to return the favour.

"Gladly!" Homais had replied. "I ought to get out and about more, I'm too entrenched here. We'll go to a show, a restaurant, we'll have a gay old time!"

"Oh, my dear!" mumbled Madame Homais fondly, frightened by the obscure dangers that he was about to expose himself to.

"What? Do you think I'm not damaging my health enough with the constant fumes in the pharmacy! Isn't that just like a woman: they're jealous of science, then object when you quite rightly want to have some lawful entertainment. Still, no matter, you can count on me: one of these days I'll descend on Rouen, and you and I will go out and *paint the town red*."

As a rule the apothecary would have been careful to avoid such expressions, but now he put on a whimsical, Parisian manner that he felt was in the best possible taste, and like his neighbour Madame Bovary he questioned the clerk closely about the ways of the capital; to impress him he even spoke slang... townsfolk said: "digs", "shambles", "gaff", "gafferoo", "Tin Pan Alley" and "I'll sling my hook" for "I'm going".

So one Thursday Emma was surprised to bump into Monsieur Homais in the kitchen of the Lion d'Or wearing his travelling attire, which consisted of an old coat that she had never seen before, with a suitcase in one hand and the foot-warmer from his shop in the other. He hadn't told anyone where he was going, for fear people would be alarmed if he wasn't there.

He was clearly excited at the thought of going back to his youthful haunts, because he held forth about it all the way; then no sooner had the coach stopped than he leapt out and set off in search of Léon; and however much the clerk protested, Homais dragged him off to the grand Café de Normandie where he swept in regally without taking his hat off, regarding it as most provincial to bare one's head in public.

Emma waited for Léon for three quarters of an hour. In the end she hurried over to his office and, lost in all kind of imaginings, reproaching him for not caring and herself for being feeble, she spent the afternoon with her forehead pressed to the window.

At two o'clock the two friends were still at table. The large dining room was emptying; the pipe of the stove, shaped like a palm tree, spread its gilt leaves in a circle on the white ceiling; in the sunlight outside a window near where they were sitting, a small fountain murmured in a marble basin where three drowsy lobsters as plump as partridges lay piled on their sides among watercress and asparagus.

Homais was thoroughly enjoying himself. Although the luxury had gone to his head more than the food, the Pommard wine was nonetheless making him loquacious, and when the *omelette au rhum* appeared he began airing some less than ethical opinions about women. What attracted him particularly was *chic*. He loved to see a stylishly dressed woman in a well-furnished apartment, and when it came to physical attributes he wasn't averse to *a nice bit of stuff*.

Léon stared at the clock in despair. The apothecary ate, drank, talked.

"You must feel deprived in Rouen," he said suddenly. "Still, she's not far away."

And as the other blushed:

"Come on, be honest! You're not going to deny that in Yonville you..."

The young man just stammered.

"That in Madame Bovary's house, you're courting?..."

"Who?"

"The maid!"

He wasn't teasing; but pride getting the better of prudence, against his better judgement Léon protested. Besides, he preferred brunettes.

"I admire your taste," said the pharmacist. "They have stronger personalities."

And leaning towards his companion he described the signs by which it was possible to tell if a woman had a strong personality. He even went off on an ethnological tangent: German women were ethereal, French women licentious, Italians hot-blooded.

"What about Negresses?" asked the clerk.

"They appeal to artists," Homais replied. "Waiter! Two small coffees!"

"Shall we go?" Léon finally asked, now impatient.

"Yes."*

But before they left Homais asked to see the head waiter so as to give him his compliments.

In order to get away, the young man made an excuse about having business to attend to.

"I'll come with you!" said Homais.

And as they walked down the street he talked about his wife and children, their future, the pharmacy, how it had been in decline and the state of perfection that he had brought it up to.

When they reached the Hôtel de Boulogne Léon suddenly left him, rushed upstairs and found his mistress in a state of agitation.

When she heard the pharmacist's name she lost her temper. Yet he had plenty of excuses ready: it wasn't his fault – after all, she knew what Monsieur Homais was like. Did she imagine he preferred his company to hers? But she turned away; he held on to her, and sinking to his knees put his arms round her waist with a languorous, pleading gesture full of lust.

She just stood there; her big fiery eyes looked at him gravely, with an almost terrifying expression. Then they clouded with tears, her reddened eyelids closed, she gave him her hands, and Léon was pressing them to his lips when a bellboy came in and told Monsieur that someone was asking for him.

"Are you coming back?" she asked.

"Yes."

"When?"

"Straight away."

"Just *something*," the pharmacist said when he saw Léon. "I'm going to cut short my visit, because I seem to be in your way. Let's just go to Bridoux's and have a glass of garus."*

Léon insisted that he had to get back to work. The apothecary teased him about bumf and procedure.

"Can't you leave Cujas and Bartolo* for a minute, dash it! What's to stop you? Be a good chap! Let's go to Bridoux's, you can see his dog. It's most peculiar."

But as the clerk was insistent:

"I'll come too then. I'll read the paper while I'm waiting, or take a look through the Code."

Head spinning from Emma's anger, Homais's prattling and the

after-effects of lunch, Léon wavered, almost bewitched by the pharmacist who kept saying:

"Come on, let's go to Bridoux's! It's just next door in the Rue Malpalu."

So, like a coward, like a fool, propelled by one of those indefinable states of mind which make us do the most disagreeable things, he let himself be dragged off to Bridoux's. They found him in his courtyard, supervising three assistants who were out of breath from turning the large wheel of an apparatus for making seltzer. Homais offered them advice, greeted Bridoux with a kiss; they drank the garus. Léon tried to leave a dozen times, but the apothecary held him back by the arm:

"Just a minute!" he said. "I'm coming. We'll go and see the gentlemen at the *Fanal de Rouen*. I'll introduce you to Thomassin."

But the clerk managed to shake him off and rushed straight back to the hotel. Emma wasn't there.

She had just left in a rage. She hated him now. His breaking his word offended her, and she looked for other reasons to be rid of him: he was devoid of heroism, feeble, mediocre, limper than a woman, as well as being greedy and faint-hearted.

But once she had calmed down she decided she might be maligning him. Yet disparaging those we love puts distance between them and us. Never tamper with an idol: the gilding rubs off on your fingers.

They soon reached the point where what they talked about was of no importance to their love; in the letters Emma wrote him it was flowers, poetry, the moon and stars, which fading passion uses in a naïve attempt to rekindle itself by turning to the external, the superficial. She was forever promising herself utmost bliss for their next meeting, then had to admit to not feeling anything out of the ordinary. But her disappointment soon gave way to new hopes, and she came back more voracious, more impassioned than before. She would undress violently, ripping the laces of her corset, which slipped over her hips like a snake. Tiptoeing in bare feet she would check the door was locked then throw aside her clothes in a single movement – and pale, silent, serious, she collapsed into his arms with a shudder.

Yet over this forehead bathed in icy droplets, the faltering lips, the wildly staring eyes, the tight embrace, hung something intemperate, ill-defined and sombre which Léon sensed was insinuating its way between them, as if to force them apart.

He daren't ask questions, but, acknowledging her experience, he told himself she must have been through every ordeal of pain and pleasure. What had once delighted him now frightened him. And he was revolted by the way her personality swallowed him up more and more each day. He resented Emma for this abiding conquest. He tried not to love her so intensely, but at the merest creak of her boots his courage deserted him, like a drunk at the sight of a bottle.

It was true that she constantly lavished attention on him, from exquisite food to a coquettish appearance, to giving him long, smouldering looks. She brought roses from Yonville hidden in her breast which she threw at him, worried about his health, advised him how to behave, and in order to hold on to him even tighter, hung a locket with an image of the Virgin round his neck in the hope that Heaven might intervene. Like a good mother she made enquiries about his friends.

"Don't mix with them," she told him. "Stay here, think only of us; love me!"

She would have liked to keep constant watch over his life, and considered having him followed. Outside the hotel there was a type of vagrant who waylaid travellers and who certainly wouldn't say no... But her pride rebelled against it.

"Oh, never mind! Let him be unfaithful, I don't care! What is it to me?"

One day when they had parted early and she was walking along the boulevard by herself, she saw the walls of her old convent, and she sat on a bench under the elm trees. Life was so peaceful then! How she had longed for those inexpressible feelings of love that she had tried so hard to conjure up from books!

The first months of married life, the rides in the forest, the waltzing Vicomte, Lagardy singing, it all passed before her eyes... And suddenly Léon was there, as distant from her as the others.

"But I still love him!" she thought.

Yet what did it matter! She wasn't happy, she never had been. So all life's meagreness, the way things disintegrated the moment she started to depend on them... where did it come from? But if there was a strong, handsome man somewhere, a dauntless character as full of rapture as he was sophisticated, with the heart of a poet in the body of an angel, a lyre with strings of bronze playing plaintive wedding hymns to the heavens, then why had fate never led him to her? No, it was impossible!

It wasn't worth searching for; everyone lied. Behind every smile was a world-weary yawn, beneath every joy a curse, in every pleasure a bitter aftertaste, and the most perfect kisses left your lips with the vain desire for even more sensual delights.

A metallic clanging sound drifted through the air; the convent clock struck four. Four o'clock! It was as if she had been sitting on this bench since time began. Yet an infinite number of passions can be contained within the course of a single minute, like a crowd in a small space. Emma was utterly absorbed with her own; she was no more concerned about money now than an archduchess.

One day, however, a puny-looking bald man with a ruddy face came to the house, saying he had been sent by Monsieur Vinçart in Rouen. He took out the pins that held the side pocket of his frock coat together, stuck them in his sleeve and politely handed her a piece of paper.

It was a bill of exchange for seven hundred francs, signed by her, and which despite all her remonstrations Lheureux had made payable to Vinçart.

She sent the maid to his shop. He couldn't come.

Meanwhile the stranger, who was standing glancing round curiously from beneath heavy blond eyebrows, asked her innocently:

"What reply shall I give to Monsieur Vinçart?"

"Ah," said Emma, "tell him... I haven't got it... that it'll be next week... yes, he should wait... till next week."

And the man went off without another word.

But at midday the next day she received a formal demand; the sight of the document with its official stamp, across which was written several times in bold letters: "Hareng, Master Bailiff, Buchy", gave her such a fright that she rushed to the draper's shop as fast as she could.

Lheureux was wrapping up a parcel at the counter.

"Good day to you!" he said. "How can I be of service?"

He carried on with what he was doing, helped by a girl of about thirteen with a slight hump, who was his assistant as well as his cook.

Clogs clattering on the wooden floor, he took Madame upstairs to a cramped little office where some ledgers held together by an iron bar with a padlock stood on a large pine desk. Against the wall under rolls of printed calico was a safe, so large it must have held more than just money and bills of exchange. For Monsieur Lheureux was also a pawnbroker; this was where he kept Madame Bovary's gold watch

241

chain and the earrings belonging to poor old Tellier, who, finally forced to sell up, had bought a small grocer's shop in Quincampoix where he was dying of catarrh, surrounded by candles that were a paler shade of yellow than his face.

Lheureux sat on his large woven-straw armchair:

"What news?"

"This."

And she showed him the piece of paper.

"What can I do about it?"

She lost her temper, reminding him that he had promised not to pass on any of the bills of exchange, and he had to admit this was true.

"But I didn't have any choice, I had a gun to my head."

"So what's going to happen now?" she asked.

"Oh, it's quite simple: a court order, then the bailiffs... *voilà*!"

It was as much as Emma could do not to hit him. But she just asked if there was any way to placate Monsieur Vinçart.

"What! Placate Vinçart? You don't know him. He's worse than a pit bull terrier!"

But Lheureux still couldn't help but get involved.

"Listen, I think I've always been good to you up till now."

And, opening one of his ledgers:

"Look!"

Moving his finger up the page he went on:

"Let's see... let's see... The 3rd of August, two hundred francs... the 17th of June, one hundred and fifty... 23rd of March, forty-six... In April..."

But then he stopped, as if afraid of doing something foolish.

"And that's without the bills taken out by Monsieur, one for seven hundred francs, another for three hundred! As for your little instalments, what with the interest payments it just goes on and on, everything gets in a muddle. I'm not getting involved any more!"

She began to cry, called him "her good, kind Monsieur Lheureux". But he kept coming back to "that sly customer Vinçart". Besides, he didn't have a penny, no one paid their bills, everyone wanted the shirt off his back, a poor shopkeeper like him couldn't afford to go advancing money to people.

Emma said no more. Lheureux, who was chewing the barbs of his quill pen, must have been alarmed by her silence, because he added:

PART THREE • CHAPTER 6

"If I saw some money coming in… then I might be able to…"

"Well actually," she said, "as soon as what's outstanding from the sale of Barneville…"

"What?"

He seemed surprised to hear that Langlois still hadn't paid. Then he said unctuously:

"So… you're saying we can come to an arrangement?"

"Whatever you want!"

He closed his eyes and thought for a moment, wrote down a few figures, and then, telling her that it pained him, that it was a tricky business and that he was *bleeding himself white*, he made out four bills of exchange each for 250 francs, payable one after another at monthly intervals.

"That's providing Vinçart will listen! Still, we've got an agreement, and I won't keep you waiting. I'm as straight as a die."

After this he casually showed her some new items, although in his opinion none of them were good enough for Madame.

"When I think of this dress here at seven sous a metre, guaranteed not to run! And they swallow it hook, line and sinker! I don't give them any sales patter of course, as you can imagine," he said, thinking that by admitting to pulling the wool over other people's eyes he would convince her of his honesty.

Then he called her back to show her three ells* of guipure that he had recently found "in a public sale".

"Isn't it beautiful!" he said. "People use it on the facings of chairs a lot nowadays, it's quite the thing."

And quicker than a conjurer he wrapped the guipure in blue paper and put it in Emma's hand.

"As long as I know that—"

"Later!" he said, and walked away.

As soon as Bovary came home that evening she urged him to write to his mother to ask her to send everything they were owed from the estate as quickly as possible. Her mother-in-law wrote back saying there was nothing left; the settlement was complete, and apart from Barneville they were left with six hundred livres a year, which should do them nicely.

So Madame sent out accounts to several of the patients, and since this worked she was soon doing it regularly. She made a point of adding a note at the bottom: "Please don't mention this to my husband, you know how proud he is... Forgive me... I remain your humble servant..." There were a few protests but she intercepted them.

To bring in some money she started selling off her old gloves, her old hats, any old iron; and she drove a hard bargain – it was her peasant blood showing itself. When she went into town she dabbled in second-hand knick-knacks, which Lheureux would buy if no one else did. She bought ostrich feathers, china and chests; she borrowed from Félicité, Madame Lefrançois, the landlady of the Croix Rouge, from anyone anywhere. With the money she eventually received from the sale of Barnevile she paid two of the bills of exchange, while the remaining fifteen hundred francs just melted away. So she set to all over again, yet always with the same result!

She did sometimes try to keep account, it was true; but when she saw the outrageous prices she couldn't believe it. So she began anew, but soon became confused, gave up and forgot about it.

The house was in a sorry state! Tradesmen came away with angry expressions. Handkerchiefs lay around on the stove, and to Madame Homais's horror little Berthe went around with holes in her stockings. If Charles ventured an opinion she replied bluntly that it wasn't her fault!

Why these fits of temper? He attributed everything to her old nervous illness and, reproaching himself for seeing her frailties as failings, he blamed his own selfishness, and then wanted to rush off and kiss her.

"No!" he thought. "That would annoy her!"

So he just stayed where he was.

After dinner he would go for a walk in the garden by himself; or he would sit young Berthe on his lap, open his medical journal and try and teach her to read. But the child, who never had lessons, soon started to rub her big sad eyes and cry. To cheer her up he found the watering can and made rivers in the sand, or snapped off branches to plant trees in the flower beds, which made little difference to the look of the garden, which was overgrown in any case; they owed Lestiboudois so much! Then the little girl said she was cold and asked for her mother.

"Go and find nanny, my darling," said Charles. "You know Mummy doesn't like being disturbed."

Autumn was coming, the leaves were falling already – like two years ago, when she was ill! When would it end?... And he walked off down the garden, hands behind his back.

Madame was in her room. No one else went in there. She would stay there all day long, somnolent and half-dressed, sometimes burning grains of exotic harem incense that she had bought in an Algerian shop in Rouen. So as not to have to lie beside a sleeping man all night, her pained expression had eventually consigned him to the second floor; she would read until daybreak, outlandish books with pictures of bloody, orgiastic scenes. Often she would cry out in horror, and Charles would come running.

"Oh, go away!" she would say.

At other times, breathless, overwrought, filled with lust, consumed more than ever by that inner flame which is kindled by adultery, she would open the window, inhale the cold air, shake her mass of long hair in the breeze and, gazing up at the stars, wish for a prince as her lover. And she thought of him, of Léon. At that moment she would have given anything for just one of their meetings, and this always appeased her.

For her they were feast days. She liked them to be sumptuous! Whenever he couldn't afford to pay for everything, which was nearly always the case, she made up the rest unstintingly. He tried to make her realize that they would be just as happy somewhere else, in some modest hotel; but she always objected.

One day she took six small gilt silver spoons from her bag (they were a wedding present from old man Rouault), and asked him to take them to the pawnshop for her; Léon did as she asked, although he found it distasteful. He feared for his reputation. Because if he stopped to think about it, his mistress was beginning to behave peculiarly. It might not be a bad idea to break with her.

The fact was, someone had sent an anonymous letter to his mother, warning her that he was "squandering himself on a married woman", and so, immediately detecting that spectre which haunts every family, that nebulous and baleful creature known as the siren, a fantastical monster that has its dwelling in the deepest depths of love, the woman had written to his employer, Maître Dubocage, who handled the matter perfectly. He spoke to him in private for three quarters of an hour, tried to open his eyes, turn him back from the brink. An affair of this kind could damage the practice. He implored him to break it off, and if he wouldn't make this sacrifice for his own sake, then he could at least do it for him, Dubocage!

Léon eventually promised to stop seeing Emma, and when he thought of the difficulties and ill opinions that this woman might still cause for him, not to mention ribbings from his colleagues when they all gathered round the stove in the mornings for a chat, he reproached himself for not having kept his word. Not only that, he was going to be senior clerk; it was time to behave sensibly. So he gave up the flute, abandoned extravagant emotions, fantasies, because, bourgeois that he was, in the heat of his youth – albeit only for a day, a minute – he had thought himself capable of prodigious passion, noble deeds. The merest philanderer dreams of Eastern promise; every lawyer has the makings of a poet.

So when Emma burst into tears in his arms now, it irritated him, and like those people who can only bear to listen to a certain amount of music, his now indifferent heart fell asleep at the strident sound of a love to whose subtle delights it was no longer receptive.

They knew each other too well to marvel at the sense of possession that makes pleasure all the more intense. She was as repelled by him as he was weary of her. In adultery Emma was confronted with the mediocrity of marriage.

But how was she to be rid of him? As humiliated as she felt by such a tawdry love, she clung to it out of habit or wantonness; she struggled more and more each day, draining it of every last drop of bliss by trying to make it more profound. She blamed Léon for her frustrated hopes as if he had betrayed her; she wished for some disaster to force them apart because she lacked the courage to do it herself.

She didn't write him any fewer love letters, on the principal that a woman should always write to her lover.

Yet in writing she discovered another man, a shadow born of her most impassioned memories, the most beautiful books she had read, her fiercest desires, and eventually he became so real, so attainable, that her heart raced in wonder, despite being unable to picture him clearly – because like a god he was almost invisible beneath his many attributes. He lived in that blue-tinted land where silken ladders hang from balconies in the sweetly scented breath of flowers in the moonlight. She felt him nearby, he would come and sweep her away body and soul with a kiss. But then she came crashing down again; for these obscure transports of love exhausted her more than the wildest debauchery.

Emma felt a constant aching sensation now. She sometimes received summonses with official seals but barely glanced at them. She would have liked not to be alive, or to be permanently asleep.

On the third Thursday of Lent she didn't come back to Yonville; that night she went to a masked ball. She wore velvet pantaloons and red stockings, a wig tied in a bow at the neck and a tricorn hat over one ear. She danced all night to the frenzied sound of trombones; people gathered round her in a circle; and in the morning she found herself in the columned entrance of the theatre with a group wearing masks, sailors and buxom young women dressed as dockers, some of Léon's friends who were talking about going on for supper.

All the nearby cafés were full. They managed to find a barely passable restaurant on the harbour, where the owner opened up a small upstairs room for them.

The men conferred in the corner, doubtless about the cost. There was a clerk, two medical students and a shop assistant: what companions for her! As for the women, from their accents Emma knew immediately that they were from the lower orders. And so she was frightened, pushed her chair back and sat looking at the floor.

The others began eating. She didn't touch a thing; her forehead was burning, her eyes stinging, her skin cold as ice. In her mind the dance floor was still pulsing to the rhythm of a thousand dancing feet. The smell of punch and cigar smoke went to her head. She fainted, and they carried her over to the window.

It was almost daybreak, and a great patch of crimson was spreading across the sky over Sainte-Catherine. The purplish-blue river shivered in the breeze; the bridges were deserted; the street lamps were going out.

In the meantime she came round, and thought of Berthe asleep at home in the maid's room. But then a wagon carrying long strips of iron drove past, making a deafening metallic echo between the houses.

She quickly slipped away, took off her costume, told Léon she had to be getting home, and then at last she was alone at the Hôtel de Boulogne. Everything, herself included, was too much for her to bear. She would have liked to fly away like a bird, to become young again in some far-distant and unsullied place.

She left the hotel, went across the boulevard, the Place Cauchoise, and through the working district all the way to a street that overlooked some gardens in the open. She walked quickly, the fresh air calmed her – and gradually the faces of the crowd, the masks, the quadrilles, the chandeliers, the supper room, the women all disappeared like morning mist. When she got back to the Croix Rouge she collapsed onto the bed in the little room on the second floor with its prints of *La Tour de Nesle*. At four o'clock Hivert came and woke her.

When she got home, Félicité pointed to a sheet of grey paper behind the clock. It said:

In accordance with the engrossment, by way of executory judgement...

Which judgement? But the day before another document had been delivered, one she didn't know about. So she was astonished to read:

In the name of the King, justice and the law, to Madame Bovary...

Skipping a few lines she saw:

Within a period of twenty-four hours...

What?

To pay the total sum of eight thousand francs.

Further down it said:

She will be compelled by every due process of law, in particular the executory distraint of her furniture and effects.

What was she to do?... It was in twenty-four hours: tomorrow! She thought Lheureux was just trying to frighten her again, because suddenly she saw through all his ploys, the reason for his obliging attitude. What reassured her was actually the inflated amount itself.

Yet as a result of buying, not paying, borrowing, taking out bills of exchange then renewing those same bills, which grew larger with each new date of payment, she had ended up creating a fund for Lheureux himself, which was now waiting impatiently for him to invest in another of his schemes.

She breezed into his shop.

"Do you realize what's happening? I suppose this is your idea of a joke!"

"No."

"What do you mean?"

He turned away slowly, folded his arms and said:

"My dear lady, did you think I was going to be your personal banker and provider for all eternity, for God's sake?! Be fair, I need to recoup my outlay."

She complained indignantly about the debt.

"That's too bad! The court has decided! Judgement has been passed! In any case it's not me, it's Vinçart."

"Couldn't you?..."

"No I couldn't."

"But... can't we discuss it."

She clutched at straws; she hadn't realized... It had caught her unawares...

"Whose fault is that?" said Lheureux with an ironic gesture. "While I've been slaving away you've been busy enjoying yourself."

"You've no sense of decency."

"I'm none the worse for it," he retorted.

She caved in; she begged; she even put her pretty white hand on the draper's knee.

"You can stop that! What are you doing, trying to seduce me?"

"You're vile!" she cried.

"Go on, insult me why don't you!" he replied with a laugh.

"I'll let everyone know all about you. I'll tell my husband—"

"Oh yes? Well I've got something to tell him, haven't I!"

And Lheureux went to the safe and got the receipt for eighteen hundred francs that she had given him when Vinçart discounted the bill.

"Poor man," he added. "Do you think he won't realize you've been thieving?"

She collapsed as if poleaxed. He walked up and down between the desk and the window, saying:

"Oh yes, I'll tell him I will... I'll tell him..."

Then he came over to her and said gently:

"I realize this is no laughing matter; even so it's not the end of the world, and since there's no other way for you to pay back what you owe me..."

"But where am I going to get it from?" said Emma, wringing her hands.

"Pah! You've got friends haven't you!"

And he gave her a terrible knowing look that shook her to the core.

"I promise I'll sign—" she said.

"I've had enough of your signatures!"

"I'll sell—"

"Come off it!" he shrugged. "You've got nothing left to sell."

And he shouted through the spyhole into the shop:

"Annette! Don't forget those three coupons for number 14."

The maid came in; Emma understood, and asked him "how much was needed to stop the legal proceedings".

"It's too late!"

"But if I give you a few thousand francs, a quarter of the amount, a third, nearly all of it?"

"There's no point!"

And he pushed her gently towards the stairs.

"I'm begging you Monsieur Lheureux, just a few more days!"

She began to cry.

"Oh dear! Tears now, is it!"

"You're driving me to despair!"

"I don't care in the least!" he said, closing the door.

7

S HE PUT ON A BRAVE FACE the next day when Hareng the bailiff came to the house with two witnesses to take an inventory for the seizure.

They began in Bovary's consulting room, without noting down the phrenological head which was regarded as an *instrument of his profession*, but in the kitchen they included the plates, the pots and pans, the chairs, the candlesticks and, in her bedroom, all the trinkets on the shelves. They inspected her dresses, the household linen, the bathroom; every last nook and cranny of her life was laid out under the gaze of the three men like a body on a slab.

Every now and then Mr Hareng, who was buttoned up in a thin black tailcoat, a white cravat and trousers with tight under-straps, would say:

"May I, Madame? May I?"

Often he exclaimed:

"Delightful!… Oh yes, very nice!"

And then he started writing again, dipping his quill into the horn inkwell in his left hand.

When they had finished in all the rooms they went up to the attic. In there was a desk in which she kept Rodolphe's letters locked away. It had to be opened.

"Ah, correspondence!" said Hareng, smiling discreetly. "May I! I have to satisfy myself that there's nothing else in the box."

And he tipped it, as if some napoleons might fall out. She was affronted at the sight of the big coarse hand with fingers like flabby red slugs touching pages that had made her heart beat faster.

Finally they left! Félicité came back; Emma had sent her to watch out for Charles and keep him out of the way. Then they quickly took the bailiff's assistant left behind to guard the seized property up to the attic, where he promised to stay.

During the evening Emma thought Charles seemed worried. She watched him anxiously from the corner of her eye, thinking that even the lines on his face were accusing her. And when she looked at the Chinese screens either side of the fireplace, the heavy curtains, the armchairs, all the things that had sweetened life's bitter pill for her, she was filled with remorse, or more precisely a profound feeling of regret, which far from extinguishing her desires only aroused them. Charles calmly stirred the fire, his feet resting on the firedogs.

At one point the bailiff's assistant, no doubt becoming bored in his hiding place, made a noise.

"Is that someone upstairs?" said Charles.

"No," she answered, "it's just a window open in the attic, blowing in the breeze."

That Sunday she went to Rouen to call on every banker she knew of. They were either away in the country or travelling. She wasn't put off, and the ones she did manage to see she asked for money, telling them she had to have it, that she would pay it back. Some of them laughed in her face. All of them refused.

At two o'clock she hurried over to Léon's house, knocked on his door. No one answered. Then finally he appeared.

"What brings you here?"

"Am I disturbing you?..."

"No... it's just..."

And he explained that the landlord didn't like them "entertaining women".

"I have to talk to you," she said.

He reached up to get his key. She stopped him.

"Not here, at our usual place."

And they went to their room at the Hôtel de Boulogne.

Once there she drank a large glass of water. She was very pale. She said:

"You have to do something for me, Léon."

And gripping his hands tightly and shaking them, she went on:

"Listen, I need eight thousand francs!"

"You're out of your mind!"

"Not yet!"

And telling him all about the bailiffs, she lay her anguish at his feet, because Charles knew nothing about it, her mother-in-law hated her, old man Rouault couldn't help; but he, Léon, was going to race off and get the money she needed...

"How do you expect?..."

"You're so feeble!" she cried.

Then he was foolish enough to say:

"You're making it sound worse than it is. If you give him a thousand écus, maybe this fellow of yours will ease off."

One more reason to try and get it; it was impossible not to be able to unearth three thousand francs. And besides, Léon could borrow it on her behalf.

"Go on! Do it! You have to! Quick!... Oh, try, try! I'll love you for ever!"

He went out, came back after an hour with a serious expression on his face:

"I went to see three people..." he said. "It was pointless!"

They sat facing each other either side of the fireplace, not moving, not speaking. Emma shrugged, tapped her feet. He heard her mutter:

"If I were in your position, I'd be able to get it!"

"Where?"

"From your office!"

And she stared at him.

There was diabolical effrontery in her fiery eyes, the heavy eyelids that drooped suggestively, persuasively, and the young man felt himself weakening beneath the silent willpower of this woman who was asking him to commit a crime. It frightened him, and so to stop matters going any further he tapped his forehead and exclaimed:

"Morel will be back tonight! He won't say no – I hope not anyway" (He was a friend of his whose father was a wealthy businessman.) Then he added: "I'll give it to you tomorrow."

Emma didn't seem as delighted with his plan as he had expected. Had she guessed that he was lying? Blushing, he went on:

"If I'm not back by three o'clock, don't wait for me, my love. Forgive me, but I must be going. Goodbye!"

He squeezed her hand, but it felt lifeless. Emma had no strength left for emotions.

Four o'clock struck; like an automaton she got up to go back to Yonville, obeying the force of habit.

The weather was beautiful; it was one of those bitterly clear March days when the sun shines out of a pure white sky. Happy townsfolk were out walking in their Sunday clothes. She came to the Place du Parvis. Vespers had just finished; the crowd flowed out of the three doors like a river between the arches of a bridge, and in their midst stood the Swiss Guard, as solid as a rock.

She remembered the day when, full of hopes and fears, she had walked into the great nave, which for all its size wasn't as vast as her love, and she walked on past, crying beneath her veil, head spinning, legs failing, almost fainting.

"Make way!" shouted a voice from a carriage entrance whose doors were just opening.

She stopped as a black horse came out, pawing at the ground between the shafts of a tilbury carrying a gentleman in a sable coat. Who was it? She recognized him... But then the carriage sped off and disappeared.

It was the Vicomte! She looked back: the street was empty. And she was so overcome that she leant against the wall to stop herself collapsing.

She thought she had made a mistake. It was the only thing she could be sure of now. Everything in and around her had deserted her. She felt lost, rolling around aimlessly in one nameless abyss after another, and when she arrived at the Croix Rouge she was almost overjoyed to see the good Homais, who was watching as a large box of pharmaceutical supplies were loaded onto the *Hirondelle*; in his hand were six *cheminots* wrapped in a handkerchief.

Madame Homais was particularly fond of these doughy rolls shaped like turbans which were eaten with salted butter during Lent: they were the last scion of medieval food, perhaps going back to the time of the Crusades, and which hearty Normans used to fill themselves up with, thinking they saw Saracens' heads waiting to be devoured among the flagons of hippocras* and vast plates of charcuterie in the yellow torchlight on the table. Despite her appalling teeth the apothecary's wife munched at them like people used to, heroically, and so every time Homais went into town he made a point of bringing some back for her, and always bought them from the big baker's shop in the Rue Massacre.

"Delighted to see you!" he said, offering Emma his hand to help her into the *Hirondelle*.

Then he hung the *cheminots* on the straps of the net, took his cap off and sat with his arms folded in a thoughtful Napoleonic pose.

But when the blind man appeared at the bottom of the hill as usual, he burst out:

"I can't understand why the authorities still allow such deplorable activities! Poor souls like that should be shut away and made to do some work or other. Goodness me, progress moves at a snail's pace! We're still floundering around in the Dark Ages!"

The blind man held out his hat, which was flopping up and down on the coach door like a flap of peeling wallpaper.

"Now there's a case of scrofula!" said the pharmacist.

And despite the fact that he knew the poor devil, he pretended it was the first time he had seen him, muttering words such as *cornea*, *opaque cornea*, *sclerotic*, *facies*, and then asked him in a fatherly way:

"How long have you had this frightful affliction, old chap? Instead of getting drunk in the tavern it would do you more good to go on a diet."

And he encouraged him to only drink proper wine, proper beer, eat proper roast meat. The blind man carried on singing; in fact he seemed half-witted. Eventually Homais took out his purse.

"Here's a sou, give me two farthings' change – and don't forget my suggestions, you'll feel better for them."

Hivert expressed doubt about how effective these would be. But the apothecary assured him that he would cure him himself with an anti-inflammatory ointment of his own making, and gave him his address.

"Monsieur Homais, near the covered market, most people know me."

"Well then," said Hivert, "for our trouble you can *do your little turn for us*."

The blind man went down on his haunches, and tipping his head back, rolling his greenish eyes and sticking out his tongue, he rubbed his belly with both hands and let out a kind of muffled howl like a starving dog. Filled with revulsion, Emma tossed him a five-franc piece over her shoulder. It was all she had. She thought it was a fine gesture to give it away.

The coach had set off again when Homais suddenly leant out the window and shouted:

"No starchy food or dairy products! Wear wool next to your skin and steam the infected parts with the fumes from juniper berries!"

The sight of all the familiar scenery going past helped take Emma's mind off her sufferings. She was overwhelmed by exhaustion and arrived home in a daze, disheartened, almost asleep.

"What will be, will be!" she thought.

Because who could say? Something extraordinary might happen at any moment. Why, Lheureux might even die.

At nine the next morning she was woken by the sound of voices in the square. A crowd had gathered in the covered market to read a large notice that had been put up on one of the pillars, and she saw Justin climbing on a bollard to tear it down. But at that moment the village policeman grabbed him by the collar. Monsieur Homais came out of the pharmacy, and in the thick of the crowd old mother Lefrançois appeared to be holding forth.

"Madame!" cried Félicité as she came in. "Madame, it's awful!"

Overcome, the poor girl held out a sheet of yellow paper that she had just torn off the front door. Within the space of a second, Emma read that all her furniture had been put up for sale.

They stared at each other in silence. Between maid and mistress there were no secrets. After a moment Félicité sighed:

"If I were you Madame, I'd go and see Monsieur Guillaumin."

"You think so?..."

What she meant was: "You know the house through the servant, has the master ever mentioned me?"

"Yes, go, it's the best thing to do."

She got up, put on her black dress with its hood edged with jet, and then, so no one would see her (there were still a lot of people in the square), she headed out of the village along the path by the river.

By the time she reached the notary's gate she was out of breath; the sky was dark and it was snowing slightly.

Théodore answered the doorbell in a red waistcoat; he invited her in almost informally, as if he knew her personally, and showed her to the dining room.

A large porcelain stove was rumbling away beneath a cactus that filled the recess, and in dark wooden frames on the mock-oak wallpaper were Steuben's *Esméralda* and Chopin's *Putiphar*.* Everything – the laid dining table, the pair of silver plate-warmers, the crystal doorknobs, the wooden floor and the furniture – gleamed with fastidious English cleanness; each window pane had a section of coloured glass in the corners.

"This is the type of dining room I ought to have," thought Emma.

The notary came in, holding his palm leaf-patterned dressing gown across him with his left hand, taking off his brown velvet cap with the other then quickly putting it back on again, tilted affectedly over his right ear where three tufts of blond hair were brushed forward from the back of his bald head.

When he had offered her a seat he sat down and began eating his breakfast, apologizing for being so rude.

"Please Monsieur," she said, "I have something to ask you…"

"What is it, Madame? Do go on."

And she explained.

Maître Guillaumin had heard about it already, because he had a secret arrangement with the draper, from whom he was always able to obtain funds to finance the mortgages that people asked him to draw up for them.

So he knew (better than she did) the long history of these bills of exchange, modest to begin with, guaranteed by various people, taken out over long periods and repeatedly renewed, until eventually the shopkeeper collected up all the formal demands and, not wanting his fellow villagers to think he was a rapacious beast, asked his friend Vinçart to take the necessary legal proceedings in his own name.

Her account was punctuated with complaints about Lheureux, which the notary acknowledged with the occasional inconsequential remark.

He continued eating his cutlet and drinking his tea, chin resting on a sky-blue cravat fixed with two diamond pins held together by a thin gold chain, and smiled his peculiar smile, which was both mawkish and equivocal. Then he noticed her feet were wet.

"Come over by the stove... Yes, closer... Sit right next to it."

She was worried about making it dirty – to which the notary gallantly replied:

"Beauty never spoils anything."

She did her best to win him over and, becoming emotional in the process, described the constraints of married life, her inner conflicts, her needs. He understood: she was a woman of style! And without stopping eating he turned towards her so that his knee brushed against her boot, which was beginning to curl up and steam from being so close to the stove.

But when she asked him for a thousand écus he pursed his lips, and told her he was aggrieved not to have been asked to manage her finances before, because even for a lady there were many convenient ways to make her money work for her. They could have invested it in some first-rate and almost certainly safe ventures, such as the peat bogs at Grumesnil or some land at Le Havre, and he let her fume to herself about the colossal profits she would undoubtedly have made.

"How is it that you didn't come to me?" he went on.

"I don't really know," she replied.

"Why, eh?... Do I frighten you that much? Because I'm the one who has something to be upset about! We hardly know each other! Yet I'm most devoted to you; I hope you're not unaware of that?"

He reached out and took her hand in his, kissed it avidly, and then held it on his knee, playing gently with her fingers while whispering sweet nothings.

His insipid voice babbled on like a stream; behind the mirror of his glasses there was a glint in his eye, and his hands moved up her sleeve and began fondling her arm. She could feel his heavy breathing on her cheek. The man was making her appallingly embarrassed.

She leapt up:

"Monsieur! I'm waiting!"

"What for?" said the notary, who suddenly turned pale.

"The money."

"But..."

Then giving in to his uncontrollable desires:

"Yes, well!..."

And paying no heed to his dressing gown he shuffled towards her on his knees.

"For pity's sake stay! I love you!"

He grabbed her round the waist.

Madame Bovary flushed bright crimson. She moved back, a terrible look in her eyes, and exclaimed:

"You have the effrontery to take advantage of my misfortunes, Monsieur! I may be pitiable but I'm not for sale!"

And she left.

The notary just stood there, astonished, staring at his handsome tapestry slippers. They were a present from a lady friend; just looking at them made him feel better. In any case, an affair of that kind might have become too complicated.

"What a swine!" she said to herself agitatedly as she rushed headlong down the road under the aspens. "What a churl!... It's outrageous!" The disappointment at her lack of success affronted her already wounded modesty even more; it was as if Providence itself was conspiring against her, and bolstering herself up with pride, never had she thought so much of herself and so little of others. She seethed with aggression. She would have liked to lash out at all men, spit in their faces, grind them to dust, and on she strode, pale, trembling, fuming, searching the empty horizon with tear-filled eyes, almost revelling in the hatred that was choking her.

But when she saw her house she was suddenly filled with inertia. She couldn't go on, yet she had to – besides, where else was there for her to run to?

Félicité was waiting at the door.

"Well?"

"No!" said Emma.

And for a quarter of an hour the two of them tried to think of people in Yonville who might be prepared to help her. But every time Félicité mentioned a name, Emma said:

"Impossible! They wouldn't want to!"

"But Monsieur's due back!"

"I know... just leave me on my own."

She had tried everything. There was nothing more she could do; so when Charles came in she would tell him:

"Take yourself away somewhere. The carpet you're standing on doesn't belong to us any more. In the whole house you haven't got a stick of furniture, not a stitch, and it's me who's ruined you, you poor dear man!"

There would be a great sob, he would shed floods of tears, and then once he had got over the shock he would forgive her.

"Oh yes," she mumbled, grinding her teeth, "he'll forgive me; he would give me a million to make me forgive him for having met me, and still not think it was enough... Never! Never!"

The thought of Bovary being superior to her infuriated her. But whether she liked it or not he was going to find out about this mess sooner or later, so she just had to wait for the appalling scene and bear the brunt of his magnanimity. She felt a sudden urge to go back to Lheureux – but what was the point? Write to her father? It was too late for that. She might even have been regretting not giving the other man what he wanted when she heard a horse trotting down the lane. It was him, he was opening the gate, ashen-faced. Dashing down the stairs she hurried out into the square where the mayor's wife, who was talking to Lestiboudois, saw her go into the tax-collector's house.

She rushed off to tell Madame Caron. The two ladies went up to the attic and, hidden by the washing hanging from poles, they took up a comfortable position from where they could see into Binet's apartment.

He was alone in his garret, busy making a wooden version of one of those indefinable ivory sculptures that are shaped like an obelisk and made up of crescents and hollow spheres one inside the other, and which serve no purpose; he was just starting the last piece, the end was in sight! In the chiaroscuro of the workshop, pale golden dust showered from his lathe like sparks from the hooves of a galloping horse; the two wheels were turning, humming; Binet was smiling, head down, nostrils flared, seemingly given over to one of those states of pure bliss that are the preserve of mundane activities which occupy the mind with facile problems, gratifying it with a sense of achievement beyond its wildest dreams.

"Ah, there she is!" said Madame Tuvache.

But it was virtually impossible to hear what she was saying because of the lathe.

Eventually the women thought they made out the word *francs*, and old mother Tuvache whispered:

"She's asking if she can delay paying her taxes."

"So it appears!" said the other.

They watched her walking up and down, studying the napkin rings, candlesticks and banister knobs ranged along the walls, while Binet stroked his beard in satisfaction.

"Is she ordering something from him?" wondered Madame Tuvache.

"He doesn't sell anything!" her neighbour replied.

The tax-collector appeared to be listening, eyes wide as if in incomprehension. She was talking in an amorous, imploring way. She came closer to him, breast heaving; they weren't speaking now.

"Is she making advances?" said Madame Tuvache.

Binet blushed to the roots of his hair. She took him by the hands.

"Oh, this is too much!"

She was undoubtedly making unspeakable propositions, because the tax-collector – who was a brave man, he had fought at Bautzen and Lützen,* in the French campaign, had even been *recommended for the Croix d'Honneur* – suddenly leapt back:

"Madame! What are you suggesting?..."

"Women like that ought to be flogged!" said Madame Tuvache.

"Where's she gone?" replied Madame Caron.

While they were speaking she had disappeared; then, catching sight of her heading down the Grande Rue and turning right as if going to the cemetery, they were left to their speculations.

"I can hardly breathe, Mother Rolet!" she said when she got to the wet nurse's house. "Undo me!"

She collapsed on the bed, she sobbed. Old mother Rolet covered her with a petticoat and stood beside her. Then as she didn't say anything more, the woman went back to her spinning wheel.

"Oh, do stop it," Emma mumbled, thinking she could still hear Binet's lathe.

"Whatever's troubling her?" wondered the nurse. "Why come here?"

She had been impelled there by the same sense of dread that had driven her out of her house.

Lying motionless on her back, eyes vacant, she could only vaguely make out the things around her, despite concentrating with a sort of imbecile obstinacy. She gazed at flaking patches on the wall, burning brands smouldering end to end, a big spider scuttling about in the crack in the beam above her head. Then at last she gathered her thoughts. She remembered... a day with Léon... oh, how long ago it was... the sun was shining on the river, the clematis filled the air with fragrance... And, swept away by memories as if in a raging torrent, she recalled the events of the day before.

"What time is it?" she asked.

Old mother Rolet went outside, held up two fingers of her right hand to where the sky was clearest, then came back and said:

"Almost three o'clock."

"Oh, thank you, thank you!"

Because he would come. There was no doubt! He would have the money. But not realizing that she was here he might go to her house; so she told the nurse to hurry over and bring him back with her.

"Quickly!"

"I'm going, Madame, I'm going!"

She was amazed that she hadn't thought of him before – he had given his word, he wouldn't go back on it – and she saw herself in Lheureux's shop already, laying the three banknotes on his desk. But then she would have to make up something to tell Bovary. What?

Meanwhile the wet nurse hadn't come back. Since there wasn't a clock in the little cottage Emma thought she might be overestimating how long it was taking. She walked slowly round the garden a few times; she went along the footpath by the hedge, then hurried back, hoping the woman might have come home another way. Eventually, tired of waiting, beset by misgivings which she dismissed, not knowing whether she had been there for an eternity or an instant, she sat in a corner, closed her eyes and covered her ears. Then the gate creaked; she leapt up; but before she could ask her, old mother Rolet had said:

"There's no one at your house!"

"What?"

"No, no one. Monsieur's crying. He's calling you. They're looking for you."

Emma didn't reply. She looked round, eyes rolling, chest heaving, and, frightened by the expression on her face, the peasant woman shrank back instinctively, thinking she had gone mad. Then suddenly she struck her forehead and let out a cry: she had just remembered Rodolphe, the memory of him flashed through her like lightning on a dark night. He was so kind, so sensitive, so generous! And if he were unsure whether to help her or not it would only take a second for her to make him do it, by reminding him of their love. So she set off for La Huchette, not realizing that she was about to offer herself to someone who had made her pain much worse, and without imagining for a moment that this was called prostitution.

8

A S SHE WALKED ALONG she wondered: "What am I going to say? Where shall I begin?" Soon she recognized bushes, trees, the seagrass on the hill, the chateau in the distance. Her earliest tender feelings were reawoken, her poor crushed heart swelled with love. A warm breeze wafted over her face; droplets of snow melted one by one onto the grass.

She went through the little gate into the grounds like she used to, then came to the main courtyard, which was bordered by two rows of bushy lime trees. The dogs barked in the kennels, yet despite the noise no one appeared.

She climbed the wide straight staircase with its wooden balusters, which led to the dusty flagged corridor lined with doors like in a monastery or an inn. His room was at the far end on the left. When her hand touched the handle, her strength suddenly deserted her. She was afraid he might not be there, almost wanted him not to be, yet he was her only hope, her last chance of salvation. She paused to gather her thoughts, and then drawing courage from the well of necessity, she went in.

He was sitting by the fire, feet on the rail, smoking a pipe.

"Well well!" he said, jumping up. "It's you!"

"Yes, it's me!... I'd like to ask your advice, Rodolphe."

Try as he might, he was unable to tear his lips from hers.

"You haven't changed, you're as delightful as ever!"

"But they're empty delights now, since you chose to spurn them," she replied bitterly.

So then he attempted to explain his behaviour, making up vague excuses for want of anything better.

She let herself be carried away by his words, and especially his voice, the sight of him; to the point where she pretended to believe, or perhaps even did believe the reason for their separation; that it was a secret upon which the honour, even the life of a third person depended.

"It doesn't matter!" she said, looking at him sadly. "I've suffered a great deal!"

"Such is life!" he replied, philosophically.

"But since we parted," Emma went on, "has it at least been good for you?"

"Oh... neither good nor bad!"

"Perhaps it would have been better if we had never split up."

"Yes... perhaps!"

"Do you think so?" she said, coming closer.

And she sighed.

"O Rodolphe! If only you knew!... I loved you so much!"

She took his hand, and for a while they stood with their fingers entwined – just like the first time, at the Agricultural Show! With a proud gesture he struggled against his tender feelings. But collapsing into his arms she said:

"How did you expect me to live without you? It's not possible simply to stop being happy, like breaking a habit! I was in despair! I thought I was going to die! I'll tell you all about it, see if I don't. But... you ran away from me!..."

Because for three years, with the instinctive cowardice of the stronger sex, he had carefully avoided her; meanwhile Emma was moving her head playfully from side to side like the sweetest of kittens:

"Admit it, you loved other women! Oh, come on, I can understand them! And I forgive them – because you seduced them like you did me. After all, you're a man! You know how to make people worship you. But we'll make a fresh start, won't we? We'll be in love? See, I'm laughing, I'm happy!... Say something then!"

She was magnificent to behold, eyes brimming with tears like a blue chalice filled with rainwater after a storm.

He sat her on his lap, stroked the back of his hand over her smooth headbands, which reflected a last beam of sunlight like a shaft of gold in the dusk. She lowered her head; gently he brushed her eyelids with his lips.

"You've been crying!" he said. "Why?"

She burst into tears. He thought it was an effusion of love, but since she said nothing more he assumed her silence was a last vestige of modesty, and then he exclaimed:

"Oh, please forgive me! For me you're the only one. I've been a fool, a wicked fool! I love you, I always will!... So what's the matter? Tell me!"

And he went down on his knees.

"It's that... I've lost everything, Rodolphe! You have to lend me three thousand francs!"

"But... but..." he said, slowly getting up, his face becoming solemn.

"My husband put all his money in the hands of a lawyer, you see," she went on quickly, "who then ran off. We borrowed; our patients didn't pay their bills. Not only that, the bankruptcy proceedings aren't over: there's more to come. As it stands, for want of three thousand francs all our possessions are going to be sold off – it's happening today, at this very moment – so I've come to you as a friend."

"Ah!" thought Rodolphe, who had turned pale. "So that's why she's here!"

And he said calmly:

"I haven't got it, dear lady."

He wasn't lying. Had he had it, he would certainly have given it to her, however distasteful it is to perform such noble deeds; because, of all the storms that blow through lovers' hearts, a request for money is the most wintry, the most violent.

At first she just stared at him.

"You haven't got it!"

And she said it several times:

"You haven't got it!... I should have spared myself this last indignity. You never loved me! You're no better than the rest!"

She was betraying herself, foundering.

Rodolphe interrupted, telling her that he was also "financially embarrassed".

"I pity you!" said Emma. "Oh yes, very much so..."

Then her gaze fell on a rifle made of damascened steel gleaming on the gun rack:

"The poor don't have rifles with silver butts! They don't buy clocks inlaid with tortoiseshell!" she went on, pointing at a Boulle* timepiece, "or have gilded silver whistles on their whip handles" – and she felt them! – "or bracelets for their watches! Ah, he wants for nothing, not even a decanter stand for his bedroom; you're fond of yourself aren't you, you live well, you have a chateau, farms, woodland; you ride to hounds, you go to Paris... Even these," she cried, picking up his cufflinks from the mantelpiece, "the merest of all these silly things, you could get money for them! Oh, I don't want them! You can keep them!"

And she hurled them across the room, breaking the gold chain on the wall.

"But I would have given you all I had, I would have sold everything, worked my fingers to the bone, begged in the street, just for a smile, a glance, to hear you say 'Thank you'! And you sit there calmly in your armchair as if you haven't caused me enough pain already! Don't you realize that without you I might have been happy! Who made you do it? Was it for a wager? Yet you loved me, you told me so... again, just now... Oh, it would have been better to throw me out! My hands are still warm from your kisses, there's the spot on the carpet where you went down on your knees and vowed to love me for ever. You had me believing it: for two whole years you carried me off into the most wonderful, the sweetest of dreams!... Do you remember that journey we planned, eh? And the letter, that letter of yours! It broke my heart! Then when I come to him, to him who is wealthy, happy, free, to beg him to do something for me, something that anyone would do, imploring him, offering him all my love and affection, he rejects me because it would cost three thousand francs!"

"I haven't got it!" said Rodolphe with that utter calm with which philosophical anger always shields itself.

She left. The walls shook, the ceiling bore down on her; she walked back down the long avenue, slipping on the piles of dead leaves that the wind was blowing around. Finally she reached the ditch by the gate; she was in such a hurry to open it that she broke her nails on the catch. After she had gone a short way she stopped, out of breath, almost collapsing. Turning round she saw it again, the impassive chateau, the grounds, the gardens, the three courtyards, the many windows of the façade.

She stood there in a daze, only registering her existence from the pulsing of the blood in her arteries, which seemed to fill the surrounding countryside with a deafening drumbeat. The ground beneath her feet was so soft it was like walking on water, the ploughed fields looked like vast brown waves breaking. Everything inside her head, her memories, thoughts, ideas, suddenly burst out like an enormous fireworks display. She saw her father, Lheureux's office, the hotel room in Rouen, a different landscape. She was seized with madness, she was frightened, barely managing to control herself, and then only hazily, because she had quite forgotten what it was that had got her into this terrible position: money. She was suffering from love, nothing else, she felt her soul escaping from her body through the hole made by this memory, like an injured man feels his life trickling away with the blood from his wound.

Night fell, crows flew past.

Suddenly it was as if fiery balls were exploding in the air like bullets, spinning furiously round and round, raging, smashing, landing on the snow between the trees then melting. In the centre of every one of them was Rodolphe's face. There were more and more, they came closer, plunged into her; then they disappeared. She recognized the lights of the houses in the distance, shining through the mist.

And then her situation opened up in front of her like an abyss. Her chest heaved violently. In a sudden heroic frenzy that almost made her feel happy, she ran down the hill, across the plank used by the cattle, along the footpath, the lane, and then past the covered market to the pharmacist's shop.

It was empty. She was about to go in, but they might have heard the bell and come out; and so slipping through the gate, holding her breath, feeling her way along the wall, she went up to the kitchen window and saw a candle burning on the stove. Justin, in shirtsleeves, was just taking in a dish.

"Ah, they're having dinner. I'll wait."

He reappeared. She tapped on the glass. He came out.

"The key! The one for upstairs, where he keeps the—"

"What?"

And he stared at her, amazed at the paleness of her face, which stood out white against the black of the night. She looked incredibly beautiful, as stately as a ghost; he couldn't quite understand what she wanted, but had a feeling that it was something terrible.

She went on excitedly, in a quiet, gentle, melting voice:

"I want it! Give it to me."

The partition wall was thin, and the clattering of knives and forks on plates could be heard from the dining room.

She told him she needed something to kill the rats that were stopping her from sleeping.

"I'll have to ask Monsieur."

"No! Stay here!"

Then she added, casually:

"There's no need, I'll tell him later. Come on, put the light on!"

She went down the passage that led to the laboratory. Hanging on the wall outside the door was a key with a label saying *inner sanctum*.

"Justin!" called the apothecary, getting impatient.

"Let's go up!"

And he followed her.

The key turned in the lock, and her memory led her straight to the third shelf, where she grabbed the blue jar, pulled out the stopper, reached in and took a handful of white powder then started to eat it.

"Stop!" he cried, grabbing hold of her.

"Be quiet! Someone will come…"

He was beside himself, wanted to call for help.

"Don't say a word – your master will get in trouble!"

And then she went home, suddenly reconciled, as if at peace in the knowledge that she had done her duty.

When Charles came home, devastated to hear about the public sale, Emma had just gone out. He called, wept, collapsed in a faint, but she didn't appear. Where could she be? He sent Félicité to the Homais', to Monsieur Tuvache, Lheureux, the Lion d'Or, everywhere – and between fits of anxiety he saw his reputation ruined, all their money gone, Berthe's future in tatters! But why, what had caused it?… Not a word of explanation! He waited until six in the evening, and then, unable to bear it any longer and thinking that she had probably gone to Rouen, he walked along the main road for about half a league, didn't see anyone, waited for a while then went home.

She was there.

"What's happened?… Why?… Tell me!…"

She sat at her desk and wrote a letter, sealed it slowly, putting the date and the time. Then she said in a formal voice:

"You are to read it tomorrow; from now on please don't ask me any questions!… No, not a single one."

"But—"

"Just leave me alone!"

And she lay on the bed.

She was woken by a harsh, bitter taste in her mouth. She caught sight of Charles and closed her eyes again.

She waited in suspense, curious to see if she was going to feel any pain. But no, not a thing! She could hear the clock ticking, the fire crackling, Charles's breathing from beside the bed.

"There's nothing to it, dying!" she thought. "I'll just fall asleep and it'll all be over!"

She drank some water and turned to face the wall.

The dreadful taste of ink wouldn't go away.

"I'm thirsty!... So thirsty!" she sighed.

"What's the matter?" said Charles, offering her the glass.

"Nothing!... Open the window... I can't breathe!"

Then suddenly she felt sick, and only just had time to get her handkerchief from under the pillow.

"Take it away!" she snapped. "Get rid of it!"

He started asking questions; she didn't answer. She lay completely still, afraid that the slightest display of emotion would make her vomit. In the meantime she felt an icy-cold sensation moving up from her feet towards her heart.

"Ah, it's beginning!" she mumbled.

"What did you say?"

She moved her head from side to side, gently but fearfully, constantly opening her mouth wide as if there was something heavy stuck to her tongue. At eight o'clock the vomiting started again.

Charles noticed what looked like white grit at the bottom of the china basin.

"Extraordinary!" he kept saying. "Most odd!"

But she cried angrily:

"You're wrong!"

Carefully, almost caressing, he ran his hand over her stomach. She gave a shriek. He leapt back in fright.

Then, quietly at first, she began to moan. Her shoulders gave a great shudder, she went whiter than the sheet that her fingers were gripping so tightly. By now he could barely feel her irregular pulse.

Her bluish face, which seemed to be set rigid in the metallic fumes of its own breath, was covered in beads of sweat. Her teeth chattered, her now enormous eyes looked vacantly round the room, and to every question she just nodded: once or twice she even smiled. Gradually her groans got louder. She gave a muffled howl; she told him she was feeling better and would soon be able to get up. But suddenly she went into convulsions, and screamed:

"Agh! My God, it's awful!"

He dropped to his knees by the bed.

"What did you eat? Tell me! For Heaven's sake say something!"

And he stared at her, his eyes filled with a love that she had never seen in them before.

"Oh... there!... Over there!..." she said, her voice faltering.

He rushed to the desk, tore open the sealed letter and read out: "No one else is to blame..." He stopped, put his hand over his eyes, then read it again.

"What!... Help!... Help me!"

All he could do was keep repeating the one word: "Poisoned! Poisoned!" Félicité ran off to fetch Monsieur Homais, who shouted the news across the square; Madame Lefrançois heard him in the Lion d'Or, people went to tell their neighbours, and the whole village was wide awake all night.

Charles paced round the room, hysterical, gabbling, on the point of collapse. He stumbled into the furniture, tore at his hair; the pharmacist couldn't believe he was witnessing something so appalling.

He went home and wrote to Monsieur Canivet and Doctor Larivière. He was beside himself; he produced more than fifteen rough drafts. Hippolyte set off for Neufchâtel, and Justin rode Bovary's horse so hard that he had to leave it on the hill by Guillaume woods, almost dead from exhaustion.

Charles tried to consult his medical encyclopedia, but he couldn't see what he was reading; the words were dancing up and down.

"Keep calm!" said the apothecary. "It's simply a matter of administering a powerful antidote. Which poison is it?"

Charles showed him her letter. It was arsenic.

"Right!" said Homais. "We'll have to do an analysis."

For he knew that in any case of poisoning you had to carry out an analysis; and Bovary, who didn't understand, just replied:

"Do it! Do it! Save her..."

Then going over to her he sunk to the floor, put his head on the bed and knelt there, sobbing.

"Don't cry!" she told him. "I won't be plaguing you for much longer!"

"Why? What made you you do it?"

"It had to be done, my love," she replied.

"Weren't you happy? Is it my fault? But I've done everything I can!"

"Yes… that's true… but then, you're a good person."

Slowly she ran her fingers through his hair. This sweet sensation was too much for his unhappiness to bear; he felt his whole being caving in in despair at the thought that he was going to lose her at the very moment when she had told him she loved him more than ever. He couldn't think of anything to say; he didn't know how, he didn't dare; the need to find a solution immediately, urgently, had turned his world upside down.

Emma was telling herself that it was all over, all the betrayals, the vileness, the countless lustful desires that had tormented her. She hated no one now; her mind sunk into a twilit daze; among the music of the earth, all she could hear was the fitful, faint and gentle lament of this poor dear heart, like the last notes of a symphony echoing into the distance.

"Bring me my little girl," she said, raising herself on her elbow.

"So you're not feeling so bad now?" asked Charles.

"No, no!"

Carried in by the maid, the child was wearing a long nightshirt with her bare feet sticking out, and looked serious and almost still asleep. She stared in amazement at the chaos in the room, screwing up her eyes, blinded by the candles that were burning everywhere. It reminded her of New Year or mid-Lent, when she was woken up early by candlelight and climbed into bed with her mother to be given her presents, because she asked:

"Where are they, Mama?"

But as no one answered she went on:

"I can't see my little shoe!"

Félicité carried her over to the bed, but she kept looking at the fireplace.

"Has the nurse got it?" she asked.

Hearing this name, which brought back memories of her adultery and her ordeals, Madame Bovary turned her head away, as if it were a worse poison than the one in her stomach. Meanwhile Berthe was sitting on the bed.

"You've got such big eyes, Mama. You're so pale! And you're all sweaty!..."

Her mother stared at her.

"I'm frightened!" said the little girl, shrinking back.

Emma took her hand to kiss it, but she pulled it away.

"That's enough!" cried Charles, who was sobbing in the alcove. "Take her back to bed!"

For a short while the effects of the poison abated; Emma seemed less distressed; and at the slightest word, every less rasping breath, his hopes were raised. When Canivet finally arrived he threw his arms round him and wept.

"You're here! Oh, thank you! You're so kind! But she's getting better now. Look..."

His colleague didn't share this opinion and, not being one – as he himself admitted – *to beat about the bush*, he prescribed an emetic to void her stomach.

It wasn't long before she was coughing up blood. Her lips clamped together even tighter. Her arms and legs were rigid, her body covered in brown blotches, her pulse felt as weak as a harp string on the point of snapping.

Then she began to scream horribly. She cursed and railed against the poison, begged it to do its work quickly, and her stiff arms thrust aside anything that Charles, who seemed closer to death than she was, tried to get her to drink. He stood with his handkerchief over his mouth, groaning, crying, choked by sobs that shook his whole body; Félicité rushed round the room; Homais kept sighing and didn't move, while Canivet, although as unruffled as ever, was now beginning to worry.

"Hell's teeth!... But... she's been flushed out, and as soon as what's causing it has stopped..."

"The symptoms should stop as well," said Homais. "That's self-evident."

Without listening to Homais, who was still suggesting that "perhaps it's a beneficial spasm", Canivet was about to administer a theriac when they heard the crack of a whip; the windows rattled, and a large Berlin pulled at breakneck speed by three mud-caked horses hove to outside the covered market. It was Doctor Larivière.

The appearance of a god wouldn't have been met with such emotion. Bovary lifted his hands to heaven, Canivet stopped what he was doing, and Homais took off his silk cap before the Doctor had even walked in.

He belonged to that great school of surgery who learnt their art under Bichat,* that generation of philosopher practitioners, now long gone, who, having a fanatical devotion for their profession, exercised it with joy and discernment! Whenever he was angry the whole hospital shook, and his pupils revered him so much that they tried to follow his example in every possible way before they were even properly established; to the point where in all the towns in the area they could be seen dressed exactly the same as him, in the long merino wool overcoat and black tailcoat whose unbuttoned cuffs partly covered his plump hands, the most beautiful hands which never wore gloves so as always to be ready to thrust themselves into other people's misfortunes. Scorning decorations, titles and learned societies, a hospital doctor, open-minded, a father to the poor and practising rather than preaching virtue, he might have been taken for a saint had his keen wit not made people fear him like the Devil. Sharper than one of his scalpels, his gaze sliced straight into your soul to cut out the illusions from among the assertions and airs and graces. Thus it was that he lived his life, filled with that easy-going and regal dignity that comes from the knowledge of having talent, wealth and forty years of painstaking, impeccable service.

The moment he came in and saw Emma lying on her back, with her mouth open and her face deathly pale, he frowned. Then, to all appearances listening to Canivet, he ran his forefinger under his nose and said:

"Very good, very good."

Yet he gave a little shrug. Bovary watched him; their eyes met; and this man who was so accustomed to the sight of pain couldn't prevent a tear from trickling onto his ruff.

He took Canivet into the next room. Charles followed.

"She's very bad, isn't she? Maybe if you applied a mustard poultice? I don't know! Please find something, you've saved so many people!"

Charles put his arms round him and gave him a wild, imploring look, almost swooning against his chest.

"There there, my dear fellow, be brave! There's nothing more that can be done."

And Doctor Larivière turned away.

"You're going?"

"I'll come back."

He went out to give instructions to the coachman, accompanied by Canivet, who was equally unconcerned about having Emma die in his care.

The pharmacist caught up with them in the square. There was something in his character that made him crave the company of famous people. He begged Monsieur Larivière to do him the singular honour of lunching with him at his house.

They quickly sent to the Lion d'Or for pigeons, to the butcher's for all the cutlets he had, cream from Tuvache's, eggs from Lestiboudois, and the apothecary helped get everything ready himself, while, tightening the strings of her smock, Madame Homais said:

"You must excuse us, Monsieur: if you don't warn people the day before in this wretched village of ours—"

"The stemmed glasses!!!" whispered Homais.

"If we lived in town, at least we'd be able to get calves' feet."

"Be quiet!... Lunch is ready, Doctor!"

Once they had started eating he thought it was a good moment to provide some details about the terrible situation.

"To begin with we felt it might be desiccation of the pharynx, followed by unbearable pains in the epigastrium, hyper-purgation, coma."

"How did she poison herself?"

"I've no idea, Doctor – I can't imagine where she came by arsenic acid."

Justin, who was just bringing a stack of plates, started to shake.

"What's the matter?" asked the pharmacist.

At this the young man dropped them on the floor with a great crash.

"Idiot!" shouted Homais. "Clumsy, oafish, blithering ass!"

Then controlling himself he went on:

"I wanted to attempt an analysis, Doctor, and so, *primo*, I carefully inserted a tube—"

"It would have been better to put your fingers down her throat," said the surgeon.

His colleague remained silent, having just been given a severe private reprimand about his use of an emetic, and so the good Monsieur

Canivet, who had been so arrogant and vociferous about the club foot, was very reticent today; he just kept smiling in approval.

Homais's pride blossomed in his role as the bountiful host, and the pathetic thought of Bovary in distress somehow added to his enjoyment, swelling his self-esteem in comparison. Not only that, the Doctor's presence sent him into raptures. He put all his learning on display, referred to cantharides, upas, manchineel and adder in no particular order.

"I've even read that people have been poisoned, and almost fatally, Doctor, by blood sausage that had been smoked in too strong a smoke! At least that's what it said in a most excellent report by a leading light of the pharmaceutical profession, one of our great authorities, the renowned Cadet de Gassicourt!"

Madame Homais came in with one of those unsteady contraptions that are heated over a spirit burner, because Homais insisted on making coffee at the table, having roasted, ground and blended it himself.

"*Saccharum*, Doctor," he said, passing him the sugar.

Then he sent for the children, interested in hearing the surgeon's opinion on the state of their health.

Monsieur Larivière was finally on the point of leaving when Madame Homais asked his professional advice about her husband. He was making his blood thicker by falling asleep after dinner.

"Oh, it's not his blood that's thick."

And with a little smile at this unnoticed pun of his, the doctor opened the door. The pharmacist's shop was bulging with people; he had difficulty shaking off the Tuvache man, who was afraid his wife had an inflammation of the chest because she was always spitting in the ashes; and then Monsieur Binet, who sometimes got cravings for food; and Madame Caron who had a tingling sensation; Lheureux, who got dizzy spells; Lestiboudois, who suffered from rheumatism; Madame Lefrançois, who had heartburn. But finally the three horses sped off, and the overall feeling was that he hadn't been very obliging.

Then people's attention was caught by the appearance of Father Bournisien coming through the covered market carrying the holy oils.

Faithful to his principles, Homais likened priests to crows who are attracted by the smell of death. The mere sight of a clergyman was objectionable to him, because a cassock reminded him of a shroud, and it was partly his horror of the second that made him vilify the first.

Nonetheless, not shrinking from what he called *his mission*, he went back to Bovary's house with Canivet, who had been strongly advised to do so by Monsieur Larivière before he left, and had it not been for his wife's remonstrations he would have taken both his sons with him, to get them used to stressful situations, something that would be a lesson for them, an example, a sombre scene that would be engraved on their memories.

By the time they arrived the room was plunged in funereal gravity. On the work table, which was covered with a white cloth, were five or six balls of cotton wool on a silver dish, next to a large crucifix between two burning candlesticks. Emma, her chin on her chest, had her eyes open unnaturally wide, and her poor hands hung limply on the sheets in that grim yet gentle way characteristic of the dying, who seem impatient to pull the shroud over their heads. Pale as a statue, eyes as red as burning coals yet dry of tears, Charles stood facing her at the foot of the bed, while down on one knee the priest mumbled quietly.

She slowly turned her head, and seemed overjoyed at the sight of the purple stole, probably recalling in this atmophere of uncommon calm the vanished sensual delights of her earliest soarings into mysticism, its visions of imminent eternal bliss.

The priest got up and fetched the crucifix; she craned her neck as if thirsty, and pressing her lips to the figure of the Son of God, with all that remained of her strength she offered it the most loving kiss she had ever given. After that he said the *Misereatur* and the *Indulgentiam*,* dipped the thumb of his right hand in the oil and began the unction: first on the eyes, which had coveted worldly opulence; then the nostrils, hungry for warm breezes and the fragrance of love; then the mouth, which had opened to tell lies, cooed with pride and cried out with lust; then the hands, which had luxuriated in the touch of soft, sweet things; and finally the soles of the feet, which had once run to satisfy her desires but which walked no more.

The Father wiped his fingers, threw the pieces of oil-soaked cotton wool onto the fire, sat beside the dying woman and told her that she must now unite her sufferings with those of Jesus Christ and give herself up to divine mercy.

Once he had finished his exhortations he tried to put a blessed candle in her hand, symbolizing the heavenly glory that would soon surround her. But Emma was too weak to hold it, and were it not for Bournisien the candle would have dropped on the floor.

She wasn't so pale now, and her face wore an expression of serenity, as if the sacrament had healed her.

The priest made a point of mentioning this; he even told Bovary that the Lord sometimes allows people to live a little longer if he judges it expedient for their salvation, and Charles remembered the time before when she was close to death, and had taken Communion.

"Perhaps I shouldn't give up hope," he thought.

And at that moment she looked round slowly, like someone waking from a dream; in a clear voice she asked for her mirror, and looked into it for a while until great tears started to flow from her eyes. Then she gave a sigh and her head fell back onto the pillow.

Immediately her chest began to heave frantically. Her tongue protruded from her mouth; the whites of her eyeballs rolled back, like the glass shades of a lamp that is going out, and they might have thought she was already dead were it not for the terrifying tossing of her ribcage as it shook with a violent exhalation, as if her soul were leaping up and down to free itself. Félicité knelt in front of the cross, even the pharmacist bent his knees slightly, while Canivet looked vacantly out of the window. Bournisien started to pray again, head bent over the edge of the bed, his long cassock trailing across the floor behind him. Charles knelt on the other side, holding out his arms to Emma. He took her hands, gripped them tightly, shuddering with every beat of her heart as if at the reverberations of a ruin collapsing. As the death rattle grew louder the priest's orations came faster and faster; they mingled with Bovary's suppressed sobs, and at times everything seemed lost beneath the dull murmur of the Latin words, which chimed like the tolling of a bell.

Suddenly they heard the sound of heavy clogs on the pavement, the light tapping of a staff, and then a voice began to sing, a hoarse, raucous voice:

"On hot days when it's nice and sunny
The young girls start to feel lovey-dovey."

Emma sat up like a corpse springing back to life, her hair falling loose, eyes vacant, gaping.

"To carefully, quickly gather in
The corn at harvest time,

My Nanette went down a-bendin'
In them furrows we'd dug in line."

"The blind man!" she cried.

And Emma began to laugh, a terrible, frenzied, desolate laugh, thinking she saw the poor devil's hideous face rising out of the eternal shades like the horror of horrors.

"There was a good strong wind on that fine day,
And her dear little petticoat blew clean away!"

Convulsing, she collapsed back onto the bed. They all came closer. The life was gone from her.

9

AFTER SOMEONE'S DEATH there always follows a sense of bewilderment, so difficult is it to comprehend the sudden onset of oblivion and to come to terms with it. Yet when he noticed that she had stopped moving, Charles threw himself at her and cried:

"Farewell! Farewell!"

Homais and Canivet took him out of the room.

"Calm yourself!"

"Yes, all right," he said, wresting himself free from them, "I'll be sensible, I won't do any harm. But leave me alone! I want to see her! She's my wife!"

And he burst into tears.

"Go on, cry," the pharmacist told him, "let nature take its course. It'll make you feel better!"

Now weaker than a child, Charles let himself be taken downstairs to the dining room, and then Homais went home.

On the square he was waylaid by the blind man, who, having hauled himself all the way to Yonville in the hope of getting the anti-inflammatory ointment, was asking every passer-by where the apothecary lived.

"Really, as if I didn't have bigger fish to fry! Oh, too bad! Come back later!"

And he hurried into the pharmacy.

He had two letters to write, a sedative potion to make up for Bovary, a lie to invent to conceal the truth about the poisoning and an article to draft for the *Fanal*, to say nothing of the people who were waiting to hear the details from him; and once the residents of Yonville had all heard his story about the arsenic which she had mistaken for sugar while making *crème à la vanille*, Homais went back to Bovary's house.

He found him all on his own (Monsieur Canivet had just left), sitting in the armchair by the window gazing stupidly at the tiles of the dining-room floor.

"You'll need to make a decision quite soon as to when the service is going to be."

"Service? What service?"

Then he added, his voice faltering and frightened:

"No, certainly not! I want to keep her."

Without replying, Homais picked up a jug from the shelf and started to water the geraniums.

"Oh, thank you," said Charles, "you're so kind."

But his voice tailed off, choked by the many memories that were stirred up by what the pharmacist was doing.

To take his mind off things, Homais thought it might be a good idea to discuss horticulture; the plants were getting dry. Charles just nodded in agreement.

"And the warmer weather's on its way."

"Oh!" said Bovary.

Running out of conversation, the apothecary opened the little curtains slightly.

"Ah, there's Monsieur Tuvache walking past."

"Monsieur Tuvache is walking past," Charles repeated mechanically.

Homais daren't say any more about the funeral arrangements; it would be up to the priest to make sense of all that.

Charles shut himself away in his consulting room, picked up his pen and, after sobbing for a moment, wrote:

I wish her to be buried in her wedding dress, with white shoes and a circlet of flowers. Her hair is to be spread out on her shoulders; three coffins, one of oak, one of mahogany, one of lead. If people leave

me in peace, I'll find the strength. Everything is to be covered with
a large piece of green velvet. This is what I want. Do it.

The men to whom it was addressed were amazed at Bovary's romantic
notions. The pharmacist was quick to say:

"The velvet seems excessive to me. Besides, there's the cost—"

"What has it got to do with you?" cried Charles. "Leave me alone!
You didn't like her! Go away!"

The cleric took him by the arm and they went for a walk in the
garden. He spoke to him at length about worldly vanities. God was
great, God was good; we must accept his edicts without a murmur,
give thanks to him.

"I despise your God!" Charles blasphemed angrily.

"The spirit of rebellion is still in you," sighed the clergyman.

But Bovary had walked off. He strode up and down by the wall, near
the steps; he ground his teeth, his eyes shot cursing looks heavenward;
but not a single leaf stirred.

It began to rain slightly. Charles was in shirtsleeves and was soon
shivering, so he went and sat in the kitchen.

At six o'clock there was a rattling noise in the square: the *Hirondelle*
had arrived; he stood with his forehead on the window, watching the
passengers get out one by one. Félicité put a mattress in the drawing
room for him; he threw himself down on it and fell asleep.

Philosopher though he was, Monsieur Homais nonetheless had
respect for the dead. So, bearing no grudge against poor Charles, he
came back in the evening to keep vigil over the body, bringing three
large tomes and his notebook to write in.

Father Bournisien was already there, and two tall candles were
burning at the head of the bed, which had been moved out of the
alcove.

It wasn't long before the apothecary, who found the silence oppressive, was expressing regrets about the "ill-fated young woman". The
priest replied that all they could do now was pray for her.

"Nonetheless," Homais went on, "two things, of which the first
is: either she passed away in a state of grace (to use the Church's
expression), in which case she has no need of our prayers; or she
died unrepentant (I believe that's the ecclesiastical term), in which
case—"

Bournisien stopped him, retorting gruffly that it was still necessary to pray.

"But if God knows everything we need," countered the pharmacist, "what point is there in praying?"

"I beg your pardon!" said the cleric. "Not pray? Aren't you a Christian?"

"Excuse me!" said Homais. "But I'm an admirer of Christianity. It emancipated slaves for one thing, introduced a moral doctrine into the world and—"

"There's more to it than that! All the texts—"

"The texts? Ha! Just look in the history books; we all know they were fabricated by the Jesuits."

Charles came in, and going over to the bed he slowly pulled the curtains.

Emma's head was tilted to one side. Her mouth, which was still open, was like a black hole in the lower half of her face; her thumbs and fingers were unclosed; there was a form of white dust sprinkled over her lashes, and her eyes were slowly subsiding into a glutinous pallor as if spiders had spun a fine web over them. The sheet formed a hollow between her breasts and her knees, and then rose again to her toes; to Charles it seemed as if some vast weight, an immense mass were bearing down on her.

The church clock struck two. They could hear the dull murmur of the river in the darkness at the bottom of the garden. Every now and then Father Bournisien blew his nose loudly, while Homais's pen scratched across the paper.

"There there, my dear chap," he said. "Go to bed, all this is breaking your heart!"

Once Charles had gone, the pharmacist and the priest went back to their discussion.

"Read Voltaire!" said the one. "Read d'Holbach, read the *Encyclopédie*!"

"Read *The Letters of Certain Jews to Monsieur Voltaire*!" said the other. "Read *Christian Reason* by Nicolas, a former judge!"*

Things began to get heated, they were red in the face, both talking at once without listening to each other; Bournisien was outraged by such effrontery; Homais was astonished at such stupidity; they were almost on the point of hurling abuse when Charles suddenly reappeared. He kept coming upstairs, drawn by some fascination.

He sat in front of her so as to see her better, and sunk into a meditation that was no less harrowing for being deep and heartfelt.

He remembered the stories about catalepsy, miracles performed by hypnotism, and he told himself that with a great act of will he might be able to bring her back to life. At one point he leant towards her and called out quietly: "Emma! Emma!" The draught from his breath made the candle flames flutter against the wall.

At daybreak Madame Bovary senior arrived; as he kissed and embraced her, Charles went into more floods of tears. As the pharmacist had done, she tried to make suggestions about the cost of the funeral. But he became so angry that she gave up; he even told her to go into town that instant and buy what was needed.

Charles was left on his own all afternoon; Berthe had been taken over to Madame Homais; Félicité stayed upstairs in the room with mother Lefrançois.

That evening he received visitors. He stood up, shook people's hands without managing to say anything, and then everyone sat down in a semicircle by the fire. Heads down, legs tightly crossed, they jiggled their dangling foot and sighed at regular intervals, all bored beyond belief; yet no one wanted to be the first to leave.

When Homais came back at nine o'clock (for the last two days he had been the only one to show his face in the square), he was laden with supplies of camphor, benzoin and aromatic herbs. He also brought a jar of chlorine to dispel the smell of putrefaction. The maid, Madame Lefrançois and old mother Bovary were gathered round Emma, just finishing dressing her; they lowered the long stiff veil which reached down to her satin shoes.

"My poor dear mistress! My poor dear mistress!" sobbed Félicité.

"Look at her," sighed the landlady, "she's still so pretty! You'd swear she was just about to get up."

Then they leant over to put the circlet in her hair.

They had to lift her head slightly, and black fluid streamed out of her mouth like vomit.

"Oh my Heavens, be careful of the dress!" cried Madame Lefrançois. "Come on then, help me!" she said to the pharmacist. "You're not frightened by any chance?"

"Me, frightened?" he shrugged. "Hardly! I saw enough of them while I was studying pharmacy! We used to make punch in the operating theatre during dissection classes! Eternal oblivion holds no terror for a philosopher, and as I often say, I intend to bequeath my body to the hospitals, in the interests of science."

When the priest arrived he asked how Monsieur was feeling; hearing the apothecary's reply he said:

"Of course, he hasn't had time to get over the shock yet."

Homais told him that he was lucky not to have a beloved spouse to lose like everyone else; from which ensued a discussion about the celibacy of the priesthood.

"It's not natural for a man to go without a woman!" said the pharmacist. "There have been crimes committed—"

"Give me strength!" the cleric burst out. "How do you expect a married man, with all that that entails, to keep the secret of the confessional, for example?"

Homais attacked confession. Bournisien defended it; he spoke at length about the wrongs it had caused to be put right. He quoted instances of thieves who had renounced their life of crime overnight. And soldiers who, on appearing before the judgement seat of penitence, felt the scales fall from their eyes. At Fribourg there was a minister who...

But his companion was asleep. And feeling rather suffocated in the oppressive atmosphere he opened the window, which woke the pharmacist.

"Let's have a pinch of snuff!" he said to him. "Do join me, it clears your head."

Somewhere in the distance there was the sound of barking.

"Can you hear a dog?" asked the pharmacist.

"People say they can sense when there's been a death," replied the priest. "Like bees: they leave the hive when someone dies."

But Homais didn't challenge these preconceptions because he had dropped off to sleep again.

Being of a stronger constitution, Father Bournisien carried on mumbling to himself for a while, and then slowly but surely his head began to nod, he dropped his big black book and was soon snoring.

And so, after all their disagreements, there they sat opposite each other, stomachs protruding, faces puffy and scowling, finally united in the same human weakness; they were as motionless as the corpse beside them, which looked as if it were asleep.

When Charles came in he didn't wake them. It was his last visit. He had come to say his farewells.

The aromatic herbs were still burning, swirls of blue-tinged smoke mingled with the mist that drifted in through the window. There were a few stars, it was a mild night.

The candles wept big wax tears onto the bed. Charles watched them burning, and his eyes grew tired with the brilliance of the yellow flames.

The watered satin of her dress shimmered white as moonlight. Emma vanished into it; it was as if she were rising up out of herself, and had in some obscure way become part of everything around her, the silence, the night, the breeze, the moist fragrances that filled the air.

And then he saw her in the garden at Tostes, on the bench beside the thorn hedge, or in Rouen, in the street, in the doorway of their house, in the yard at Les Bertaux. He could still hear the lads laughing merrily as they danced under the apple trees; the room was filled with the scent of her hair, her dress rustled as it shimmered and sparkled in his arms. That was the very same woman as this one!

He took a long time recalling all the lost joys, her manner, her gestures, the sound of her voice. Yet no sooner had he stopped despairing over one than there came another, then another, in never-ending waves like a rising tide.

Then he was seized with a terrible curiosity: with the tips of his fingers he slowly lifted her veil. But he gave a cry of horror that woke the others. They took him downstairs to the dining room.

Then Félicité came up to say that he was asking for a lock of her hair.

"Cut some then!" retorted the apothecary.

But since she daren't, he found some scissors and did it himself. He was shaking so much that he broke the skin on her temples in several places. Eventually, bracing himself, Homais made two or three snips at random, which left white patches in the beautiful black hair.

The pharmacist and the priest reimmersed themselves in their individual occupations, still dropping off occasionally and berating each other for the fact when they woke up. Then Bournisien sprinkled the room with holy water and Homais tipped chlorine on the floor.

Félicité had thought to leave some brandy, cheese and a large brioche on the chest of drawers for them. And so at four in the morning, unable to bear it any longer the apothecary sighed:

"I wouldn't say no to a bit of sustenance!"

The cleric didn't need to be asked twice: he went off to celebrate Mass then came back, and they both tucked in with the odd nervous giggle, not quite sure why, carried away by that ambivalent mood of cheerfulness that takes hold of us after a sad occasion – and over their last glass the priest clapped the pharmacist on the shoulder and said:

"We'll see eye to eye eventually!"

When they went downstairs they met the carpenters in the hall. For two hours Charles was tortured by the sound of hammers ringing on wood. Then they brought her down in her oak coffin, which was fitted into the other two, but as the outer casket was too large they had to fill the gaps with stuffing from a mattress. Finally, once the three lids were planed, nailed down and sealed, it was put on a stand by the front door; the house was thrown open and the people of Yonville came flocking.

Then old man Rouault arrived. When he saw the black pall he passed out in the square.

10

H E HAD ONLY RECEIVED THE PHARMACIST'S LETTER thirty-six hours after the event, and to spare his feelings, Homais had phrased it in such a way that it was impossible to know quite what to make of it.

At first the man collapsed as if he were having a stroke. But then he realized she wasn't dead. Although she might be... So in the end he put on his smock, got his hat, fixed spurs on his ordinary shoes and set off at a split-arse gallop; and all the way, gasping for breath, old man Rouault was consumed with dread. Once he even had to dismount. He couldn't see where he was going, he heard voices everywhere, he thought he was going mad.

Dawn broke. He saw three black hens sleeping under a tree: the omen made him shudder with horror. So he promised the Holy Virgin that he would buy three chasubles for the church, and go barefoot all the way from the cemetery at Les Bertaux to the chapel at Vassonville.

As he rode into Maromme he was already shouting ahead to the people at the inn, where he barged the door open with his shoulder, grabbed a sack of oats, poured a bottle of sweet cider into the feed trough then jumped back on his old nag, who shot off like lightning.

He told himself that they would save her; the doctors were sure to come up with a cure. And he remembered the miraculous recoveries that he had heard about.

But then she appeared before him, dead. She was lying on her back in the middle of the road in front of him. He reined in his horse and the hallucination vanished.

At Quincampoix he drank three cups of coffee to raise his spirits.

He wondered if they had sent the letter to the wrong person. He put his hand in his pocket, touched it but daren't open it.

Then he came to the conclusion that it might be a hoax, someone taking revenge, something dreamt up for a tasteless joke; because if she were dead people would know about it! No, of course she wasn't! There was nothing odd about the scenery around him: the sky was blue, the trees were swaying, a flock of sheep went by. He caught sight of the village; they saw him gallop past, hunched over his horse's neck, whipping it furiously with blood dripping from its sides.

When he came round he fell into Bovary's arms, weeping:

"Emma! My daughter! My child! Tell me what happened…"

With a sob the other replied:

"I don't know, I don't know! We've been cursed!"

Then the apothecary stepped in.

"These ghastly details don't serve any purpose. I'll explain everything to Monsieur. There are people arriving. Show some dignity for goodness' sake! Be philosophical!"

Poor Charles wanted to be strong, and several times he said:

"Yes… be brave!"

"Quite right!" cried the older man. "I will be! Hell's teeth, I'll see it through to the end."

The bell began to toll. It was time. They had to be making their way.

Sitting side by side in the choir stalls, they watched the three cantors walk back and forth in front of them, chanting. The bass horn intoned mightily. Father Bournisien, fully robed, sang in a high voice; he bowed to the tabernacle, lifted up his hands, raised his arms. Lestiboudois wandered round the church with his whalebone staff; the coffin stood near the pulpit, between four rows of candles. Charles wanted to go and blow them out.

Nonetheless he did his best to give himself over to his devotions, to soar upwards in the hope of an afterlife where he would see her once again. He told himself that she was on a long journey, far away. But when he remembered that she was down there, that it was over, that they were going to put her in the ground, he was seized with a savage and despairing black rage. At times he thought he couldn't feel anything, and he delighted in how this eased his pain, while rebuking himself for being such a wretch.

There was the sharp, regular sound of a steel-tipped walking stick tapping on the flagstones. It came from the back then stopped abruptly in the side aisle. A man in a coarse brown jacket knelt down awkwardly. It was Hippolyte, the stable lad from the Lion d'Or. He was wearing his best leg.

One of the cantors came round to take the collection, large coins jingled onto the silver dish.

"Hurry up, will you! I'm going through agony here!" Charles burst out angrily, tossing down a five-franc piece.

The man thanked him, bowing deeply.

They sang, they knelt, they stood up again, it went on for ever! He rememembered a time when they were first married, they had come to Mass and had sat on the other side, on the right by the wall. The bell began to toll again. There was a sound of chairs moving. The bearers slid their poles under the coffin, and everyone followed out of the church.

Just then Justin came to the door of the pharmacy. But, pale and trembling, he quickly went back inside again.

People stood at their windows to see the cortège go by. At the head, Charles threw back his shoulders. He put on a show of being brave, and nodded greetings to members of the crowd that came from alleys and doorways.

The six men, three on either side, inched their way along slightly out of breath. The priests, the cantors, the two altar boys recited the *De Profundis*;* their voices drifted away over the open countryside, rising and falling. At times they disappeared round a bend in the path, but the large silver cross was always there, standing up beneath the trees.

The women followed on behind, heads covered with black mantillas with the hoods pulled up; in their hands were large lit candles, and Charles felt himself growing faint from the constantly repeated prayers and the flaming candlesticks, the dulling smells of wax and cassocks. A cool breeze was blowing, the fields of rye and rape were lush and green, dewdrops quivered on the thorn hedges along the lane. All manner of cheerful sounds filled the surrounding countryside: the rattle of a cart trundling over ruts in the distance, a cock that kept crowing or a foal galloping under the apple trees. The clear sky was strewn with pink clouds; gentle wreaths of bluish smoke hovered over thatched cottages surrounded by irises; as he walked past, Charles recognized the yards. He remembered other mornings like this one, when he had been to see a patient and then went home to see her.

Every so often the corner of the black pall, sprinkled with white droplets, lifted up and revealed the coffin. Tiring, the bearers slowed down, and she moved forward in halting little movements like a rowing boat pitching about on the waves.

They arrived.

The six men went on to the far end, where a grave had been dug in the grass.

They all gathered round it in a circle, and as the priest was speaking the reddish soil piled up on the edges trickled silently back in again.

Once the four tapes were laid out, they slid the coffin onto them. He watched it go down. Down and down.

There was a bump; with a scraping noise the tapes were pulled back out. Bournisien took the spade that Lestiboudois held out to him and, still sprinkling with his right hand, he threw in a large shovelful of earth with his left, and as the stones fell onto the wooden lid it made that fearsome sound that we imagine to be the echoes of eternity.

The cleric handed the sprinkler to the person beside him. It was Homais. He shook it solemnly then passed it to Charles, who sunk to his knees in the dirt and threw in great handfuls, calling out: "Farewell!" He blew kisses; he crawled towards the grave so he could be swallowed up in it with her.

They led him away, but it didn't take him long to calm down; for perhaps like all the others he felt a vague sense of satisfaction in getting it over with.

On the way back old man Rouault calmly started smoking his pipe, which privately Homais felt to be somewhat unseemly. He also noted that Monsieur Binet had failed to put in an appearance, that Tuvache had "slipped away" after the Mass, and that Théodore, the notary's manservant, was wearing a blue tailcoat, "as if you couldn't get a black one, after all, it's the custom, dash it!" And in order to share his reflections he went from group to group. People were bemoaning Emma's death, especially Lheureux, who had made a point of coming to the funeral.

"Poor dear lady! How distressing for her husband!"

"If it hadn't been for me, you know," the apothecary pointed out, "he would have tried to do away with himself."

"Such a good person! And to think she was in my shop only last Saturday!"

"I didn't have time to write a few words to say at the graveside," added Homais.

When they got back Charles changed his clothes, and old man Rouault put his blue smock back on again. It was new, and because he had kept wiping his eyes with his sleeve during the ride, the colour had come out on his face, and the tracks of his tears traced streaks through the layer of dust that still covered it.

Madame Bovary senior sat with them. None of them spoke. Eventually the old man sighed:

"Do you remember the time I came to Tostes, my dear fellow; when you had just lost your first lady wife. I was able to comfort you back then! I could find something to say – but now…"

And with a deep groan that made his chest heave he went on:

"It's all over for me, you know! I've seen my wife go… then my son… and now today my daughter!"

He wanted to go straight back to Les Bertaux, because he said he wouldn't be able to sleep in this house. He even refused to see his granddaughter.

"No no! It would grieve me too much. Just give her a big kiss from me! Goodbye!… You're a good lad! And don't worry, I won't forget!" he said, slapping his thigh. "You'll still get your turkey."

Yet when he reached the top of the hill he stopped and looked back, as he used to on the road from Saint-Victor after he had left her. The windows in the village were ablaze with the glancing rays of the sun, which was setting over the meadows. He shaded his eyes, and on the skyline he made out an area enclosed by walls where trees made dark clumps among the white stones; then he went on his way at a gentle trot, because his nag was going lame.

Despite being tired, Charles and his mother sat chatting until late that night. They talked about times past and times to come. She would move to Yonville, keep house for him, they would stay together from now on. She was shrewd and solicitous, inwardly rejoicing at regaining an affection that had eluded her for so long. Midnight struck. The village was silent as usual, but Charles was wide awake and thinking of her.

Rodolphe, who had spent all day cutting wood to take his mind off things, was fast asleep in his chateau; and in Rouen, Léon was sleeping soundly as well.

But there was someone else who wasn't asleep.

On the grave among the fir trees, a boy knelt crying, his breast racked with sobs in the shadows, weighed down by an infinite sorrow that was gentler than the moon and more unfathomable than the night. Suddenly the gate creaked. It was Lestiboudois, come to fetch the spade that he had left behind that afternoon. He recognized Justin clambering over the wall, and so now he knew who the culprit was who had been thieving his potatoes.

11

T HE NEXT DAY Charles had his daughter brought home. She asked for her mother. She was told that she was away, that she would bring her some toys. Berthe mentioned her again several times, but as time went by she forgot all about her. Bovary found the child's sunny disposition distressing, as well as having to endure the pharmacist's insufferable efforts at comforting him.

The problems with money soon resurfaced; Lheureux was spurring on his friend Vinçart again, and Charles borrowed vast amounts at exorbitant rates; because he would never allow even the smallest piece of furniture that had belonged to *her* to be sold. It drove his mother to distraction. But he got angrier than she did. He had changed completely. So she gave up and went home.

Then people began *taking advantage*. Mademoiselle Lempereur demanded payment for six months' lessons, although Emma had only ever had one (in spite of the receipt she had shown Bovary): there had been an understanding between them; the book-lender claimed three years' subscriptions; old mother Rolet wanted paying for delivering twenty or more letters, and when Charles asked her to explain she was discreet enough to say:

"Oh, I don't know anything about it! It was some business of hers."

With every debt he paid, Charles thought he had seen the last of it. But others kept cropping up.

He demanded details of the arrears for goods and services that had been provided. They showed him the letters that his wife had sent them. So he was forced to apologize.

Félicité wore Madame's dresses now – although not all of them, because he had kept a few and would shut himself away in her dressing room to look at them – the girl was more or less the same size, and if he saw her from behind Charles was often seized with imaginings, and cried out:

"Oh, don't go! Don't go!"

But at Pentecost she packed her bags and left Yonville, and ran off with Théodore, taking the remainder of the wardrobe with her.

It was around this time that the widow Dupuis was pleased to inform him of "the marriage of her son, Monsieur Léon Dupuis, notary at Yvetot, to Mademoiselle Léocadie Lebœuf of Bondeville". Among the congratulations he sent her, Charles wrote these words:

"My poor dear wife would have been so pleased!"

One day while he was wandering aimlessly round the house he went up to the attic, where he felt a piece of thin, crumpled-up paper under his slippered foot. He unfolded it and read: "Be brave, Emma! Be brave! I don't want to bring unhappiness to your life..." It was Rodolphe's letter, which had fallen between some crates, where it had stayed until a breeze from the skylight blew it towards the door. Charles stood there, not moving, gaping, on the same spot where, all that time ago, much paler than he was now, and in despair, Emma had wanted to die. Then he noticed a small "R" at the bottom of the second page. Who was it? And he remembered Rodolphe's attentiveness, his unexpected departure and his rather strained manner on the two or three occasions when he had bumped into him since. But he was deceived by the letter's respectful tone.

"Perhaps they loved each other platonically," he thought.

Charles wasn't one to go into things too deeply; he baulked at any sign of proof, and his dim feelings of jealousy were swallowed up by the enormity of his grief.

People must have adored her, he thought. Men had lusted after her, that was for certain. It made her seem all the more beautiful, and he contrived to feel a crazed and unceasing state of desire for her that kindled his despair, and which knew no bounds since it could now never be consummated.

To please her he took on her likes and dislikes, her ideas, as if she were still alive; he bought patent-leather boots, took to wearing white cravats. He used lotions on his moustache, signed bills of exchange like she had. She was corrupting him from beyond the grave.

He was forced to sell off the silver piece by piece, and then the furniture in the drawing room. Gradually all the rooms emptied, but the room, her room, remained just as it had always been. After dinner Charles would go up there. He put the round table by the fire and brought up *her* armchair. He sat facing it. A candle burned in one of the gilt candlesticks. Next to him Berthe would colour in engravings.

It pained the poor man to see her so badly dressed, with no laces in her boots and the armholes of her smocks torn to the waist, because the housekeeper took very little care of her. And yet she was so sweet, so nice, with her little head tilted forward so charmingly and her beautiful blonde hair tumbling over her rosy cheeks, that he was overcome with utter delight, a pleasure mingled with bitterness, like those bad wines that taste of resin. He mended her toys, made jumping jacks for her out of cardboard, stitched up her dolls' torn stomachs. If he happened to glance at the workbox, a piece of ribbon lying around or even a pin stuck in a crack in the table, he would begin to dream – and he would look so sad that she was sad too.

No one came to see them now; Justin had run off to Rouen and found a job as a grocer's boy, while the apothecary's children spent less and less time with the little girl because, given the differences in their social position, Monsieur Homais wasn't keen for the friendship to continue much longer.

The blind man, whom he had been unable to heal with his ointment, had gone back to the hill by Guillaume woods, where he would tell travellers about the pharmacist's fruitless attempt, and it had reached the point where if Homais went into town he would hide behind the curtains in the *Hirondelle* to avoid meeting him. He loathed him, and for the sake of his reputation, wanting to be rid of him at any cost, he waged a secret campaign against him, which revealed the depths to which his mind could sink and the heights of iniquity to which vanity could take him. For six months in a row short articles appeared in the *Fanal de Rouen* phrased in terms such as these:

Anyone who journeys to the fertile regions of Picardy will have undoubtedly noticed a poor wretch afflicted with appalling facial injuries. He harasses you, plagues you, levies a veritable tax on travellers. Are we still in the abominable era of the Middle Ages, when in our public squares vagrants were allowed to flaunt the leprosy and scrofula that they had brought back with them from the Crusades?

Or even:

Despite the laws against vagrancy, the outskirts of our large towns continue to be overrun with gangs of paupers. There are some who wander around on their own, but who are no less dangerous for that. What are our elected representatives thinking of?

And then Homais would make up little stories:

Yesterday, on the hill by Guillaume woods, a skittish horse...

And there would follow the account of an accident caused by the blind man.

It worked so well that the man was put in prison. But then he was released. He started again, and so did Homais. It was a battle – and he emerged victorious, because his enemy was shut up in the poorhouse for life.

Success emboldened him, and from then on a dog couldn't be run over, a barn set alight or a wife battered without him immediately letting the public know about it, always guided by his love of progress and his hatred for the priesthood. He drew comparisons between State primary schools and those run by the Ignorant Brothers,* to the detriment of the latter, reminded people of the Massacre of St Bartholomew when there was talk of a hundred-franc grant for the church, drew attention to injustices and sallied forth witticisms. It was his moment. Homais was out to undermine the existing order; he was becoming a dangerous man.

Yet he soon found journalism constraining; what he needed was a book, a work! So he produced a *General Statistics of the Canton of Yonville, Followed by Climatological Observations*, and statistics led him to philosophy. He concerned himself with major issues: social problems, the moral education of the poor, fish-farming, rubber, the railways, etc. He was ashamed of his bourgeois origins now. He adopted an *artistic lifestyle*, took up smoking! He bought two Louis XV statuettes – *très chic* – for his drawing room.

Yet he didn't give up his pharmacy: quite the reverse! He kept himself up to date with the latest innovations. He monitored activity in the growing market for chocolate. He was the first to introduce *choca* and *revalenta* to the Lower Seine region. He became wildly enthused with Pulvermacher's hydroelectric chains;* he wore them himself; and at night when he took off his flannel vest, Madame Homais was dazzled at the sight of the gold spirals that completely covered him, and felt herself falling in love all over again with this man who was more bedecked than a Scythian and as magnificent as one of the Magi.

He had wonderful ideas for Emma's tomb. At first he suggested a truncated column draped in hangings, then a pyramid, then a temple of Vesta, a form of rotunda... or even "a pile of ruins". And among all these different projects Homais insisted on there being a weeping willow, which he regarded as the prerequisite symbol of sadness.

He and Charles made a trip to Rouen to look at tombs at a monumental mason's, accompanied by a painter friend of Bridoux's by the name of Vaufrylard, who never stopped making puns. Eventually, having studied hundreds of designs, having asked for an estimate and made another trip to Rouen, Charles settled on a mausoleum with "a spirit holding an extinguished torch" on both sides.

When it came to the inscription Homais could think of nothing finer than: *Sta viator*, and so he decided on that. Then he racked his brains to think of something more; he repeated it over and over: *Sta viator*... and finally came up with: *amabilem conjugem calcas,** which was what was used.

The odd thing was that by thinking constantly of Emma, Charles forgot her, and it filled him with despair to feel her image slipping away from him despite his efforts to keep it in his memory. Yet he dreamt of her every night; it was always the same dream: he was walking towards her, but when he put his arms round her she crumbled to dust.

For a whole week he was seen going into the church every evening. Father Bournisien visited him two or three times, but then gave up. According to Homais the priest was becoming intolerant, a fanatic; he inveighed against the spirit of the age, and in every other Sunday sermon he made a point of describing Voltaire on his deathbed, who as everyone knew had died eating his own excrement.

Despite living frugally, Bovary was unable to pay off his old debts. Lheureux refused to renew any more bills of exchange. A visit from the bailiffs was impending. So he turned to his mother, who agreed to let him take out a mortgage on her property, although she complained bitterly about Emma. In return she asked for a shawl that had escaped Félicité's pillaging. Charles refused. They fell out.

It was she who made the first moves towards reconciliation by offering to let his daughter come and live with her; the girl would be a comfort to her all alone in her house. Charles agreed. But just as she was about to set off, his courage deserted him. And so their relationship broke down permanently.

The more his attachments faded, the more tightly he clung to his love for his child. And yet she worried him; she sometimes coughed, or had red blotches on her cheeks.

Across the street meanwhile, blossoming and beaming for all to see, was the pharmacist's family, for whom nothing seemed to go wrong. Napoléon helped him in the laboratory, Athalie made him a new silk cap, Irma cut out round pieces of paper to cover the jam jars, while Franklin could recite Pythagoras's theorem in one breath. He was the happiest of fathers, the most fortunate of men.

Wrong! Because he was consumed with a nagging ambition: Homais wanted the Croix d'Honneur. And he had all the right qualifications:

"1. During the cholera outbreak, distinguished myself by unbounded dedication; 2. having published at my own expense various works of public benefit, such as..." (and he evoked his dissertation, titled: *Cider, Its Production and Effects*, plus his observations on the lanigerum aphid, sent to the Academy, his volume of statistics, and even his pharmaceutical thesis), "not to mention the several learned societies of which I am a member" (he belonged to only one).

"After all," he exclaimed, pirouetting, "it can only show me in a good light!"

And so Homais gravitated towards power. Secretly he was of great service to the Prefect during the elections. In a word he prostituted himself. He even petitioned the sovereign, begged him to *give him due recognition*, addressed him as *our good King* and likened him to Henri IV.

Every morning the apothecary rushed to the newspaper to see if his nomination had come through; it never appeared. Finally, unable to bear it any longer, he had the lawn of his garden laid out like the star of the Croix d'Honneur, with two small strips of grass at the top to represent the ribbon. And he would walk round it with his arms folded, reflecting on the government's lack of competence and mankind's lack of gratitude.

Out of respect, or from a sensuality in his nature that made him prolong his investigations, Charles still hadn't opened the secret compartment in the rosewood desk that Emma had always used. Then one day he sat down at it, turned the key and pressed the spring. In it were Léon's letters. This time there was no doubt! He read them all, right to the last word, he rummaged through every corner, every piece of furniture, every drawer, behind the walls, sobbing, wailing, distraught and raving. Then he unearthed a box, gave it a kick. Out fell Rodolphe's portrait, among a jumble of love letters.

His state of despondency astonished people. He no longer went out, he wouldn't receive visitors, he even refused to go and see his patients. Word went round that he had *shut himself away with a bottle.*

Yet sometimes an inquisitive soul would stand on tiptoe and look over the garden hedge, and would be amazed to see a wild man with a long beard dressed in filthy ragged clothes, walking up and down and crying.

On summer evenings he went to the cemetery with his little girl. They came back once it was dark, when the only light in the square was from Binet's attic window.

Yet the self-indulgence of his grief lacked something, because he had no one to share it with, and he would go and see Madame Lefrançois so as to be able to talk about *her.* But the landlady only half-listened, for she had troubles of her own: Monsieur Lheureux had now finally set up his *Friends of Commerce* stagecoach, and Hivert, who had made a name for himself by running errands, was demanding more money and threatening to go and work for "the competition".

One day when he had gone to Argueil market to sell his horse – a last resort – he bumped into Rodolphe.

When they saw each other they both turned pale. Rodolphe, who had only ever sent his card, mumbled excuses, but then became bolder and even had the audacity (being August it was very hot) to ask him to join him for a beer in the inn.

Elbows on the table, he puffed away on his cigar and chatted while Charles, confronted with the face she had loved, was sunk in reverie. It was as if he were seeing part of her. It was incredible. He would have liked to have been this man.

Meanwhile this man was talking about farming, livestock, manure, filling every gap in the conversation with platitudes to prevent the slightest clue from slipping out. Charles wasn't listening; Rodolphe noticed, and watched the memories flitting back and forth across his face. Gradually it turned crimson, his nostrils twitched, his lips quivered; there was even a moment when Charles, full of dark rage, stared straight at Rodolphe, who stopped talking as if seized with terror. But his face soon reassumed its look of doleful world-weariness.

"I don't bear a grudge against you," he said.

Rodolphe didn't reply. And, head in hands, Charles went on in a voice that was faint and resigned to endless sorrow:

"No, I don't bear a grudge against you any more!"

And then he said a grand phrase, the only one he had ever used:

"Fate was to blame!"

Rodolphe, who was the instrument of this fate, thought this was mightily good-natured for a man in his position, laughable even, and rather contemptible.

The next day Charles sat on the seat under the arbour. Sunlight shone through the trellis, vine leaves traced shadows on the sand, the scent of jasmine filled the air, Spanish flies buzzed round the flowering lilies, and like a boy still in adolescence, he could barely breathe with the fragrant waves of love that swelled his grieving heart.

At seven o'clock, young Berthe, who hadn't seen him all afternoon, came to fetch him for dinner.

His head was leaning back against the wall, his eyes were closed, his mouth was open, and in his hand were some strands of long black hair.

"Come on, Papa!" she said.

And thinking he was playing a game, she gave him a gentle push. He fell on the ground. He was dead.

Thirty-six hours later, at the apothecary's request, Monsieur Canivet hurried over. He opened him up but didn't find anything.

Once everything had been sold there were twelve francs and seventy-five centimes left, which paid for Mademoiselle Bovary's journey to her grandmother's house. The woman died the same year, and since old man Rouault was paralysed, an aunt agreed to take her in. Being poor, she sends her out to earn her living in a cotton mill.

Since Bovary died there have been three doctors in Yonville, none of whom made a success of it, so swiftly did Homais demolish them. His practice goes from strength to strength; the authorities treat him with respect and public opinion protects him.

He has just been awarded the Croix d'Honneur.

Note on the Text

This translation is based on the Folio edition of *Madame Bovary* (Paris: Éditions Gallimard, 1972).

Notes

p. 5, *czapka*: The headgear of the Polish cavalry, adopted by the French under Napoleon.

p. 7, *Quos ego*: The words uttered by Neptune to quell the furious winds in the first book of Virgil's *Aeneid*.

p. 7, *ridiculus sum*: "I am ridiculous" (Latin).

p. 9, *angelus*: In the Roman Catholic Church, a devotion commemorating the Incarnation of Christ said three times daily, as well as the name given to the ringing of bells to announce this.

p. 9, *viaticum*: The Eucharist when given to a terminally ill person.

p. 10, *Anacharsis*: The *Voyage du jeune Anacharsis en Grèce* (1788), a work describing ancient Greece, by Abbé Barthélemy (1716–95).

p. 10, *remove year*: Flaubert refers to this as Bovary's "*troisième*" – the fourth year in the French system, in which pupils begin in the "*sixième*" and progress to the "*première*" (the penultimate year) before completing their secondary education in the "*terminale*". Although the meaning of "remove" varies from institution to institution in English public schools, it often refers to a group in their fourth year of secondary education (or Year 10, as it is now known in most British schools).

p. 10, *baccalauréat*: Examinations taken at the end of secondary education in France, roughly equivalent to British A levels.

p. 11, *Béranger*: Pierre-Jean de Béranger (1780–1857), a popular poet and songwriter known for his liberalism and criticism of the Bourbon monarchy during the period of the Restoration (1814–1830).

p. 12, *livres*: An old French currency, divided into twenty sols (or sous), which existed before decimalization occurred in 1795. The novel mentions several other such defunct currencies, such as the écu, the sou and the louis, even though the action takes place after decimalization.

p. 14, *galette des Rois*: A cake eaten to celebrate the Epiphany (6th January).

p. 17, *the Ursulines*: A Roman Catholic order of women founded in 1535 at Brescia, Italy, which, uniquely at the time, was dedicated to the education of girls.

p. 20, *pots de crème*: Custard served chilled in ramekins.

p. 23, *the time of Saint-Michel*: Michaelmas (29th September).

p. 26, *eau de vie*: Brandy.

p. 26, *bouchons*: A game once especially popular among Breton fishermen, in which coins or other valuables are placed on top of a large cork. Standing at some distance from it, the contestants toss disks; the player who first overturns the cork takes the coins.

p. 29, *boc*: A Normandy term for a small horse-drawn carriage.

p. 31, *Paul et Virginie*: A romantic novel by Bernardin de Saint-Pierre (1737–1814), published in 1788. Set in Mauritius, it is a tragic story of two adolescent lovers.

p. 31, *Mademoiselle de la Vallière*: Françoise Louise de La Baume Le Blanc (1644–1710), later Duchesse de la Vallière et de Vaujours, was one of Louis XIV's mistresses. She bore him four children, the younger two of whom were later legitimized. She took monastic vows and spent the last thirty-six years of her life in a Carmelite convent in Saint-Jacques, where she is buried.

p. 32, *Abbé Frayssinous's... Génie du christianisme*: Denis-Luc Frayssinou (1765–1841) was a priest and statesman during the Restoration. His lectures, published in 1825, contributed to the Christian revival during that period. *Le Génie du christianisme* was a defence of the Christian religion by François-René de Chateaubriand (1768–1848), published in 1802.

p. 33, *Héloïse... praises of Louis XIV*: Héloïse d'Argenteuil was a twelfth-century monastic and theologian whose letters to Peter Abelard are one of the best-known examples of romantic love. Agnès Sorel was the favourite of Charles VII. La Belle Ferronière (whose husband was either called Ferron or was a *ferronier*, a craftsman in wrought iron) was one of François I's mistresses, whose sudden death left him inconsolable. According to legend, Clémence Isaure was a wealthy citizen of Toulouse who died unmarried towards the end of the fifteenth century. Sometimes known as the Lady of the Troubadours, she is attributed with leaving money to fund an annual poetry prize, the Académie des Jeux Floraux, which is still awarded in Toulouse. Louis IX (1215–70), known as St Louis, is said to have sat beneath an oak tree to pass judgements. Pierre Terrail LeVieux, Seigneur de Bayard (1473–1524), usually known as the Chevalier Bayard, was a nobleman from the Dauphiné who distinguished himself during the Italian Wars in the fifteenth and sixteenth centuries. St Bartholomew refers to the massacre of thousands of French Protestants (Huguenots) on St Bartholemew's Day 1572. "Le Béarnais" was the popular name for Henri IV (1553–1610), who was a native of the old province of Béarn at the foot of the Pyrenees. The white plume that he wore in his hat was a rallying point for his troops in battle.

p. 34, *bayadères; Giaours*: A bayadère is a Hindu dancing girl. "Giaour" is a derogatory Turkish term for an infidel. It was popularized via Lord Byron's long poem *The Giaour*, which appeared in 1813.

p. 34, *Lamartine-like*: Alphonse de Lamartine (1790–1869), a poet best known for *Le Lac* (1820), an autobiographical poem about the passing of romantic love.

p. 37, *rince-bouche*: A bowl of warm perfumed water served after a meal to rinse the mouth and clear the palate.

p. 41, *the Battle of Coutras… Saint-Vaast-la-Hougue*: The characters mentioned are fictitious, although the battles are real. The Battle of Coutras, part of the period of conflict during the late sixteenth century known as the French Wars of Religion, was fought between an army under the Huguenot Henry of Navarre (the future Henry IV) and the Catholic royal army led by Anne, Duke of Joyeuse. In May 1692, during the Nine Years' War (fought from 1689 to 1697 between France under Louis XIV and an Anglo-Dutch "Grand Alliance" led by William III), the waters around Saint-Vaast-la-Hougue in Normandy were the site of a major naval battle, in which the French suffered a major defeat.

p. 43, *barège*: A simple and loosely woven light woollen cloth used for making shawls, scarves and dresses, produced in the town of Barèges in south-western France.

p. 49, *La Marjolaine*: A popular folk song.

p. 49, *La Corbeille… Le Sylphe des salons*: *La Corbeille* (*The Basket*) was a female fashion magazine which ran from 1836 to 1878. *Le Sylphe des salons* (*The Sylph of the Salons*) ran under different names from 1829 to 1882.

p. 50, *Eugène Sue*: Eugène Sue (1804–57), author of popular sensation novels such as *Les Mystères de Paris* (1842–43).

p. 52, *La Ruche médicale*: Literally, "the medical hive".

p. 54, *Érard piano*: Sebastian Érard (1752–1831) was a famous piano-maker.

p. 63, *the Charter*: The Charter of 1814 was a constitution granted by King Louis XVIII of France during the Restoration. It guaranteed certain rights and imposed limitations on the monarch. The Charter was retained in modified form after the revolution of 1830 and during the ensuing July Monarchy under Louis-Philippe.

p. 63, *Bengal lights*: A kind of firework.

p. 63, *Raspail medicines... Regnault paste*: Medicines named after famous chemists: François-Vincent Raspail (1794–1878), Jean Darcet (1724–1801) and Henri Victor Regnault (1810–1878).

p. 65, *Poland... victims in Lyon*: During the years following the defeat of an uprising against Russian rule in Warsaw in 1830, many attempts were made in France to raise funds for Polish refugees. There were floods in Lyon in 1840, allowing us to date the Bovarys' arrival in Yonville-l'Abbaye to shortly after this time.

p. 67, *Supreme Being*: In 1994, Robespierre declared the deist "Cult of the Supreme Being" to be the new state religion.

p. 67, *La Profession... of '89*: *La Profession de foi du vicaire savoyard* (*The Profession of Faith of the Savoyard Vicar*) is an argument for natural religion comprising Book IV of Rousseau's *Émile* (1762). By the "principles of '89" Homais refers to the *Déclaration des droits de l'homme et du citoyen* (*Declaration of the Rights of the Man and the Citizen*), which was adopted by the National Constituent Assembly during the early stages of the Revolution, and was one of its defining documents.

p. 70, *In winter... Fahrenheit*: The Réaumur temperature scale is named after René-Antoine Ferchault de Réaumur (1683–1757). It was established in 1730, but had fallen into disuse by the late nineteenth century. In fact, Homais's calculations here are faulty: twenty-five degrees centigrade is equivalent to seventy-seven degrees Fahrenheit, not fifty-four.

p. 71, *L'Ange gardien*: A popular romance by Pauline Duchambre (1778–1858).

p. 73, *Delille... Fanal de Rouen*: Jacques Delille (1738–1813) was a poet famous for his translations of Virgil. The *Écho des feuilletons* is a journal containing serialized novels (*feuilleton* meaning "serial").

The *Fanal de Rouen* (*The Rouen Beacon*) is based on the *Journal de Rouen*, whose editor would not allow the paper's name to be used.

p. 75, *19th Ventôse, Year XI*: 10th March 1803 in the French Republican Calendar, which was adopted in 1793 and abolished in 1805.

p. 77, *Athalie... French theatre*: *Athalie* (1691) was Racine's final play

p. 78, *Le Dieu des bonnes gens*: An anticlerical poem by Béranger (see note to p 9 above).

p. 78, *La Guerre des dieux*: An irreligious epic of 1799 by the poet by Évariste-Désiré de Forges de Parny (1753–1814).

p. 78, *forty days*: in the original French, "les six semaines de la Vierge" ("the six weeks of the Virgin"). This refers to the period after childbirth during which the Christian Church, drawing on the Judaic tradition, regards a woman as being ritually impure and thus not allowed to take holy communion or go to church. She was expected to stay at home, preferably remaining indoors, resting, praying and looking after her newborn child. At the end of the six weeks she would attend a service of purification, after which she was released from her confinement.

p. 80, *Mathieu Laensberg*: An astrological almanac first published in Lièges around 1635.

p. 84, *trente-et-un... écarté*: *Trente-et-un* is a card game on the same principle as pontoon or twenty-one. *Écarté* was a card game similar to Whist popular in the nineteenth century.

p. 85, *L'Illustration*: A periodical concerned with Parisian society and fashion.

p. 91, *La Sachette in Notre-Dame de Paris*: In Hugo's novel of 1831 (often known in English as *The Hunchback of Notre-Dame*), the name of the mother is Paquette, not Sachette.

p. 99, *Caribs or Botocudos*: The Caribs are a tribe from the Caribbean, the Botocudos a tribe from Brazil.

p. 100, *grisettes*: Young, working-class women.

p. 125, *Cincinnatus... cabbages*: According to legend, the Roman statesman Cincinnatus (b. *c.*519 BC) was discovered working a plough when he was called upon to become dictator in 458 BC, during Rome's war with the Aequi. Diocletian (245–316), Roman emperor from 284 to 305, is famous for growing cabbages on his farm after his retirement from office.

p. 126, *Flemish fertilizer*: Based on human excrement.

p. 127, *Croix d'Honneur*: In other words, the Légion d'Honneur, a military and civil order of merit created by Napoleon Bonaparte in 1802.

p. 144, *picots*: A Normandy expression for a female turkey.

p. 146, *tenotomy*: The surgical cutting of a tendon as a remedy for club foot.

p. 146, *Doctor Duval's great tome*: *Traité pratique du pied-bot* (*Practical Treatise on the Club Foot*) (1839) by Vincent Duval (1796–1876). The technical vocabulary in the following paragraph comes from this book.

p. 148, *Ambroise Paré... Gensoul*: The physician Ambroise Paré (1510–90) is seen as the father of modern surgery. Guillaume, Baron Dupuytren (1777–1835) and Joseph Gensoul (1797–1858) were famous French surgeons in the nineteenth century.

p. 152, *strabismus... lithotripsy*: Strabismus is a squint. Lithotripsy is a treatment in which kidney stones are broken up in order that they can be passed.

p. 157, *cold cream*: In English in the original text.

p. 159, *Peter and Paul*: A festival celebrating the martyrdom of St Peter and St Paul, observed on 29th June.

p. 159, *napoleons*: Gold coins worth twenty francs each.

p. 159, *Amor nel cor*: "Love in my heart" (Italian).

p. 161, *Duke of Clarence in his vat of malmsey*: According to tradition, George, Duke of Clarence (1449–1478) was drowned in a butt of malmsey at the command of his brother Richard, Duke of Gloucester (later Richard III), who wished to claim the throne for himself.

p. 175, *sternutator*: A substance causing irritation to the nose.

p. 176, *That is the question*: In English in the original text.

p. 180, *Monsieur de Maistre... Use of the Young*: Joseph de Maistre (1753–1821), a moralist and polemicist famous for his reactionary and authoritarian views in the period after the Revolution. The books listed here are fictitious.

p. 180, *la Vallière*: See second note to p. 29.

p. 183, *Castigat ridendo mores*: "It corrects morals by laughter" (Latin).

p. 183, *Le Gamin de Paris*: A popular vaudeville by Jean-François Bayard (1796–1853) and Émile Vanderbruch (1794–1862).

p. 186, *Lucia di Lammermoor*: An opera by Gaetano Donizetti (1797–1848) based on Walter Scott's novel *The Bride of Lammermoor* (1819).

p. 197, *Code Civil*: The Code Civil or Code Napoléon (Napoleonic Code) is the French civil code, enacted in 1804 under Napoleon Bonaparte.

p. 201, *La Tour de Nesle*: A play by Alexandre Dumas (1802–70), which was first performed in 1832. Set in the eponymous tower, part of Paris's old city wall, it concerns the adultery of the daughters-in-law of King Philip IV.

p. 204, *Swiss Guard*: Swiss Guards are a division of Swiss soldiers whose mission is to protect the Pope and who have served as guards in the Vatican and at other European courts since the early sixteenth century.

p. 204, *Dancing Marianne*: A carving in Rouen cathedral representing Salomé dancing before Herod, as described in Mark 6:21*ff*.

p. 211, *Fabricando fit faber, age quod agis*: "Practice makes perfect, despite what you do" (Latin).

p. 218, *One night... recall*: From Lamartine's poem 'Le Lac'. Lamartine was referred to previously on p. 32.

p. 225, *L'Odalisque... Barcelone*: Names designed to evoke typical Romantic themes rather than those of particular works. Examples of *L'Odalisque au bain* ("the bathing odalisque") are *La Baigneuse Valpinçon* (1808) or *La Grande Odalisque* (1814), both by Ingres.

p. 238, *Yes*: In English in the original text

p. 238, *garus*: A form of digestif based on cinnamon, nutmeg and saffron.

p. 238, *Cujas and Bartolo*: Jacques Cujas (1522–1590) was a French legal expert and humanist. Bartolo da Sassoferrato (1313–1356) was an Italian lawyer and jurist.

p. 243, *ells*: An ell was a unit of length used mostly for textiles. It varied from country to country, the English ell being about forty-five inches.

p. 254, *hippocras*: A sweetened fortified wine mulled with cinnamon, cloves, vanilla, etc., very popular in the Middle Ages.

p. 256, *Steuben's... Putiphar*: Charles-Guillaume Steuben (1788–1856) painted two works based on Hugo's *Notre-Dame de Paris*: *La Esmeralda et Quasimodo* (1839) and *La Esmeralda donnant une leçon de danse à sa chèvre Djali* (1841). Chopin is Henri-Frédéric Chopin (1804–1880), although it is likely that *"Putiphar"* here is a reference to Steuben's *Joseph et la femme de Putiphar* (1843).

p. 260, *Bautzen and Lützen*: Lützen and Bautzen, in, respectively, the German states of Saxony-Anhalt and Saxony, were both sites of battles in May 1813 between Napoleon I's French army and the Russo-Prussian army.

p. 264, *Boulle*: André-Charles Boulle (1642–1732), a famous French cabinet-maker known for skills in the field of marquetry.

p. 272, *Bichat*: Marie François Xavier Bichat (1771–1802), a renowned French anatomist and physiologist, known as the founder of histology, the study of the microscopic structure of tissues.

p. 275, *Misereatur... Indulgentiam*: Prayers of absolution in the Roman Catholic Church.

p. 280, *d'Holbach... a former judge*: Paul-Henri Dietrich, baron d'Holbach (1723–1789), famous amongst other things for his contribution of many articles on scientific subjects to Denis Diderot's *Encyclopédie*, published in France in the late eighteenth century. Here attributed to J.J. Nicolas, *La Raison du christianisme* (its original title) was in fact written by M. de Genoude and first published in 1834.

p. 286, *De Profundis*: Psalm 130.

p. 292, *Ignorant Brothers*: In the French, *frères ignorantins*. Monks belonging to the Order of Saint-Jean-de-Dieu took this name as a mark of humility. As a result, whether out of confusion or hostility, clergy who taught in religious schools were often referred to by the same name. A further misnomer also arose from the fact that the Brothers based at Saint-Yon were known as "*Frères Yontains*", which Voltaire and his followers delighted in changing to "*frères ignorantins*".

p. 293, *Pulvermacher's hydroelectric chains*: Otherwise known as "Pulvermacher's Galvanic Belt", a quack remedy intended to provide relief for a variety of illnesses and increase physical strength. It consisted of a series of coils powered by a battery and worn around the waist.

p. 293, *Sta viator... amabilem conjugem calcas*: "Traveller halt: here lies buried a worthy wife" (Latin).

Extra Material

on

Gustave Flaubert's

Madame Bovary

Gustave Flaubert's Life

Gustave Flaubert was born on 12th December 1821, in Rouen, one of the most thriving industrial and cultural centres of France, and the administrative capital of Normandy. His father, Achille-Cléophas, was director and senior doctor of the Hôtel-Dieu, the major hospital of the city, where he and his family occupied a wing provided for the residential use of senior staff. Flaubert was born here, as his brother – also named Achille – had been almost nine years previously, and his sister Caroline would be two and a half years later. Flaubert always had a protective and loving relationship towards Caroline, and he was devastated when she died at the age of twenty-one. In addition, there had been a sister who died in infancy in 1818 and a brother who died aged eight months in 1819, as well as a further brother who was born in 1819 but died in 1822, just a few months after Flaubert's birth. Achille the son later succeeded his father as director and senior doctor of the Hôtel-Dieu.

Achille-Cléophas Flaubert and his wife, Anne-Justine (née Fleuriot), had throughout their married life made numerous astute purchases of land in the surrounding region. This land was let out to tenant farmers, so that, by the time their children were born, Flaubert's parents were among the most wealthy and respected families of the entire district.

Flaubert recounts in some of his adult letters how his parents – perhaps believing that he too would become a doctor – made no attempt to prevent him or Caroline from roaming through the hospital and watching patients who were severely ill, or even from entering the morgue and being present at the dissection of corpses. Furthermore, Flaubert was taken to visit the local mental asylum at the age of six or seven, and recalls later seeing the lunatics chained to the wall, screaming and tearing at their naked flesh. He wrote: "These are good impressions to have when young: they make a man of you." One wonders whether he was being ironical. Jean-Paul Sartre, in his massive unfinished study of the novelist, tries to prove that Flaubert did indeed have all kinds of psychological problems dating from his childhood.

Flaubert claims to have been very late in learning to read, something that apparently caused severe concern to his family. He was already, however, prone to thinking deeply, making up tales and listening to elderly neighbours reading stories aloud, including *Don Quixote* in French translation. He also loved attending the theatre with his parents. However, when he finally did overcome this apparent mental resistance to reading, around the age of eight or nine, he began to devour literature, and also to write letters which already displayed a facility for observation and literary expression; from that moment on he would dispatch thousands of missives to friends, and these reveal his innermost thoughts on life, philosophy, the purpose of culture and the art of writing. By the age of ten he was already creating dramatic sketches, which he, Caroline and his friends would put on at a makeshift theatre in their hospital residence.

Schooling and Early Writing   Just after his tenth birthday, Flaubert was sent to be a boarding pupil at the local Collège Royal, a fee-paying grammar school – it was the custom for children of the educated classes to board at these institutions, even if their home was very near. He remained there till just past his eighteenth birthday, frequently winning prizes for such subjects as French grammar, translation into Latin, geography, history, philosophy and overall excellence in his studies. His schoolmates were enthusiastic readers of the latest French Romantic writers, principally Chateaubriand, Hugo, Lamartine, Musset and Vigny – all supporters of social and political reform, making the school a hotbed of agitation as these young men tried to emulate their heroes. In addition, during the later years of Flaubert's schooling, Balzac began to produce the first volumes of his vast series of realist novels and stories, and Flaubert voraciously consumed these too. He also loved Shakespeare, Homer and Cervantes, admiring what he saw as their objectivity, their ability to cover the whole of human life without passing judgement on any character or taking sides on any issue.

His parents often spent their holidays at the seaside, and in 1836, on vacation with them at the fishing village of Trouville when he was still not quite fifteen, he developed an infatuation with the twenty-five-year-old Élise Schlésinger, the wife of a successful entrepreneur and publisher. This was the first of many such turbulent passions in his life. Many years later, as a student of law in Paris, Flaubert reacquainted himself with the Schlésingers, enjoying a close friendship with them. This early erotic fascination, as well as his later pursuit of an intimacy with both husband and wife, would much later form the basis for the novel *Sentimental Education*, with Élise herself providing the model for the alluring Madame Arnoux.

He was by now churning out essays and short stories, two of which appeared in a Rouen literary magazine – the only work of his to be published before *Madame Bovary*. Many of these stories, and the theatrical melodramas he was also composing in large numbers, were at first staple Romantic fare, full of ghosts and mad monks and generally set in the Middle Ages, but gradually, under his reading of Balzac, Shakespeare, Cervantes and Homer, this exaggerated Romantic element was weeded out, to be replaced by more reflective and realist subject matter, and a style which became progressively less prolix and more limpid and precise.

In 1839, the year which was meant to lead up to his taking the *baccalauréat*, the series of exams which would have provided him with entrance to higher education, Flaubert was thrown out of the school, along with several of his friends. The reasons are obscure, but it seems that during this final year the very popular philosophy teacher began to miss more and more lessons as a result of ill health (Flaubert had always received excellent marks in philosophy due to this man's excellent teaching); an incompetent and tyrannical teacher was appointed in his place, who constantly doled out unreasonable punishments with which the class refused to cooperate. The headmaster singled out the pupils he considered to be ringleaders, including Flaubert, and expelled them. Flaubert was just two days past his eighteenth birthday. However, he continued to study privately, and passed the *baccalauréat* in August 1840.

As a reward his parents sent him on a tour of southern France and Corsica for a couple of months, along with a family friend, a medical doctor. Flaubert was fascinated by the

Later Education and Travels

311

classical remains in southern France, and he now developed an urge to travel further on at some stage, perhaps to Africa and the Orient.

Flaubert had made it quite clear to his parents that he had no desire to become a doctor, but they insisted that he follow some profession. However, he still remained interested only in art and writing. Finally, he enrolled in the law department of Paris University in November 1841, and began studies there the following autumn. However, he attended very few lectures, and told his parents categorically that, even if he did graduate in this subject, he had no intention of earning a living by it.

Illness and Move to Croisset Despite these assertions he does seem to have worked extremely hard cramming for exams; in addition, he was still trying intensively to pursue his literary vocation by writing stories and plays and carrying out research for various plans he had for future works. He also attempted simultaneously to live a full social life. As a result of all this he was exhausted when he went home to Rouen for the Christmas holidays in December 1843. In January 1844, on a return to his parents' residence from a visit in the locality with his brother Achille, he suddenly fell writhing to the floor of the carriage with what was probably a form of epilepsy. He continued to suffer these fits throughout his life, as well as other mysterious ailments, including regular outbreaks of virulent boils, which would cover his entire body.

Just a week or so later, he managed to return to Paris in an attempt to continue his studies, but immediately had another seizure and so came home. His father promptly imposed on him a strict diet and prolonged rest, and bought a large house to the west of Rouen, on the river at Croisset, where his son could live peacefully and be attended to by doctors and servants. The family was wealthy enough to support him without his having to earn a living, and so he gave up permanently any idea of the law, or indeed of any other profession, and spent almost the rest of his life at Croisset devoting himself to thought, observation and writing – at least, when his epileptic seizures and generally poor health would allow. Over the years he built high walls all around the house and extensive gardens, so that he would be cut off from noise and disturbances and be able to think and write in almost monastic seclusion.

Two further disasters followed in swift succession. In March *Deaths of Father and*
1845 Gustave's beloved sister Caroline had married Émile *Sister*
Hamard – a man whom the whole family regarded as below her
in intelligence and social standing, and whom Gustave detested
and considered an idiot. His sister's health, like Gustave's, was
also deteriorating. On 15th January 1846, their father died
after a short illness, and just six days later Caroline gave birth
to a daughter, also to be named Caroline. But the mother
immediately fell ill with puerperal fever and eight weeks later
she too died. The family managed to gain legal custody of
the baby, and Gustave, his widowed mother and the child all
commenced living together at Croisset.

It was around this time, in 1846, that Flaubert first encountered
the poet Louise Colet, who was posing for a sculptor he had
become acquainted with in Paris. Colet was married to the
musician Hippolyte Colet, but nevertheless she and Flaubert
embarked on a passionate affair, during which they corresponded
frequently, before parting company for ever in October 1854.
Colet later described her tempestuous relationship with Flaubert
in her novel *Lui*, which appeared in 1859.

Flaubert had no time for politics and, although he held
authority in contempt, he also regarded those he considered
the common people with a kind of patrician disdain. When
in February 1848 the July Monarchy was brought down by
an alliance of the middle classes and the radicals, Flaubert,
although pleased to see the authoritarian monarch Louis
Philippe go, had no sympathy for those who replaced him
– a combination of, as he saw it, the philistine bourgeoisie,
fanatical revolutionaries and the uncouth working masses.

Following Caroline's marriage, the entire family, including *Italy*
Gustave, had accompanied the married couple on their
honeymoon to Italy, where, in the Palazzo Balbi in Genoa, he
had been overwhelmed by *The Temptation of St Anthony*, a
painting ascribed to Pieter Breugel the Elder. Flaubert – possibly
inspired by Goethe's *Faust* – had immediately conceived the
idea of a play on the subject. He took some eighteen months to
compile material and write the work, which grew to mammoth
proportions. The cast of characters was enormous, and
some speeches were ten pages long. On completion he read
it to two friends, Maxine Du Camp and Louis Bouilhet. Du
Camp claimed later that the entire reading had taken in total
some thirty-two hours spread over four days. They were both

313

profoundly discouraging, even contemptuous, and told him to throw the whole thing on the fire and stick to subjects he was familiar with.

Tour of Middle East   Despite this blow to his confidence as a writer, Flaubert bore no ill will to Du Camp, and the pair set off in October 1849 to explore the Middle East; this had been one of Flaubert's dreams since his teenage years, and he hoped to gain fresh material from this journey for his writing. They spent time in Cairo, sailed up the Nile, visited the Holy Land, Beirut, Rhodes and Constantinople, and, on the way back, paused in Greece to see the ancient remains. Flaubert came back prematurely ageing: he was losing his hair and putting on weight. He had also contracted syphilis from a visit to a Beirut brothel.

Writing of Madame   They returned to France in June 1851, and almost immedia-
Bovary, Controversy   tely Flaubert took up a new project: a novel based on the
and Trial   down-to-earth subject of an ordinary medical official and his wife's adultery and eventual suicide.

He completed the novel, *Madame Bovary*, in April 1856. It was serialized, albeit in bowdlerized form, from October to December that year, something that resulted in accusations of obscenity and a failed attempt to prosecute the author for offending public morals and blasphemy. The controversy had the perverse effect of guaranteeing the two-volume edition, which appeared in April 1857, best-seller status.

Flaubert now attempted a wholesale revision of *The Temptation of St Anthony*, but delayed any publication of this work because he knew that its subject matter, the sexual temptation of a holy figure, might make it, like *Madame Bovary*, liable for prosecution. He then turned to a new project, one whose subject was equally far-removed from the provincial realism of *Madame Bovary*: a novel set in third-century Carthage to be entitled *Salammbô*.

During his writing of this volume, he began once again to suffer from serious seizures. These episodes occasionally involved severe injury, as he would collapse writhing on the pavement, hitting his head and limbs.

He completed *Salammbô* on 20th April 1862, and promptly suffered a virulent outbreak of boils all over his body. The novel was generally successful among the public and intellectuals: Victor Hugo, Hector Berlioz, George Sand and Théophile Gautier sent him adulatory letters. Some critics and historians, however, attacked the story for what they saw as its prolixity and inaccuracy of historical detail. But Flaubert now found himself an honoured guest at literary salons, and he formed friendships with such literary luminaries as the Goncourt brothers and the Russian novelist Ivan Turgenev, who was resident in France at the time. He also became acquainted with the younger set of French writers, including Émile Zola, Alphonse Daudet and Guy de Maupassant. Indeed, the intensity of his friendship with Maupassant was so strong that it has been seriously speculated that Maupassant was Flaubert's illegitimate son.

On 15th August 1866 Flaubert received the Légion d'Honneur – an award reserved for France's most eminent individuals in all fields.

Flaubert began to consider in earnest what he described as his "Parisian novel" on his forty-first birthday, 12th December 1862, two weeks after the publication of *Salammbô*. Over six years later, in May 1869, *Sentimental Education*, about a young man living through the revolution of 1848 and the foundation of the Second Empire, was finished. Although the novel sold reasonably well, it was vilified by the critics for its perceived shapelessness. Furthermore, it was criticized by the conservative sections of the press for its theme of political radicalism; at the same time the radicals attacked the novel for what they considered its unsympathetic portrayal of them.

In July 1870, war broke out between France and Prussia. *Franco-Prussian War* On 1st September, the French army was crushed at the Battle of Sedan, something that resulted in the capture of Emperor Napoleon III, the collapse of the Second Empire and the formation of a new republican government. The fastidious Flaubert, with his contempt for politics, found himself appointed to the rank of lieutenant in the local Rouen Home Guard, which had been formed to defend the region against the Prussian invasion.

Paris withstood the Prussian siege that followed the defeat at Sedan, but the lands to the north capitulated almost immediately. Prussian soldiers were billeted in Flaubert's house at Croisset from December 1870 to April 1871, and Flaubert, despising what he saw as the barbarous and uncouth German soldiers, fled for the period to the house in Dieppe of his niece Caroline, who in 1864 had married an incompetent timber merchant named Ernest Commanville. Flaubert called the period of the Prussian invasion the worst of his life.

Death of Mother In April 1872, a year after Flaubert's return to Croisset, his mother died, leaving Croisset not to Gustave but to her grandchild Caroline; it was only after lengthy negotiations that Caroline allowed her uncle to continue living there. Over the next couple of years he yet again extensively revised and abridged *The Temptation of St Anthony*, and it was at last published in this final version in April 1874. It sold well, but was nevertheless lambasted by the drama critics as being unperformable – it still had a huge cast, was extremely static and, like the first version written so many years before, still contained many speeches that continued unbroken over several pages.

In April 1875, the timber company of his niece's husband collapsed, leaving the couple with enormous debts, and, to help them, Flaubert immediately sold some of the family property that had provided him and his relations with a secure rental income for so long; he estimated that he had bailed the young couple out to the tune of a million francs, and there was even a possibility at one time that Croisset would have to be sold too, though this was averted.

Paris and Later Life However, because Croisset was expensive to keep, and to light and heat during winter, and his income was now severely curtailed, Flaubert moved to cheap lodgings in Paris. This also enabled him to be near Caroline and her husband, who had also moved to the capital. Gustave constantly feared that Croisset, his lifelong retreat, would have to be sold, and this worry, and his attempts to keep up his writing in his cramped and noisy lodgings, caused his health to worsen alarmingly.

He had begun a new novel, *Bouvard and Pécuchet*, in August 1872, but owing to his family problems and ill health, he abandoned it in the summer of 1875 and turned to writing short stories. However, these too went very slowly, and over the next eighteen months he managed to produce only three that he considered worthy; these were issued in one volume, under the title *Three Tales*, in April 1877. At this point he resumed work on *Bouvard and Pécuchet*, but it was never completed.

, In 1879 he was awarded a small state pension for his literary work, which alleviated his comparative penury somewhat, but still did not allow him to resume residence permanently at Croisset. Nevertheless, he did manage to visit his old house occasionally, especially when the weather was warmer, in order to inspect it and make sure it was not falling into total disrepair. It was on one of these brief visits to Croisset, on 8th May 1880, that he suffered what seems to have been an apoplectic stroke – although there has been speculation that he committed suicide in a state of depression. The servants summoned a doctor, but Flaubert, who was in a coma, died soon afterwards.

Zola, Daudet, Maupassant and other major French writers and cultural figures attended the funeral service and procession, and Flaubert was interred at the Cimetière Monumental in Rouen.

Gustave Flaubert's Works

Although Flaubert pondered a great deal over aesthetics and the significance and aims of literature, he wrote very little about his ideas on these subjects. His views are therefore to be gleaned from chance remarks in his letters, and from the style of his works themselves.

Although seeming to like people individually, and to have many friends, he possessed a pessimistic, even contemptuous view of the human race overall, and in particular of its preoccupation with what he saw as mediocrity and trivia. He told some of his correspondents that he found life boring, ugly and even hideous.

As for metaphysics, religion and politics, he thought that we can know nothing for certain, and therefore that one ought not to take sides, put forward any viewpoint in one's writing or pass judgement on any of the characters' behaviours in one's stories, however reprehensible their conduct might seem.

Much of the art of the time dealt with social and political themes, but Flaubert stood aloof from these currents: he wrote in his letters that a work has importance only by virtue of its eternity, and that the more it represented humanity as it is and has always been, the more beautiful it would be. Furthermore, he believed, it is of paramount importance that this Olympian impersonality and detachment should be represented through beauty and clarity of style, to emphasize that life could be lived in a different way from what he saw as the ugliness of reality.

Therefore, his chosen subject matter in his mature works is predominantly that of ordinary human beings who, although mediocre in intelligence and understanding, have aspirations that are constantly thwarted by the circumstances and people they are surrounded by. Instances of such sad individuals in Flaubert's writings are Emma Bovary, Frédéric Moreau and the two old clerks, Bouvard and Pécuchet. As Flaubert's style matured, the narrator more or less vanished altogether from his works; everything is merely "shown", and the reader is left to make up his or her own mind. Of *Madame Bovary*, Flaubert wrote that he hoped that the reader would not notice all the psychological effort that he'd put into representing the characters, but would still be deeply affected by their portrayal.

Flaubert revered science for its objective means of analysis of the world, and its progressive accumulation of details of the make-up of reality. This may explain too the vast amount of research he did for all his projects, sometimes amounting to reading over one hundred volumes for a planned work, and taking painfully long periods to write it. However, in this striving for total objectivity and a transparent style that made exclusive use of what he termed "*le mot juste*" (the most apt or appropriate word for any context), he stressed that the perfection of the writing always had to take precedence over mere documentation and detail.

Madame Bovary Flaubert sat down to write *Madame Bovary*, his most famous novel and first large-scale work to be published, in 1851, after the savaging by two friends of his manuscript for *The Temptation of St Anthony*, as mentioned above.

He may have obtained the original germ of the idea for the novel on his return to France, when he heard the tale of Eugène Delamere, a mediocre former student of his father's who had failed to pass all his medical exams and therefore had to be satisfied with a post not as a doctor, but as a public-health officer. Delamere's wife Delphine committed numerous infidelities, ruined him financially, and then committed suicide by taking poison, leaving him with their child. Devastated, Delamere had in his turn taken his own life.

Whether or not this was the inspiration, Flaubert's idea is first mentioned on 21st July 1851, in a letter to Flaubert from Du Camp – although it should be noted that this might imply that the topic had been discussed between them previously, possibly on their travels in the Middle East. He began writing in earnest on 16th September that year.

He spent some five years over this project, developing the meticulousness, precision and objectivity for which his prose is known. In a letter to the poet Louise Colet, his lover at the time, dated January 1852, Flaubert explains his intention to write a book in which style is predominant and the subject irrelevant. In another letter to Colet from April of the same year, he described his ambition of creating a form of prose as precise as scientific language and as musical as poetry, later telling her that he thought that a well-turned prose sentence ought to be as immutable as a line of verse.

However, this commitment to *le mot juste* came at a price. According to friends such as Louis Bouilhet, Flaubert found progress on the novel desperately slow, and he would frequently fly into rages, bellow and swear while working on it. Over the course of a week he would perhaps agonize over just one page of his fiction, and yet over the same period he would churn out dozens of affable and informative letters to friends – occasionally containing some quite coarse language. For instance, in a letter to Colet of January 1852, Flaubert confessed to being "depressed" and "harried" by the novel, as well as occasionally wishing for death. In April of the same year he described the ascetic, austere life he was leading while writing, telling Colet that he had written twenty-five pages in six weeks, and that he felt that his arms could drop off and his brain disintegrate with the fatigue.

The prosaic theme – a story of everyday provincial life – enabled Flaubert to develop his gift for clinical observation of human beings and move away from the youthful melodramatic excesses and verbosity of *The Temptation of St Anthony*. Over five years he wrote and rewrote *Madame Bovary*, progressively honing his style and constantly paring the text to remove both superfluities of language and authorial judgements and subjectivity.

We are introduced first to Charles Bovary at school; he is a misfit: clumsy, awkward and shy. He grows up to be a mediocre country doctor earning a modest income. A first, unhappy marriage to a local widow ends with the death of his wife.

Meanwhile, Emma Rouault, the pretty farmer's daughter whose mind is filled with aspirations beyond her reach – caused perhaps by reading popular romantic literature – longs to escape. She meets Charles and he falls in love with her. She, perhaps to escape her stifling background, marries him, but soon begins to feel that her marriage to her hard-working and unromantic husband has not matched her visions, derived from her reading, of luxurious aristocratic mansions and travel to exotic foreign locations, and she grows restless and unsatisfied. She builds up enormous debts, and begins to commit adultery – first with the law student and aesthete Léon Dupuis and then with the wealthy and caddish Rodolphe Boulanger. Charles, however, never suspects any of this, and is almost pathetically happy in her presence.

With mounting debts, and following the failure of an attempt to run off with Boulanger – who does not have the courage or interest to go through with it – Emma undergoes a long period of mental illness, during which she is nursed devotedly by her loving husband – who, however, still has no idea that he himself, and her life with him, might be part of the underlying problem.

Finally, Emma commits suicide by poisoning herself with arsenic she has stolen from the local chemist. At her death, Charles is devastated to discover letters from her secret lovers and loses all interest in life. He abandons his medical practice, neglects his personal appearance and well-being, and finally dies suddenly, apparently from natural causes.

After the novel's completion in April 1856, it was published in serial form in the weekly periodical *La Revue de Paris* between October and December that year. However, due to the climate of moral censoriousness at the time, the editorial board made extensive cuts – both with and without the author's permission – and so, after several instalments had been published, Flaubert insisted on inserting a note in the journal denying responsibility for the confused and mutilated state of his story.

Despite all these precautions by the editorial board, both they and Flaubert were prosecuted for immorality and insulting religion. However, although the work was castigated in court by the judge, the charges were thrown out and, inevitably, when the novel was finally published in two volumes in April 1857, it enjoyed enormous sales – although Flaubert made little money from it, since he'd sold the entire publishing rights for the book format for a few hundred francs. It generally received excellent reviews, although the more conservative sections of the press did indeed lambaste what they perceived as its immorality.

When asked once whether Emma Bovary was modelled on any real person, Flaubert is alleged to have responded: "*Madame Bovary, c'est moi!*" However, it is very difficult to pin down precisely where this story came from and, besides, Flaubert told a number of correspondents that there had been no model for either the story of the novel or any of its characters. Therefore, many commentators have cast doubt on the authenticity of this quotation. Furthermore, it is difficult to see exactly what it refers to, even if true: does it mean that this character is based on Flaubert himself? Or was Flaubert in fact referring to *Madame Bovary* the novel, and therefore trying to imply that he had put the best of himself into it?

For his next work, Flaubert settled on a totally different *Salammbô* subject: ancient Carthage. He researched the background intensively, claiming to have read over one hundred volumes on the theme, and spent three weeks from April to May 1858 visiting the supposed sites of the ancient city in North Africa. Like his previous novel, it took more than five years to write: he began work on 1st September 1857, and completed it on 20th April 1862. It was published in late November that year.

The novel is set over the period 241–238 BC, when Carthage had just suffered a crushing defeat in a war against Rome. Following this rout, the city could not pay off its enormous mercenary army, and as a result these hired soldiers launched a mutiny against the Carthaginian government to try to obtain payment. The human interest in the foreground is provided by the fictional love of Matho, the general of this insurgent army, for Salammbô, the daughter of the city's military leader, Hamilcar.

Salammbô flees the violence in the city, but Matho manages to find his way to her quarters. However, she is torn between her love for him and her revulsion at his enmity for her father and the Carthaginian people. She utters a triple curse against him, declaring that she wishes him to be asphyxiated and then rent asunder, and finally for his body to be burnt. He runs away. She seems to develop some kind of mental illness – akin to Emma Bovary – as a result of the ambivalence of her feelings towards Matho.

When Matho is eventually caught and executed, Salammbô is taken to see his body, and to watch his heart being ceremonially removed by her father. He has indeed been asphyxiated and torn apart, and his corpse is to be burnt.

Perhaps stricken by the belief that he has died in this way as a result of her malediction, Salammbô collapses and dies.

Although differing considerably from the preceding novel in that it is set in a major capital of antiquity, during events of extraordinary importance for the Western world of the time, the novel utilizes the same precision of style and objectivity of observation as *Madame Bovary*.

Despite being disparaged by some critics for its incoherence, and by a number of historians for its inaccuracy, *Salammbô* sold well, and attracted admiring letters from, among other cultural figures, Victor Hugo and Hector Berlioz.

Sentimental Education On his forty-first birthday, 12th December 1862, two weeks after the publication of *Salammbô*, Flaubert jotted in a notebook that he had begun to address himself seriously to his "Parisian novel" – what was to become *Sentimental Education*. This work, to be concerned with the politically radical generation of young Parisians of the 1840s and 1850s, would incorporate extensive reminiscences from Flaubert's own youth. In particular, the novel would make use of Flaubert's relationship with Élise Schlésinger, the beautiful, married woman whom the author had encountered at the age of fourteen on a holiday with his parents in the fishing village of Trouville, and whom he had deliberately sought out later in his life while studying law in Paris.

Once again, the novel took far longer to research and write than he thought, and Flaubert's health was declining rapidly. He completed the last page on 16th May 1869 – over six years after first referring to the project.

The reader is introduced to Frédéric Moreau, a young man whose family is distantly related to aristocracy and consequently highly respected in Nogent-sur-Seine, the town in Normandy where they live. He is full of the romantic clichés of the literature of his day, and is inflamed with the drive for social and political reforms current among his own generation. On a journey by boat from Paris to Nogent-sur-Seine, his provincial home town, he sees and falls in love with Madame Arnoux, the beautiful wife of a businessman. Returning to Paris, where he enrols at the university to study law, Frédéric penetrates the social circle of M. Arnoux, eventually succeeding in making contact with his wife.

When his mother's financial situation deteriorates sharply and she is forced to halt his allowance, Frédéric is compelled to interrupt his studies and go home. He embarks on various mundane tutoring jobs in Nogent-sur-Seine, and it is only after several years that the death of a wealthy uncle leaves him at last financially independent. He immediately returns to Paris, only to discover that Madame Arnoux has moved. However, he finds her again, and his intermittent infatuation with her resumes. Along the way, Frédéric becomes involved with Rosanette, the mistress of M. Arnoux; eventually she becomes his own lover and becomes pregnant. He also contemplates with marriage with Louise, the daughter of a friend of his mother's.

All this takes place during the 1848 revolution and the foundation of the Second Empire, a time of increasing violence. Frédéric ends up having made one woman pregnant, and with both her and another woman wanting to marry him; to make things worse, he has increasing financial problems. He marries one of these ladies more for her wealth and social position than from any love towards her, then shortly afterwards leaves her, since they are mutually incompatible. He is now completely alone, having lived an aimless and rootless life and failed to commit himself in any way in the political turmoil taking place around him. He is at this point in his late forties, and the title of the novel, *Sentimental Education*, is now shown to be heavily ironical – neither he nor his friends have learnt anything from life, but have become sad, pathetic and lonely middle-aged people, living meaningless existences.

Sentimental Education was published in November 1869. It met with a hostile reception, firstly from the literary critics for its perceived shapelessness and incoherence, then from the right-wing press for having dared to mention radicalism at all, and finally from the radicals for its unsympathetic portrait of them – for, although contemptuous of the political right and of authoritarianism, Flaubert viewed militant republicans and socialists with disdain too.

Although the finished work was not published until 1874, Flaubert had first had the idea of writing *The Temptation of St Anthony* upon seeing Pieter Bruegel the Elder's representation of the subject, as mentioned above. The story of St Anthony of Egypt (*c.*251–356), a religious hermit who was, according to his biographer, Athanasius, plagued by supernatural visions sent by the Devil during his self-imposed solitude on a mountain near the Nile called Pispir, had proved popular with

The Temptation of St Anthony

writers and artists over the centuries, and, immediately on his return to France, Flaubert began to carry out intense and wide-ranging research, intending to create his own theatrical version.

In Flaubert's treatment, Anthony has vowed to save his soul by a life of prayer in a remote cave, but is constantly suffering enticements to break his vows of dedication to God with a succession of alluring maidens sent by the Devil to seduce him. He resists successfully. But the huge canvas of the drama is populated with a vast number of ancient pagan divinities, Christian heretics, figures from classical and heathen legend, and, in a device reminiscent of medieval mystery plays, personified representations of the vices, all of whom struggle to wrest the soul of the hermit away from God.

The Devil himself appears and tries to persuade Anthony that his view of the divine being as a personal god who loves humanity is false. Anthony appears to have resisted all these allurements, but the Devil promises at the end of the play to return again and again, implying either that Anthony will ultimately fall, or that he will remain subject to temptations throughout his life and that the struggle to escape them is futile.

Having abandoned work on the play after the unwieldy 1848–49 draft, Flaubert undertook a drastic revision of the *The Temptation of St Anthony* before starting work on *Salammbô*, cutting it down by more than half and trying to make the language less febrile. However, it was still far too long to perform, or even to publish in full, although a few very brief extracts from it appeared in the magazine *L'Artiste* in late 1856 and early 1857.

He took up the manuscript of this work once again as late as July 1870, some six months after the publication of *Sentimental Education*, and subjected it to yet another radical revision. He continually read out extracts from this greatly pared-down third version to his friends, but they still found it appallingly prolix and unoriginal – though they didn't tell him so to his face.

He managed to complete the project once and for all on 20th June 1872. This final version, published at last in April 1874, had not only been drastically abridged but also revised from a philosophical point of view: for instance, instead of the former conclusion, with the Devil threatening to return

324

repeatedly in the attempt to tear Anthony from God, this third and final rewriting ends with the saint experiencing a vision of Christ; now at the end of the play, he can settle down uninterrupted to his devotions, presumably never to be subject to diabolical temptation again.

Although the project may overall be said to be a failure, it is instructive that Flaubert returned to the theme again and again through a period of some twenty-five years, signifying how much this motif of a hermit subjected to continual temptations fascinated Flaubert, and how much perhaps he identified with St Anthony.

In 1872 Flaubert began his next major work, a novel to be *Three Tales* called *Bouvard et Pécuchet*, which he had planned as far back as 1863. However, bored and frustrated by the tedious progress he was making, and perhaps thwarted by deteriorating health, he suspended work on this project for eighteen months from September 1875 to February 1877, and instead turned to short stories set in different periods and with very different themes; he did this to experiment with different styles, extend his range and further hone his style into that necessary for the short-story form.

He published three of these tales in one volume, in April 1877, under the title *Three Tales*. These stories, in the order in which they appear in the book, are 'A Simple Heart', 'The Legend of St Julian the Hospitaller' and 'Herodias'. They take place, respectively, in modern times, the Middle Ages and the beginning of the Christian era.

The first story, 'A Simple Heart', is set in Flaubert's own time. Critics consider this tale a masterpiece on a par with *Madame Bovary*. Like that novel, the story is not concerned with distant times or vast historical canvases, but rather with what he knew. It employs Flaubert's memories of the region in which he was brought up, and the central figure is based partly on that of a very aged family servant who was still alive when he wrote the tale.

Félicité is a young, reliable, hard-working servant girl; as she spends year after year in the job she seems to become dry and drained of feeling. But this is not true: she has her own feelings, her own inner world, largely unknown to her bourgeois employers. For instance, in her early life, she loves a young man to distraction, but when he abandons her for another woman, she transfers her affections to her employer's children and a worthless nephew who turns up out of nowhere. They all take her love for granted, and the nephew dies in the West Indies. Finally, she becomes fixated on a pet parrot, which almost takes on a religious significance to her: it is, significantly, the only thing ever to talk to her in her later years – albeit with a fixed repertoire of three phrases. It too finally dies.

Félicité has had little communication with the outside world and has bestowed her love on subjects who either do not notice it, are unworthy of it, or simply die, like the parrot. She becomes deaf and progressively aged and frail, finally dying of pneumonia. She remains content to the last in her simple, devout religious belief. As she reaches the point of death, she sees heaven opening and what is possibly an angel or the Holy Spirit coming to receive her soul – in the form of a gigantic parrot. The old servant's life has apparently been pointless, but she herself dies in bliss and convinced that her vision is real.

The second tale, 'The Legend of St Julian the Hospitaller', is derived from a medieval religious tale. The young Julian inherits from his army-general father aggressive, militaristic tendencies, and from his mother a gentle, religious outlook on life. His father intends him to have a military career, and trains him when still very young to hunt wild animals in a bloodthirsty and cruel manner. Julian accordingly slaughters vast numbers of animals quite senselessly until finally, on one such hunting expedition, a stag, just before being killed by him, utters a prophecy that he will murder his own parents. Julian feels he can tell nobody about this, and falls seriously ill as a result of this repression of his anxiety.

When recovered from his sickness, Julian hurls a javelin at what he thinks is a bird, only almost to kill his mother. Horrified by the possibility that the prophecy may come true, he flees from his parents' castle and enlists as a common soldier, hoping to avoid the curse by dying in battle. He rescues an Eastern emperor from death and marries his daughter. Finding himself at peace mentally at last, he longs to see his parents again. One day he goes out hunting, but fails to kill any animals; inflamed with rage and frustrated bloodlust, he returns home. However, in the mean time his parents have come at last to visit him, and his wife has put them into a bed to recover from their journey. Julian, seeing a male and a female head on the pillows, and thinking the female is his wife and the male is a lover, kills them both, thereby fulfilling the prophecy.

He abandons his home and to expiate his crime decides to devote his life to the service of others. He tends the sick and dying, and spends many years caring for a repulsive leper, until finally the leper is revealed to be Jesus Christ. Julian dies and is transported to heaven, his early crimes obviously redeemed by his subsequent saintly life. In the last sentence of the tale the narrator laconically reminds us that this is a legend, the details of which are depicted in a stained-glass window in the wall of a church near his home. There is in fact a window in Rouen Cathedral that tells this story.

The final story, 'Herodias', deals with the last days of John the Baptist, as related in the Gospels of Matthew and Mark, set against the background of the politics of contemporary Palestine. Herodias throws a birthday banquet for her second husband, Herod Antipas. She schemes to have her husband fall in love with her daughter by her first marriage, Salomé, as part of a plan to kill John the Baptist. Salomé dances for Herod and, infatuated, he promises her whatever she wants: she demands John's head on a salver, which he accordingly gives her, although very reluctantly. Following John's execution, his followers set off into the desert to await the Messiah whose coming the ancient prophets and John have foretold.

Like the legend of St Julian, Salomé's dance is depicted on a window in Rouen Cathedral, and it was possibly from this image that Flaubert derived his inspiration for this story set in biblical times.

Flaubert returned to the novel that was to become *Bouvard and Pécuchet* in 1877, although it remained unfinished at the time of his death in May 1880. Even without the eighteen-month break, during which he wrote *Three Tales*, Flaubert took over six years to write fewer than ten chapters of what was apparently intended to be a very long philosophical novel, possibly indicating that he was finding it more and more difficult to write as a result of his deteriorating health.

The original inspiration for this work seems to have been a humorous novel by Barthélemy Maurice entitled *Les Deux Greffiers* (*The Two Court Clerks*), in which two

Bouvard and Pécuchet and The Dictionary of Received Ideas

court copyists, having spent their entire lives in their boring occupation, devote their retirement to the attempt to find the meaning of life. They step back from their endeavour on the edge of madness, and decide to resume their old, rather boring life, having realized that, tedious though it is, they enjoy it. But, inevitably, Flaubert, having adopted this idea, resolved to make his own work based on it extremely long, realistic and philosophical. He once declared he was going to write an angry book against human stupidity.

Like *Madame Bovary*, *Bouvard and Pécuchet* is set in modern Normandy. Its titular protagonists work as legal copyists in different parts of the town. They are middle-aged, unmarried mediocrities. They meet by chance, become friendly, and, when one inherits a fortune, decide to retire and engage in intense study of all fields of human endeavour, delving profoundly into questions such as the meaning of life, the existence of God and other knotty subtleties.

Yet they talk in clichés and are physically inept and clumsy. They drift from one subject to another: philosophy, metaphysics, medicine, politics, religion, geology, physiology, natural sciences, literature, aesthetics – indeed, the whole spectrum of human knowledge. They begin to infuriate the people of Chavignolles in Normandy, where they have settled, as, full of their own superficial learning and inflated notions, they pass judgement on what they perceive as the coarseness and obtuseness of those around them.

The surviving notes and plans do not make it clear how the novel would have continued. However, according to Flaubert's notes, at least one plan was for their neighbours to force Bouvard and Pécuchet out of the area or have them committed, and for Bouvard and Pécuchet to return to their former occupation. It is also possible that Flaubert intended to add to the novel as an appendix a separate work entitled *The Dictionary of Received Ideas*, an encyclopedia of platitudes and clichés designed to satirize bourgeois French society that the author compiled throughout the 1870s. The latter work was eventually published separately many years later.

What had been completed of *Bouvard and Pécuchet* was published in instalments in literary journals shortly after Flaubert's death.

Adaptations

The earliest French version appeared in 1933, adapted and directed by Jean Renoir, starring Valentine Tessier as Emma and Pierre Renoir (the director's elder brother) as Charles Bovary, and featuring music by composer Darius Milhaud.

French-language Screen Adaptations

Critics consider what remains of this version superbly shot and acted. Unfortunately, because Renoir's original print was three and a half hours long, the American distributors cut it by around ninety minutes, leaving the story disjointed and incoherent; furthermore, much of the depth of characterization has been lost. The excised scenes have never come to light. Despite its mutilated state, however, this early French version is still more involving than any of the later cinematic takes on the theme, either in French or in English.

Claude Chabrol's film of the novel was released in 1991, starring Isabelle Huppert as Emma and Jean-François Balmer as Charles. The critical consensus was that Huppert was cold and wooden in the title role, and that the film as a whole was dull, lifeless and totally forgettable. One review described it as "a complete turkey". However, despite these negative views in the press, the film was nominated in 1992 for a Golden Globe award for best foreign-language film, and an Academy Award for best costume design, although it won neither.

A feature-length adaptation was made for French television in 1974, directed by Pierre Cardinal, with Nicole Courcel as Emma, and Jean Boise playing Charles. The general view was that the characters were under-developed and badly acted, and that the screenplay and direction were very poor.

Perhaps the most notable English-language cinematic adaptation of *Madame Bovary* is the 1949 MGM version directed by Vincente Minelli and starring Jennifer Jones as Emma and Van Heflin as Charles. Ingeniously, the film is framed by Flaubert's trial. Flaubert – played by James Mason – is depicted in the witness box at the beginning of the film, beginning his defence of the novel. Following the story's tragic conclusion, we return to the courthouse, where Flaubert is acquitted, to the congratulations of his friends. In the audience, there are several women who look like Emma Bovary: the message is that there are lots of women in small-town France suffering what she had to suffer.

English-language Screen Adaptations

Although Mason is considered to be brilliant in the court scenes, the adaptation was not well received. Significantly, because of the strict censorship in the United States of the time, the precise details of Emma's transgressions, and the reasons why the novel was being prosecuted, are only dealt with in a very oblique fashion, leaving any viewer who had not read the novel none the wiser as to its original subject matter.

David Lean's *Ryan's Daughter*, released in 1970, transposes the theme of *Madame Bovary* to Ireland during the troubles of 1916. A village girl, Rosy Ryan, played by Sarah Miles, marries the boring, middle-aged village schoolmaster, but, feeling unfulfilled, has an affair with a young officer of the occupying British army, something that leads to tragic repercussions when she is accused by the locals of collaborating with the enemy.

The first of two television adaptations by the BBC appeared in 1964, consisting of four forty-five-minute episodes. It was directed by Rex Tucker and adapted by Giles Cooper. Nyree Dawn Porter starred as Emma, with Glynn Edwards as Charles. This version is spoken of highly by critics, with Nyree Dawn Porter coming in for especial praise.

A second, feature-length version was produced by the BBC in 2000, directed by Tim Fywell with a screenplay by Heidi Thomas. Shot mainly at Ashridge Park, Hertfordshire, it featured Frances O'Connor as Emma and Hugh Bonneville as Charles. The film was nominated for two BAFTAs in 2001, one for best costume design and the other for best make-up and hair design, but won neither. Frances O'Connor was nominated in 2001 for a Golden Globe award for her role as Emma, but was unsuccessful.

The general view is that, although the settings are superb, the photography excellent and the acting in general very good, the adaptation failed to convey much of the subtlety of the novel's characterization and story. We see simply the banality of the characters and the mundane theme of small-town adultery, but not the desperate longing of Emma or the other characters to escape from their limitations and find happiness.

Literary Spin-offs   Turning now to literary adaptations, a distant spin-off is the graphic novel *Gemma Bovery* by the cartoonist Posy Simmonds, first issued in 1999. This is a reproduction in book form of Simmonds' strip cartoons, which appeared in the *Guardian* newspaper over several years under the same title. Gemma, an average London girl, marries a boring furniture designer who is divorced with children. Fed up with her life, and with being used as an unpaid babysitter, Gemma persuades her husband to relocate with her to Normandy, where, inevitably, she has affairs with the local men. The essence of the cartoon, which received glowing reviews, was its absolutely spot-on portrayal of the typical English person living abroad, and of the attitude of the French towards them. The first edition sold some 43,000 copies, and it has gone through many reprints since.

An even more distant spin-off is by the British francophile novelist Julian Barnes. In 1984 he produced what he termed a "work in progress" under the title *Flaubert's Parrot*, which purports to be the first-person musings of a depressive modern British doctor, Geoffrey Braithwaite, who is obsessed with Flaubert, and travels to France to explore the regions connected with the great French writer. His ponderings on Flaubert's works, style and life are interwoven with accounts of Braithwaite's trivial and boring existence in London and his visits to the Flaubert sites.

Select Bibliography

Standard Editions:
The most authoritative editions of Flaubert's works in the original French are the two-volume *Œuvres complètes*, published by Éditions du Seuil, Paris, in 1964, and the sixteen-volume edition of the same name, published by Club de l'Honnête Homme, Paris, from 1971 onwards. The latter edition contains Flaubert's complete correspondence as well as unedited manuscripts.

Biographies:
Bart, Benjamin F., *Flaubert* (Syracuse, NY: Syracuse University Press, 1967)
Lottman, Herbert R., *Flaubert: A Biography* (London: Methuen, 1989)
Oliver, Hermia, *Flaubert and an English Governess: The Quest for Juliet Herbert* (Oxford: Clarendon Press, 1980)
Sartre, Jean-Paul, *The Family Idiot: Gustave Flaubert 1821–1857*, tr. Carol Cosman, 5 vols. (Chicago, IL, and London: University of Chicago Press, 1981–1993)
Spencer, Philip, *Flaubert: A Biography* (London: Faber, 1952)
Starkie, Enid, *Flaubert: The Making of the Master* (London: Weidenfeld & Nicolson, 1967)

Starkie Enid, *Flaubert the Master* (London: Weidenfeld & Nicolson, 1971)

Wall, Geoffrey, *Flaubert: A Life* (London: Faber, 2001)

Additional Recommended Background Material:

Barnes, Julian, *Flaubert's Parrot* (London: Jonathan Cape, 1984)

Barnes, Julian, *Something to Declare* (London: Picador, 2002)

Bart, Benjamin F., ed., *Madame Bovary and the Critics* (New York, NY: New York University Press, 1966)

Bloom, Harold, ed., *Gustave Flaubert's Madame Bovary* (New York, NY, and Philadelphia, PA: Chelsea House, 1988)

Brombert, Victor, *The Novels of Flaubert* (Princeton, NJ: Princeton University Press, 1966)

Donaldson-Evans, Mary, *Madame Bovary at the Movies* (Amsterdam and New York, NY: Rodopi, 2009)

Fairlie, Alison, *Flaubert: Madame Bovary* (London: Edward Arnold, 1962)

Heath, Stephen, *Flaubert: Madame Bovary* (Cambridge: Cambridge University Press, 1992)

LaCapra, Dominick, *Madame Bovary on Trial* (Ithaca, NY, and London: Cornell University Press, 1982)

Lloyd, Rosemary, *Madame Bovary* (London: Unwin Hyman, 1989)

Lowe, Margaret, *Towards the Real Flaubert: A Study of Madame Bovary* (Oxford: Oxford University Press, 1984)

Roe, David, *Gustave Flaubert* (London: Palgrave Macmillan, 1989)

Simmonds, Posy, *Gemma Bovery* (London: Jonathan Cape, 1999)

Steegmuller, Francis, *Flaubert and Madame Bovary* (London: Macmillan, 1968)

Tillett, Margaret G., *On Reading Flaubert* (London: Oxford University Press, 1961)

Unwin, Timothy, ed., *The Cambridge Companion to Flaubert* (Cambridge: Cambridge University Press, 2004)

Vargas Llosa, Mario, *The Perpetual Orgy* (London and Boston, NY: Faber, 1987)

On the Web:

www.univ-rouen.fr/flaubert

perso.wanadoo.fr/jb.guinot/pages/accueil.html

ALMA CLASSICS

ALMA CLASSICS aims to publish mainstream and lesser-known European classics in an innovative and striking way, while employing the highest editorial and production standards. By way of a unique approach the range offers much more, both visually and textually, than readers have come to expect from contemporary classics publishing.

1. James Hanley, *Boy*
2. D.H. Lawrence, *The First Women in Love*
3. Charlotte Brontë, *Jane Eyre*
4. Jane Austen, *Pride and Prejudice*
5. Emily Brontë, *Wuthering Heights*
6. Anton Chekhov, *Sakhalin Island*
7. Giuseppe Gioacchino Belli, *Sonnets*
8. Jack Kerouac, *Beat Generation*
9. Charles Dickens, *Great Expectations*
10. Jane Austen, *Emma*
11. Wilkie Collins, *The Moonstone*
12. D.H. Lawrence, *The Second Lady Chatterley's Lover*
13. Jonathan Swift, *The Benefit of Farting Explained*
14. Anonymous, *Dirty Limericks*
15. Henry Miller, *The World of Sex*
16. Jeremias Gotthelf, *The Black Spider*
17. Oscar Wilde, *The Picture Of Dorian Gray*
18. Erasmus, *Praise of Folly*
19. Henry Miller, *Quiet Days in Clichy*
20. Cecco Angiolieri, *Sonnets*
21. Fyodor Dostoevsky, *Humiliated and Insulted*
22. Jane Austen, *Sense and Sensibility*
23. Theodor Storm, *Immensee*
24. Ugo Foscolo, *Sepulchres*
25. Boileau, *Art of Poetry*
26. Georg Kaiser, *Plays Vol. 1*
27. Émile Zola, *Ladies' Delight*
28. D.H. Lawrence, *Selected Letters*
29. Alexander Pope, *The Art of Sinking in Poetry*
30. E.T.A. Hoffmann, *The King's Bride*
31. Ann Radcliffe, *The Italian*
32. Prosper Mérimée, *A Slight Misunderstanding*
33. Giacomo Leopardi, *Canti*
34. Giovanni Boccaccio, *Decameron*
35. Annette von Droste-Hülshoff, *The Jew's Beech*
36. Stendhal, *Life of Rossini*
37. Eduard Mörike, *Mozart's Journey to Prague*
38. Jane Austen, *Love and Friendship*
39. Leo Tolstoy, *Anna Karenina*
40. Ivan Bunin, *Dark Avenues*
41. Nathaniel Hawthorne, *The Scarlet Letter*

42. Sadeq Hedayat, *Three Drops of Blood*
43. Alexander Trocchi, *Young Adam*
44. Oscar Wilde, *The Decay of Lying*
45. Mikhail Bulgakov, *The Master and Margarita*
46. Sadeq Hedayat, *The Blind Owl*
47. Alain Robbe-Grillet, *Jealousy*
48. Marguerite Duras, *Moderato Cantabile*
49. Raymond Roussel, *Locus Solus*
50. Alain Robbe-Grillet, *In the Labyrinth*
51. Daniel Defoe, *Robinson Crusoe*
52. Robert Louis Stevenson, *Treasure Island*
53. Ivan Bunin, *The Village*
54. Alain Robbe-Grillet, *The Voyeur*
55. Franz Kafka, *Dearest Father*
56. Geoffrey Chaucer, *Canterbury Tales*
57. Ambrose Bierce, *The Monk and the Hangman's Daughter*
58. Fyodor Dostoevsky, *Winter Notes on Summer Impressions*
59. Bram Stoker, *Dracula*
60. Mary Shelley, *Frankenstein*
61. Johann Wolfgang von Goethe, *Elective Affinities*
62. Marguerite Duras, *The Sailor from Gibraltar*
63. Robert Graves, *Lars Porsena*
64. Napoleon Bonaparte, *Aphorisms and Thoughts*
65. Joseph von Eichendorff, *Memoirs of a Good-for-Nothing*
66. Adelbert von Chamisso, *Peter Schlemihl*
67. Pedro Antonio de Alarcón, *The Three-Cornered Hat*
68. Jane Austen, *Persuasion*
69. Dante Alighieri, *Rime*
70. Anton Chekhov, *The Woman in the Case and Other Stories*
71. Mark Twain, *The Diaries of Adam and Eve*
72. Jonathan Swift, *Gulliver's Travels*
73. Joseph Conrad, *Heart of Darkness*
74. Gottfried Keller, *A Village Romeo and Juliet*
75. Raymond Queneau, *Exercises in Style*
76. Georg Büchner, *Lenz*
77. Giovanni Boccaccio, *Life of Dante*
78. Jane Austen, *Mansfield Park*
79. E.T.A. Hoffmann, *The Devil's Elixirs*
80. Claude Simon, *The Flanders Road*
81. Raymond Queneau, *The Flight of Icarus*
82. Niccolò Machiavelli, *The Prince*
83. Mikhail Lermontov, *A Hero of our Time*
84. Henry Miller, *Black Spring*
85. Victor Hugo, *The Last Day of a Condemned Man*
86. D.H. Lawrence, *Paul Morel*
87. Mikhail Bulgakov, *The Life of Monsieur de Molière*
88. Leo Tolstoy, *Three Novellas*
89. Stendhal, *Travels in the South of France*
90. Wilkie Collins, *The Woman in White*
91. Alain Robbe-Grillet, *Erasers*
92. Iginio Ugo Tarchetti, *Fosca*
93. D.H. Lawrence, *The Fox*
94. Borys Conrad, *My Father Joseph Conrad*
95. James De Mille, *A Strange Manuscript Found in a Copper Cylinder*
96. Émile Zola, *Dead Men Tell No Tales*

97. Alexander Pushkin, *Ruslan and Lyudmila*
98. Lewis Carroll, *Alice's Adventures Under Ground*
99. James Hanley, *The Closed Harbour*
100. Thomas De Quincey, *On Murder Considered as One of the Fine Arts*
101. Jonathan Swift, *The Wonderful Wonder of Wonders*
102. Petronius, *Satyricon*
103. Louis-Ferdinand Céline, *Death on Credit*
104. Jane Austen, *Northanger Abbey*
105. W.B. Yeats, *Selected Poems*
106. Antonin Artaud, *The Theatre and Its Double*
107. Louis-Ferdinand Céline, *Journey to the End of the Night*
108. Ford Madox Ford, *The Good Soldier*
109. Leo Tolstoy, *Childhood, Boyhood, Youth*
110. Guido Cavalcanti, *Complete Poems*
111. Charles Dickens, *Hard Times*
112. Charles Baudelaire and Théophile Gautier, *Hashish, Wine, Opium*
113. Charles Dickens, *Haunted House*
114. Ivan Turgenev, *Fathers and Children*
115. Dante Alighieri, *Inferno*
116. Gustave Flaubert, *Madame Bovary*
117. Alexander Trocchi, *Man at Leisure*
118. Alexander Pushkin, *Boris Godunov and Little Tragedies*
119. Miguel de Cervantes, *Don Quixote*
120. Mark Twain, *Huckleberry Finn*
121. Charles Baudelaire, *Paris Spleen*
122. Fyodor Dostoevsky, *The Idiot*
123. René de Chateaubriand, *Atala and René*
124. Mikhail Bulgakov, *Diaboliad*
125. Goerge Eliot, *Middlemarch*
126. Edmondo De Amicis, *Constantinople*
127. Petrarch, *Secretum*
128. Johann Wolfgang von Goethe, *The Sorrows of Young Werther*
129. Alexander Pushkin, *Eugene Onegin*
130. Fyodor Dostoevsky, *Notes from Underground*
131. Luigi Pirandello, *Plays Vol. 1*
132. Jules Renard, *Histoires Naturelles*
133. Gustave Flaubert, *The Dictionary of Received Ideas*
134. Charles Dickens, *The Life of Our Lord*
135. D.H. Lawrence, *The Lost Girl*
136. Benjamin Constant, *The Red Notebook*
137. Raymond Queneau, *We Always Treat Women too Well*
138. Alexander Trocchi, *Cain's Book*
139. Raymond Roussel, *Impressions of Africa*
140. Llewelyn Powys, *A Struggle for Life*
141. Nikolai Gogol, *How the Two Ivans Quarrelled*
142. F. Scott Fitzgerald, *The Great Gatsby*
143. Jonathan Swift, *Directions to Servants*
144. Dante Alighieri, *Purgatory*
145. Mikhail Bulgakov, *A Young Doctor's Notebook*
146. Sergei Dovlatov, *The Suitcase*
147. Leo Tolstoy, *Hadji Murat*
148. Jonathan Swift, *The Battle of the Books*
149. F. Scott Fitzgerald, *Tender Is the Night*
150. Alexander Pushkin, *The Queen of Spades and Other Short Fiction*
151. Raymond Queneau, *The Sunday of Life*

152. Herman Melville, *Moby Dick*
153. Mikhail Bulgakov, *The Fatal Eggs*
154. Antonia Pozzi, *Poems*
155. Johann Wolfgang von Goethe, *Wilhelm Meister*
156. Anton Chekhov, *The Story of a Nobody*
157. Fyodor Dostoevsky, *Poor People*
158. Leo Tolstoy, *The Death of Ivan Ilyich*
159. Dante Alighieri, *Vita nuova*
160. Arthur Conan Doyle, *The Tragedy of Korosko*
161. Franz Kafka, *Letters to Friends, Family and Editors*
162. Mark Twain, *The Adventures of Tom Sawyer*
163. Erich Fried, *Love Poems*
164. Antonin Artaud, *Selected Works*
165. Charles Dickens, *Oliver Twist*
166. Sergei Dovlatov, *The Zone*
167. Louis-Ferdinand Céline, *Guignol's Band*
168. Mikhail Bulgakov, *A Dog's Heart*
169. Rayner Heppenstall, *The Blaze of Noon*
170. Fyodor Dostoevsky, *The Crocodile*
171. Anton Chekhov, *The Death of a Civil Servant*
172. Georg Kaiser, *Plays Vol. 2*
173. Tristan Tzara, *Seven Dada Manifestos* and *Lampisteries*
174. Frank Wedekind, *The Lulu Plays and Other Sex Tragedies*
175. Frank Wedekind, *Spring Awakening*
176. Fyodor Dostoevsky, *The Gambler*
177. Prosper Mérimée, *The Etruscan Vase and Other Stories*
178. Edgar Allan Poe, *Tales of the Supernatural*
179. Virginia Woolf, *To the Lighthouse*
180. F. Scott Fitzgerald, *The Beautiful and Damned*
181. James Joyce, *Dubliners*
182. Alexander Pushkin, *The Captain's Daughter*
183. Sherwood Anderson, *Winesburg Ohio*
184. James Joyce, *Ulysses*
185. Ivan Turgenev, *Faust*
186. Virginia Woolf, *Mrs Dalloway*
187. Paul Scarron, *The Comical Romance*
188. Sergei Dovlatov, *Pushkin Hills*
189. F. Scott Fitzgerald, *This Side of Paradise*
190. Alexander Pushkin, *Complete Lyrical Poems*
191. Luigi Pirandello, *Plays Vol. 2*
192. Ivan Turgenev, *Rudin*
193. Raymond Radiguet, *Cheeks on Fire*
194. Vladimir Odoevsky, *Two Days in the Life of the Terrestrial Globe*
195. Copi, *Four Plays*
196. Iginio Ugo Tarchetti, *Fantastic Tales*
197. Louis-Ferdinand Céline, *London Bridge*
198. Mikhail Bulgakov, *The White Guard*
199. George Bernard Shaw, *The Intelligent Woman's Guide*
200. Charles Dickens, *Supernatural Short Stories*
201. Dante Alighieri, *The Divine Comedy*

To order any of our titles and for up-to-date information about our current and forthcoming publications, please visit our website at:

www.almaclassics.com